THE PRICE WAS RIGHT....

Or was it? Mechanic Maggie Muldoon had her doubts
about wealthy playboy Wyatt Sommersby—
until a family business she didn't know she had
fell in her lap. She knew she needed all the help
she could get...preferably in the form of a husband,
in Ginna Gray's *The Bride Price*.

"...Ginna Gray gifts readers with...
provocative romance."
—*Rendezvous*

❤ ❤ ❤

And as far as Brody Smith was concerned,
at first all he was to Jessica Lockhart
was a hired bodyguard. But once the lovely
heiress proposed a new bargain, he realized he'd better
start protecting his own heart, in
Husband: Bought and Paid For, by Laurie Paige.

"Laurie Paige doesn't miss...."
—*New York Times* bestselling author Catherine Coulter

GINNA GRAY

A native Texan, Ginna Gray lived in Houston all her life until 1993, when she and her husband, Brad, built their "dream home" and moved to the mountains of Colorado. Coming from a large, Irish/American family, in which spinning colorful yarns was commonplace, made writing a natural career choice for Ginna. "I grew up hearing so many fascinating tales, I was eleven or twelve before I realized that not everyone made up stories," Ginna says. She sold her first novel in 1983 and has been working as a full-time writer ever since. She has also given many lectures and writing workshops and judged in writing contests. The mother of two grown daughters, Ginna also enjoys other creative activities, such as oil painting, sewing, sketching, knitting and needlepoint.

LAURIE PAIGE

"One of the nicest things about writing romances is researching locales, careers and ideas. In the interest of authenticity, most writers will try anything...once." Along with her writing adventures, Laurie has been a NASA engineer, a past president of Romance Writers of America and is a mother and a grandmother. She was twice a Romance Writers of America RITA® Award finalist for Best Traditional Romance and has won awards from *Romantic Times* for Best Silhouette Special Edition and Best Silhouette. Recently resettled in Northern California, Laurie is looking forward to whatever experiences her next novel will send her on.

MARRIED ON DEMAND

GINNA GRAY
LAURIE PAIGE

Silhouette® Books

Published by Silhouette Books

America's Publisher of Contemporary Romance

SILHOUETTE BOOKS

ISBN 0-373-21737-4

by Request

MARRIED ON DEMAND

Copyright © 2002 by Harlequin Books S.A.

The publisher acknowledges the copyright holders of the individual works as follows:

THE BRIDE PRICE
Copyright © 1995 by Virginia Gray

HUSBAND: BOUGHT AND PAID FOR
Copyright © 1997 by Olivia M. Hall

Visit Silhouette at www.eHarlequin.com

Printed in U.S.A.

CONTENTS

Dear Reader,

As a writer, the most frequently asked question I hear is, "Where do you get your ideas?" My answer is always, "From anywhere and everywhere." Anything can spark a writer's imagination—a song, a news story, interaction with another person, observing others in action, even an overheard snippet of conversation or a session of introspection (in which I am often prone to indulge).

For instance, once, after the dust had settled following a family crisis, I started thinking about what it means to be part of a close-knit and loving family. To know that there is a group of people in the world who will always be there for you, will always love, support and accept you, come what may, is a comfort and joy beyond measure. To know that you will always have "a soft place to fall" gives you a secure feeling and brings peace to your soul.

However, membership in a family, indeed, when you receive love of any sort, carries with it certain responsibilities and obligations. There are times when we would all like to "soar like an eagle" with no ties, no one else to consider, no need to account for our actions to anyone, but that lonely existence is a poor substitute for love. For belonging.

This train of thought naturally led me into my "what if" mode. I began to wonder what it would be like to feel you didn't belong in a family. What if that feeling of rejection drove you to seek absolute independence? What if you did not understand that loving and being loved was a complicated paradox that brings incredible freedom and joy, and at the same time tethers you to the beloved by your heartstrings? What if, eventually, you came to realize that curtailed freedom is a small price to pay for the blessing of love?

From these musings came *The Bride Price*. I hope, dear reader, that you enjoy my heroine's journey of discovery as much as I enjoyed writing it.

Enjoy.

Ginna Gray

THE BRIDE PRICE
Ginna Gray

Chapter One

The first inkling of trouble occurred about twenty miles northwest of Houston on a lonely country road.

The sound was no more than a slight knock—enough to bring Wyatt Sommersby's black eyebrows together for an instant, but no great cause for concern. The high-powered Aston-Martin was notoriously temperamental. Merely keeping it tuned required almost constant attention from a master mechanic who had the fine touch of a surgeon and the hourly rates to match.

That's what came of driving a vintage, fireball car in Houston traffic. Wyatt knew it was a foolish self-indulgence, but some things were worth the price, no matter how high. From the moment he'd seen the silver antique sports car he'd known that he had to have it—and Wyatt Sommersby was a man who always got what he wanted.

One moment he was driving along the country highway, his agile mind miles away, sorting through various business matters. The next moment a loud eruption of coughs and wheezes from beneath the hood jarred him from his thoughts.

"Aw, damn. Not now," he groaned. He pumped the gas pedal, but the classy little car continued to lose speed, knocking and shuddering ominously. Wyatt pounded the leather-covered steering wheel with his fist and cursed.

"Great. Just great." He was in the middle of nowhere. On either side of the two-lane country road an impenetrable forest of tall pines grew right up to the shoulder. There wasn't a house in sight.

Since passing through the town of Tomball he had encountered few other cars. It was Saturday afternoon. Back in Houston the traffic would be bumper to bumper, but this road was empty.

His mechanic's shop was closed for the Memorial Day weekend. He wouldn't be back until Tuesday.

"Dammit to hell. Now what?"

He supposed he could use the car phone and call Asa's place for assistance, but he didn't relish that idea. With preparations for the party underway, it was probably bedlam out there.

More important, where Asa Hightower was concerned it never paid to show the slightest weakness.

Most of the guests would not be arriving until much later, not even the ones who would be staying overnight. Wyatt had come early to try once again to negotiate a deal to buy into Asa's company. The wily old coot was one of the shrewdest businessmen Wyatt had ever run up against. Asa could turn any situation to his advantage, even something as minor as his opponent being stranded in a stalled car.

A sardonic half smile twitched Wyatt's mouth.

Still…he couldn't help but admire the crusty old bastard. Hell, at times he actually liked him. Maybe, Wyatt mused ruefully, because they were so much alike.

Over the next ten minutes a few cars zoomed by. Each time, Wyatt flashed his headlights and honked, but no one so much as slowed. "Great," he muttered. "Where are the Good Samaritans when you need them?"

By the time Wyatt made it to Magnolia, the town closest to Asa's country place, and spotted the service station, the car was sputtering along at about three miles an hour and the noise coming from under the hood sounded more like a thrashing machine than a precision-made automobile.

He coaxed the car into the station and brought it to a stop. A man wearing greasy overalls and a baseball cap turned backward stood in the doorway leaning against the jamb, watching his approach. His homely face resembled a sleepy hound dog's and showed about as much animation.

On the raised area next to the door, a teenage girl with a mane of wildly curling red hair sat on an old-fashioned chest-type soft-drink machine, swinging her legs and sipping an orange soda out of a can.

Not trusting the engine to start again, Wyatt left it running and climbed out of the car. "Good afternoon. As you can see, I'm having some trouble."

"Yep. Sure sounds like it," the man said. He rolled the toothpick he held between his lips to the other side of his mouth and hooked his thumbs under the straps of his overalls. "You want me to take a look-see under the hood? I ain't never worked on one of these fancy Ass-tin Martins, but I 'spect they's pretty much like any other car."

Wyatt barely suppressed a shudder. The thought of this

hick mechanic touching his vehicle made him break out in a cold sweat. But what choice did he have? "Yes. I'd appreciate it. And if you would, please hurry." Wyatt glanced at his watch. "I'm running late."

The girl perched on the soft-drink machine took in every word, her amused gaze bouncing back and forth between him and the mechanic. Wyatt ignored her.

"Sure thing." The man hitched up his overalls and ambled out to where the silver Aston-Martin sat shaking and wheezing.

Wyatt followed right on the man's heels. "You don't need to worry about doing a major overhaul. If you can just patch it together enough to last a few days, I'll take it to my mechanic on Tuesday."

"Hmm" came the laconic reply from under the hood. The sound did nothing to calm Wyatt's anxiety. Peering over the mechanic's shoulder, he watched him pump the throttle linkage. Wyatt grimaced when the car wheezed and coughed even more.

The next several minutes he stood helplessly by, while the man tinkered with the engine and muttered under his breath.

Perspiration beaded Wyatt's upper lip and forehead, and his shirt began to stick to his back. According to the large thermometer hanging in the window of the service station office, the temperature was ninety-seven. The humid air made it feel more like a hundred and ten.

A sluggish breeze wafted through the bay, swirling the sand and grit on the concrete into little dust devils and intensifying the pungent scents of gasoline, diesel fuel and motor oil.

A car whizzed by on the highway, adding a blast of hot exhaust fumes to the oppressive mugginess. Wyatt wiped the sweat from his brow with the back of his forearm and looked around. He wondered what kept Magnolia alive. As far as he could tell, the town consisted of a school, a church and a hodgepodge of small businesses and houses strung out for a few blocks, mainly along one side of the highway. On the other side, train tracks ran parallel with the paving. Whether or not they were still in use was difficult to tell.

As Wyatt finished his inspection of the little burg his gaze met that of the girl's sitting on the soft-drink chest. Instead of looking away, as he expected, she continued to study him, her bright blue eyes wide with curiosity.

He raised one eyebrow, but the imperious gesture did not intimidate her. To his astonishment, she flashed him a grin and winked, and he felt a tiny shock zing through him.

Before he could analyze the reason for the reaction, the station attendant straightened. He wiped his hands on a rag he pulled from the rear pocket of his overalls and shook his head. "Sorry, Mister, but there just ain't no way I can put a Band-Aid on that engine. What you need is a new fuel pump."

"Can you install one?"

"Yep. That is…I could if I had one. I don't stock parts for these fancy foreign jobs."

Wyatt gritted his teeth. Patience was not one of his virtues, and he was holding on to what little he had by a thread. "I see. How long would it take you to get one and do the job?"

"Well, let's see now." The attendant fished an old-fashioned pocket watch from a small slot in the bib of his overalls and flicked open the top with a grease-encrusted thumbnail. "Ain't nobody here but me right now, but if I can run down that boy of mine and send him over to Houston to pick up a pump I could have 'er ready by say...ohhh...nine or ten tonight.''

"Nine or ten!"

"'Fraid so. That is, if Billy Ray can make it to the auto parts store before they close.''

"Great. Just great. I'm suppose to be at the Hightower place by three. Is there anywhere around here where I might rent a car? Or any other vehicle that runs,'' he added, remembering where he was.

"Nope.''

"I thought not. I don't suppose this town has such a thing as a taxi service, either?''

"Nope. But as it happens, you're in luck. Maggie here is on her way out to the Hightowers' herself. She just stopped in to chat and have a cool drink.'' He turned to the girl perched on the soft-drink chest. ''You wouldn't mind givin' this here feller a ride, would you, Maggie?''

Wyatt's gaze turned sharply on the girl. This child could drive an automobile?

Tipping her head to one side, she pursed her lips and had the temerity to give him another thorough once-over, as though deciding whether or not he might be a serial killer. Finally she shrugged. "Sure. Why not?''

She chugalugged the last few swallows of orange soda, lobbed the can into a trash barrel with a casual overhand shot Michael Jordan would have been proud of, and hopped down from the cooler, cocky as you please.

She was a tiny thing. Even tinier than he'd thought. Perhaps five feet tall—five-one at most—and she couldn't have weighed a hundred pounds soaking wet. She looked about fourteen.

However, her trim little figure was perfectly proportioned, he realized a bit uneasily. She looked like a pint-sized Venus with the pixie face of a mischievous child.

Silently he questioned the wisdom of going off alone in a car with a minor.

"C'mon. Let's go." Sticking her fingertips in the back pockets of her tight jeans, which molded a disturbingly enticing heart-shaped bottom, the saucy teenager sauntered across the concrete drive toward the most battered pickup Wyatt had ever seen. At one time it might have been brown, but now it was mottled with so many different shades of primer and paint and rust it resembled a camouflaged army vehicle. One fender was missing and so was the outside handle on the passenger door. From front to back scratches and dents covered the body.

Wyatt rolled his eyes. Of course. What else? It was too much to ask that this impudent child would drive a respectable vehicle.

She glanced back over her shoulder and cocked her auburn eyebrows. "Well? You coming, or not?"

Wyatt hesitated, weighing his options.

Oh, what the hell. "Yeah, I'll be right with you. Just give me a minute to get my things," he called after her.

"Okay, but shake a leg. I'll catch hell if I'm late."

"Look, my name is Wyatt Sommersby," he told the attendant as he snatched his case from the car. "Here's my card. I'll be out at the Hightower place for the next couple of days." He stopped and patted his shirt pocket. "Now where'd I put that phone number?"

"That's okay," the man said. "I know the number at the Hightowers'. I'll give you a ring when the car's ready."

"Thanks, I—"

The dilapidated truck started up with a roar. The girl gunned the motor and blasted the horn.

Wyatt scowled at her over his shoulder, but the attendant laughed. "You'd better hurry if you're gonna catch a ride with Maggie. When that little gal decides to hit the road, she goes, and she don't wait for nuthin' er nobody.''

Wyatt snatched up his cases and sprinted for the truck.

He swung his things into the back, reached inside the open window to unlatch the door and climbed into the cab. Before he could close the door completely she took off, peeling out of the station as though she were being pursued by a division of state troopers.

"Holy—'' Wyatt ground his teeth and held on.

In moments they reached the other end of town where the highway ended at a T intersection. She didn't even slow down. Executing a sharp right, she bumped over the railroad tracks and hung a left just beyond. Wyatt bounced so high he hit his head on the roof then slammed into the door.

"Damnation!'' He shot her a dark look, but the girl merely grinned and drove blithely on. "Are we going to a fire?'' he asked through clenched teeth.

"What? Oh. Sorry. If you recall, though, I did say I was in a bit of a hurry.''

"A hurry to get us killed. Did anyone ever tell you that you drive like a maniac?''

"A few,'' she said with maddening unconcern. "I'll stop, if you want to get out.''

He fixed her with a narrow-eyed look. "Cute.''

They rode in silence for several minutes after that—he with his jaw set, her with that damned, cheerful half smile on her pixie face.

"You don't have to worry, you know,'' she said out of the blue.

Wyatt turned his head and looked at her. That amused smile still hovered around her mouth. "Excuse me?''

"About Lester. I could tell you would've sooner swallowed a rotten egg than left your Aston-Martin in his care. But don't worry, he's a top-notch mechanic. Actually, I'm not bad myself, and he taught me everything I know about engines. I do most of the work on this truck, and what I can't handle, I take to Lester.''

One corner of Wyatt's mouth curled as he glanced around the interior of the shabby pickup. ''I wonder why I don't find that comforting.''

She chuckled, not in the least offended. ''Ahhh, His Nibs is embarrassed to be seen riding in this old truck, is he? Well, too bad. Beggars can't be choosers, me old granny used to say.''

Wyatt blinked at her, stunned. ''Are you implying that I'm a snob?''

''No, not at all.'' She flashed him a guileless grin. ''I'm telling you so straight-out.''

''Now, look here, just because a person has certain standards, that doesn't mean he's a snob.''

''Och, forget it. From the look of you, you were born to money. You can't help it if you don't know any better.''

''Now wait just a damned min—''

''But do yourself a favor and take a piece of friendly advice. Don't be lettin' appearances fool you. This machine may not look like much to a man of your obvious means, but she runs like a top, she does.''

Why, the impertinent brat. Wyatt was so stunned he could not reply for a moment. No one, *no one,* had ever talked to him the way this presumptuous child had.

Glancing sideways, he noted she had to sit on a pillow to see over the steering wheel, and she had her seat scooted all the way forward in order to reach the pedals. He frowned.

''Do you have a license to drive this thing?''

She sent him another grin. "Of course. I've had a driver's license since I was sixteen."

"When was that? Two days ago?"

He expected adolescent indignation, but he got laughter. Not the inane giggle of a girl, but a low, husky sound that reminded him of smoke and honey. It feathered over his skin like a caress, raising a host of unwelcome and inappropriate sensations, most of which were located below his belt. Annoyed with himself, *and* with the audacious teenager, Wyatt gritted his teeth and stared straight ahead. He didn't see what was so damned funny.

When her laughter subsided, she replied with a chuckle, "There you go, judging by appearances again. Don't you be letting my size fool you. I've had my license for ten years."

Wyatt's head whipped around. "*Ten years!* You mean you're *twenty-six?* I don't believe it."

She shrugged. "Believe what you like. 'Tis no difference to me."

He stared at her. He tried to tell himself that she was lying, but her disinterest was more convincing than vociferous insistence. In spite of himself, he was intrigued.

In profile, her delicate features had an almost angelic clarity. Freckles dotted her little tilted nose and spread out over pink cheeks. And those eyes. Lord, if they didn't make a man believe in innocence nothing could. They were big as saucers and the brightest blue he'd ever seen. The auburn lashes that surrounded them were so thick and long they almost looked fake. Her stubborn little chin had a hint of a cleft in the center, and when she flashed that impudent grin, twin dimples dug holes in her cheeks. The whole picture was one of angelic impertinence.

Yet, there were signs of maturity—subtle and slight, but visible if you looked hard enough; the finest tracery of lines at the outer corners of her eyes, the firm ripeness of her mouth, the ease with which she handled herself. And, of course, that lush little body.

"You must have a helluva time getting a glass of wine at a restaurant."

That smoky laugh flowed out once again, raising gooseflesh along Wyatt's arms, much to his annoyance. "Sometimes, but it's not that much of a problem. Lucky for me, a burger and a Slurpy are more to my taste, anyway."

What the devil was a Slurpy? Wyatt wondered, but he refused to ask.

"You said you'd be in trouble if you were late. I assume you work at the Hightower ranch."

Her lips twitched. "No, not really."

"I see. Then you're just helping out because of the party?"

"You could say that."

She fell silent again, but that amused smile still hovered about her lips. Wyatt gritted his teeth.

"By the way, my name is Wyatt Sommersby."

"Sommersby? Of Sommersby Enterprises?" At Wyatt's yes, she nodded. "Ahh, well then…that explains a lot."

"What, exactly?" Wyatt demanded with an edge to his voice.

"Just that your family is not only as rich as nabobs, they're the cream of Houston society." She gave him another once-over out of the corner of her eye. "You must be Daphne's soon-to-be fiancé."

"Good God, no! That's my younger brother, Eric."

Not that Daphne and her grandfather hadn't tried to hook him. When Wyatt had first approached Asa about Sommersby Enterprises buying into his chain of discount stores the old rascal had made it clear that he would consider the proposition only if there were a family connection between them. Then the sly old dog had introduced his granddaughter.

Daphne was a beauty, Wyatt would give her that. She was also spoiled, shallow, vain and vapid. When she'd begun to pursue him he had told her in the bluntest terms that he had no interest in marriage, but that he might consider a brief affair. She had reacted with outrage and immediately turned her sights on Eric.

"Hmm. Sounds to me as though you're not pleased about the match."

"Not at all. I'm merely grateful I'm not the prospective groom."

Actually, Wyatt had reservations about the union. It would provide the "in" he needed with Asa. However, he never would have asked that kind of sacrifice of his brother, not even for a chunk of BargainMart.

Fortunately, his brother seemed besotted with Daphne, though for the life of him, Wyatt didn't know why. She was blond and pretty and socially adept, but so were thousands of other women. Personally, she would have him climbing the walls within a month—if she didn't bore him to death first. Most women did.

"Have you got something against Daphne Hightower?"

"No. Just against marriage." Wyatt had never met a woman he could imagine spending a month with, much less the rest of his life. The very thought made him shudder.

"Ahh, like that, is it?"

Wyatt responded with a grunt and she chuckled.

"Your mechanic friend called you Maggie. I assume

that's short for something else,'' he prodded after another lengthy silence.

Her dimples winked again. "Aye. My name is Margaret Mary, but that's too much of a mouthful. Besides, Maggie suits me, I'm told, and I like it."

He studied her cheerful profile. The women in his social circle would shudder at the thought of being stuck with a common name like Maggie. The females in the country club set had names like Buffy, Blair, Whitney and Sabrina.

"I detect a slight accent to your speech. You weren't born in this country, were you?"

"Ah, 'tis a keen ear you have, Mr. Sommersby. After all these years with you Yanks I thought I'd lost all trace of my native tongue. And 'tisn't an accent, 'tis a brogue. Some even call it a lilt. I was born in Ireland. In a wee, lovely place called Innishmore."

"How old were you when you came here?"

"Fourteen."

"Did your parents immigrate?"

"No. Ah, here we are." She turned between two pillars that supported a swinging sign bearing the Rocking H brand. Immediately the truck bumped over a cattle guard, effectively ending the conversation.

The stab of disappointment surprised Wyatt. He wanted to know more, though he had no idea why.

The rattle-trap truck barreled up the gravel lane, trailing a plume of dust like a rooster's tail. Wyatt gazed out the window at the prime Angus cattle grazing in the pastures on both sides of the drive. By Texas standards, the Rocking H was a small ranch, a mere two thousand or so acres. Unlike Blue Hills—Wyatt's thoroughbred farm near Brenham and his passion and most prized possession—for Asa this spread was mainly a tax write-off that just happened to have the convenient plus of being a handy weekend getaway. Nevertheless, the small ranch was kept in pristine condition and the animals were top-notch.

The lane forked just before reaching the main house, the left branch forming a circular driveway before the entrance, the right looping around the house and grounds toward the barns and corrals out back.

"You want me to drop you off behind yonder tree and let you walk the rest of the way? It'll save you the humiliation of arriving in a lowly pickup."

Wyatt shot her a quelling look, but it merely increased her amusement. Her eyes danced and sparkled like two sapphires in the sun.

"The front will do nicely, thank you."

"Just thought I'd ask. I wouldn't want to ruin your image." She wheeled the old truck into the circle and brought it to a halt in front of the veranda steps. Leaving the engine running, she flashed him that saucy grin. "Have a nice weekend, Mr. Sommersby."

"Thanks. And thanks for the lift."

"'Twas nothing."

Wyatt climbed from the truck and hefted his bag from the back. She shifted gears and was about to drive away when, driven by an urge he didn't understand, he put his hand on the open window. "Wait. You never told me your last name."

She laughed as though he'd said something funny, her blue eyes twinkling. "'Tisn't important. But if you must know, 'tis Muldoon. Margaret Mary Muldoon at you service, Your Nibs."

And with that, she drove away.

He stared after her and shook his head. Cheeky brat. Asa Hightower was a crusty, no-nonsense old tyrant. Wyatt was surprised that a free spirit like Maggie Muldoon had managed to get a job on his domestic staff, even a temporary one. With her sassy mouth and irrepressible spirit he doubted she'd last the weekend.

He found the household in an uproar. A harried housekeeper greeted him at the door with the news that Asa had had to fly back to Houston in his helicopter to deal with an urgent matter that had cropped up, but that he would be back in time for the party.

Wyatt barely bit back a curse. That damned wily old fox. He'd give odds there was no emergency; it was simply another of Asa's evasive tactics. Wyatt had been trying to pin him down about cutting a deal for months, but he was as slippery as an eel.

Neither Daphne nor Eric, nor Corinne, Daphne's mother, had arrived yet. Tyson, Daphne's artist brother, was there, but he was in his studio painting. There was nothing left to do but allow the housekeeper to show him to his room.

The view from the wing in which his room was located gave an unobstructed view of the rear of the main section of the house, the back gardens and the barn and the corrals and the rolling pastures beyond. Wyatt barely noticed. Angry and out of sorts, he slung his suitcase on the bed and began to pace the room and curse. On his second pass by the windows he spotted Maggie's truck parked beside the corrals.

He halted and stared at the dilapidated vehicle. An instant later Maggie came out of the barn and headed for the kitchen door. Her red hair seemed to take fire in the sunlight. Wyatt watched her, fascinated.

Even at that distance, there was an effervescence about the woman that was tangible. She seemed to exude a bubbly joy at merely being alive. Everything about her was upbeat and bouncy, her twinkling eyes, that constantly smiling mouth, her untamed mane of bright curls. Even her walk was sassy and carefree.

Watching her, it occurred to him that a man would never be bored with a pint-sized pixie like that in his life. Of course, he'd probably never have a calm day, either.

Spotting an elderly gardener working in the rose garden that separated the backyard and pool area from the corrals, she yelled something and broke into a run.

The old man straightened, and his weathered face lit up. He dropped his hoe and held out his arms, and when she catapulted herself against his chest he patted her back fondly. Within seconds what appeared to be the entire kitchen staff came pouring out the back door to surround her. Maggie immediately bestowed hugs and kisses on them all.

Wyatt frowned, inexplicably irked by her open-handed show of affection. Hell, didn't the woman even know the meaning of the word *restraint?*

Making an aggravated sound, he spun away from the window and resumed his pacing. He made several restless circuits of the room but he felt more out of sorts by the second. Finally, he spat out a curse and headed for the door.

On the first floor he found the household staff scurrying around like ants, preparing for the party that was to take place in a few hours. The few people he encountered were so distracted they barely noticed him.

Outside the swinging double doors that led into the kitchen, he paused and listened. Over the hum of voices and clatter of pans he heard Maggie's smoky laugh. Firming his mouth, he pushed the doors open and stepped inside.

The five women and two men in the kitchen looked

around at his entrance, stricken expressions on their faces—all, that was, except Maggie.

She sat perched on one of the kitchen counters, hands braced on either side of her hips, idly swinging her legs, much as she had been doing when he'd first seen her.

She shot him a cheeky grin. "Hi, Mr. Sommersby. What're you doing here? You lost or something?"

"No, I am not lost. My tuxedo needs pressing. Everyone I've run into seems to be busy."

A plump woman in a cook's apron stepped forward, wringing her hands. "Oh, 'tis sorry I am, Mr. Sommersby. I'll find someone and send them up right away."

"Miss Muldoon doesn't appear to be overworked." Wyatt's gaze swung to Maggie. "Why don't you come get the tux and press it? While you're there, you can also unpack my things."

The cook's jaw dropped. "Oh, but Mr. Sommersby—"

"That's all right, Mrs. O'Leary."

"But—"

Maggie hopped down from the counter and put her hand on the older woman's arm. "Really. I don't mind." She looked at Wyatt and grinned. "I'll be right there."

"Fine."

Wyatt knew that he was being insufferable and overbearing, but he wasn't sure why. Never in his life had he spoken to anyone on his own or anyone else's household staff in that way.

But what the hell. After the lousy day he'd had, who could blame him? Anyway, she ought be happy it was him and not Asa who had caught her loafing, otherwise she'd be out on her ear.

With a nod to the other members of the domestic staff, he turned on his heel and stalked out.

Mrs. O'Leary stared after him, her eyes round as saucers. The others were struck equally dumb.

When the doors finally stilled the plump cook snapped her gaping mouth shut, planted her fists on her ample hips and turned a disapproving look on Maggie. "Och, shame on you, Maggie Muldoon, you naughty girl, you. Imagine how that poor man is going to feel when he finds out that you're Mr. Asa's granddaughter."

Chapter Two

Shrugging, Maggie plucked a banana from the bowl in the middle of the table and began to peel it. "Embarrassed, probably. But that's what happens when you jump to conclusions."

"Margaret Mary Muldoon, 'tis a naughty girl you are. The man is a guest in your grandfather's home. You should have explained that he'd made a mistake."

"Before he made a fool of himself, you mean?" Maggie's grin flashed and her dimples dug deep. "Mrs. O'Leary, darlin', if Mr. Sommersby is such a snob as to judge someone by externals, that's his problem, not mine."

She was not about to admit that at least part of the reason she was bent on embarrassing Wyatt Sommersby was that she didn't care for her reaction to him. From the instant he had climbed into her truck her skin had felt all prickly and her breathing had been constricted, as though she had a weight on her chest.

"Externals? What does that mea— Oh, dear. Don't be tellin' me he saw that old wreck of a truck you drive? Saints preserve us! No wonder the poor man thought you were a maid."

"He not only saw it, I gave him a ride in it. He had a bit of mechanical trouble and had to leave his car with Lester."

Pegeen O'Leary put her hand over her heart and moaned. Chuckling, Maggie hugged her. "Now, darlin', it'll all straighten itself out. There's no need to get in a dither."

"Humph. All the same, I've a mind to tell your grandfather about this little shenanigan. He'll be none too happy about it, I'm thinkin'."

Maggie wasn't in the least worried. For one thing, Asa didn't scare her. She had long ago discovered that beneath his bark and bluster, her grandfather was an old softy. So was Pegeen O'Leary. The motherly woman would sooner cut out her tongue than cause Maggie a moment's discomfort.

Twelve years ago, when Asa had brought her into this household, Maggie had been terrified. She had felt as though she'd been dropped, all alone, into an alien world. The people, the way they spoke, their ways, the clothes they wore, the magnificent mansion in Houston, this grand country house, had all been strange to her.

She had viewed this new family she'd been thrust into with the healthy wariness and suspicion of a young wild animal. Her instinct had been to avoid them, to seek the solitude and freedom of the outdoors, as she had done most of her life in Ireland.

The morning after her arrival, while trying to sneak out through the kitchen, she'd heard Mrs. O'Leary talking to her helpers. The cook had left her native land over forty years ago, but her faint Irish brogue had been music to Maggie's ears, one blessedly familiar thing in an unfamiliar world, and she had gravitated naturally toward the plump woman.

Mrs. O'Leary had immediately taken Maggie under her wing. Growing up, she had spent most of her spare time in the kitchen chattering away with the help.

Asa was a fair man. He'd seen to it that Maggie had the same advantages as Daphne; the best schools, the best clothes, dancing lessons, art lessons, piano and voice lessons and whatever else young ladies of good families required. As a result, Maggie could hold her own in any social setting.

Yet, she had always been more comfortable with the staff. She still was, much to Daphne and Corinne's dismay.

Maggie popped the last bite of banana into her mouth and lobbed the peel across the room toward the garbage can. "Go ahead, if that's what you want to do. Personally, I don't see why you're so upset. Wyatt Sommersby will find out who I am soon enough."

Mrs. O'Leary rolled her eyes heavenward and crossed herself. "Saints preserve us, that's what I'm worried about."

Twenty minutes later, Maggie knocked on Wyatt's door. He snatched it open at once. "You certainly took your time."

She shrugged and sauntered past him with her hands in her pockets. Her expression remained blasé, but her fingers curled into fists and prickles rippled over her skin when she caught his scent. "Patience is a virtue, you know. You ought to try cultivatin' it sometime, Your Nibs. 'Tis good for the character they say."

Wyatt ground his teeth. "So is a little humbleness. And would you stop calling me that ridiculous name?"

"What? Your Nibs? 'Tisn't so ridiculous. It's what we called all the high muckity-mucks back in Ireland."

"You're not in Ireland, now."

"Aye, an' that's the truth, more's the pity," she said over her shoulder, making for the suitcase on the bed.

"It won't take me but a minute to put your things away, Mr. Sommersby. Then I'll take your tux and be gettin' out of your way." She unsnapped the locks on the mono-grammed case and spread it wide. Scooping up shirts, handkerchiefs and socks, she headed for the dresser and dumped the items into a drawer. "You see, that wasn't so difficult, was it? I'm sure if you tried you could do it yourself."

"No doubt, I could," he replied tightly. "But since that's what you're getting paid for, I don't see why I should."

She shrugged and strolled back to the open case. Picking up a pair of underwear, she held it between two fingers, turning it this way and that. They were black silk bikini briefs. "Mmm. Nice. I'll bet the ladies love these."

To Wyatt's consternation, he felt himself blushing. He was an experienced man of the world, a man of consider-able clout and sophistication. Yet he couldn't remember anyone discomfiting him they way this scrap of a woman did.

He scowled. "I sincerely hope that you don't plan to make domestic work your life's career."

"Oh? And why is that?" She pawed curiously through the rest of his things and lifted his maroon silk robe from the case. Holding it up by the shoulders, she gave it a thorough inspection, then her gaze went from the garment to him, and back. A slow, wicked grin punched her dimples deep.

"Because," Wyatt snapped, snatching the robe from her hands. "Your manner leaves a lot to be desired."

"Oh, I'm so sorry, sir. What should I do? Keep my mouth shut and my head down? Scurry about the room like a ghost so you can pretend I'm not here?"

"No, of course n—"

"Oh! I know. How about this?" Holding out an imaginary skirt, she bowed her head and bobbed a curtsy.

Wyatt's jaws clenched. "A simple attitude adjustment would be sufficient," he growled. "I merely meant that you need to control that ebullient nature of yours a bit. Be less impulsive. Less…conspicuous. And perhaps make more of an effort."

"Ah, now, the less conspicuous part would be difficult. With my red hair an' all, I stick out like a neon sign in church."

"I *mean* your manner should be more circumspect. And, by the way, you can count yourself lucky that I was the one who walked into the kitchen and found you loafing. Asa probably would have bellowed the house down."

"Mmm. You're right about that. Ah, well. I'm new at this job. I guess I'll just have to work on my deportment."

Her mouth twitched with what looked suspiciously like laughter. Wyatt frowned, and she ducked her head and scurried back to the dresser with an armload of clothes.

He ground his teeth. The little minx wasn't in the least repentant. She was merely stringing him along. And laughing.

"Do you find something amusing?"

"Oh, aye," she said cheerfully, shooting him a full-fledged grin over her shoulder.

He waited several seconds. "Would you care to share it?"

"No, I don't think so."

The pleasant but implacable statement brought Wyatt up short. For several moments he stared at her, speechless. He had not expected her to refuse. As a rule, whenever he asked a question, people gave an answer.

He snapped his mouth shut and went to stand by the window. He pretended an interest in what was going on below, but every few seconds his gaze strayed over his shoulder to Maggie. She darted back and forth between the bed and dresser with his things, humming off key and still smiling to herself as though she had a delicious secret. The wild mane of red curls that hung past her shoulders bounced with every step.

"Where do you live?" The question came out of nowhere, startling Wyatt as much as it did her.

Maggie cocked her head and gave him a wary look. "Why do you want to know?"

"I don't know. Just curious, I guess."

"I see," she murmured, and turned back to the suitcase.

"So where do you live?"

Lord, but the man was tenacious. "Oh…not too far from here," she said with a casual wave of her hand.

"In Texas that could mean anywhere from a mile to fifty."

"That's right." She hung the last garment in the closet, stowed the suitcase on the shelf, picked up the tux from the bed where she'd left it and headed for the door. "If there's nothing more, I'll take this with me. Someone will return it in plenty of time for the party."

"Wait! You didn't answer my question."

She stopped with her hand on the doorknob and looked

at him over her shoulder. Her devilish grin flashed. "I know."

Before he could speak, she darted out and hightailed it down the hall. She ducked into her own room, barely a split second before she heard his door open again.

Collapsing back against the door, she closed her eyes. "Whew. That was close."

"What was close? What have you done now? And what are you doing with that tuxedo? Honestly, Margaret Mary, if you've been up to mischief again—"

"Daphne!" Maggie's eyes popped open and focused on her sister. "What're you doing in my room?"

"I came to talk to you about tonight, but first tell me what you've done."

"Oh, that. 'Twas nothing. Forget it. You look upset. Is something wrong?" Maggie had learned over the years that the surest way to sidetrack Daphne was to turn the conversation to her favorite subject: Daphne. This time was no exception.

She twisted her hands together and began to pace. "Not upset, exactly. Just…well…concerned."

"Oh? About what?" Maggie tossed the tux into a chair, then crossed the room and flung herself backward onto the bed, bouncing twice. Daphne rolled her eyes and sighed.

"About you. Margaret Mary, you've got to give me your solemn vow that you will behave tonight. This party is important to me. And to Grandpère. He wants this tie with the Sommersby family very much. If you do something to wreck the party or my engagement to Eric, I'll…I'll just die. And there is no telling what Grandpère will do."

Maggie sighed at the affectation. Ever since they had attended that finishing school in Switzerland and learned French, Daphne had taken to calling Asa by that ridiculous title, at least when he wasn't around. Asa hated it, and had told Daphne so in no uncertain terms, but she seemed to think sprinkling her conversations with French words made her sound worldly and sophisticated.

"I see. Afraid I'll embarrass you?"

"Well…yes," she admitted in an abashed tone, then added huffily, "It *has* happened before."

"If you say so. But tell me, what, exactly, are you afraid I'll do?"

"That's just the trouble. You're so…so…uninhibited one never knows what you'll do next. Or what you'll say. It's unnerving. I want tonight to be perfect."

"Heavens, Daph. If you feel that way, why did you even invite me to the party?" Given a choice, she would have gladly stayed away. The brittle, chic affairs that her stepmother threw were not at all Maggie's cup of tea.

"Because you're my sister. Of course I would invite my own sister to my engagement party," Daphne insisted, her voice sharp with indignation. Then she spoiled it by adding, "Anyway, Grandpère insisted that you be here. You know how he feels about family occasions."

"Yes." Maggie's mouth twisted wryly. She should have known it was Asa, not Daphne or Corinne, or even Tyson, who had issued the invitation.

Asa was big on family. Maggie didn't particularly share her grandfather's sentiments on the subject. She valued freedom and independence much more than familial relationships. Why should she feel bound to a person just because they happened to share the same gene pool?

Family ties were too confining for Maggie. Close relationships of any kind made her feel trapped. She did not want the responsibility or the limitations that went with kinship or romantic love. The more strings someone tried to put on her, the more suffocated and panicky she felt and the harder she fought them.

Still, she was fond of Asa, so for his sake she occasionally gritted her teeth and bore get-togethers such as this one. At least for as long as she could.

"I'm serious, Maggie. You have to promise you won't do anything crazy tonight, not just for my sake, but for Grandpère's. He's delighted that I am going to marry Eric. He's been trying to establish a connection with the Sommersbys for years."

"Why?"

"He's looking for someone to succeed him in the business. You know that Tyson is helpless when it comes to business. Since I can't do it, and you won't, Grandpère's hoping one of us will marry a man capable of taking over for him when he retires."

Maggie gave a little shudder. "Then it will have to be up to you. I'm not interested in marriage."

"Don't be silly, Margaret Mary, every woman wants to get married."

"Not this one. Anyway, I don't see what Asa's worried about. First of all, that old warhorse will never retire. He'll probably die at his desk when he's one hundred. Secondly, he has a whole army of top executives to run the business if by some miracle he did retire."

"I know, but he wants someone in the family to be in control, someone he can trust who has experience and know-how. Since Eric's older brother Wyatt took over Sommersby Enterprises twelve years ago he's more than tripled their family's fortune."

"I see. So you're marrying Eric to please Asa."

"Of course not!" Daphne snapped. Maggie cocked one auburn eyebrow and met her sister's glare with a skeptical look. Daphne's irate expression quickly turned to chagrin.

"Oh, all right. I admit Asa did encourage me to date Eric. But I'm marrying him because I love him, so you needn't act so disapproving."

"Hey. 'Tis your life. I've no stake in it." For her sister's sake, however, she did hope that Daphne truly cared for Eric and hadn't merely convinced herself that she did in order to please Asa. Maggie didn't think much of love herself, but it was better than cold calculation.

"If Eric's brother is the one in charge, I'm surprised that Asa didn't sic you on him."

A guilty look flickered over Daphne's face. She looked away and began to fiddle with a perfume bottle on the dresser.

Maggie jerked to a sitting position, her eyes nearly bugging out of her head. "Sweet Mary and Joseph. Don't tell me you actually tried your luck with Wyatt Sommersby?"

"Yes. No! That is…I did try to interest him, but then I realized that he's not my type. He's too…too…overpowering."

I'll say, Maggie thought. She was amazed that her sister ever got up the nerve to even approach the man. Daphne was not shy, but she was accustomed to having men chase after her. "Ah, Daph, you goose, you. 'Tis a wonder he didn't tear you to shreds and have you for breakfast."

Folding her arms, Daphne hugged herself and shivered. "I know. He's very frightening. And rude, too. But he is the head of the family so I have to be nice to him. He's going to be here tonight. That's why I want you to promise you won't do or say anything inappropriate."

"Don't worry, Daphne. When I meet Mr. Sommersby tonight I'll be the soul of decorum. Cross my heart." Maggie saw no point in telling her that she'd already met Wyatt Sommersby, or under what circumstances. Daphne would only get in a tizzy and make herself sick, and what good would that do? What was done was done and there was no undoing it.

Mr. Sommersby might even see the whole thing as funny. Assuming the man had a sense of humor.

Wyatt searched the room for a mane of red curls, but none of the maids circulating among the guests with trays of drinks even remotely resembled a certain pint-sized pixie.

"Well, what do you think, my boy? Some shindig, huh?"

"Yes. Yes, it is," Wyatt agreed, abandoning his search. Standing between Asa and Corinne Hightower, he sipped champagne and studied the milling throng that filled the living room and spilled out through the three sets of French doors onto the patio and pool area at the back of the house. He had to admit, for a man who had jerked himself up by his bootstraps, Asa knew how to throw one helluva party.

The champagne was superb, the musicians were top-notch and the buffet in the dining room rivaled the menu at Maxim's.

Wyatt's gaze swept the room, and a cynical smile tugged at his mouth. The guests included the upper echelon of Texas society. Some had flown in from Dallas and San Antonio and West Texas, others from as far away as Paris and the Riviera. Wyatt knew that most had come because Eric's name had been on the invitation. Which, he suspected, was at least part of the reason Asa was so eager for this marriage to take place.

Asa Hightower was a diamond in the rough. His wealth had gained him a toehold in Houston's society, but he was more tolerated than accepted. The cachet of the Sommersby name would go a long way toward changing that.

A black-and-white uniform caught Wyatt's eye. His

gaze darted to the woman serving drinks on the other side of the room, but immediately his mouth tightened. The hair beneath the frilly white maid's cap was brown.

"Wyatt! There you are."

He looked around and saw Daphne bearing down on him with Eric and her brother Tyson in tow. Wyatt managed a tight smile. "Hello, Daphne. Tyson. Little brother."

"Sorry we weren't here when you arrived," Eric said, thumping his older brother on the back. "I heard you had some trouble with the Aston-Martin."

"A little, but it's being taken care of."

"Why don't you get rid of that money pit? It's in the shop almost as much as on the road."

"True. But some things are worth the trouble."

Eric glanced down at Daphne and his face softened. "Yeah. I know." He draped his arm around her shoulders and pulled her against his side. Smiling up at him, she snuggled close.

The look on his brother's face was so besotted Wyatt almost gagged. It was sickening. Hell would freeze over before he turned to mush over any woman. Especially not a gushy one like his brother's fiancée.

"We've been looking all over for you, Wyatt," Daphne said, slipping her arm through Eric's.

"Really? I've been right here with your grandfather all along."

"Oh, well. I guess we just missed each other. I hope you're enjoying the party. I do think it's a success, don't you?" she asked, sending an anxious glance around the room.

"It'd damned well better be," Asa snapped. "I told these two women not to spare the horses. I want all these hoity-toity snobs to know when Asa Hightower throws a party it's a humdinger."

Tyson chuckled, but his mother looked pained. "Father Hightower, really," Corinne admonished softly. "What a thing to say. Please excuse my father-in-law, Mr. Sommersby. He was just joking."

Asa snorted and muttered under his breath, "The hell I was."

"The reason Eric and I weren't here to meet you," Daphne said, "is that we were in Dallas, picking out rings. I told your brother I would be happy with a simple gold band but he insisted that I have this one."

The hand she held out sported a diamond ring of at least five carats. Wyatt thought it was gaudy as hell, but he murmured a dutiful "Very nice," and his future sister-in-law preened like a peacock.

"I'm marrying the most beautiful woman in the world. Only the best is good enough."

"Oh, Eric. You say the sweetest things."

Wyatt had to grit his teeth to keep from groaning. His brother was gazing at his fiancée like a lovesick pup. What the devil did he see in the woman?

"Where is that girl?" Corinne fretted. Craning her neck, she searched the room. "I haven't seen her all evening. She gets more irresponsible by the day. I told her that we wanted to make the announcement at precisely ten. It's five till, and she's not here yet. You really should talk to her, Asa. This is simply intolerable."

"Ah, Mom, don't worry." Tyson patted his mother's arm. "She'll be here."

"Maybe we should go ahead without her," Daphne suggested.

"No! Not without Maggie," Asa snapped.

Wyatt's head snapped around. "Who?"

"But, Grandpère—"

"Dammit, girl, I told you not to call me that! And I meant what I said. No announcement until she gets here."

"Now, Asa, be reaso—"

"Here she comes," Tyson announced.

Wyatt's head swiveled in the direction that Asa's grandson was looking, and his mouth dropped open.

The dainty vision in emerald green silk making her way toward them, red curls piled elegantly atop her head and glittering in the soft light, was none other than one Maggie Muldoon.

Chapter Three

Maggie saw the shock that spread over Wyatt Sommersby's face. She grinned and waggled her fingers at him.

Even from a distance she could see his jaws clench and his face tighten and darken, but he recovered his composure quickly and forced his expression into impassive lines.

He didn't fool Maggie for a minute. He was angry, all right. She could see it in the set of his mouth and the icy glitter in his narrowed gray eyes. Her grin widened. Poor man, she thought cheerily. No sense of humor a'tall.

He was a good-looking devil, though. Black hair and silver gray eyes were a stunning combination, Maggie decided. Especially when combined with a face that looked as though it had been chiseled out of rock.

He was no shrimp, either. Her grandfather was a big man, but standing beside him, Wyatt topped Asa's six foot one by a good inch or more. And those shoulders looked as though they were at least an ax handle wide. Altogether, he was a gorgeous specimen—rich, good-looking and oo-dles of animal magnetism. Women probably tripped over themselves trying to interest him, she thought, chuckling.

"It's about time you got here, young lady," Asa thundered when she drew near. "Where the devil have you been?"

"Oh, here and there. Have you been looking for me?"

"Of course I've been looking for you. Humph! A fine thing. I haven't seen you in over a month and you didn't even bother to come say hello when you arrived."

"Because you weren't here. Mrs. O'Leary said you'd taken the chopper to Houston." Ignoring Wyatt, Maggie went up on tiptoes and gave her grandfather's chin a kiss. "Hello, Asa, you old grump."

"Cheeky brat," the old man grumbled, but his eyes were filled with pride and love.

She greeted her sister and Corinne with a hug and complimented them on their appearance before finally turning her gaze on Wyatt.

To meet that glittering stare she had to tip her head back at a sharp angle. Up close she could see the frustration and outrage in his eyes, and she found herself battling a strong urge to laugh. She managed to assume a polite expression but she knew the slight curl of her lips and the amusement in her eyes gave her away. "Hello, Mr. Sommersby."

He nodded. "Maggie," he said softly—too softly. "I'm surprised to see you here, as I'm sure you can imagine."

Oh, yes. He was definitely angry, she thought, feeling a bubble of laughter sliding up her throat.

"What's this? You mean you've already met my grand-daughter?"

In a fraction of a second Wyatt's hard-fought composure deserted him again. His head snapped around, and he stared at Asa. "Your *granddaughter?*"

"That's right. Didn't she tell you?"

"No. No, as a matter of fact, she didn't." He zeroed in on Maggie again. "That's one item you neglected to mention."

Not one whit intimidated, Maggie chuckled. "I don't believe we got around to exchanging life stories, Mr. Sommersby. As I recall, you didn't seem to have any doubts as to who—or should I say, what—I was."

"When did you and Margaret Mary meet? And how? And why didn't you tell me you knew Wyatt?" Daphne demanded.

"Maggie and I met this afternoon. She gave me a ride from Magnolia." Throughout the explanation, Wyatt's gaze never left Maggie.

"Oh, dear Lord. You mean in that horrid old truck of hers?" Daphne covered her face with both hands and groaned against her palms. "I don't believe it. Margaret Mary, how *could* you? I begged you to get rid of that disreputable vehicle ages ago. I don't know how you can bear for anyone to see you in it."

She sent Asa a desperate look. "You see! What did I tell you? I knew she would do something to ruin my engagement party. I just knew it! Ever since she first came into this house she's been doing things like this to me."

"Oh, hush up, girl. Nobody's doing anything to you. And your party isn't ruined. Why, I'll bet you Wyatt even enjoyed that little ride. Didn't you, my boy?"

Wyatt tore his laser stare away from Maggie long enough to cast a sardonic glance Asa's way. "I wouldn't exactly say *enjoy.* However, I did appreciate the lift.... I thought you had only one granddaughter, Asa."

"Humph! I might as well have. This one's never around. She's always flitting off somewhere or another. You might as well try to hold on to a rainbow as try and control her. She's got a restless soul, just like her grandmother.''

A faraway look entered Asa's eyes. ''Until the last few years, when the sickness sapped her strength, my sweet Jessie was the same. She was like a beautiful wild bird, one no man could ever tame completely, yet you knew you were blessed that she allowed you to be part of her life.''

''Why, Asa,'' Maggie said, staring at her grandfather with amazement. ''You never told me that. I always thought I was just…I don't know…different.''

Asa blinked his misty eyes and cleared his throat. ''I thought it was obvious,'' he said gruffly.

She grinned at his discomfort and surged up on tiptoes and kissed his chin again. ''Not to me, it wasn't. Thank you for telling me.''

Wyatt frowned. ''Wait a minute, you said your name was Muldoon.'' He glanced at Maggie's left hand. ''I don't see a ring. I suppose that means you're divorced.''

''Och. There you go again, jumping to conclusions.'' Maggie shook her head and tsked.

''Don't let the name fool you. She's my granddaughter, all right. Stubborn as a mule, too. I've talked until I'm blue in the face, but she refuses to use my name.''

''Because I'm not a Hightower. I was born on the wrong side of the blanket, you see,'' she said matter-of-factly to Wyatt.

''Margaret Mary!'' Corinne gasped. She couldn't have looked more shocked if Maggie had stripped naked and done a tap dance on her prize rosewood dining table.

Daphne moaned and buried her face against Eric's chest.

Ignoring her sister's hysterics, Maggie went on in the same cheerful voice. ''You see, after he graduated from Harvard, Asa's son, John—''

"Your father," Asa snapped. "Which makes you as much a Hightower as Daphne. You're just too stubborn and too full of stiff-necked pride is all."

"Asa, we've been all over this a hundred times. If your son didn't think enough of my mother and me to give us his name, then I don't want it."

"You see," Asa thundered, looking to Wyatt for support. "Mule stubborn. Independent as hell, too, and full of sass. Enough to drive a preacher to drink."

Other than flicking her grandfather a droll look, Maggie ignored the outburst and forged right on. "Anyway, as I was saying…after graduation John Hightower went on a world tour before settling down to marry his fiancée. While he was in Ireland he had a fling with a young Irish artist named Colleen Muldoon. I'm the result."

Her sister made a sound as though she were in mortal pain.

"For heaven's sake, Daphne. What're you getting so hysterical about? Everyone in your crowd knows about me. It's not as though I'm revealing some deep, dark secret."

"I didn't know," Wyatt put in softly.

"Ah, but then, you're not really a member of my sister's crowd, are you?"

From what little she had gleaned since arriving, Wyatt Sommersby, though one of the wealthiest and most eligible bachelors in the state, was more interested in business and investing than living the life of one of the idle rich, which, Maggie conceded reluctantly, was a point in his favor.

According to Daphne, he was a financial genius and a tough-as-nails tycoon who spent almost no time playing. If he attended a party it was usually for a business reason. This engagement party was a rare exception.

Or was it? Maggie studied him, her lips pursing. Perhaps

Mr. Sommersby saw his brother's upcoming nuptials as more of a business merger than a marriage.

"True. But if you knew that, then you were also aware there was a possibility that I wouldn't know about you."

"Actually, I didn't. I hate to disappoint you, Mr. Sommersby, but until this afternoon, I'd never even heard of you. The name Wyatt Sommersby meant absolute nothing to me." Even if she had known who he was, she could not have cared less, was the message that hung in the air, unspoken. That Wyatt had received it was evident.

His eyes narrowed. Maggie's danced with laughter.

Beside them, Daphne carried on as though it were the end of the world.

"Darling, it's all right," Eric crooned, patting her shoulder. "These things happen. No one blames you. Anyway, this is the nineties. These days no one cares."

"I care," Daphne wailed. "It's so humiliating. And Margaret Mary is always doing things like this. She's so brazen about it. If she would just keep her mouth shut, people might forget. Oh, Lord, what must your brother think of us?"

"Now, darling, don't be upset," Corinne soothed. "It's an old scandal. One that people forgot about years ago. I'm sure Wyatt understands."

"Okay, that's enough. Maggie, you and Wyatt can settle this later. And for pity's sake, Daphne, shut up that caterwauling," Asa commanded. "You're making a spectacle of yourself. Our guests are beginning to stare. Anyway, it's time to make our announcement."

Corinne looked stunned. "Now? But, Father, Daphne's so upset—"

"Nonsense. Put a smile on your face, girl, and let's get this show on the road."

Daphne was too accustomed to catering to her grandfather to disobey. Her whining cut off as quick as shutting off a faucet. Hastily, she patted her hair and smoothed her dress. Linking her arm through Eric's, she beamed up at him as though he had just handed her the world on a platter.

Throughout the announcement and the well-wishing and toasts that followed, Maggie stood quietly to one side, ignoring Wyatt's steady stare. When the band struck up a tune and the happy couple took to the floor she started to ease away, but before she'd taken two steps Wyatt grasped her hand.

"Dance with me, Maggie." It was a command, not a request.

Cocking her head to one side, she studied his tight smile. She could tell he expected her to argue. She grinned and answered with a cheery "All right" and led the way.

"Although, this really isn't such a good idea, you know," she added over her shoulder as they approached the cleared area that served as a dance floor.

"Oh? And why is that?"

"You're much too tall to be my dancing partner. It'll be awkward as the very devil. I'll probably wind up with a crick in my neck."

"I think we'll manage," he said dryly, and swept her into his arms.

He was a surprisingly good dancer, Maggie discovered, though it was every bit as awkward as she had predicted— at least for her. Her head did not even reach his bow tie and even though she had on three-inch heels, she still had to dance on tiptoes to keep her hand on his shoulder.

Somehow she had thought that because he was not a part of the social scene he would be stiff and uncomfortable dancing, but he glided to the rhythm with effortless ease.

"Why didn't you tell me who you were? You let me make a complete fool of myself."

She fought back a grin. She had been expecting the question. "Why should I have? I knew you would find out soon enough. Besides, 'tisn't my place to stop you from making a fool of yourself."

"And you weren't concerned that I'd be angry?"

"Not a'tall. Why should I be?"

He studied her face for several seconds. "You really haven't ever heard of me, have you?"

"Nope. Sorry. I don't read the society pages. Nor the gossip columns."

"Nor, evidently, the business section."

"Right. I leave that to Asa," she admitted, chuckling.

"You call your grandfather Asa?"

Maggie shrugged. "Since I didn't come into his life until late, grandfather just didn't seem appropriate."

"Mmm." He continued to study her, and for several moments they danced in silence. Since Maggie had to tip her head back painfully far to see over his shoulder, she stared at a stud on his pleated silk shirt. She couldn't help but notice that he had an impressive chest. He smelled nice, too.

"So. Why don't you tell me the rest of your story," he said, deftly maneuvering her around another couple. "I got the definite feeling you left a lot out."

"Why, Your Nibs. I never would have picked you for the kind who listens to juicy gossip."

"I'm not. That's why I want to hear it from you."

"Trust me, 'tisn't very interesting."

"Tell me, anyway. Unless, of course, it's too painful to talk about."

"Painful?" Maggie thought that over. "No. Not for me, at any rate. For my mother 'twas agony."

"Did John know she was pregnant when he left Ireland?"

"Oh, yes. He even claimed to love her, but she was just a poor Irish lass with no money, no breeding and none of the social skills of his set. He told her she would never fit into his world. It crushed her, but he went back to his eminently suitable fiancée anyway."

"Corinne?"

"Yes. Three weeks after he returned they were married. Even then my mother did not give up hope that he would change his mind. But a year later, six months after I was born, Daphne came along. Mother knew then that he would never marry her. When Tyson was born three years later she died a little.

"Actually, John Hightower was probably right," she mused, glancing at the elegantly dressed, well-heeled people around them. "My mother would never have fit in with this crowd."

"Why not? You've managed to."

"You think so?" Maggie flashed him a wry look. "If by that you mean I know which fork to use, I guess you could say that, but mainly I just go my own way. In any case, my mother didn't have the opportunities that I've had. She wouldn't have had a chance with these people. They would have eaten her alive. It's too bad she never realized that. If she had, maybe she would have forgotten John Hightower and gotten on with her life, instead of wasting it pining away for something that could never be."

"What did she do after he abandoned you?"

"Oh, he didn't abandon us. Not completely, anyway. There was a check every month, and he came to visit three or four times a year. All on the QT, of course. No one in the States knew about us. He traveled a lot for Asa's company so 'twas easy for him to stop by Ireland now and then.''

"I'm surprised your mother would have any more to do with him.''

"Aw, well, she still loved him, the poor soul. Mother lived for those times. Between visits she scarcely left our cottage for fear he would call or show up and she wouldn't be there. She spent the next ten years grieving and waiting.''

"What happened after ten years?''

"She died,'' Maggie said baldly, and Wyatt winced.

"I'm sorry.''

"Don't be. 'Twas a long time ago. The doctor said 'twas pneumonia that took her, but I think 'twas a broken heart. John Hightower came to the funeral, you know. Wept like a baby, he did,'' she said in a distracted voice, her gaze fixed, unseeing, on his shirt front.

"Then what happened?'' he prodded after a moment.

"What? Oh. I went to live with relatives in Galway—distant cousins. The checks continued to come every month, but he never returned. Then about four years later the checks stopped coming, too. My cousin wrote to him to find out why, but John had been killed in an auto accident so it was Asa who got the letter. It was the first he or anyone here had heard of me.''

"That must of been quite a shock.''

"Yes, I imagine. But to give him his due, Asa came and fetched me right away. He may be a hard businessman and a crusty old coot, but family is important to him. He said I belonged here with him and my grandmother. Unfortunately, I never really got to know her. She was ill when I arrived, and she passed on eight months later.''

"It must have been a little awkward with Corinne and her children living with Asa, too.''

"A bit at first. But they've always been nice to me. Tyson is a sweetie. Despite what you saw tonight, Daphne and I get along well enough and Corinne has been remarkably tolerant."

She didn't tell him what she had always suspected—that Asa had given them no choice. Corinne was a member of an old, socially prominent but impoverished family. She and Maggie's half sister and brother were dependent on Asa for the cushy life-style they enjoyed. They all bent over backward to please him, and when he gave an order they jumped.

"So tell me, Margaret Mary Muldoon. Since you're not a part of the country club set and you're obviously not a maid, what do you do?"

"I guess you could call me a free-lance writer."

"Ah. And what is it that you write?"

"Oh, this and that. Nothing that would interest you."

He frowned, clearly not pleased with being so summarily cut off. He was accustomed to having his questions answered.

Before he could say more the music ended and she pulled out of his arms, flashing an amused smile. "Thank you for the dance, Mr. Sommersby."

"Maggie! There you are, I've been looking all over for you."

Annoyance rippled through Wyatt at the interruption, but Maggie whirled and let out a whoop. "Philip!"

Frowning, Wyatt watched her cover the short space and hurl herself into a man's open arms with utter abandon.

Wyatt recognized him. Philip Townsend was the scion of an old Texas family whose fortune had been made in oil during the boom days. Though a nice enough sort, he was a jet-setting playboy who drifted aimlessly through life, drinking, partying and seducing women, not necessarily in that order.

"Ah, Maggie, my love, you're a sight for sore eyes," Philip said, holding her at arm's length. "Where have you been? I've been trying to call you ever since I returned from the Riviera last week."

"I've been on the road for a few days. I came back yesterday just so I could attend this party."

Philip sighed. "When are you going to give up that nonsense and marry me? You know I love you madly. I'll give you the moon and stars, my darling. Just say the word."

Wyatt watched them, his jaw tight. Townsend was looking at her like a gourmet eyeing a delicious treat, and Maggie's mischievous grin flashed indiscriminately.

Laughing, she went up on tiptoes and kissed Philip's cheek. "You know you'd keel over in a faint if I said yes."

For an instant Philip's perpetually devil-may-care expression slipped and something hot and intense burned in his eyes. The look vanished as quickly as it had come, and he turned on his sleepy-eyed grin.

"Try me."

"What? And give your sainted mother a heart attack? I couldn't live with that on my conscience."

He tweaked her upturned nose and gave her a soulful look. "One of these days I'm going to wear you down."

"Have you congratulated Daphne and Eric yet?" she asked, deftly changing the subject. At Philip's no, she linked her arm with his and turned to lead him toward the group where her sister and Eric stood. But when she noticed Wyatt, she stopped.

"Oh. Philip, have you met Wyatt Sommersby?"

Wyatt gritted his teeth. She had forgotten he was even

there. That was a first, and he didn't particularly like the experience.

"Yes, of course. We've known each other for years." Philip smiled and stuck out his hand, and Wyatt had no choice but to take it. "How are you, Wyatt? I haven't seen you around for a while."

"I've been hard at work. Business has taken up most of my time lately," he replied, squeezing Philip's hand harder than necessary.

It was a deliberate dig, and he watched the younger man for signs of discomfort, but Philip didn't turn a hair.

"C'mon, Philip, before the happy couple are swamped," Maggie said, tugging him toward the sidelines. "You can say hello to Asa while you're there, too."

Wyatt followed along behind the pair, feeling like a fifth wheel—another new experience he found less than pleasing.

After a few minutes of well-wishing and small talk, Philip dragged Maggie back out onto the dance floor. Wyatt watched them, frowning.

He took Maggie through an intricate dance maneuver, whirling her round and round. She threw back her head and laughed, and Wyatt's eyes narrowed as they traced over the graceful arch of her neck.

"You're probably wondering why I didn't introduce you to Maggie instead of Daphne."

He looked around and found Asa standing beside him, watching his granddaughter. "The thought has crossed my mind."

"Would it have made any difference if I had?"

"Ultimately, no. I'm not the marrying kind."

"Mmm. That's what I thought, so I didn't see any sense in bothering. Besides, Maggie's not as biddable as Daphne. If she thought I was matchmaking she'd have my head."

Wyatt chuckled and cast Asa an amused look, but his eyes returned at once to the pixie on the dance floor. He could feel Asa watching him, his pensive gaze flickering back and forth between him and Maggie, but he ignored the older man.

"Take my advice. Don't set your sights on Maggie."

The comment was not at all what Wyatt had expected. He'd been sure the old fox was plotting ways to get the two of them together. The concern in Asa's voice was sincere, however, and Wyatt was surprised by the look of compassion in the old man's eyes.

"She's a free spirit who goes where the wind blows her. A will-o'-the-wisp as elusive as a leprechaun. The more you try to hold on to her or tie her to you, the more she pulls away. So if you've got ideas in that direction, my advice to you is to forget them. She'll break your heart, my boy."

Wyatt started to give a scornful snort, until he saw Asa's expression. He could not imagine any woman meaning that much to him, but he could see that the old man meant every word.

"Don't worry about me, Asa," he said with a droll smile. "I promise you, my heart is safe. Even from leprechauns."

"Humph. Just don't say I didn't warn you."

Wyatt shrugged off Asa's warning. He was confident of his ability to resist any woman's charms. Nevertheless, all evening his gaze followed Maggie wherever she went.

She fascinated him. He'd never met a woman quite like Maggie. She seemed so…so alive. She practically vibrated with vitality. A smile rarely left her lips, and her eyes had a perpetual twinkle.

Of course, whenever she was in his vicinity she seemed

to be laughing at him. It was annoying and frustrating as hell, but still he found her thoroughly captivating.

Around midnight, after having danced his duty dances with his future sister-in-law and her mother, Wyatt stood on the sidelines with Asa, watching Maggie talking with a group of women on the other side of the room. She looked like a tiny, brightly colored parakeet in a roomful of crows. It was at that precise moment that he decided he wanted Margaret Mary Muldoon.

"Uh-oh. Looks like Philip's had a few too many."

Asa's comment drew Wyatt's attention to the younger man. His lips thinned as he watched Philip stagger over to Maggie and sling an arm around her shoulders, nearly toppling her. He murmured something in her ear and took advantage of the opportunity to nibble her neck at the same time.

Wyatt was about to go over and jerk him off her, when Maggie started leading her inebriated friend their way. Philip leaned heavily on her. She nearly went down under his weight twice before they reached them.

"Philip isn't feeling too well, I'm afraid," she announced with a rueful grimace when she drew near.

Wobbling on his feet, Philip gave them a sloppy smile and held up one hand, his thumb and forefinger an inch apart. "Had a leeetle too mussh of the bu-bubbly."

"As you can see, he's in no shape to drive, so I'm takin' him home. With the hangover he's going to have, he wouldn't enjoy the rest of the weekend anyway."

"Issch been one...*hic*...one he-helluva party."

Wyatt shot Philip a disgusted glare and had to clench his fist to keep from punching the goofy grin off his face. "Surely one of the ranch hands could drive him," he said tightly. "It's a long way to Houston and back, and it's late already."

"Oh, I'm not coming back. I was going home tonight, anyway. I only came for the party."

"I suppose I should be grateful you stayed as long as you did," Asa grumbled. "All right, all right. Go on with you. But you drive careful, girl, you hear? And tell Philip I'll have one of my men drive his car home tomorrow. That is, if he's sober enough to understand when you get him home."

"Have him drive my truck instead. I'm driving Philip's Jag." She wrinkled her nose and grinned. "You don't think I'd risk having him throw up in my truck, do you? Now, come along, Philip, you jughead. Let's go pour you into the car."

"'Night all. Wonnerful par...*hic*...ty."

"You mean you're just going to let her go off with him? Alone?" Wyatt demanded. "The man's skunk drunk, for God's sake. What if he gets violent."

"Philip? Naw, he gets sloppy and mushy, but there's not a mean bone in his body. Besides, if anyone can handle him, it's Maggie. They've been pals since they were fourteen. Don't worry about it. Maggie knows what she's doing."

Wyatt's gaze followed the bright curls as the pair wove an erratic path through the room. For all he knew, they could be lovers. It was none of his business.

His jaw clenched and a muscle jumped in his cheek. The hell it wasn't.

Chapter Four

There had to be some mistake. Maggie couldn't live here.

Wyatt brought his Aston-Martin to a halt by the curb and stared at the number on the building. It was the correct address, all right. But it was a warehouse, for Pete's sake.

He looked around, scowling. An old warehouse in a rundown part of downtown Houston. Hell, nobody lived downtown—nobody in their right mind, at any rate.

Oh, he'd heard about the latest trend among the yuppie crowd of buying a loft apartment in a converted warehouse, but that was a recent brainstorm of a slick developer who didn't seem to realize that Houston wasn't New York.

After the offices and stores closed there was a mass exodus for the suburbs, and except for a few exclusive restaurants, hotels and theaters, the downtown area of Houston shut down tighter than a drum. There were no little neighborhood stores or bars or restaurants in the heart of town. Hell, there were no neighborhoods. Except for theatergoers and concertgoers, about the only people on the streets after dark were winos, perverts, crooks and cops.

Even all those fashionable converted warehouses were congregated together a mile or so away on the perimeter of the downtown area. This cavernous old dinosaur appeared to still be a working warehouse.

A wino lay curled up on the sidewalk down the block. In the alley beside the building a half dozen scrawny cats meowed indignantly at a bag lady poking through a Dumpster.

Wyatt's lips curled at one corner. Dammit, didn't that woman have a lick of sense? And what the hell was the matter with Asa, letting her live here?

Wyatt cut the engine and started to open the car door, then paused with his hand on the handle, his gaze skimming the street once again. Damn, he hated to leave his car parked in this neighborhood. He'd probably find it gutted and sitting on its axles when he got back. Hell, what he ought to do was just drive away and forget about the aggravating woman.

With a sigh, he climbed out and activated the car alarm.

He entered the small door beside the wide bay doors on the loading dock and found himself in a tiny vestibule. Straight ahead a flight of metal stairs went up at a sharp angle. Through the glass-paneled wall at the back a cluttered office was visible. A quick look through the barred window in the steel door to the right revealed the ground floor of the warehouse. A freight elevator was to his left.

On Sunday no one was there, but the place was stacked high with crates and boxes and several forklifts sat in the aisles. In one corner, Wyatt spotted Philip's fire engine red Jaguar parked beside a motor home. His mouth tightened.

The guy could be in Maggie's bed at that very moment.

What would he do if he was? Grim-faced, Wyatt took the stairs two at a time. Throw him the hell out, that's what.

As he suspected, the freight elevator opened onto the small landing at the top of the stairs. Directly across from the open shaft was a windowless metal door with a brass knocker in the center and a tiny nameplate above it inscribed M. M. Muldoon.

Wyatt banged the knocker hard three times. He tapped his foot and counted to ten, then banged the knocker again as hard as he could without letup.

It seemed he'd been rapping for five minutes before the door finally opened. Through the inch-and-a-half crack a bleary blue eye peered out. "Yes? Oh. It's you."

Her tone prickled, and he was suddenly furious. "Do you always answer the door without checking first to see who's on the other side? Good Lord, woman, this is a dangerous part of town. Haven't you any sense at all?"

"I know everyone around here and they know me. I'm perfectly safe," she mumbled over a yawn.

"Even the wino down the street and the bag lady pawing through your garbage?"

"Fred and Agnes? Sure. Mmm, I hope she finds that blouse I put out there for her."

"You leave handouts for the bag lady to find? Why am I not surprised? Look, I'd rather not carry on this conversation out here. I have this uneasy feeling I'm going to be mugged at any moment."

The bleary eye narrowed. "What're you doing here, anyway? You're suppose to be at Asa's. The engagement party isn't over until tomorrow evening."

"I told your grandfather an urgent business matter needed my attention. He understood."

She grunted. "Asa would."

"Let me in, Maggie."

"Oh, all right." Sighing, she pulled the door open.

Wyatt stepped inside and found himself in a small raised entryway, separated from the rest of the apartment by an iron railing. Three steps down, the cavernous apartment seemed to stretch away forever. Curious, he scanned the open space.

Windows wrapped around the apartment on two sides and massive skylights dotted the high ceiling, flooding the space with sunlight. Several groupings of furniture rested on colorful rugs, which formed small islands on the great expanse of polished hardwood floors. At the far end of the loft, a set of stairs led up to a raised platform, which Wyatt assumed was Maggie's bedroom. The wall of the bedroom overlooking the rest of the apartment was only about six feet high and was made up entirely of stacked aquariums.

Wyatt stared at the wavering images coming through the sunlit water.

"What're you doing here, anyway, Your Nibs?"

"I want to talk to you—" He swung to face her, as she turned from closing the door, and froze in his tracks.

"About what? I can't imagine what you would need to speak to me about."

Wyatt gaped, speechless. She was wearing bunny slippers! Big, fuzzy things with glass eyes and whiskers and gigantic floppy ears!

Slowly, his stunned gaze rose from her feet up over a pair of shapely calves, but just above her knees he received another shock. Her nightgown was an enormous blue-and-white Houston Oiler football jersey. It wasn't one you buy at souvenir stands, either. This was the real thing.

The neck opening drooped over one shoulder, exposing an expanse of creamy white skin covering incredibly delicate bones. The hem came down to the top of her knees, and the short sleeves hung almost to her wrists. Made for a two-hundred-fifty-pound-plus football player, the shirt could have wrapped around Maggie twice with material left over.

Her mane of red curls stuck out wildly in all directions. Scrubbed free of makeup, her face was rosy from sleep and shiny in the morning sun coming through the wrap-around windows and skylights. Amber freckles dotted the bridge of her nose and her cheeks still bore pillow marks.

Standing there disheveled and half-asleep, wearing that enormous jersey and bunny slippers, she should have looked ridiculous.

What she looked was adorable…and sexy as hell.

Lust slammed through Wyatt. His nostrils flared and his jaws clenched. He had to knot his hands into fists to keep from snatching her up and carrying her back to bed.

He frowned. "Where did you get that jersey?"

"A friend gave it to me. He used to play on the team." Running her fingers through her tangled hair, she turned and trudged down the steps and headed for the open kitchen area, bunny ears flopping. The name A. Petrantonio was stenciled across the back. Wyatt followed on her heels, his jaw clenched and his gaze flicking back and forth between the name and the enticing movement of her derriere beneath the jersey.

"This had better be important, to get me up so early."

"It's ten after nine. What's this friend's name?"

"Anthony Petrantonio. And nine is early when you didn't get to bed until dawn."

What had she been doing all night? Remembering the sports car down stairs, his mouth tightened.

He shot a look around. "Where is Townsend, by the way?"

"Philip? By now, probably hanging over a toilet wishing he were dead." She rounded the end of the counter that separated the kitchen from the rest of the loft, crossed to the refrigerator and stuck her head inside. "I hope you're not expecting coffee, because I don't have any" came the muffled announcement from inside the fridge.

"I phoned his apartment. He wasn't there."

"Who? Oh, you mean Philip. I know." She straightened with an apple in her hand and shot him an inquiring look. "Wanna apple? I've got two."

"No, thanks," he replied tightly.

Shrugging, Maggie bit into the apple and munched.

"So where is Philip?"

"I took him to his mother's house. She'll scold him when he wakes up, but then she'll fuss over him and wait on him hand and foot until he's feeling better."

She cocked her head. "What do you want with Philip?"

"Nothing. I just wanted to know where he was."

"Why?"

"I thought he might be here."

"Here? Why would I bring him— Oh. I see."

"Are you lovers?"

"Philip and me?" She laughed. "Of course not. Where'd you get an idea like that?"

"I heard him propose to you."

"Oh, that. 'Twas nothing." She bit off another chunk of apple and munched. A drop of juice escaped her lips and she caught it with her fingertip and licked it off.

Wyatt nearly ground his back teeth off.

When she'd swallowed the bite she grinned at him. "Philip is always proposing to me. It stops his mother from nagging him about getting married. He told her he would only marry for love, and as long as she thinks he's in love with me she leaves him alone. She's too scared of pushing him into marrying me to do otherwise."

Wyatt studied her guileless face. She really believed that

nonsense, but he didn't. He'd seen the way Philip looked at her. "She disapproves of a match between you and Philip?"

"Disapproves? Och, the poor woman gets heart palpitation at the thought." Maggie's dimples deepened and she said sotto voce, "I'm not a'tall suitable, don't you know. Given the circumstances of my birth an' all."

"That's absurd." He experienced a surprising flash of anger. Philip's mother was the biggest snob he'd ever met. The woman never missed an opportunity to let everyone know that her ancestry could be traced back to the *Mayflower*. Normally he ignored her, but somehow the thought of her looking down her nose at Maggie made him burn.

"But 'tis true. Asa's a successful man, but he's still considered a bit of an upstart by Houston society. The only reason many of them tolerate him is his money. His bastard granddaughter is just a bit too much for Emaline to stomach."

She finished the apple, tossed the core into a trash can and licked the juice off her fingers.

Wyatt nearly groaned. Was the woman deliberately trying to drive him nuts?

Maggie yawned and stretched, arching her back, arms reaching high over her head. He watched the hem of the jersey ride to the tops of her thighs and his mouth went dry. For such a little thing, she had legs that went on forever.

"So what was it you wanted to talk to me about?" she asked, knuckling her eyes and stifling another yawn. "It must be important. You had to have left Asa's at the crack of dawn to get here at this hour."

She didn't know the half of it. After a sleepless night he'd dragged Eric out of bed before daybreak and made his brother drive him to Lester's house in Magnolia. The mechanic hadn't been any more pleased than Eric had been about being rousted out of bed just so Wyatt could retrieve his car.

She stopped mid-yawn and gave him a sharp look. "Come to think of it, how did you get my address?"

"I got it from Daphne."

"You did what? Ah, saints preserve us, you might as well have asked Asa for it, because she's sure to have told him."

"So?"

"Och, man, you've no idea what you done. Asa will think you're interested in me." She groaned and ran her hand through her wild mane. "Holy Mary and Joseph, the man's probably orderin' wedding invitations as we speak."

Wyatt chuckled. "I doubt that. Anyway, so what if he is? It'll do him no good."

"*I* know that and *you* know that, but try telling that to Asa. One of his main goals in life is to see me married and settled, perish the thought."

Maggie made a face and shuddered eloquently and Wyatt laughed outright this time. "Look, forget about Asa. If he gets any ideas in that direction I'll set him straight. Right now, why don't you get dressed and I'll take you out to breakfast and we'll talk."

"No, thanks. I just had breakfast."

"An apple isn't breakfast."

"'Tis for me. Anyway, I don't have time to go out. I've work to do, and since I'm up, I might as get to it. So why don't you just tell me what it is you want to discuss."

"I want to talk to you about Daphne and Eric."

"What about them?"

"The truth is, I'm not entirely sure I'm in favor of this marriage. I consented to the engagement only to stall for time. But now they're talking about getting married soon. I don't think that's such a good idea.''

''*You* consented? Eric's a grown man. He doesn't need your permission to get married.''

''No he doesn't. However, I do control his trust fund until he's thirty-five. I also run Sommersby Enterprises. Eric has a job there only because I allow him to have one.''

''So you control him with the purse strings, is that it?''

''When it's for his own good, yes. My brother tends to be impulsive. A case in point is this engagement.

''He and Daphne have known each other a grand total of two months. I think it would be wise if they got to know each other better before they take that leap. I want you to talk to them, especially Daphne. Help me convince them to wait.''

''Sorry, I'm afraid I can't do that.''

He looked stunned. Clearly he had not expected her to refuse. Wyatt was a man accustomed to getting his way.

Biting back a grin, Maggie wandered over and sat down on the high stool before the drafting table located beneath a skylight along the north wall of windows. She studied the sketch pinned to the surface, her eyebrows drawing together in a frown of concentration.

''Why not?''

''What? Oh. Because I make it a rule never to interfere in anyone else's life.''

''Sometimes we have no choice.''

''Sure you do. You just butt out and leave people to their own devices. You should try it sometimes.''

''Don't you want your sister to be happy? What if it turns out this isn't the real thing? What if they marry, then later divorce. How would you feel then?''

''Sad for them, of course, but not responsible, so you can quit trying to make me feel guilty. Of course I want my sister to be happy, but not enough to stick my nose into her business. Live and let live, I always say.''

She picked up a broad-nibbed pen, dipped it into a bottle of ink and stroked it over the paper on the drafting board.

Wyatt paced the room. She glanced at him once, and her lips twitched. He seemed to be counting under his breath. Poor man. He was going to pop a blood vessel if he didn't calm down.

''That's fine for strangers, but this is your sister, for Pete's sake.'' Maggie shot him an ironic look and he spread his hands wide. ''All right, all right, she's your half sister, and maybe you're not all that close, but she's still your family.''

Before he'd finished, Maggie's attention had drifted back to the drawing. She heard Wyatt's words but they didn't truly register. She dipped her pen into the ink again, and with a few quick strokes gave the knobby-kneed crane a comically shocked expression.

''…understand that you have an obligation to— Are you listening to me?''

''Mmm,'' Maggie mumbled, and stroked in a few ruffled feathers on the duck.

''Oh, for— Will you stop that scribbling and pay attention. What're you doing, anyway?''

''Mmm,'' she replied again absently.

''Dammit, woman, I asked you a question,'' he barked, and Maggie jumped.

She glanced at his angry face and replayed his last words in her mind. ''Oh! Uh…just a little finish work.''

He crossed the room and looked over her shoulder. ''What is— Hey, wait a minute. I recognize this. Those are the characters from those children's books. What are they called?'' He snapped his fingers. ''Damn. I know that series. I've read those books to my niece, Melissa, a dozen times. What the devil is it?''

She grinned, ridiculously pleased that he not only knew her work, he seemed to like it.

"The Adventures of Mergatroid and Arbuckle," she supplied, adding quick strokes to the drawing.

"Right! The knock-kneed crane and the cross-eyed duck who travel the world together in search of adventure. They're my four-year old niece's favorite books. My sister and brother-in-law think they're terrific. They live in the Orient so we have to send them the books. They say this Professor Everything who writes them is the greatest author of children's literature since Dr. Seuss.''

He gave her a sharp look. "Wait a second. Don't tell me you illustrate them.''

"I write *and* illustrate them.''

"You're kidding." He looked astounded. Maggie laughed.

"I told you I was a free-lance writer.''

"Yeah, but I thought you meant you dabbled in poetry or something. I didn't know you were famous.''

"I'm not, thank heavens. Professor Everything is becoming moderately well-known among the younger set, but I'm not being hailed as a literary lion just yet.''

"I see. You use a pseudonym to protect your privacy.''

"Yes," Maggie said cautiously. She didn't like the calculating gleam in his eyes. Shrewd businessmen like Asa and Wyatt had a knack for turning the simplest things to their own advantage. She had the uneasy feeling he was storing away that piece of information to use later. "If I were recognized I wouldn't be able to travel around the country doing my research with anonymity.''

He glanced around at the loft again. Maggie had the

feeling he was assessing her belongings, even the clothes she wore. "Does writing children's books pay well?"

"I'm not getting rich, if that's what you mean, but I manage to earn a comfortable living."

"Mmm, I see."

He saw what? Suddenly Maggie felt an urgent need to get him out of her apartment.

"Look, Mr. Sommersby—"

"Wyatt," he insisted.

"All right…Wyatt, if you'll excuse me, I've got a lot of work to do."

Wyatt stared at her. He wasn't accustomed to being dismissed, certainly not by a slip of a woman like Maggie. She was the antithesis of the women with whom he had associated in the past—irreverent, sassy, uninhibited and impulsive. She was also fascinating. And adorable. And the sexiest, most innocently alluring female he'd ever met.

"Have dinner with me tonight, Maggie."

"What?" Maggie blinked up at him, for once at a loss for words. His tone, more than the request, sent a little frisson through her. It was low and husky, dark with masculine intensity. "I-I'm sorry. What did you say?"

"I said have dinner with me."

"Why? If you think I'll change my mind about Eric and Daphne—"

"This has nothing to do with them."

"Then why—" Her eyes widened. "You didn't come here to talk about Daphne and Eric at all, did you?"

"Not really," he confessed, without a flicker of remorse or embarrassment. "I am concerned about my brother, but mainly I wanted to see you again." He leaned forward, bracing one hand on the back of her chair and the other on the drafting table, hemming her in. The look in his eyes made Maggie's heart stutter, then take off at a gallop.

"The truth is, like it or not, I'm attracted to you, Maggie. Very attracted."

For an instant she experienced a rush of panic, but Maggie's sense of humor was never far from the surface. The absurdity of the statement struck her, and she tipped her head back and gave a throaty chuckle.

Whatever reaction Wyatt expected, it obviously wasn't that one. His black eyebrows jerked together.

"You find that funny?"

"Hilarious," she sputtered, fighting laughter.

It was a losing battle, and finally she surrendered to the overwhelming urge. She laughed so hard her eyes streamed and her shoulders shook. After a while she folded her arms on the drawing board, put her head down and let the gales of mirth fill the room.

Long before her laughter ran its course she became aware of the ominous silence from Wyatt. She knew he was furious, but she couldn't seem to stop.

Finally, weak with laughter, she raised her head and wiped her cheeks with the backs of her hands. She tried to look contrite but her lips still quivered. "I-I'm sorry."

"Are you quite through?"

It hurt her throat, but Maggie swallowed down another bubble of laughter and nodded, biting her lower lip.

"May I ask just what it is that you find so amusing?"

"Everything. Oh, Wyatt, you can't be serious. I'm not your type at all."

"You think I don't know that?" he said between clenched teeth.

"We're opposites in every way."

"I know."

"Your life is making deals, acquiring things, nailing everything down in black-and-white. I value freedom, the unexpected. I hate being tied to anyone or anything."

"I'm aware of that," he agreed, but she could see that he wasn't budging. Frustration and amusement mingled in her voice.

"Look, Wyatt, be reasonable. You're an intense, dominant man who has to be in control. You make things happen. I blow where the wind takes me. I let life happen. For me, every day is a new experience, a grand surprise to be relished."

"I'm beginning to gather that."

"I'd drive you crazy in a week."

"Dammit! I know that, too!" he roared. "Don't you think I've told myself that? I spent the better part of the night telling myself all those things and more. But it doesn't change a thing. I'm still attracted to you."

"Well, saints above, get over it, man! It'll never work."

"How do you know if you won't give it a try?"

"Don't be daft. I've no need to walk through fire to know I wouldn't like the experience." On the surface Maggie appeared calm, even amused, but her brogue grew thicker with every word she spoke, a sure sign of nerves.

"Interesting that you equate this thing between us with fire." His gaze zeroed in on her mouth and narrowed. His silvery eyes darkened to a stormy gray. "It is hot."

"You *are* daft." She chuckled. "There's nothing between us. Nothing a'tall. Nor is there going to be."

"You're wrong. Like it or not, you're just as attracted to me as I am to you. What's more, you know it."

"Now you're dreamin'. You really should get a grip, Your Nibs."

A hard smile split Wyatt's handsome face. "You think this is all one-sided, do you? Why don't we put it to the test?"

Before she could evade him he bent his elbows and

swooped. She barely had time to suck in a breath before his mouth captured hers.

Maggie had been kissed before, many times—at least she'd thought she had—but she had never experienced anything like this. The heat was incredible. Her blood seemed to be rushing through her body like molten lava. She wouldn't be at all surprised to learn that the insides of her veins were blistered.

It wasn't a forceful kiss, but soft, wooing, breathtakingly tender. The feather-light caress sent a current of electricity zinging through her. Every cell in her body sprang to attention, every nerve ending sizzled.

Maggie's toes curled in her bunny slippers. Her hands knotted into the soft jersey material covering her thighs. Otherwise she didn't move a muscle. She didn't even breathe.

Her head was beginning to spin when he finally ended the kiss. He drew back only a few inches and looked into her eyes, smiling.

"Well?"

She sucked in a deep breath. As her head cleared she quickly gathered her composure. Pursing her lips, she pretended to ponder a moment. "'Twas very nice. You're a good kisser, I'll give you that. But 'twas nothing I'd lose my head over."

For an instant Wyatt's face hardened. Then he paused and studied her flushed face, and his smile returned, slow and self-satisfied. "Little liar."

"I'm no such th—"

"Shh." He put his forefinger over her mouth, silencing her. "We won't argue the point. You'd lose, anyway."

Before Maggie could find her tongue he straightened and headed for the door. With his hand on the doorknob he turned and looked at her, and even across the vast width of the loft Maggie could see the determined glitter in those silvery eyes. "This isn't over, Maggie. Count on it."

When the door clicked shut behind him Maggie expelled a long, pent-up breath and slumped in her chair. "Sweet Mary and Joseph, the man is lethal." She touched trembling fingers to her lips and closed her eyes. If she were the kind of woman who pined for love and romance she could wind up with a broken heart.

The thought no sooner flickered through her mind than her eyes popped open and she laughed. Picking up a pen, she turned her attention back to the drawing.

"'Tis a good thing you're made of stronger stuff, Maggie Muldoon," she announced to the room in general. "Otherwise, my girl, you'd be in big trouble. Big trouble, indeed."

Chapter Five

"Dammit, I thought we had a deal."

"We do." Asa smiled innocently at Wyatt. "As soon as the vows are said I'll gift Daphne and Eric with one percent of the stock in BargainMart and give him the option to purchase five percent more. In return, you will appoint me to the board of directors of Sommersby Enterprises."

"But you failed to mention that Eric wouldn't be allowed to turn the stock over to me."

Asa shrugged. "BargainMart was set up as a family owned company. The articles of incorporation forbid sale or transfer to a nonfamily member. Your brother will be a member of my family by marriage, but I'm afraid that status doesn't stretch to you."

"You own ninety-five percent of the shares. You could vote to change the articles of incorporation."

"I could, but I won't. What I worked my tail off to create is damned well going to stay in my family."

Wyatt ground his teeth. It wasn't often he was bested on a deal, but the old coot had done it. "All right, you win. But I'm warning you, the wedding had better not take place for at least a year. If it does you can forget that board of directors appointment."

"Don't worry, Daphne will do as I say. She's a biddable girl. Unlike that sister of hers," Asa grumbled.

Wyatt's jaws clenched at the mention of Maggie. He hadn't seen her in three weeks, not since that morning at her loft. He had flown to Paris the next day to deal with an urgent matter and had returned only four days ago.

And he had been fighting the urge to see her again ever since.

While he'd been away she had been on his mind constantly. Thoughts of her had kept him awake at night, and when he had slept he'd dreamed about her. In the middle of meetings his mind had wandered to that pixie face and saucy grin.

His preoccupation with Maggie angered him. On the flight back he'd decided he wouldn't see her again after all.

It was a wise decision, he told himself. There were plenty of other women around. He didn't need a royal pain in the posterior like Maggie Muldoon complicating his life. He was definitely better off without her.

He returned his signed copy of their agreement to his briefcase and needlessly shuffled several other papers. "So...how is Maggie?" he asked casually.

"How the devil would I know? Hell, you've seen her since I have. You tell me."

Wyatt's head snapped up. "How did you know about that?"

"Never mind. I have my ways." Asa took a cigar from the box on his desk, unwrapped it and leaned back in his chair. Taking his time, he lit up and puffed contentedly. "So…you're interested in Maggie, are you?"

"Not really," he lied. "I was curious about her, is all."

"Mmm." Asa blew a puff of smoke toward the ceiling. "That's too bad. I plan to gift the man who marries her with ten percent of the company and an option on ten percent more."

Wyatt tried not to let his shock show. "Twenty percent? That's almost four times what you're offering Eric. You must be desperate to get Maggie married off. Which raises the question of why."

"Let's just say I worry about her more than Daphne. Oh, I know she's sassy and self-reliant, but she's also too free spirited and too damned trusting of her fellow man for her own good. I want to see her married to a strong man who'll watch over her and take good care of her, see that she doesn't come to harm." Asa grimaced. "One, of course, who has the good sense not to let her know he's doing it."

"From what I've seen of your granddaughter, I'm sure that would be wise. I must admit, your offer is tempting, but I'm not your man. Not even for twenty percent of BargainMart."

With one eye squinted against the smoke, Asa puffed on his cigar and studied Wyatt. "Mmm. You're probably right. The man who marries Maggie should be gentle and easygoing and have the patience of Job. He's going to need it."

Wyatt gritted his teeth. The thought of Maggie with another man didn't set well with him for some reason.

He snapped his briefcase shut and rose. "I think we're

finished here. If you'll excuse me, I've got another appointment.'' He shook Asa's hand and headed for the door.

He had barely reached it when Asa said, ''Tell me something, Wyatt.''

He looked over his shoulder. ''Yes?''

''Did you satisfy that curiosity?''

Wyatt's jaw clenched but he met the older man's gaze without flinching. ''No.''

''I thought not,'' Asa said, grinning around his cigar.

After pounding on Maggie's door for ten minutes Wyatt had given up and was on the verge of climbing back into his car when he spotted her coming around the corner.

Leaning his hips back against the Aston-Martin's spotless fender, he folded his arms over his chest, crossed his legs at the ankles and waited, drinking in the sight of her like a thirsty man at a well.

She strolled down the sidewalk without a care, licking an ice cream cone. She applied herself to the task, enjoying the treat as much as any eight-year-old would.

Keeping ahead of the summer heat was a losing battle. Her pink tongue flicked and swirled, but the vanilla ice cream still dripped down her fingers, and every now and then she had to stop and lick those, as well.

She wore shorts and a halter top. Wyatt's gaze trailed over those long legs and bare midriff and settled in the shadowy cleft between her breasts, where her skin glowed with perspiration. His nostrils flared. All the blood in his body seemed to rush to his loins and settle there, hot and heavy.

Her hair was subdued in a French braid, though errant curls had pulled loose and stuck out in all directions. The strap on one sandal had slipped off her heel and with every step the shoe slapped against the bottom of her foot.

None of it bothered Maggie. She was too busy enjoying herself. Never had Wyatt met anyone so totally unaffected.

Maybe that was why she fascinated him, he mused. With Maggie, what you saw and heard was genuine. There wasn't an ounce of artifice or guile in her. She said what was on her mind and did as she pleased, however the spirit moved her, and laughed if you were surprised or shocked or disapproving.

She was the opposite of most of the women he knew. Pretentious, shallow women whose very lives revolved around superficial things—wearing the right designer label, attending the right parties, frequenting the right places with the right people, living in the right neighborhoods and driving the right cars. Vain women who spent hours with personal trainers and hairdressers, who'd sooner die than allow anyone to see them without the armor of full makeup or looking anything less than perfect. Sly, artificial women who smiled and said what they thought you wanted to hear.

Like a breath of clean air, Maggie was a refreshing change from all that. One he intended to enjoy…and to bloody hell with all the reasons he'd given himself for staying away.

He would not, of course, be taking Asa up on his offer. Marriage was out of the question. Fact was, Asa might well want to string him up from the nearest tree for what he intended, but so be it. He wanted Maggie, and he was damn well going to have her.

She was about fifty feet away when a wino stumbled out of the alley beside the warehouse and hailed her.

Wyatt tensed and pushed away from the car, but to his astonishment, Maggie stopped and chatted with the man. It was clear that she knew him. Her face was animated and cheerful, and from her expression you would have thought the filthy old bum was a dear friend. After a moment she handed him her ice cream cone, dug into the pocket of her shorts and gave him something else. What, Wyatt couldn't be sure but from the old derelict's reaction, he had a hunch it was money.

Maggie waved to the man and resumed her leisurely stroll and he staggered down the street in the opposite direction avidly devouring the remainder of her ice cream cone. Wyatt settled back against the car, shaking his head.

Intent on licking the ice cream from her fingers, she had yet to notice him. Anticipation tightened Wyatt's body, and as she strolled nearer his mouth curved in an unyielding smile.

Ten feet from the doorway Maggie looked up, and her heart gave a funny little skip. She jerked to a halt in the middle of the cracked sidewalk.

There in front of the warehouse, leaning against his car, legs crossed at the ankles, was Wyatt, watching her in that steady, determined way that sent a chill rippling through her.

She had obviously underestimated him.

Three weeks ago she had dismissed Wyatt's warning with the cocky ease of a woman who had managed to remain heart-whole for all of her twenty-six years.

She was a novelty to him, she had decided, a breed of female outside his experience, and therefore a challenge to his dominant nature. His reaction to her rejection had merely been a face-saving bluff to soothe his bruised ego. His remarks were not to be taken seriously.

Maggie had chalked up her startling and intense response to him to nothing more than old-fashioned male-female chemistry. Annoying, but perfectly normal and healthy. Nothing for her to worry about, certainly.

Within minutes of Wyatt's leaving she had dismissed the episode and again become absorbed in her illustrations.

Over the next few days she submerged herself in work. If she thought about Wyatt and their last encounter at all it was with amusement and a strange, vague regret. After a week, she'd forgotten about the incident completely.

Now she realized that she'd obviously been foolish to dismiss him so quickly. She should have known that a man as dominant and determined as Wyatt would not give up so easily.

"What're you doing here? I thought I'd seen the last of you."

"Charming." He pushed away from the car and covered the space between them in a few lazy steps. Touching her cheek with a fingertip, he pushed back a corkscrew curl. "You really know how to turn a guy's head, don't you, sweetheart?"

Maggie shrugged. "I'm not your sweetheart. And if you want someone to pander to your ego there's a massage parlor around the corner," she added with her old twinkle. Tilting her head slightly to the left, she avoided his touch.

"Did you miss me?" He toyed with the lock of hair. Fascinated, he watched the curl twine around his finger and cling as though it had a life of its own.

"Were you gone?"

Wyatt's gaze snapped up. He had expected denials, even taunting, but the look in her eyes left no doubt that she really hadn't known he'd been out of the country. He didn't know whether to curse or laugh.

"Ouch. It's a good thing I've got a tough hide. You're really murder on a guy's self-esteem."

"Sorry. It wasn't intentional. You didn't answer my question though. What're you doing here?"

"Isn't it obvious? I came to see you." He looped his

arm around her shoulders and tried to steer her toward the door on the loading dock, but Maggie dug in her heels.

"Wait a minute! All that's obvious to me is you're a stubborn man who won't take no for an answer."

"That's right. If I were the kind of fool who did that, Sommersby Enterprises would have gone belly-up years ago. When I want something I go after it. And I don't stop until it's mine."

The statement, issued in that soft but implacable voice, sent a shiver down Maggie's spine. She shot him a wary look. "I don't think I like the sound of that."

She didn't care for the enigmatic look he gave her, either. But when he nudged her shoulder and said, "Come on, Maggie. We have to talk," she sighed and allowed him to lead her inside. It was probably best to clear the air and get the matter settled once and for all.

How in the world had she gotten herself into this tangle, anyway? One minute she'd been sitting there minding her own business, enjoying a cool drink and shooting the breeze with Lester. Then Wyatt Sommersby had rolled into the station in that wheezing car, and her life hadn't been the same since.

Disgust compressed Maggie's mouth as they stepped into the freight elevator. See if she gave anyone a lift again.

Neither spoke as they made the slow ascent. Wyatt stood with his feet braced wide, his jaw set in that determined way that she was beginning to recognize. Maggie sighed again. This wasn't going to be easy.

Instinctively from the start she had known that this was a man she should avoid at all costs. He represented danger simply because she found him so outrageously attractive. And because he tempted her the way no other man ever had. Just the sight of him made her feel giddy and excited, and the sound of that gravelly voice never failed to send gooseflesh rippling over her skin and make her heart go pitty-pat.

None of which was a good sign. She absolutely could not allow herself to become emotionally attached to Wyatt.

Love was a trap, one she intended to avoid. Not that she believed for a moment that Wyatt would ever fall in love with her. It was her own foolish heart she did not trust.

Maggie was not, nor had she ever been, in the market for a man. Since her early teens she had made it a practice to steer clear of serious romantic involvements.

She liked men. She liked them a lot. She enjoyed their company, their attention, that exciting little spark of electricity that flowed between a man and woman when the chemistry was right. Some of the men she had met had even made her feel all fluttery and weak in the knees, though not enough to abandon her freedom. None of them, however, had ever affected her the way Wyatt did.

Maggie sighed, disgusted with herself. If she had tried, she could not have picked a man more unsuitable for her. Like Asa, Wyatt was an acquisitive man. Maggie knew herself too well; she needed freedom as much as she needed oxygen.

She could not abide ties or restrictions or commitments. She did not want to feel responsible for anyone else's happiness or have to stop and consider someone else before making a decision.

For those reasons, she knew she couldn't survive within the restrictions of a serious affair. And marriage with anyone was out of the question. To even consider either with a possessive man like Wyatt would be insane.

The best way to ensure that she remained heart-whole and footloose was to avoid temptation.

Deciding that the best defense was an offense, the instant they stepped inside her apartment she mentally braced herself and turned to Wyatt. "Listen to me—"

That was as far as she got. In one swift motion his arms encircled her and scooped her up against his chest, lifting her clear off the floor. At the same time his mouth closed over hers, cutting off her words in mid-sentence. Which was just as well, because at the first touch of his lips her thought processes shut down.

For that moment in time Maggie operated as a purely sensual creature, responding mindlessly to a seemingly endless bombardment of stimuli. As though her sensory perception had been suddenly fine-tuned, she became aware of even the most minute sensations and tactile pleasures. Her entire being was attuned to this man, absorbed by him—touch, taste, smell.

The savage hiss of his breathing reverberated in her ears like a roar and sent puffs of moist warmth skipping over her cheek. Against her almost-bare back she felt the slight abrasive rub of the sleeves of Wyatt's suit coat and the hard warmth of his hands splayed across her skin, right down to the surprising calluses that ridged his palms. She was aware of each individual shirt button imprinted against the tender flesh of her midriff and his belt buckle pressing intimately into her belly. Her soft breasts, pressed flat against the solid wall of his chest, absorbed the thunderous beat of his heart, and her nipples hardened in response. An intoxicating mixture of aromas filled her head and made it spin; citrusy cologne, starched linen, soap and potent male. At some time her arms had found their way around his neck, and as her hands caressed his nape she felt the delicious prickle of hair stubble against her fingertips.

With a little moan, Maggie melted against him, her body conforming to his like wax in the sun. The loose sandal slipped off her foot and hit the ceramic tile floor of the entry with a small thud. Seconds later the other one followed.

Wyatt's tongue plunged in and out of her mouth, staking a claim with sure, erotic strokes, twining in a seductive dance with hers. Tiny sparks shot through Maggie. Every cell in her body tingled, and a fire ignited in the core of her femininity. She felt weak and wobbly, and her stomach went deliciously woozy. All she could do was hang there and let the heady experience absorb her.

Maggie embraced life and all its experiences and she eagerly accepted this one, relishing each new sensation that quivered through her. It was mindless, heart-thumping, skin-tingling, breath-stealing pleasure, and she wondered distantly why she had never experienced anything like it before. Mainly, though, she simply held on and savored the glorious bliss.

How long the kiss lasted she had no idea, but when his lips lifted slowly from hers she groaned a weak protest. She hung in his arms, her eyes closed, her moist lips parted. Her heart thundered and her body vibrated like a plucked string on a cheap guitar. She felt on fire.

Slowly, as though weighted with lead, her eyelids lifted partway, and through the fog of passion she met Wyatt's glittery stare. His pupils were dilated until only a narrow band of silver showed around the outer edges. His nostrils were flared, his face flushed with fierce passion.

Maggie swallowed hard and licked her lips. His eyes followed the action and narrowed. "Wh—"

"That was so we wouldn't waste any more time arguing about whether or not you're attracted to me. I think we just established that you are."

His arrogance took away what little breath Maggie had, but she couldn't deny his claim, nor the effectiveness of his strategy—not when she was hanging in his arms like a wet rag.

"A-all right, so I do find you attractive," she admitted grudgingly. "So what? I find a lot of men attractive—Pierce Brosnan, Tom Cruise, Warren Moon, Carl Sagan, Stone Phillips. That doesn't mean I'm going to run out and have a flaming affair with any of them."

"I doubt that you know any of them, so that reasoning doesn't apply. Anyway—" He frowned. "Carl Sagan?"

Maggie grinned. "I think intelligent men are incredibly sexy." She was beginning to regain her equilibrium, and with it her sass.

"Really. Interesting. Remind me to tell you my IQ sometime. Right now, however, we've got a lot to discuss. I have to catch a plane in just a little over an hour, and I want to get this settled before I leave."

Maggie wanted the same thing, but she had a sinking feeling that they were after different results.

She pushed against his shoulders. "Fine. But I really think I could discuss this more comfortably if you would put me down. My legs are going to sleep, just hanging here."

His mouth quirked. "Too bad. I was enjoying myself." For a second his arms tightened. Then, watching her, he loosened his hold just enough to let her slide slowly downward.

The erotic rub of her body over his took her breath away. Her breasts molded to the contours of his chest, soft to hard. Against her belly she felt first the scrape of his belt buckle, then the hard ridge of his maleness. Her nipples hardened into taut, tingling buttons and her heart began to pump so hard a flush spread over her from her bare toes to the roots of her hair. Maggie felt as though she were on fire. Even her earlobes burned.

She knew by the blaze of heat in Wyatt's eyes and the rigid set of his features that he was aware of what he was doing to her, but she was powerless to hide her reaction. Dazed, all she could do was cling to his shoulders and stare into those mesmerizing silver eyes.

At last her toes touched the floor, then her heels, but for a moment he continued to hold her. Afraid her knees would give way without support, Maggie didn't protest.

"Maggie." He whispered her name like a caress, and her heart skipped a beat. It started up again and took off at a gallop when his gaze dropped to her mouth. "Maggie," he repeated. His head tilted to one side and began to descend, but from somewhere she gathered her resolve and took a quick step backward, pulling out of his arms.

"Oh, no. No more of that," she said in a shaky but adamant voice, backing down the steps. "You said you wanted to talk. So talk."

Wyatt sighed. "I can think of things I'd rather do with you, but you're right. We do need to settle a few matters first."

What matters? Maggie wondered.

He walked to the grouping of furniture that defined the living room, but instead of taking a seat he stood in the middle of the rug with his hands in his trouser pockets and jingled his change and keys. Finally his gaze lit on her.

"I want us to be together, Maggie."

"Now, Wyatt, I told y—"

"No, wait, let me finish. I don't want you to think that all I want is a brief affair or some cheap one-night stand. That's not what I'm after at all."

"Well, that's a relief," she quipped drolly, but her heart began to boom like a kettledrum. Surely he wasn't leading up to... She gave a little shudder and shook off the thought. No, of course not. Heavens, they barely knew each other.

Wyatt paced back and forth across the rug twice, scowling. Finally he seemed to come to a decision and swung to face her. "Look, I know you women like all the hearts and flowers, all those ritual preliminaries—the dating, the phone calls, the gifts and romantic gestures—but I'm a busy man. I don't have time for all that nonsense. Besides, I want you too much to wait any longer, so I'm going to cut right to the chase."

Maggie didn't like the sound of that at all.

"First of all, you should know that I happen to be a man who likes stable relationships."

Oh, no. Please, Sainted Mother Mary, don't let him do this. Don't let him propose, she prayed fervently, but Wyatt forged right ahead.

"Even if I weren't, in today's world I'd have to be a fool to sleep around. That's why I practice serial monogamy."

Maggie blinked. "Excuse me?"

"I maintain an exclusive relationship with one woman for an extended period of time. Before I begin a new relationship I insist that my new partner be tested, and for her peace of mind I do the same, of course."

Astounded, Maggie dropped down on the arm of the sofa, her mouth agape.

"As long as you and I are together, I'll take excellent care of you, Maggie. I think you'll find that I'm a generous man." He glanced around at her apartment and his mouth turned down at one corner. "It's obvious that you don't have access to Asa's wealth—although I must admit, that surprises me. I didn't expect the old man to be such a skinflint with his family. However, that doesn't matter.

"The first thing I want to do is move you into a nicer

place. Maybe a condo over by the Galleria. I'll buy it and put the deed in your name, of course, as a sort of security for you for later.''

''Later?''

''Yes. When we decide to go our separate ways.''

''Now wait just a min—''

''Of course, I would also provide a generous monthly allowance, charge accounts at all the stores and a maid, if you want one. Oh, and a car to replace that old clunker of a truck you drive. Pick out whatever you want and have the bill sent to me.'' He rubbed the back of his head and thought for a moment. ''I think that about covers everything. Except, of course, that in return I expect exclusivity.'' He looked at her and raised one eyebrow. ''Perhaps there's something else you'd like? If so, now's the time to say so.''

Bemused, Maggie stared at him. When she realized her mouth was hanging open she snapped it shut. A chuckle threatened, but she fought it back. Barely.

''Let me get this straight. You're asking me to be your mistress?''

Wyatt frowned. ''That's an outdated word that carries negative connotations. I prefer…*romantic liaison.* Or just *lover,* if you like.''

''Call it whatever you want, a kept woman is still a kept woman,'' Maggie said with a wry smile. ''Since it's not a position to which I've ever aspired, I'm afraid I must decline.''

He looked stunned. ''You're saying no? Without even thinking it over?''

''I don't have to think it over. Your offer is more than generous, I'm sure, but I'm simply not interested.''

''Now, Maggie, don't be hasty. Perhaps I put it badly. I don't think you fully realize what I'm offering.''

"You're offering me a gilded cage. You're offering me exactly what John Hightower gave my mother. Holy Mary and Joseph! Did you really think I'd go for that?"

Wyatt stiffened as though she'd slapped him. "It's not the same thing at all. Your father took advantage of a naive girl. He used her for his own pleasure then left her to face the consequences alone. He was irresponsible and unbelievably selfish, and even after he left her for someone else he continued to keep her on a string.

"I'm being honest and open with you, and I think very fair. Times are different now. You won't suffer from our relationship. There will be no children nor will any hearts be broken. And when either of us decides to end it, the break will be a clean one, with no regrets on either side."

"Och, what a great loobie you are, Wyatt Sommersby." The scornful amusement in Maggie's voice was unmistakable. "You think by laying it all out like one of your business deals that makes it all right. Well, I'm telling you, 'tis still an insult."

"*Insult!* For your information, there are plenty of women who would jump at the chance to be my woman," he roared.

"Fine. Why don't you offer one of them your deal."

"Because I want you. And it's not a deal, damn you. It's a sensible arrangement that will be mutually advantageous and satisfying. And what the bloody hell is a loobie?"

"A loobie is a loobie—an idiot, a fool, an ass."

His mouth dropped open. "You're calling me an ass?"

Maggie burst out laughing, and Wyatt glared. "What's the matter, Your Nibs. Hasn't anyone ever called you that to your face before? I don't know why not. It certainly fits."

"Very funny," he snapped. She could almost see him

grinding his teeth and calling on his last reserve of patience. "Look, Maggie, you haven't thought this thing through. You could have a better apartment, a new car, all the latest fashions. You said yourself your writing hasn't made you rich."

"Difficult as this may be for you to understand, becoming rich is not a priority for me. I happen to like my apartment. And my truck runs like a top. For heaven's sake, man, if I wanted to lead the life of the idle rich I'd move back into my grandfather's home. Believe me, nothing would tickle Asa more.

"Oh, and just so you'll know, he's not a'tall stingy. Asa has offered me the same allowance he gives Daphne and Tyson, but I refused it. I prefer to be on my own."

Wyatt's mouth tightened into a straight line. "You do realize, don't you, that I could buy this warehouse and have you evicted?"

She laughed. "You could try, but I don't think it would work, since I own it."

"You? But you just said—"

"My grandmother Hightower left it to me." Maggie shrugged. "I have no idea why. I barely knew her. However, 'tis mine, and between my writing and the income this place generates, I have everything I need."

She cocked her head to one side. "I am curious, though. Do you truly believe that having me tossed out on the street will somehow endear you to me?"

He made a sharp, dismissive gesture with his hand. "Dammit, you know I didn't mean that."

Turning away, he paced to the other end of the loft. For several minutes he stood with his feet braced wide, his hands bracketing his hip bones, staring out the wall of windows. The stance held his suit coat thrust back and emphasized the tautness of his body. Frustration radiated from him.

Suddenly he swung around. "Dammit, Maggie. Why are you being so stubborn about this? What are you holding out for? If it's a wedding ring, forget it. Surely you must realize that I can't marry you. I'm not the marrying kind."

Maggie laughed. "Thank the Dear Lord for that."

Wyatt looked taken aback, then affronted. "What, exactly, is that supposed to mean?"

"It means I have no more desire to get married than you. Less, most likely. I like my freedom too much to tie myself to another person. And for life, yet." She gave a little shudder at the thought, and Wyatt's scowl deepened.

"You needn't act as though you just escaped a foul fate worse than death, you know. For your information, there are plenty of women who'd kill for the chance to marry me."

"Then aren't you lucky you met me?"

If that made him happier, it wasn't evident by his expression. She wasn't positive, but she thought he was grinding his teeth.

"Dammit, Maggie, if it's not marriage you want, then why won't you consider my offer? I can't be the first man who's ever wanted to take you to bed."

"That's true. But I said no to all of them, too."

His head snapped up. "What?"

Maggie's eyes danced with laughter. "None of the others have been quite so bold as you, but I gave them all the same answer."

His eyes widened, then narrowed. "Every one of them?"

"Every last one."

"Are you saying...? No, that's impossible. You can't be a...a..."

With an impish twinkle in her eyes she leaned forward and whispered, "I think the word you're groping for is *virgin*."

Chapter Six

Maggie burst out laughing at Wyatt's stupefied look. He opened his mouth, closed it, then opened it again, but no sound came out.

"Go ahead. You can say it out loud," she prodded with a devilish grin. "'Tisn't a naughty word, you know."

"Dammit, you can't be a virgin!" he finally bellowed.

"Oh? And just why not?"

"You're twenty-six years old, for Pete's sake."

"So? Is there a legal age limit on virginity? If so, I'm not aware of it."

"Of course not! But…but…" He raked a hand through his hair. "Dammit, women simply don't reach your age without having at least one sexual experience. It's just not normal. Hell, these days, you can hardly find a teenager who's not sexually active."

"True," Maggie said without the least concern. "But then, I've never craved to follow the herd." She slid off the sofa arm onto the cushions. Stretching out full-length, she propped her head on a pile of decorative pillows, her feet on the pile at the opposite end of the sofa.

"What the hell was wrong with the young men you met in college? Were they all dumb and blind? Or gay?"

"Hardly," she said with a chuckle, recalling some of the seduction attempts made by those very same young men. "I simply never met anyone who interested me that much." Nor did she feel comfortable about allowing anyone that close.

"I find that difficult to believe."

"Believe it or not, 'tis true," she said with a maddening unconcern that made Wyatt's jaw clench.

"I don't understand how this could happen. It doesn't make any sense. I know you're not frigid. Just the opposite. One kiss and you go up like a gasoline fire. There had to be at least one male in all those years who turned you on. Or at the very least aroused that insatiable curiosity of yours."

The remark brought a blush to Maggie's face, but she brazened it out. Pretending her cheeks weren't blazing, she looked Wyatt right in the eye and said, "Maybe I'm a late bloomer. What difference does it make? The decision was mine, I made it, and 'tis no one else's business."

He stared at her. "Good Lord. A virgin," he repeated in a stunned voice. "You really are a virgin."

"That's what I've been telling you."

He dropped down on the overstuffed chair opposite the sofa as though someone had suddenly cut his legs out from under him. Perching on the edge of the seat, elbows propped on his spread knees, forearms and hands dangling limp between, he sighed. "The only twenty-six-year-old virgin on the North American continent and I have to get an itch for her. Hell."

"Oh, dear. Does my chaste condition put a kink in your seduction plans?"

Wyatt tipped his head up slightly and gave her a long look from beneath his eyebrows. A touch of unease whispered through her and her amusement dissolved like cotton candy in the rain. "So you find this whole thing funny, do you? As a matter of fact, I didn't have seduction plans. I didn't think they'd be necessary. But now...perhaps..."

He let the words trail away and looked her over, from her toes up to the halo of red curls that had pulled free of her braid and framed her face. He smiled.

That look instantly wiped away her smug expression. She had been certain that her inexperience would protect her from his advances. Had he been a proper gentleman it would have, she thought indignantly. The heat in those silver eyes, however, told her she had grossly misjudged his character; Wyatt Sommersby was no gentleman.

Maggie sat up and shot him an annoyed look. "Don't you have a plane to catch?"

For several taut moments he did not reply. He merely continued to watch her with that faint smile on his lips and an unholy gleam in his eyes. Finally he shot back his cuff and glanced at his watch. "You're right, I do."

Sighing, he stood up and crossed the rug. Before she realized his intent, he bent, took hold of her hands and jerked her to her feet.

"I don't want to leave you," Wyatt murmured, slipping his arms around her. He pulled her close and settled her snugly against him. His gaze roamed her upturned face. The gentle massage of his hands on her bare back felt warm and relaxing, almost mesmerizing. "Especially not with things still unsettled between us."

"Wyatt—" Maggie pushed at his chest, but it was a token protest at best. She knew she should resist his embrace, but being held in his arms was oddly pleasurable. It shouldn't have been, she thought ruefully, but it was. Despite the disparity in their sizes, their bodies seemed to fit together. It felt…right, somehow.

She frowned at that.

"Quit fighting it, Maggie," Wyatt admonished. "I have. God knows I didn't want to get involved with you. Common sense tells me you're trouble. I tried my damnedest to stay away, but it's no use. An attraction this strong doesn't just happen. Whether we like it or not, some things are meant to be. You and I are one of them. You've got to know that."

Maggie wanted to deny the statement, but she couldn't. For the first time in her life, she'd met a man she couldn't ignore or dismiss. Lord knew, she'd tried to do both.

Never had she experienced anything like the sensations that he aroused in her—the dreamy fascination that overtook her at odd moments, the strange, lighter-than-air feeling, the tightness in her chest, the antsy anticipation at the thought of seeing him again, the burst of foolish elation when she did. It was disconcerting, but even when she was absorbed in her work, thoughts of him intruded. She found it was annoying…and wonderful. And it scared the bejesus out of her.

To admit as much to herself was one thing, however, and to do so to Wyatt, quite another. Jaw clenched, she stared straight ahead at the third button on his shirt, her hands curled into fists against his chest.

He nudged the small of her back and ducked his head, forcing her to look at him. "Well? Don't you?"

She sighed. She should have know he wouldn't let her off that easy. "All right. I'll admit there's…I don't know…something there," she said with elaborate unconcern.

"Something worth exploring."

Her auburn eyebrows jerked together again. "You know, Your Nibs, you really are a stubborn pain in the posterior."

"When I have to be. Now, quit trying to distract me and answer the question. I haven't got much time."

"Oh, all right. Perhaps it wouldn't hurt to see each other now and then. Nothing regular or permanent, mind you," she added in a rush. "I can't abide to be tied down. Just an occasional casual date when we both have time."

Wyatt narrowed his eyes and studied her mulish expression. He looked ready to argue, but after a moment he nodded. "All right. I guess I can live with that. For now."

"What does that mean? Now look, if you th—"

"Hush and kiss me goodbye."

He didn't give her a choice. She started to argue but he pulled her against him, bent his head and caught her open mouth in a hot, thoroughly carnal kiss that instantly short-circuited Maggie's brain and sent fire racing through her.

She melted against him with a little moan. Lacing her fingers together at his nape, she gave herself up to the voluptuous pleasure, her protest forgotten. At that instant there wasn't one thing in the universe about which Maggie would have complained.

Time ceased to exist. There was nothing but pleasure—exciting, hot, delicious pleasure. The passionate embrace went on and on. Lost in sweet delirium, Maggie had no concept of time or place, only the pounding of her heart and the tactile delight of their bodies straining together and his tongue mating with hers, his big hands roaming over her back, clutching her bottom.

Their lips clung as he slowly ended the kiss. Instinctively, she moaned and pressed closer, but Wyatt exerted gentle pressure on her waist to ease her away. Dazed, she remained as she was, her arms looped loosely around his neck, head arched back, eyes closed, lips parted and wet and kiss swollen. At that moment she could not have moved had they come under nuclear attack.

She felt the soft brush of Wyatt's lips on hers again, and slowly, as though weighted down with lead, her eyes lifted partway. Wyatt studied her dreamy expression with blatant masculine satisfaction and possessiveness.

"You look besotted. I like that."

Maggie blinked. It took a few seconds for her brain to decipher his statement and that look. When she did she stiffened momentarily, but she quickly made herself relax and forced a scornful chuckle. "Besotted? Me?" she drawled, giving him an amused look. "Sorry to disappoint you, Your Nibs, but I was merely enjoying a physical sensation." She shrugged and tried to casually pull from his embrace. He grinned and planted another kiss on the tip of her nose, then released her so suddenly she stumbled backward.

His mouth twitched, and he lightly cuffed her chin. "I'll be back in four days. I'll see you then."

He headed for the door, leaving her standing there staring after him, her mouth working like a beached fish.

For a few seconds she sputtered and fumed, but Maggie had the unique ability to see the humorous side of almost any situation, and her sense of humor was never far from the surface. Barely had the string of Gaelic curses begun to roll from her tongue than they turned to laughter.

The arrogant, overbearing devil. The nerve of the man, giving her orders like she was one of his lackeys. Or one of his doxies. Was he so spoiled from getting whatever he wanted he thought he could snap his fingers and she would fall in line with his wishes?

Of course he was, silly, she thought, answering her own question, which produced another round of chuckles.

Och, the poor man. He had no idea with whom he was dealing...or what he was letting himself in for, she added with a wicked smirk. "I'll be back in four days. I'll see you then," she mimicked in a singsong. "Huh. We'll just see about that."

Not that she had any illusions about avoiding him completely. It was apparent she no longer had that option, given their response to one another.

Besides, he had piqued her curiosity. She wanted to explore these new sensations he aroused. If those steamy kisses were anything to go by, the experiment promised to be pleasurable, and she fully intended to enjoy it to the fullest, as she did most new experiences. However, she would do so in her own time and on her own terms, she decided, wandering over to her drawing board.

Plopping down on the stool, she picked up a pen, dipped it into the ink bottle and began to sketch. If Wyatt didn't like it, he could whistle in the wind. Maggie Muldoon was a free woman. She followed her own drummer and answered to no one, least of all an arrogant, take-charge, possessive, avaricious man the likes of Wyatt Sommersby.

Maggie lived for the moment. She took life as it came and rarely fretted over what "might" happen, and she didn't do so now. She would deal with Wyatt when they met again. In the meantime, she had work to do.

Catching her lower lip between her teeth, she sketched in a throbbing knot on the top of Mergatroid's noggin and crinkled his beak like an accordion. She drew his eyes unfocused and filled with stars and his knocked-kneed legs wobbling. Standing next to the crane, a smashed vase lying beside his webbed feet, Arbuckle wrung his wing tips and tried to focus his crossed eyes on his tall friend.

When Maggie zeroed in on something, whether work or play, her focus was absolute. All her concentration centered on whatever held her attention at the time, to the exclusion of all else. Within moments of Wyatt's departure she was immersed in the illustration.

She worked straight through dinner without letup. At three in the morning the last brush stroke went onto the final illustration. Yawning, Maggie rinsed out her brushes, trudged up the stairs and fell, fully dressed, across her bed.

She awoke at nine, refreshed and full of restless energy. She went through her apartment like a whirlwind, straightening and cleaning. A few hours later the place was sparkling and in apple-pie order, but the fidgety feeling still hung on. She paid her bills, did her laundry, cleaned out dresser drawers and changed the oil in her truck, amid hoots and hollers from the workmen in the warehouse. Afterward she showered and washed her hair, then paced the loft.

She turned on the stereo, and as the mellow tones of Harry Connick filled the open space she made another circuit of the apartment, returned and snapped the music off again.

She felt confined. Maggie recognized the antsy feeling. It was one she knew well; the call of the open road, the siren song of freedom whispering in her ear, tugging at her, beckoning her to follow. There was only one cure.

She stopped pacing. She hadn't intended to take another trip just yet, not with Asa's birthday coming up in a couple of weeks. On the other hand...

A grin spread over her face as she made her decision. Letting out a whoop, she took off at a gallop up the stairs to her bedroom and began to gather what she would need.

Wyatt rang the doorbell until his forefinger was numb. "She ain't there."

He spun around. The wino he'd seen Maggie talking to before stood on the third step from the top on the stairs watching him, his rheumy eyes filled with suspicion. Wyatt had been so preoccupied with his efforts to rouse Maggie he had not heard the old bum shuffle up the iron steps.

"Are you by chance speaking to me?" he asked in his most cutting voice. Holy hell. He could smell the man from where he stood.

"Yeah." The derelict jerked his head toward Maggie's door. "I said, Miss Muldoon ain't there."

"I gathered as much," Wyatt said dryly, looking the filthy creature up and down. "The question is, what're you doing skulking around in here?"

"I ain't skulkin'. Miss Muldoon asked me to look after the place."

Wyatt's jaw tightened. He agreed that someone needed to watch out for her, but this bum couldn't protect a fly. Knowing Maggie, she had probably assigned him the chore just so she'd have an excuse to give him money.

"Agnes feeds her fish for her," the old man added.

"Agnes?"

"She lives around here, same as me."

"Ah, yes, Agnes. The person I saw digging in the Dumpster the other day." Wyatt frowned. "Wait a minute. Why would Maggie need anyone to feed her fish?"

"'Cause they'd die if she didn't. Miss Muldoon, she headed out three days ago."

"Headed out?"

"Yeah. In that motor home of hers."

"You mean she left?" At the bum's nod Wyatt planted his balled fists on his hips, tipped his head back and spewed a string of curses at the ceiling. She had left the day after they'd had their talk.

A look of horror spread over his face. Good Lord. To

feed the fish while Maggie was gone, that disreputable old woman had to have a key to the apartment. Holy— Just wait until he got his hands on Maggie. The crazy little fool.

Eyeing Wyatt, the derelict began to ease down the stairs.

"Hold it. Don't leave yet. You said she left in a *motor home?*"

"Yeah, the one she keeps in the warehouse. You must'a seen it when you was here before."

Surprise flickered through Wyatt. So, the old bum did keep a watch on the place. "I saw it, but I had no idea it belonged to Miss Muldoon. Did she say where she was going?"

"Naw. You could check with the guys in the warehouse. Could be they'd know, but I kinda doubt it. When the urge comes over Miss Muldoon, she usually just takes off and goes where the wind blows her."

Wyatt's jaw clenched. "I see. I don't suppose you would have any idea when she'll be back, either, then."

"Nope. She'll be back when she gets back. Maybe today, or it could be a week or two or next month. Two or three months, even. Once she stayed on the road all winter and clear into spring. She's a restless one, that little lady."

"I see." Wyatt reached into his inside coat pocket and withdrew a pen and a card and scribbled something on it. "This is my business card, and I'm writing my home number on the back. I want you to call me as soon as Maggie returns—and I do mean the minute she drives in," he said, shoving the card into the old man's grime-encrusted hand.

"Well, now…I don't know…"

"There's fifty dollars in it for you if you do."

A buzz interrupted Asa's concentration. He looked up from the report he was reading and cast an irritated look at the intercom on the corner of his desk. "Damned, infernal contraption,'' he grumbled, reaching over to stab the button. "What the devil is it? Dammit, Della, I told you not to disturb me.''

Della Ledbetter had been Asa's secretary for twenty-eight years. His growls and snarls didn't faze her. "Mr. Sommersby on line one for you,'' she said.

Asa sat up straighter. "Which Mr. Sommersby?''

"Wyatt Sommersby.''

"Well why the devil didn't you say so in the first place? Put him on. Put him on.

"Wyatt, my boy! Nice to hear from you. How's the world treating you?''

"Where the hell is your granddaughter?'' Wyatt bellowed.

Asa winced and held the receiver away from his ear. He looked at the mouthpiece and raised one eyebrow, then leaned back in his chair, his features settling into a sly expression. "Daphne's attending a fashion show at Neiman's. She should be home in an hour or so.''

"Not Daphne. You know damned well I'm talking about Maggie.''

"Ah, Maggie is it?'' Asa reached for a cigar. "Well now, that I can't say. She's a hard one to keep tabs on.''

"I know. I've been trying to locate her for the past ten days. Did you know she's running around the country in that damned motor home of hers? All alone.''

"Is she now? No, I didn't know, but I can't say I'm surprised. She's real fond of doing that.''

"Are you saying this is a regular thing?'' He sounded appalled, and Asa had to bite back a chuckle. "She just goes careering off, God knows where, all alone? And you allow it?''

"*Allow* it?'' Asa snorted. "Hell, man, I don't like it any better than you do, but there's not a damned thing I or anyone else can do to stop her. If you know anything at all about Maggie you ought to know that. She's a grown woman, as she'd be the first to tell you.''

"She's a defenseless target for any criminal or pervert that comes down the pike," Wyatt shot back. "As you pointed out yourself, she's too damned trusting for her own good. Did you know she's given a bag lady a key to her apartment?''

"The hell you say!" Asa pulled his hand down over his face and gave a weary sigh. "Agnes, I suppose."

"Yes. Look, does Maggie have a cellular telephone in that rig she's driving?''

"Are you kidding? It was all I could do to talk her into putting a phone and answering machine in her apartment. Says she doesn't want to be bothered when she's out on one of her jaunts. Hell, even when she's home most of the time she lets the machine take her calls, and she returns them when she gets around to it."

"Didn't she at least leave an itinerary with you so you can reach her in case of an emergency?''

"An itinerary? Maggie? Hell no. She doesn't know herself from one day to the next where she's heading."

Wyatt growled something under his breath, and again Asa fought the urge to laugh. "Dammit, she could be lying dead in an alley somewhere and you wouldn't even know it.''

"It's not quite that bad. She calls me every few nights when she's on the road, just to make sure I'm still breathing, I think. Matter of fact, I spoke to her last night. She didn't tell me she was traveling, but I figured as much. She doesn't bother to call very often when she's in town."

"You talked to her last night?" Even over the line he could feel Wyatt's interest quicken. "Then you expect her to call back in a few days, right? When she does, tell her I said for her to call me immediately."

This time Asa didn't even try to stifle his laughter. "Oh, Wyatt, son...I don't think you want me to tell her that. You'd never hear from her again if I did."

"Dammit, I need to talk to her. And according to the wino on her block there's no telling when she'll be back."

"Ah, you've been talking to Fred. He's right, you know. With my granddaughter, one never knows. But look here, boy. If you really want to see her, come to my birthday party at the ranch next Tuesday."

"She'll be there?"

"Well now, I can't promise for sure, but she's never missed one of my parties yet. She may not go back to her apartment, and she may only stay for a few hours then be off again, but I expect she'll drop by on my birthday."

"I'll be there."

"Good. Oh, and Wyatt."

"Yes?"

"My offer on that stock still holds."

On the other end of the line the receiver banged. Chuckling, Asa replaced his gently. He leaned back in his chair, clasped his hands together at the back of his head and grinned around his cigar. "Yessiree. That young man has it bad. Real bad."

A little after eight on Tuesday evening, Maggie parked her motor home beside the barn. As usual, she entered the house through the kitchen. When hugs and greetings were exchanged with Mrs. O'Leary and the kitchen help she asked about her grandfather.

"He and the others are in the parlor." Mrs. O'Leary gave Maggie a chastising look. "Dinner's been ready this past quarter hour, but he's held it up. I'm sure he was hoping you would arrive.''

Maggie laughed and patted the older woman's plump cheek. "Well, I'm here now, darlin'. I'll go on in so your dinner won't be ruined.''

"Like that!" Mrs. O'Leary's scandalized gaze swept over Maggie's black, skintight, scoop-necked T-shirt and multicolored, gauzy peasant skirt, ending up at her strappy sandals. "The others are all dressed to the nines for the occasion and you look like a wild gypsy.''

"Oh, pooh. Asa won't care how I'm dressed. Anyway, this is the best I've got with me. If it were anyone else's birthday, I wouldn't have bothered to get this gussied up.'' She winked and headed for the door.

"Well it's about time you got here, young woman," Asa thundered the minute she sauntered into the parlor.

"Och, you knew I'd be here. Would I miss your birthday?'' Grinning, Maggie crossed to where her grandfather sat. She whipped out a foil-wrapped gift from behind her back, dropped it in his lap and planted a kiss on his forehead. "Happy birthday, Asa, you old bear.''

He turned pink and grumbled, "There's always a first time." He picked up the small box and shook it next to his ear. "What'd you bring me?''

"Och, you greedy old thing, you," she scolded, snatching the box from his hands when he began to tug at the ribbon. "You'll open it after dinner along with your other gifts and not a moment before. Saints preserve us, you're worse than a child when it comes to presents.''

Asa grumbled something under his breath, but she ignored him and turned with a smile to greet the others. "Hi, everybody.''

Eric sat on the sofa with Daphne and Corinne, and

Great-Aunt Edwina, Asa's sister, occupied the wing-back chair across from her brother's.

"Sorry I'm late, but—" Maggie drew in a sharp breath when a slight movement drew her gaze to the bay window across the room. Holy Mother Mary and Joseph! What was *he* doing there?

"Hello, Maggie," Wyatt said in a low voice that sent a tingle down her spine.

"Wyatt. I didn't expect to see you."

"Oh, I'm sure you didn't." He strolled toward her, one hand holding a drink, the other in his trouser pocket, his gaze locked with hers. Those watchful silver eyes did not so much as blink.

He was trying to intimidate her, Maggie knew. However, now that the shock had begun to fade, she was recovering her composure and with it her sense of humor.

Her eyes twinkled and she flashed him a grin. "Well…'tis a family affair, an' all. Eric, being Daph's fiancé, is almost obligated to attend, but you don't really belong here, do you?"

"Margaret Mary! Really! You're being terribly rude," Corinne chastised. "Mr. Sommersby is here as your grandfather's guest."

"Please excuse my sister, Wyatt," Daphne chimed in. "Sometimes Margaret Mary speaks before she thinks."

"Oh, I'm sure Maggie always says exactly what she thinks. But don't worry about it, Daphne. You neither, Mrs. Hightower. Your stepdaughter and I understand each other. Don't we, Maggie?"

He stopped directly in front of her and searched her features one by one before his gaze settled on her mouth. Maggie's heart began to lope. Sweet Mary and Joseph! Surely he wasn't going to kiss her right there in front of everyone?

She didn't trust him not to do exactly that. Taking a precautionary step backward, she clasped her hands behind her back and gave him a saucy look. "Maybe."

Wyatt's eyes narrowed, but before he could respond Maggie swung back to her grandfather. "Shall we go in to dinner? It's ready, and Mrs. O'Leary is fretting that it will ruin if we don't eat soon."

"Good idea. I nearly starved waiting for you," Asa barked, getting to his feet.

Wyatt took a step toward Maggie, but she pretended not to notice and linked her arm through her grandfather's. Leading the way into the dining room, she sent an impish grin over her shoulder and said sweetly, "Do be a dear and escort Aunt Edwina, won't you, Wyatt?"

"I'd be happy to." He offered his arm to the old lady with impeccable courtesy, but the look in his eyes as his gaze caught Maggie's promised retribution.

Throughout the meal Maggie thoroughly enjoyed herself. She chattered away happily about how her trip was going so far and took repeated little jabs at Wyatt, knowing how both irritated him. He smiled politely through it all, but his eyes smoldered like hot ice.

She didn't know how he'd wangled an invitation to this party. Asa had always been adamant about keeping birthdays just for family. However, she was confident that Wyatt would not dare reveal his interest in her. He knew what a matchmaking old scoundrel her grandfather was.

After dinner Mrs. O'Leary and her staff proudly brought out a huge cake ablaze with so many candles it looked like a four-alarm fire. Asa blew them out amid hoots and applause, then tore into the stack of gifts, shredding the beautiful wrappings with the utter disregard of a five-year-old.

He received the usual assortment of sweaters and ties and monogrammed handkerchiefs, for which he was dutifully appreciative. He seemed surprised and pleased by the leather-bound desk set that Eric gave him and Wyatt's gift of a bottle of fifteen-year-old Scotch, but it was her own gift, which he had saved for last, that made his eyes light up.

He lifted the plastic case filled with intricate, hand-tied fishing flies from the gift box with a reverence usually reserved for priceless works of art. He shot her a look over the top of the case and lifted one bushy white eyebrow. "Mosely Baker, right?"

She answered with a grin, and Asa shook his head. "How on earth did you sweet-talk him into selling them to you?"

"I promised to dance at his next wedding."

Asa laughed, then explained for Eric's and Wyatt's benefit, "Mosely Baker is ninety if he's a day. He ties the best flies in ten counties, but he quit selling them at least a dozen years ago, since arthritis slowed him down. Says these days he only has time to make enough for himself."

Wyatt gave Maggie a long, steady look. "I'm not surprised he made an exception in this case. I doubt there are many men who can resist your granddaughter's charms."

"Humph. She's a minx," Asa muttered fondly, and Maggie stuck her tongue out at him.

After coffee and cake they rose to return to the parlor. Maggie intended to wait a few minutes, then make an excuse and take off. As they crossed the foyer, Wyatt foiled her plan by grasping her wrist and announcing, "If you have no objection, Asa, I'd like to have a word with your granddaughter. Alone."

"But—"

"Sure. You can use my study. It's right down the hall," Asa said absently, appearing much more interested in examining his fishing flies than the reason for Wyatt's request.

"Now, wait a minute. You didn't ask me if *I* wanted to talk," Maggie protested with a nervous laugh, trying to hold back. Wyatt merely hauled her down the hallway without a word. "Wyatt, what're you—?"

"Shh. We'll talk in a minute."

"I don't understand. What does Wyatt want to talk to Maggie about?"

Daphne's confused voice floated after them, and Maggie couldn't stifle a giggle. Poor Daph. Never in a gazillion years would she be able to understand Wyatt's attraction to her. For that matter, neither did she.

"Really, Wyatt, you didn't have to use Neanderthal tactics, you know," she laughingly complained when he hustled her inside the book-lined room. He released her to lock the door, and Maggie moved to the middle of the room before turning to face him. "If you wanted to talk to me, all you had to do was say so."

"Uh-huh." Wyatt leaned back against the door and crossed his arms over his chest. "And run the risk of you bolting again. I don't think so."

"I *didn't* bolt," she hedged, but her eyes still brimmed with mirth. "I merely went on a research trip."

"Bull. I was getting too close, so rather than deal with what's happening between us you took off like a scared rabbit."

"That's not true."

"Oh, no? You promised you'd see me, go out with me. Then the moment I turn my back, you're gone."

"I *said* now and then, when we were both free. I happen to be busy right now."

"Joyriding around the country? You call that busy?"

"Ah, but you don't understand. These jaunts are business for me. I'm researching my next book."

"You write children's stories."

"Right. *The Adventures of Mergatroid and Arbuckle.* Don't you see? How can I write adventures for them if I don't experience them myself."

His expression turned so appalled she almost laughed. "You mean you drive around deliberately *courting* trouble?"

"Of course not," she replied with a giggle. "I look for exciting things to do, unique experiences, interesting new places. Then I try them and have Mergatroid and Arbuckle experience the same things in a book. You didn't think I made all that stuff up, did you?"

"Wait a minute, correct me if I'm wrong, but I seem to remember reading a story to my niece in which Mergatroid and Arbuckle did some deep-sea diving in shark-infested waters. You *did* that?"

"Uh-huh. That was in book three, I think. Or maybe it was book four," she said innocently, pretending she didn't notice the ashen shade his face had turned or the sudden fury that blazed in his eyes. His face tightened, and when he spoke again his voice was pitched low and there was a silky quality to it that did not bode well.

"I see. And then I believe there was stock-car racing at Indy and hang gliding in Big Bend and rock climbing in Washington State and hotdog skiing in the Rockies and no doubt many more escapades I don't know about, since I didn't read all my niece's books. You did all those things, too, I take it?"

Maggie shrugged and gave him a cheeky grin. "It's called research."

"It's damned well crazy!" he bellowed "Dammit,

woman! You could get yourself killed doing dangerous stuff like that.''

''Wyatt, I'm not stupid. Before I did those things I took lessons and I observed all the safety precautions. How could I write about something if I didn't experience it first-hand?''

''You could read a book about it. Interview a pro. Something other than risking your fool neck.''

''It's my neck. If I want to risk it I will. Besides, it was fun.''

He looked ready to fly apart at that, but as she watched, he clamped down on his temper and raked a hand through his hair. ''All right, I don't like it and I sure as hell don't buy it, but even supposing, for the sake of argument, that your method of research is necessary, I still think the timing of this trip had more to do with running scared than creativity.''

''Scared? Me?''

''Yes, you. I think you— What's so funny?''

Putting her hand flat against her midriff, Maggie leaned weakly against the back of Asa's big leather chair. ''You. Us,'' she sputtered between peals of laughter. ''Don't you see? This is exactly what I meant when I said a relationship between us wouldn't work,'' she said, wiping her eyes. ''I'm a creature of impulse. I eat when I'm hungry, sleep when I'm sleepy and work when inspiration strikes. And any one of those could occur at three in the morning or six in the afternoon. When I get itchy feet, I climb into my motor home and go. I let things happen, go with the flow. *You* have to be in control.

''Face it, you're the nine-to-five, dinner-at-eight type. You don't make a move, business or personal, without thinking it over, weighing the pros and cons. I doubt you've ever made a spontaneous decision in your life.

Can't you see that no matter how strong the physical attraction, we just don't mesh?''

"I can be spontaneous," Wyatt objected, clearly offended.

"Oh, pul-leeze."

"All right, you don't believe me. I'll prove it. I'll…I'll go with you on this little jaunt of yours." The words shocked him as much as her. The idea of spending days cooped up inside a tiny home on wheels appalled him.

"What?" She grabbed her middle and doubled over with laughter. "Don't be absurd," she said finally, wiping her eyes.

"It's not so crazy. It'll kill two birds with one stone. It'll demonstrate to you that I can be flexible and at the same time prove that just because we're different doesn't mean we're incompatible. It's perfect," he insisted perversely.

Maggie stopped laughing and stared. He meant it. Holy Mary and Joseph!

Her nerves began to hum like a struck tuning fork. She cleared her throat and groped for the right words to change his mind. "Look…Wyatt…it won't work. You wouldn't make it a week away from your wheeling-dealing world of big business and high finance. I'm talking about living simply in a very small space for perhaps weeks. I'm talking about kicking back and letting life happen, enjoying yourself with no cares, no worries, no schedules to keep, no agenda. When was the last time you took a vacation that didn't involve some sort of business deal, at least in some remote way?"

"What difference does that ma—"

"When?"

Wyatt gritted his teeth. "All right, never. Satisfied? But that doesn't mean I can't. Let me prove it to you."

"No. Absolutely not. Besides, I travel alone."

"What's the matter, afraid I'll prove you wrong? Or are you just afraid that you won't be able to resist me if we're together for very long?"

Her eyes widened. Then, slowly, she began to shake her head. "No. Oh, no. No you don't. I'm not falling for that."

"Falling for what? We're obviously at an impasse. I think my suggestion is the ideal way to break it." A taunting half smile tipped up one corner of his mouth. "What's the matter? Running scared again, Margaret Mary?"

"Don't be ridiculous."

"Then let me come along."

It was a direct challenge. His eyes dared her to refuse. Plucking at her gauzy skirt, Maggie chewed her lower lip and shifted from one foot to the other, forcing herself to hold that mocking stare. Damn him. How did he know she could not resist a challenge?

"I may be gone for a month or more. You can't stay away from your business that long, and you know it. Even if it ran all right without you, you couldn't stand to keep your nose out of it."

"A month?" Wyatt repeated with something less than enthusiasm.

"That's right. Maybe more."

He had not counted on that, it was plain. She watched him struggle to come to grips with the idea. Finally he clenched his jaw and gave an abrupt nod. "It won't be easy, but I can manage to be away for a while."

She sighed and gave him a disgusted look. "Oh, all right, you're on," she said against her better judgment. "Be ready to go in ten minutes."

"You mean from now? Tonight?"

A smug grin twitched her lips. "What's the matter? Too spontaneous for you?"

"No. No, I, uh…I just didn't realize you were leaving tonight is all. I assumed you'd be spending the weekend here. I'll just go grab my overnight bag and call my secretary and tell her to clear…my…" He stopped and ground his teeth as a smug grin spread over her face.

"Your schedule?" Maggie inquired sweetly.

"Yes," he snapped. "As soon as I'm done and I've said goodbye to Asa I'll be ready."

"Okay. But I'm serious. If you're not in the RV in ten minutes, I leave without you."

Chapter Seven

"Aren't you driving a little fast? This rig doesn't seem all that stable. Feels top-heavy."

Maggie glanced at him. He thought he saw her mouth twitch, but in the dim glow of the dashboard he couldn't be certain. Other than to speed up, she didn't reply.

Since leaving Asa's place an hour or so ago, she hadn't said much and he hadn't pressed her to talk. He had a hunch she was having second thoughts about allowing him to come along. If so, he didn't want to push her.

Wyatt looked out the window, but all he saw was his own reflection in the glass. He wasn't sure exactly where they were, just that they were heading generally northwest. Maggie certainly hadn't volunteered any information, either about their whereabouts or their destination. He wondered if she even knew where she was going.

He had expected to be bored out of his mind, but it was kind of nice actually. With the radio tuned to a CW station and turned low, the glow from the dash bathing the cab with warm light, the rhythmic thump of the tires on the pavement, the silence seemed almost companionable.

Of course, he was out of his mind to be doing this. His brother had thought so as well.

Eric had been present when he'd explained his abrupt departure to Asa. The old man had taken it well, considering that Wyatt had just informed him he was taking an extended trip with his granddaughter. Asa had leaned back in his chair and studied him through narrowed eyes.

"It should prove to be an interesting experiment. We'll talk when you get back."

Asa's calm acceptance had aroused Wyatt's suspicions. "You don't seem particularly upset."

"Should I be?"

"Depends on how you look at it. I'm going to be honest with you. I intend to seduce your granddaughter."

"Jeez, Wyatt," Eric groaned. "You didn't have to be *that* honest."

"It's all right, my boy," Asa assured him, never taking his eyes from Wyatt. "I think Maggie can handle the likes of your brother." He blew a puff of cigar smoke at the ceiling and sent Wyatt a Cheshire cat smile. "Have a nice trip."

"Wyatt, you can't just take off like this, with no warning," Eric protested. "What about the business?"

"You and the staff can run things for a while."

"But...what if a crisis comes up? What'll I do?"

"Handle it." He glanced at the mantel clock. "Look, I've got to go. I'll call you tomorrow."

"Wyatt, wait!" Eric followed him into the hallway and Wyatt swung back, clearly aggravated.

"What? Dammit, I don't have time to chat."

"Have you lost your mind?"

"Probably," he admitted grimly. "God knows, I'm not anxious to tour the country in an RV."

"Then tell Maggie you've changed your mind."

"I can't do that. It was my suggestion."

"Good Lord." The look of shock and revulsion on Eric's face would have been funny another time. "I think you have lost your mind. Whatever possessed you to do such a thing?"

"Hell, I don't know. She was about to leave and I was trying to stop her, and all of a sudden it just popped out. Anyway, I can't change my mind now. That's exactly what she's hoping for."

"What do you care? Why are you even doing this?"

"Because I want her," Wyatt snapped.

Eric groaned. "Oh, Lord. I've heard that tone before. Poor Maggie. She doesn't stand a chance."

"Look, I have to go."

He barely made it. Maggie was easing down the drive when Wyatt sprinted up beside the rig and jerked the door open. On the run, he slung his briefcase inside, jumped on board and collapsed in the passenger's seat.

Maggie spared him a glance. "So you made it after all."

"Jeez, you…you could have sl-slowed down a li-little," he gasped.

She shrugged. "Your ten minutes were up."

Of course, Eric had been right, Wyatt mused. He was crazy for doing this. His schedule was full through next month and there were a dozen things hanging fire that needed his attention. His secretary had nearly gone into a tailspin when he'd told her to clear his schedule indefinitely.

He would handle what he could by telephone. The rest, Eric and his staff would just have to deal with the best they could. For once they could earn their exorbitant salaries.

A short while later he was still mentally planning what to assign to whom when Maggie took an exit ramp off the highway and brought the rig to a stop in a lighted rest area. Three eighteen wheelers and a minivan with an SMU sticker on the back door were parked nearby.

"Why are we stopping here?"

Maggie propped her forearms on the steering wheel and gave him a pointed look. "If we're going to share this tiny space for the next few weeks I think it's time we set some ground rules. We should have done it before we left Asa's."

"Why? Have I done something wrong? And what do you mean 'few weeks'? Surely we won't be on the road that long."

She shrugged. "Maybe, maybe not. It all depends. If that's too long for you, you're free to leave anytime you want. Nobody's holding a gun to your head to make you stay."

"Oh, I'll stay." You can bet on it, sweetheart, he added silently.

"Fine. But as long as you do, this is how it's going to be. You are just along for the ride. I call the shots, and I don't want to hear any complaints or suggestions. We stop when and where I want. We leave when I'm ready. And I'll drive as fast or as slow as I want. Got that?"

"Loud and clear," he drawled. "Anything else."

"As a matter of fact, there is. You are not to contact your office or conduct any business."

"What! Now wait just a min—"

"No, you wait. Let me remind you that the purpose of you tagging along is to prove you can adapt to my way of life. That means no schedules, no wheeling and dealing.

"Also, just so we're clear on the subject, the bedroom is mine. You sleep in the bed above the cab. You'll do your share of the work and stay out of my way. Oh. And no hanky-panky."

"Not even a little?" Wyatt said with a lecherous grin.

"I mean it. So make up your mind now. If you don't want to abide by those rules you use that telephone over there and call Eric or whoever to come and get you right now."

"You're a hard woman, Margaret Mary," Wyatt said, both annoyed and amused. "All right. We'll play it your way." For now, he added silently. But if she thought he was going along with that no business nonsense she had another think coming. He would just have to contact his office on the sly, whenever he got the chance.

"Fine. We might as well spend the night here, then."

"What?" Wyatt looked around. "You can't be serious. These places are dangerous. You hear on the news all the time about people being robbed and murdered in rest stops."

"We'll be fine. I do it all the time."

He looked horrified, but before he could say anything, Maggie jumped out. Muttering, Wyatt got out as well.

The whole time she went about setting up the motor home he followed her around arguing his case for camping elsewhere, but she refused to budge. Most of the time she acted as though he weren't there. In the end he had no choice but to accept her decision.

"You can have first turn in the bathroom," she said when they were locked in for the night. "Just remember, our water supply is limited, so the rule is to conserve. That means get wet, turn the water off, soap up, turn it back on to rinse."

Wyatt looked so appalled Maggie laughed. "There are

other camping rules, but I'll save those for another day. I'm not sure you can handle them all at once.''

"Funny," he retorted, sounding anything but amused.

While Wyatt showered, Maggie closed the privacy curtain between the cab and the interior of the RV and all the curtains over the windows. She dug out sheets and a light blanket and tossed them onto the bed Wyatt would be using. He had probably never made up a bed in his life, but she'd be darned if she'd do it for him.

She grinned to herself as she turned back the covers on her own bed. It ought to prove interesting; there was less than three feet of clearance between the queen size bed above the cab and the ceiling, which made it a bear to make up.

Wyatt emerged from the bathroom barefoot, wearing only his trousers and drying his wet hair with a towel. He carried the rest of his clothes over one arm. He smelled of her soap and shampoo and a marvelous male scent that made her nose twitch and sent little prickles over her skin. The sensation made her uncomfortable, and she ducked her head and scuttled past him into the bathroom, locking the door behind her.

Wyatt frowned when the lock clicked. Did she really think he would force himself on her? Tossing the damp towel over the back of a chair, he walked over to inspect the high bed he would be using and spotted the folded linen. He looked at the closed bathroom door. So, that's the way she was going to play it. She probably thought he wouldn't be able to manage and come running to her for help. Which would give her the ammunition to boot him out.

He shook out the bottom sheet and held it high. Lips pursed, he studied the elasticized corners, then the high mattress. It didn't look so hard. He hoisted himself up onto the bed, scrunched up and crawled to the other side.

It took him fifteen minutes of wrestling with the mattress just to get the bottom sheet to stay on and another ten to secure the top sheet and blanket.

While he worked he heard Maggie's electric toothbrush whirring and small bumps and knocks as she moved around. Wyatt imagined her removing her makeup and slathering on night cream, brushing her wild curls a hundred strokes.

After what seemed an eternity of struggle, he got the feather pillow stuffed into a linen pillowcase. Finally, exhausted, he shed his trousers and climbed up into the bunk. With a sigh, he stretched out full-length on his back, his hands stacked beneath his head. He closed his eyes and was about to drift off when he heard the shower turn on.

Suddenly he was wide awake.

He told himself to ignore the sound, but all he could think about was Maggie standing naked in the shower, hosing herself down with the hand-held sprayer. The water shut off, and he imagined her lathering a washcloth and rubbing it all over her body, covering her skin with sudsy bubbles that slid downward in slow motion over her slick skin.

Sweat beaded his upper lip. The water came on again and he pictured the warm spray sluicing away the lather, water sheeting down satiny skin, gathering in her navel, dripping from the tips of her breasts. He clutched the sheet on either side of his thighs, and immediately the two bottom fitted corners popped loose from the mattress.

He cursed and kicked at the bunched material as the water shut off. He heard the rattle of shower curtain rings, and groaned as he imagined Maggie stepping naked from the tiny tub, reaching for the towel, long wet curls clinging to her back, her skin sleek and rosy, beaded with water. He ached to lick every droplet from every inch of her.

Wyatt's body responded predictably to the erotic thought and he groaned again. It was going to be one hell of a difficult trip.

Damn, he wanted that woman. He wanted her more than he could remember ever wanting any woman in his life. Why? He hadn't the slightest idea.

The bathroom door opened. Moist air rolled out, warm and evocative, redolent with scents that were uniquely feminine: talc and flowery soap and perfume. And sweet, clean woman. Wyatt ground his teeth as the heady combination filled his senses and sent fire streaking to his loins.

He turned his head and felt as though he'd received a punch to the midsection. All he could do was stare. Damp curls cascaded around her creamy shoulders in a fiery cloud. A provocatively cut, coffee-colored satin gown clung to every sweet inch of her delectable little body. Even with those ridiculous bunny slippers on her feet she still looked sexy.

Maggie scowled at him. "I don't have a robe with me. I wasn't expecting company, so just keep your eyes to yourself."

"Yes ma'am." Smiling, he looked back at the ceiling.

The bathroom light went off, leaving only the soft glow from the bedroom. He heard Maggie walk into the room, heard her moving around. Then her voice floated to him, soft and sleepy. "'Night, Your Nibs."

Wyatt ground his teeth. "Good night, Margaret Mary."

The bedroom light clicked off, then he heard the faint squeak of the bedsprings.

He squeezed his eyes shut. Oh, yeah. It was going to be one helluva hard trip.

* * *

It seemed to Wyatt that he had just fallen asleep when he was jerked awake by a siren that sounded as though it was right outside the RV.

He jackknifed up and banged his head on the ceiling. "What the— Ow!"

He grabbed his head, then his ears as the siren wailed on with an ear-splitting, scale-climbing *Whop-whop-whop-whop! Whop-whop-whop-whop! Whop-whop-whop-whop!*

"Holy—" The damned thing *was* right outside. "Maggie! Maggie, are you okay?" he yelled, but he couldn't hear his own voice for the screaming siren. He tried to scoot to the edge of the bed and jump down and got caught in a tangle of sheets. "Of all the stupid— Maggie! What the hell's going o—"

The siren shut off with stunning abruptness, but the magnified silence lasted only seconds before it was shattered by Maggie's voice calmly blaring over a bullhorn.

"Step away from the trailer. I repeat, step away from the trailer. NOW. If you don't step away from the trailer with your hands above your heads I will shoot you where you stand."

"Holy hell," Wyatt muttered, frantically fighting to free himself from the covers. He bucked and kicked and cursed, banging his head and knees on the overhead. "Damned...stupid...son-of-a-dirty—" Finally he freed his legs and jumped down, just as Maggie's amplified voice ordered,

"Stop! Stop at once or I'll shoot!"

Spitting out an obscenity, Wyatt tore through the RV and into the bedroom. His heart jumped right up into his throat at the sight of Maggie sprawled on her stomach, squinting down the barrel of a shotgun which was stuck out the window. The bullhorn lay on the bed beside her.

"No! Maggie, stop! Don't shoot!" Wyatt launched himself through the air in a flying dive. He landed on her with enough force to sink her petite body deep into the mattress and force the air out of her lungs with a loud *"Oof!"*

"Are you all right? Are you all right?" Frantic, he scrambled off her. Maggie didn't move. He snatched the shotgun out of her limp grasp and rolled her over onto her back. In the faint light coming in through the window he could see her face. Her eyes were bugged out so far white showed all around her pupils. She clawed at her chest and her mouth worked but no sound came out. He grasped her shoulders and shook her. "Dammit, Maggie! Speak to me!"

Air rushed back into her starved lungs with a loud rasp. She sucked in several gasping breaths. Then her eyes focused on Wyatt, and she hauled off and socked him in the chest.

"Ow!"

"Speak to you! *Speak* to you! Sweet Mary and Joseph! How am I suppose to do that when you've just collapsed my lungs! What the devil do you mean, jumping on me that way?"

"I couldn't let you shoot someone. You want to go to jail? What the hell did you think you were doing?"

She rose up on both elbows and stuck her face in his. "I was frightening the bejesus out of a couple of punks who were trying to steal my trailer, *that's* what I was doing."

He hefted the shotgun and shook it. "Where the hell did you get this thing? This is a lethal weapon. Don't you know how dangerous this is?"

She looked at the shotgun, then at Wyatt's fierce expression. She tried to maintain an angry demeanor, but after a moment her mouth began to twitch.

"I'm serious. You could kill somebody with this thing."

"Not with that, I couldn't," she sputtered, and collapsed back on the bed in a fit of giggles.

"Dammit, Maggie, don't you understa— Stop that laughing. This is not funny."

"Oh, ye-yes it…is," she sputtered. She waved at the gun. "L-look at it. It doesn't ha-have a tr-trigger…or…or a firing p-pin."

Wyatt sat up and snapped on the lamp beside the bed. He examined the gun, scowling. "Good Lord." Instead of softening, his expression hardened even more. "You confronted criminals with a disabled weapon? Are you batty? What if they'd had weapons, too? You can damn well bet *theirs* wouldn't be duds. What if they'd used them on you? Dammit, woman, you could have gotten yourself killed!"

"Oh, pooh. All I have to do is snap out a few threats and stick the barrel of that shotgun out the window and thieves run like scared rabbits."

"You mean this has happened before?"

"A few times. That's why I have the alarm system. It's connected to the trailer and all the windows and doors on the RV. Once I lock up, no one can touch anything without the alarm blasting."

"Dear God," he whispered, staring at her as though she'd taken leave of her senses.

"Wyatt, there's no need for you to be concerned." She placed her hand on his arm and looked at him sincerely. "It's perfectly safe. Honestly. Anyway, I've been looking after myself all of my life, and I've never been hurt yet. So please…don't fret. Okay?"

He looked down at her hand on his arm. Her delicate fingertips were buried in the dark dusting of short hairs. Slowly his gaze lifted and his eyes held hers. "Maggie."

In a heartbeat the atmosphere in the room changed. They became aware of the intimacy of the situation, that they were sitting together on a bed, she in her nightie, Wyatt in only his navy blue cotton briefs. The air suddenly pulsed with sensuality and awareness.

Wyatt's gaze dropped to Maggie's mouth, and her pulse skittered, then began to beat like a jungle drum. He leaned closer. She felt herself sway. Drawn by a pull neither could resist, they angled closer. Wyatt's head lowered. Maggie's lifted, and her eyes drifted shut.

The kiss, when it came, was light at first, a mere touch of flesh upon flesh, a mingling of breaths. Then Wyatt made a low, savage sound, and his arms came around her.

He lifted her tight against his chest. Maggie gave no thought to resisting. She wrapped her arms around his neck and clutched his hair with both hands as though she would never let go. Locked together, they kissed with desperate hunger, while their hearts pounded and their bodies yearned.

The sudden pounding on the door had the impact of a pistol shot. They sprang apart like two guilty children.

"Hey, Irish! You okay in there! Open up, it's Bullfrog!"

"Yeah, and Sugar Daddy and Cowboy, too," another voice hollered.

"What the—"

"Guys!" Maggie whooped and sprang off the bed.

"Maggie, come back," Wyatt yelled, bolting after her. "Don't open that d—"

Before he could stop her she flung the door wide and launched herself from the top step, right into the tattooed arms of a burly ape the size of Hulk Hogan who had a face like a blunt club.

Beside him stood two other men. The short, wiry one appeared to be in his late twenties, the other guy was bald and pot-bellied and middle-aged. All three brandished tire irons, but the gorilla dropped his to catch Maggie in a bear hug and swing her around. The other two clamored for their turn. Wyatt watched, grinding his teeth, as she was passed from one rough-looking character to the next.

When the exuberant greetings were finally over, Maggie introduced Wyatt to the three men. "They're all truck drivers," she said happily. "We became acquainted over our CB radios during my travels."

"Yeah," Bullfrog concurred. "A lot of truckers look out for Maggie. In fact," he added proudly, puffing out his chest, "that bullhorn routine Maggie used was my suggestion. The siren woke us up, but the instant I heard it blowing, I knew it was you."

"Yeah, I recognized your voice over the bullhorn and bailed outta my rig," the middle-aged man added. "I bumped into Cowboy and Bullfrog here soon as I hit the ground, and the three of us took out after them thieves."

The one called Cowboy laughed and slapped his thigh. "You should'a seen 'um, Irish. They was quakin' in their boots, looking down the barrel of that old shotgun. Then, when they seen us a'comin', waving these tire irons, why they bolted like a couple of rabbits. We chased 'um, but they hopped in a souped up pickup and hightailed it outta here like their butts was on fire."

That brought on a round of laughter and back slapping as the three congratulated one another. "Did you see that skinny one's face when he looked back at us over his shoulder?" Bullfrog gasped between guffaws. "He was so scared his eyes looked like they was bugged out on stems."

"Yeah," Sugar Daddy gasped. "He looked like he was about to pee in his pants." The other two men scowled and poked him, and he looked sheepishly at Maggie. "Sorry, Irish."

"Maggie and I appreciate your help," Wyatt interjected. "It was a dicey situation."

The three knights of the road sobered and looked Wyatt over. Eyebrows rose when they noticed he wore only his underwear, and they exchanged a look. Almost imperceptibly their stances altered, became wary, braced for trouble. "Who'd you say you were, again?" Bullfrog asked in a semigrowl.

"Wyatt Sommersby. I'm—"

"He's just a friend who came along for the ride," Maggie inserted quickly.

"You sure everything's all right, Irish? I've known you for years and in all that time you've never traveled with anyone before. Hey, if this dude's botherin' you, all you gotta do is say so. We'll take care of him."

"Yeah."

"You bet. You just say the word," the other two said in unison, stepping closer.

"Now, see here—"

"No, really, fellas. There's no problem," she assured them. "Wyatt simply wanted to experience RV travel and see some of the country, so I said he could come along with me. That's all. We were both asleep when the alarm went off."

While Maggie explained, Sugar Daddy sidled over to the open door and peeked into the RV. "It does look like he's sleepin' in the spare bunk."

"Well…in that case, I guess you're okay," Bullfrog conceded grudgingly. "You can't be too careful these days."

"I agree," Wyatt said stiffly. "That's why I've been telling Maggie it isn't safe for her to travel alone."

"Maggie's safe enough. She's got hundreds of friends like me 'n Cowboy and Sugar Daddy. When we know she's on the road we pass the word, and truckers all over this country keep an eye on her.'' His tone and the look in his eyes warned that they would be watching him, too, and not for his safety.

''I don't think those dudes will be coming back, but just to be on the safe side, I think we oughta tuck her away behind our rigs,'' Cowboy suggested, and his friends agreed.

Maggie tried to refuse their offer but they wouldn't hear of it. Her three friends climbed back into their rigs and fired them up, and moments later the three eighteen wheelers formed a tight triangle around the RV.

Wyatt watched it all with amazement. ''I've heard of circling the wagons before but this is the first time I've actually seen it done,'' he said when they were back in the RV.

''They're a good bunch of guys. Maybe now you'll believe me when I say I'm perfectly safe on the road.''

''I'll admit, it's comforting to know you've got a whole army of truckers looking out for you, but they won't always be there when you need them. Especially on the back roads.''

Maggie threw up her hands. ''There's just no satisfying you.''

Something flashed in Wyatt's eyes. Stepping close, he hooked his forefinger under her chin and tipped her face up. A wicked smile slowly curved his mouth. ''Oh, I don't know. I think you could satisfy me just fine.''

Wyatt had not expected to sleep at all, after what had happened, but he fell into an instant slumber the moment his head hit the pillow. He slept so soundly he barely moved—not until dawn when the blast of an air horn jerked him awake.

"Wha—?" He lurched up and banged his head again. "Aw, hell." This damned bed was going to give him a concussion. Rubbing the back of his head, he lay back down on his stomach just as another horn blasted, then another. The sounds were accompanied by a deep rumbling and the hiss of air brakes. Wyatt pulled back a corner of the curtain covering the windows that wrapped around the bed and peered out sleepily. One by one, the three truckers pulled away from the RV with a wave goodbye and a blast on the horn.

It had just occurred to Wyatt to wonder why they were waving, when the RV began to roll out right behind the convoy.

"Holy—" Wyatt clutched the swaying bed with both hands and cursed roundly. He felt as though he were in a rubber raft in high seas.

Why the devil was she leaving so early? And why didn't she wake him?

Out of sorts, bleary-eyed and still half-asleep, he grimly scooted to the side of the bed and jumped down. The RV bumped out onto the highway and he staggered and had to hold on to the wall. "Dammit, Maggie," he snarled, snatching open the curtain between the cab and the interior of the RV. "Would you mind telling me just what's so all-fired important that you have to leave at the crack of dawn?"

"Oh, hi. Good morning." She flashed a bright smile over her shoulder. "Sorry. To tell you the truth, I forgot you were up there," she said with deflating honesty. "I was awake, so there was no reason not to hit the road. You can go on back to sleep if you want to."

"Fat chance in that rocking bed," he mumbled.

"What?"

"Never mind."

"Well, if you're not going to sleep I'm going to listen to some music." She slipped a CD into the player and when Garth Brooks's deep voice belted out "Friends in Low Places" she bounced along to the rhythm.

"Oh, hell," Wyatt growled, heading for the bathroom. "It ought to be against the law to be that bright-eyed and bubbly at this hour."

Maggie tooled down the highway with her usual carefree abandon, sending Wyatt staggering and lurching from one side of the vehicle to the other and cursing under his breath. He quickly made the unhappy discovery that performing necessary morning functions in a bathroom that bumped and swayed was next to impossible. It took some doing, but he finally managed to take care of nature's call and brush his teeth.

"Help yourself to whatever you can find in the fridge," Maggie called when he stumbled out of the bathroom.

Holding on to anything in reach, Wyatt staggered into the tiny kitchen, but when he opened the refrigerator his jaw dropped. Except for a slice of cold pizza, a jar of dill pickles, a few limp stalks of celery, and a half a loaf of bread, it was empty. A quick check of the pantry turned up nothing more than a jar of peanut butter and what proved to be some sort of canned meat. Wyatt looked at the latter with revulsion. He hadn't even known meat was put into cans.

Deciding to forego eating until they stopped, he lurched forward to the cab and sat down in the passenger seat. Maggie shot him a curious look.

"Through eating already?"

"Hardly. There's not enough food back there to keep a mouse alive more than a day."

"Really? I hadn't noticed."

"Didn't you have breakfast?"

"Of course."

"What did you eat?"

"Um, a sandwich, I think."

"You think?"

"Yes, it was definitely a sandwich. I remember now."

"You had a sandwich for breakfast? Out of what?"

"Uh…peanut butter and pickles."

"Good God!"

"What's wrong with that? It's food. Actually, it was pretty tasty."

Wyatt shuddered. "The combination is hideous, and neither one of those things is something you want to put in your stomach first thing in the morning."

Maggie shrugged. "I'm not particular. Besides, I'm not much of a cook, so…"

"You just eat whatever is there," he said finishing for her with a look of revulsion.

"Right. It's easier that way," she agreed cheerily.

"Maybe for you, but my system demands a bit more discretion. Do me a favor. At the next town stop at a grocery store. I'm going to stock up on food."

"What for? I wouldn't know what to do with it."

"I do."

She shot him a surprised look. "You can cook?"

"Yes. Nothing fancy, but I manage to turn out a decent meal when I put my mind to it. Don't look so stunned. I don't like having live-in help, and I get tired of eating out all the time, so I learned a few kitchen skills. That's all."

"That's more than I ever managed. Not for lack of Mrs. O'Leary trying to teach me, mind you. I just never could work up much enthusiasm. I'm impressed, Your Nibs. I truly am."

"Don't be, until you've tasted my cooking."

Maggie laughed. "Ah, well, I'm no judge. To me food

is food. If it's edible and it keeps me alive, that's pretty much all that matters."

They drove along in companionable silence for several miles, until Wyatt noticed her casting glances at him out of the corner of her eye.

"What?"

"Oh, nothing. I'm just surprised that you didn't shave. You strike me as the fastidious type."

"I am, but I wasn't about to get a razor anywhere near my face with this rig lumbering all over the place. I didn't want to risk cutting my throat. Just washing my face was a major undertaking." He shot her a wry, sideways glance. "We won't even discuss how difficult it is to hit a moving target going fifty-five miles an hour."

Maggie shot him a puzzled look. "What moving target?"

"The toilet," he said dryly.

She chuckled, even as her cheeks turned a fiery red.

They reached Abilene around noon and agreed that while Maggie filled the RV with gas, Wyatt would buy groceries at the supermarket across the street.

When he climbed out of the rig, he paused to flex his shoulders and stretch, and for the first time he got a good look at the trailer Maggie was towing, the one she had gone to such lengths to protect.

"What do you have in there?" he asked, looking it over curiously. It couldn't be much. The trailer wasn't very large, barely eight-by-four, and only about five feet high.

"Just my bike," she replied, and gave the handle on the gas pump a crank. She stuck the nozzle into the tank and nodded toward the supermarket across the street. "You'd better get going if you're going grocery shopping. I want to be back on the road within an hour."

"Yeah. I guess I'd better," Wyatt agreed, but he hesitated.

Maggie grinned. "What's the matter, afraid I'll go off and leave you?"

"The thought has crossed my mind."

"Mine, too," she admitted with a chuckle. "I'll admit, it's tempting, but don't worry, Your Nibs. We made a deal, and I never break my word. I'll be waiting outside for you over there in the parking lot when you're done."

Wyatt stared into those vivid blue eyes for several seconds, then nodded. "I shouldn't be very long."

"Oh, Wyatt."

He stopped on the curb and looked back. "Yeah?"

"There's a clothing store over there by the market. While you're in a shopping mood, you'd better pick up some duds to wear."

"Good idea."

"Get some jeans, will you. Those dress slacks just don't cut it."

He went to the clothing store first and bought everything from the skin out, plus sneakers and boots. When he'd paid for the purchases he made arrangements to pick them up after he'd finished grocery shopping.

Forty-five minutes later, pushing a cart piled high with sacks of food, he came out of the grocery store, but there was no sign of Maggie or the RV.

Chapter Eight

Wyatt looked everywhere, but Maggie simply wasn't there. "Dammit to hell," he muttered, scanning the parking lot.

Two boys came walking across the parking lot, the heels of their athletic shoes flashing red and blue lights with every bouncing step. Wyatt collared them. "There's five bucks for each of you if you'll stay here with this cart for a few minutes while I run across the street."

"Hey, cool. Sure, man." The prepubescent little yuppies agreed in unison.

Wyatt trotted across the parking lot and dashed across the busy street against the red light.

"There was a woman in here an hour or so ago," he told the station attendant. "Long, curly red hair, blue eyes, about so tall." He held his hand out at chest level. "She was driving an RV pulling a trailer. Do you remember her?"

"Yeah, sure. She was a total babe," the pimply faced teenager behind the counter replied.

Wyatt's fists clenched, but he resisted the urge to plant one right in the face of Mr. Raging Hormones. "Do you happen to know which way she went?"

"Yeah, dude. She headed out the highway. She asked me about that rodeo poster in the window. Seemed real interested. Soon as she signed her credit card ticket she jumped in her RV and headed toward the fairgrounds."

Wyatt bit off a curse. What the hell was he supposed to do now?

After recrossing the street he paid the two boys and used the public telephone outside the market to call his office.

"Wyatt, how're you enjoying the trip," Eric taunted, when Wyatt's secretary put the call through.

He gritted his teeth. "Listen, I'm in no mood to—" The squeal of tires distracted him, and he turned around just in time to see Maggie come careening into the parking lot.

"Sorry, Eric, I'll have to call you back," he snapped, and slammed down the receiver.

Stepping to the curb, he folded his arms and waited. The lumbering vehicle screeched to a halt in front of him.

"I'm sorry," Maggie began, the instant he opened the door. "I didn't mean to go off and leave you. Honestly I didn't."

He responded to her chagrined expression with stony silence and began to unload the cart of groceries, setting the sacks just inside the main door of the RV. Maggie scrambled from the driver's seat and went back into the kitchen to help.

"It's just that I'm so used to traveling alone." Meeting him at the open door, she took the next sack from him and put it on the counter, then quickly returned for the next one. "When I saw that advertisement for the rodeo I got so excited I just forgot about you. I was almost to the fairgrounds before I remembered. It wasn't intentional. I swear it."

"I suppose that's something," he snarled.

"You're angry."

The look he shot her as he handed in the last sack was eloquent. Without a word to Maggie, who was watching him anxiously from the open door of the RV, he stalked next door to the clothing store to retrieve his purchases.

Damned right he was angry. And insulted. No woman had ever forgotten him. Maggie was damned hard on a man's ego.

All the way to the fairgrounds he maintained his miffed silence, but he finally realized he was wasting his time. Holding on to anger against Maggie was futile, since she didn't even seem to notice that he was still upset. For her the matter was settled; she'd made a mistake and apologized, and now she'd moved on, the gaffe forgotten. Her upbeat, sunny outlook was firmly in place once more.

Throughout the drive she chattered away about the rodeo.

"It's great, a genuine Western rodeo. I haven't been to one in years. Oh, they have that big extravaganza in Houston, but it doesn't have the real Old West flavor like this one. This is cattle country around here. And this rodeo is being held in an open-air fairground, the way they're supposed to be," she chattered gaily while he struggled to put away the groceries and his things and still remain upright in the swaying RV. "Oh, and there's an RV park next to the fairground," she called over her shoulder. "If there's space available we'll park there and stay overnight."

Her excitement was so great when she found out there were still a few camping spaces available you would have thought she'd won the lottery. The instant she had the RV set up she was raring to go and enjoy the rodeo.

"Don't you want to eat lunch first? After that pickle and peanut butter sandwich you need some nourishing food."

"Oh, I'm not hungry."

"Well, I am. I'm starved."

"Oh." Wyatt had never heard one word imbued with so much disappointment, but a second later her face brightened. "Then you go ahead and eat. I'll just go look the place over, while you have lunch."

"Maggie, you need to eat. It's not healthy to skip meals."

"Oh, pooh. I do it all the time. But if it'll make you happy, I'll have a carrot." She grabbed one from the bunch on the counter, gave it a quick rinse and bounded out the door, ignoring Wyatt's protests. Shaking his head, he watched her wind her way through the crowd, her bright head swiveling as she tried to take in everything at once. He'd never before met anyone who embraced life with such unbridled enthusiasm.

After satisfying his hunger, Wyatt shaved and changed into a pair of jeans and a Western shirt, then set out to look for Maggie.

He wandered around for a while without spotting her, but he wasn't concerned. What could happen to her at a country rodeo? Much to his surprise, he enjoyed himself. He walked around the pens and looked over the stock and stopped by the arena and watched the cutting horse competition.

Both his complacency and his good mood went up in smoke when he approached the holding chutes.

He stopped in his tracks and gaped. In one of the chutes, surrounded by adoring cowboys, all of whom were apparently giving her instructions on the fine art of bull riding,

Maggie sat astride a wild-eyed, snorting, enraged two-thousand-pound Brahma bull.

For several seconds he could not move or even breathe.

Then, with a roar of rage, he exploded. In three long strides Wyatt reached the chute, grabbed two cowboys by their shirt collars and yanked them off the side of the pen.

"Hey! What the—"

Ignoring the men's protests, he tossed them aside like sacks of potatoes and leapt up onto the rail in their place and plucked Maggie off the bull.

She shrieked and the cowboys yelled protests, but Wyatt's fury quickly silenced them all. He set her on her feet with enough force to clack her teeth together, then lit into her with a vengeance.

"What in the bloody hell do you think you're doing!" he roared. "I leave you to your own devices for half an hour, and this is what you do? Try to ride a damned wild bull! Dammit, woman, do you have a death wish?"

"Hey, now wait a minute, mister. You can't talk to the little lady thata wa—"

"The hell I can't. And as for you guys, I can't believe you would let her do this. You, of all people, know how dangerous this event is, even for an experienced competitor. Look at her, for God's sake! A puff of wind would blow her away. And you were going to let her go out there on the back of a bull. She could've been killed or maimed for life. What the hell is the matter with you?"

"Now, Wyatt—"

"Stay out of this." He jabbed the air near the end of her nose with his forefinger, and Maggie jumped. "I'll deal with you later.

"As for the rest of you yahoos, I ought to beat the tar out of all of you. You're just lucky I got here in time to put a stop to this insanity."

Embarrassed, all of the cowboys shuffled from one foot to the other and exchanged guilty glances. "We're sorry, mister. You're right. We shouldn't oughta done it," one young cowboy said, and the others muttered agreement.

"Now wait just a minute." Maggie stepped up to Wyatt and poked his chest with her forefinger. "Where do you get off, interfering in my life?"

"It's obvious that somebody has to. Otherwise you'd break your fool neck."

"Oh, yeah. Well 'tis my neck, and I won't have you buttin' your nose into my business."

"If you'd use a little sense I wouldn't have to."

"Nobody tells me what to do." Maggie bristled, giving his chest another poke.

Wyatt leaned down, fury flashing in his eyes. "It's high time somebody did. You don't seem to have an ounce of caution or common sense."

"Is that right. Well let me tell you—"

They stood toe to toe and nose to nose, shouting and gesturing wildly, while the cowboys exchanged uneasy glances.

"I was perfectly safe!" Maggie insisted.

"Dammit, woman!" Wyatt roared back. "Don't you realized you could have gotten yourself killed?"

"Uh, excuse me, mister," one brave cowboy put in cautiously. "You don't have to worry about that. We weren't gonna let her ride 'im."

"You weren't?"

Maggie crossed her arms and stuck her nose in the air. "See. I told you it wasn't dangerous."

"Naw. The lady, she wanted to but we couldn't let her 'cause it's against the rules," the fresh-faced lad explained.

Maggie groaned as Wyatt's face tightened with renewed fury.

"That cuts it," he snapped. Too angry to continue the argument, he hefted her over his shoulder and stomped toward their campsite.

"Put me down! Do you hear me, Wyatt Sommersby? Put me down this instant." Maggie kicked and pounded his back with her fists but he didn't so much as flinch.

Maggie was no match for him physically, but once he deposited her on the floor of the RV she erupted. "Why you sorry, misbegotten son-of-a-lop-eared-jackass! Who do you think you are?"

"A better question is, what the hell did you think you were doing?"

"Mindin' me own business. Which is more than can be said of you," she accused, her brogue growing thicker by the second.

For the next half hour they indulged in a wing-ding of a fight, exchanging shouted insults and accusations. At one point Wyatt tried to ignore her, but she dogged his footsteps from one end of the RV to the other, nipping at him like a terrier. Though her nature was naturally sunny, Maggie's Irish temper, once aroused, was formidable.

"Listen, you jackass. Get this through that thick head o' yours. What I do is my business an' none of yours!"

"Well I'm making it my business," he shouted back.

"Oh, is that right! Well just take your sorry hide out of here and go back to your safe corporate world where you belong."

Wyatt stuck his face in hers. "Make me."

"Ohhh." At her wits' end, she doubled up her fists and pummeled his chest.

Wyatt grabbed her hands, but Maggie hauled off and kicked him in the shin.

"All right. That's it," he growled and hauled her into his arms and clamped his mouth to hers.

The kiss was no gentle seduction, but hot and open-mouthed and full of fire. Wyatt's lips rocked over hers, hungrily taking, demanding, giving no quarter.

Maggie drummed her fists against his shoulders, but gradually the flailing blows faltered, then ceased, and the strangled sound of protest emanating from her throat became a soft moan. Her body grew relaxed and pliant and conformed to his. She wrapped her arms around his neck and hung in his arms, limp as a rag doll, her feet dangling a foot off the floor.

The kiss altered with her surrender, grew soft and tender, and so hot Maggie thought her bones would surely melt. She trembled and tightened her arms around his neck.

"Maggie. Oh, God, Maggie," Wyatt gasped, coming up for air. He strung frantic kisses down her neck, along the tender underside of her jaw.

Eyes closed, Maggie tipped her head back to give him better access. She raked her fingernails over his scalp and clutched his hair with both hands. "Ah, sweet mercy, don't stop. Don't stop."

Neither knew how they got there, but suddenly they were sprawled across the bed. They rolled together, mouths locked, legs intertwined, hands desperately clutching and roaming.

The top two buttons on Maggie's blouse gave way, and she sighed when his warm hand cupped her breast. His thumb brushed across her nipple, and the sigh became a sharp cry and her back arched off the mattress as pleasure pierced her.

"Aw, Maggie. Sweet Maggie. Do you like that?" he murmured against her ear.

"Yes. Yes!"

The pleasure was so intense the sound did not penetrate at first, but the electronic trill persisted, slowly intruding into the delicious haze. Maggie blinked several times and raised her head off the pillow. "What's that?"

In the throes of passion, Wyatt barely heard the sound and didn't care. "Forget it. It's not important."

"No, wait. Listen. That's a ringing."

"It's probably outside," he murmured, nibbling her earlobe. "Or maybe in the next camper."

"No. No, I don't think so. It's in here somewhere." She cocked her head. "It sounds like a telephone."

Wyatt stilled and listened. "Ah, hell."

Maggie's eyes grew round and her jaw dropped. "It *is* a telephone!" She socked Wyatt. "You rat! You sneaked a phone in here when I specifically said no phone calls."

She bounded off the bed and flew through the motor home, opening drawers and cabinets, riffling through them, pawing through the closet. She lifted the cushions on the couch and checked inside the oven and microwave. "Where is it? Where'd you hide it, you sneak?"

"Maggie, sweetheart, it's not like that, I swear it," Wyatt pleaded. "I forgot I had it with me. Honest."

"Ha! I bet!" She spied his briefcase, shoved between the couch and the end of the counter and pounced. "Aha!"

Snatching up the case, she held it to her ear, and let out a triumphant whoop. "I knew it! I knew it! You rotten, lying cheat."

"Now, Maggie, be reasonable. I wasn't trying to deceive you. I always carry that phone. Really."

Ignoring him, she set the case on the table, clicked open the latches and snatched up the chirping cellular telephone. "Hello?"

Two beats of silence followed. "Maggie? Is that you?"

"Yes, Eric, it's me."

"Uh…is Wyatt there?"

"Yes, he's here, but—"

"Give me that," Wyatt insisted, but she batted his hand aside and turned away.

"He's unavailable right now."

"Maggie! Give me the damned phone."

He made another grab but she kicked him in the shin.

"Ow! Ow! Ow!" Wyatt hopped on one leg, holding the other one. "That hurt, dammit!"

"What's going on?"

"Sorry, your brother won't be available for several days. Maybe weeks, so don't waste your time calling back. 'Bye."

"Why did you do tha— Wait a minute! Where are you going? Dammit, Maggie come back here with that phone!" he yelled, but she was already out the door.

By the time he stepped outside she was halfway across the campground. When Wyatt saw where she was heading he groaned, "Oh, no," and broke into a run.

He didn't make it in time. He skidded to a halt beside her as she dropped the cellular telephone into a horse trough.

Wyatt stared through the water at the high-tech instrument resting on the bottom of the trough. "I can't believe you did that," he said in a stunned voice, then in a roar. "I *can't* believe you *did that!* Woman, have you lost your mind? That was a state-of-the-art three-hundred-dollar telephone."

"When we go back to Houston I'll buy you another one. In the meantime I have peace and quiet. If you can't live with that, then hit the road."

She dusted her hands together, smiled sunnily and strolled back toward the RV at a sedate pace. Wyatt fell into step beside her, crackling with fury.

"You keep making that suggestion, but I'm not leaving. And it's not a matter of not liking peace and quiet. I can live with peace and quiet. I welcome it. It's you I can't live with.''

Her grin flashed. "I know. That's what I've been telling you all along.''

Wyatt ground his teeth. She'd tripped him up that time.

He gave her a tight-lipped smile. "I'm confident we can adjust to each other. If a certain maddening woman would just stop doing reckless things, that is.''

"Well, let that certain woman remind you that you invited yourself along on this trip and that she'll do as she darn well pleases. What I do and what happens to me is no business of yours.'' She climbed the two steps to the trailer, pausing on the top one to toss him a smug look over her shoulder and chuckle. "You're not my father or my brother or my husband, you know. You're not even my lover, so back off, Your Nibs.''

With her nose in the air and her laughing mouth curled up at the corners, she sashayed inside with an impudent little twitch of her hips.

Wyatt stared after her. "Not yet," he growled. "But soon, sweetheart. Soon.''

To give himself time to cool off and rethink his strategy, he went for a walk. The sight of the telephone booth reminded him of Eric's call. He stopped and stared at it. After two aborted calls, Eric was probably about to have a nervous breakdown trying to figure out what was going on. Wyatt glanced back in the direction of the campground, but he couldn't see Maggie's RV.

He hesitated, torn. They had a deal. But dammit, it wasn't fair of her to expect a man to just dump his business and never even check in to see that everything was all right. That kind of irresponsible behavior might work for a free spirit like her, but a lot of people depended on him. Why, for all he knew, his office could have burned down by now. A call now and then wouldn't hurt. He wouldn't do it often.

Coming to a decision, he stomped to the telephone. He fished his wallet from the back pocket of his jeans, pulled out his credit card and inserted it into the slot.

A few seconds later his secretary again put him through to Eric.

"Wyatt, is that you? What the devil is going on? Why wouldn't Maggie let me talk to you?"

"Part of our deal was I wouldn't contact the office. She seems to think that I can't go even a day without involving myself in business."

Eric chuckled. "Looks like she was right."

"This doesn't count," Wyatt snapped, frowning. "I'm returning your call because I didn't want you to worry. And I was afraid there might be an emergency."

"Not yet. But one is sure to pop up," he joked. "They always do." Three seconds of silence followed, then, in a serious voice Eric said, "Wyatt, why are you taking this crazy trip? I've never known you to put anything before business. You've never even taken a weekend vacation since you took over Sommersby Enterprises."

"Yeah, well, maybe it's time I did."

He rubbed the back of his neck and stared at a dirty limerick someone had scratched on the wall of the phone booth. For twelve long years he'd worked his buns off. The first three it had taken every ounce of energy and ingenuity he possessed just to keep the company afloat, thanks to the mess his father had made of the business.

Wyatt's grandfather had run Sommersby Enterprises until his death at the ripe old age of ninety-one. By then Wyatt's father had been well into his sixties, and though he'd been an officer of the company, it had been a titular position. Winston Sommersby had been a gentleman of leisure, a polished socialite who excelled in polo and tennis and yachting, a man who'd had excellent taste in clothes and wine and who'd possessed impeccable manners.

He had not, however, inherited the drive or business savvy of his ancestors. In the six years that Wyatt's father had been at the helm of Sommersby Enterprises he had almost succeeded in ruining a business that had grown and flourished under five previous generations of Sommersbys.

When Wyatt took over and discovered just how close they were to going belly-up, he had been forced to put in eighteen- and twenty-hour days. In those early years he had taken work home on weekends and holidays, hustled bankers, sweet-talked creditors and beat the bushes for every remote chance to turn even the tiniest profit. By the time the company was in the black again, it had become a habit, he realized now.

One it was perhaps time to break.

"The business can survive without me for a while. You just said everything was running smoothly."

"It is. We can, but… Look, Wyatt, I know how determined you get when you want something, but why Maggie? Aside from the fact that it makes it damned awkward for me to have my brother trying to seduce my fiancée's sister, I just don't get it. I mean, she's cute and all, but you go out with better-looking women all the time. And she's…well… different. What do you see—"

"Just drop it, Eric."

"But—"

"I said drop it."

An offended silence followed. "Very well. If that's what you want," Eric said in a stilted voice.

Wyatt cursed under his breath. "Look, I'm sorry, I don't want to discuss it right now. Just take care of things for me, okay? I'll get in touch in a day or so if I can."

"Of course. Whatever you say."

When he'd hung up, Wyatt stood with his hand on the receiver. Damn. He could not recall ever being so frustrated in his life.

How the devil could he explain to his brother what he didn't understand himself? All he knew was he wanted Maggie like he'd never wanted any other woman, and it had little to do with physical beauty. Although, in his opinion, Maggie's wholesome allure was a hundred times more appealing than conventional beauty, especially the pampered, polished looks of the women in their social circle.

Hooking his thumbs in his belt loops, he strolled toward the corrals, his mind whirling. The problem was he was accustomed to being in control and giving orders. When he gave those orders they were obeyed without question. Yet the little Irish imp defied him at every turn. And laughed at him when she did it.

Wyatt sighed. It didn't matter. He wanted Maggie in his life. Damned if he knew why. The well-ordered existence he'd had before the pint-sized female had breezed into it and scrambled his brain had certainly been one hell of a lot easier. And saner. Nevertheless, having Maggie had become imperative.

It wasn't just sex, either, though God knew, desire for her was eating him alive.

She mystified him and annoyed him and fascinated him. And the thought of harm coming to her terrified him. He liked being with her, he liked the way she looked, her enthusiasm and bubbly joy, her unique way of looking at the world. Her innocence.

He'd never felt this way about a woman before—this possessive, this…connected. But then, Maggie wasn't like any woman he'd ever known. Maggie was special. Maggie was…Maggie. A unique jewel and a pain in the butt.

He stopped beside a corral, propped his forearms on the top rail, one booted foot on the bottom, and stared, unseeing, at the remuda of skittish horses across the pen. God, she was so open and trusting, so naive and reckless, so full of laughter and vivacity and enthusiasm, she scared the living hell out of him. He wanted to wrap her up in cotton wool and keep her safe. Was that so wrong?

He thought of that wild spirit, the excitement that sparkled in her eyes, and he knew the answer. He sighed and rubbed his chin on the top of his hands. Yes, it was wrong. It was probably criminal.

Asa was right; Maggie was a will-o'-the-wisp. A wild little bird who needed freedom as much as she needed oxygen. But dammit, it was hard. How did a man stand back and let her have her head? When every instinct in him wanted to lock her up and throw away the key and keep her safe?

Inside the RV, Maggie sat curled up on the sofa, arms around her updrawn legs, chin on her knees, and stared out the window at the bright summer day.

What was she going to do about Wyatt? She'd tried reason and humor and now anger, but he wouldn't give up. He just kept pushing his way into her life, edging closer.

She should never have gotten within a mile of a dominant man like Wyatt. If she wasn't careful he would take over.

"The problem is, my girl, you don't want him to go away altogether," she muttered. "Face it, you want to have your cake and eat it, too. You're attracted to the bothersome man, and you want him around, but on your own terms. Much the same as he wants you. Och, what a fine pair. Two mules in harness, that's what you are."

Maybe she ought to just go ahead and have a flaming fling with him and be done with it. Get him out of her system. It was time—past time—she found out what all the fuss was about, anyway. Lord knew, if the way her body responded when he was around, she was ready. She could look at it as just another new experience.

Except that the act entailed a degree of intimacy that she found unsettling.

Was it possible to share that kind of physical closeness without becoming emotionally involved? Oh, she knew that men did it all the time. Wyatt had made it abundantly clear that a temporary relationship of limited commitment was what he wanted with her. But even that made her nervous.

Women were such creatures of emotion. Even sane, sensible women couldn't seem to resist falling in love when their hormones ran amok.

Well, not her.

Ever since Eve, emotions had been the downfall of women. Maggie didn't want to end up like her mother—wasting her life, never going anywhere, never doing anything but waiting for her lover to show up and dole out a few crumbs of affection. She shuddered. No. Love was not for her. She could not let herself fall in love with Wyatt. She wouldn't.

When Wyatt returned, Maggie was working on her laptop computer, drafting out her next book, he presumed. She didn't so much as look up when he entered the RV.

He took the chair opposite her and waited for her to acknowledge him. Finally he gave up.

"Maggie, for Pete's sake, will you stop that and listen to me for a minute? I want to say something."

At first he thought she hadn't heard him, but after a

moment her fingers stilled on the keyboard. She looked up and eyed him warily. "What?"

"I want you to know that..." He grimaced and rubbed the back of his neck. "Dammit, this isn't easy for me, but...well...I'm sorry. You were right. I had no business doing what I did. I still think it was a foolish risk," he added quickly. "But I realize that it's not my place to interfere. It won't be easy, but I promise I'll try my best not to do it again."

She stared at him, silently assessing. After a moment her remote expression softened and a grin lit up her face. "Apology accepted. Now, was that so hard?"

"Yes," he snapped, and Maggie laughed.

"No doubt that's because it's the first one you've given in a long while. Well, cheer up, 'tis good for the character they say." She gave him a vague smile and returned her attention to the computer screen.

Wyatt stared at her. She had tuned him out, just like that. Already she was so engrossed in that damned story she was writing he doubted she was even aware that he was there. He'd never in his life had any woman treat him with such breezy indifference. The woman was driving him around the bend.

He stood up and stomped into the tiny kitchen a few feet away and began to drag out what he needed to prepare dinner. Muttering under his breath, he slammed drawers and cabinet doors and banged pans with more force than necessary, but Maggie didn't so much as flinch. Her fingers flew over the keyboard and her gaze never left the screen.

Several times he had to reach around her to set the table, but she never noticed. When the meal was ready he had to shake her shoulder to get her attention.

"What is it?" she asked, blinking at the food he had put in front of her.

"Steak, baked potato and salad. Not very fancy but nourishing and easy to prepare. So eat up."

At the beginning of the meal Wyatt made several attempts at conversation, but Maggie's mind seemed to be miles away, so finally he quit trying. After eating only about half of her meal she shoved her plate aside and replaced it with her computer. Wyatt stacked and washed the dishes, to the sound of the keyboard clacking without letup.

When he'd finished in the kitchen he sat down on the sofa opposite Maggie and flipped through a magazine. He shifted positions several times. He cleared his throat loudly, then coughed. Maggie pounded on without so much as a blink.

Finally he made a disgusted sound, shot to his feet and stomped into the bathroom. Twenty minutes later he returned, smelling of soap and toothpaste and mouthwash, dressed in only his jeans, the top button of which was undone. He stretched and yawned.

"I think I'll turn in," he announced. Deliberately, watching Maggie all the while, and standing only a few feet from her, he stripped off down to his underwear.

She paid no more attention to him than she had over dinner. "Oh, for Pete's sake! Good night!"

Cursing through his clenched teeth, Wyatt climbed into the bed above the cab and yanked the privacy curtain closed.

The clack of the keyboard continued without pause as Maggie's mouth slowly curled up at the corners.

Chapter Nine

"*Ba-ba-ba-ba-ba-ba-baaad to the bone!*"

Wyatt's whole body jerked and he came up off the mattress. "What the— His forehead slammed into the ceiling so hard he went sprawling again. "Ow! Dammit to hell!"

"*Ba-ba-ba-ba-ba-ba-baaad to the bone!*"

The deep bass beat of the rock music reverberated through the RV. Wyatt groaned and grabbed his head. Grimacing, he peered over the edge of the mattress in time to see Maggie come boogying down the passageway. Dressed in her bunny slippers and that damned football jersey, eyes closed tight, she was singing along with the gravelly-voiced vocalist.

"*Baa-ba-ba-ba-ba-ba-baaad!   Baa-ba-ba-ba-ba-ba-baaad!*"

She danced around the minuscule kitchen with her arms over her head, that delicious little body gyrating in a perfect bump-and-grind to the raunchy beat. In the same way she did everything, she threw herself into the music with utter abandon and joy.

Wyatt could have watched her all day—except that it was only five in the morning, he had a lump on his forehead big enough to hang a hat on, and that damned pounding music was about to take his head off.

"For Pete's sake, Maggie, will you turn that stuff off! Or at least turn it down," he bellowed.

"*Ba-ba-ba-ba-ba-ba-baad to the bone!*" Maggie sang on in ecstasy, shimmying her shoulders to the beat. Eyes still squeezed shut, she was lost in the pounding rhythm and oblivious to anything else.

"Argh!" Pressing his palms flat over his ears, Wyatt tried to shut out the raucous music, but the whole rig shook with it. "Oh, for the love of—" He pumped his legs and kicked the cover into a wad at his ankles, rolled to the edge and jumped down.

The music was coming from the bedroom. Maggie gyrated in the tiny kitchen between there and where he stood. He tried to dodge around her but whichever way he stepped so did she. Finally he made an aggravated sound, clamped his hands around her waist and lifted her out of the way.

Her eyes popped open, and she grinned down at him from midair. "Oh, hi! Top o' the mornin', Your Nibs. Isn't it a great day?" she shouted.

Wyatt glared into her cheery face, plunked her down in the sitting area without so much as a word, and stomped into the bedroom. He located the CD player on a shelf above her bed and jabbed the Off button with enough force to scoot the unit back three inches.

He sighed and let his head fall back. Blessed relief.

The silence was thick and absolute, but it still seemed

to pulse with the heavy beat. Or maybe that was just the ringing in his ears.

The calm lasted only seconds. Maggie marched into the bedroom with her hands on her hips. "Why did you do that?"

Rubbing the knot on his forehead, Wyatt skewered her with a look. "Because it's too damned early for that kind of noise."

"Noise! I'll have you know that's one of my favorite songs. And it can't be that early. I—"

She jumped when a fist pounded on the outside of the RV. "Hey! Keep it down in there, will ya! People are trying to sleep around here, for Pete's sake!"

Folding his arms over his bare chest, Wyatt cocked one black eyebrow. "You were saying?"

Maggie grimaced and put her hand over her mouth. "Oops." She rolled her eyes and sighed. "Now you know why I don't like to stay in campgrounds. I do things when the mood strikes me. Sometimes I forget that other people live their lives by the clock."

Suddenly alert, Wyatt cocked his head to one side and studied her. "Is that why you like living above a warehouse in a nonresidential part of town? So you have the freedom to do whatever you feel like doing whenever you want without disturbing anyone?"

"I guess. But I also happen to like the place."

"Mmm. Interesting."

Maggie didn't like the sound of that at all. Squirming, she lowered her gaze to escape his searching look and found herself staring at a bare, furry chest. Belatedly she realized that she was standing there having a conversation with an almost naked man. The only article of clothing Wyatt had on was a pair of white cotton briefs.

She tried to keep her gaze focused on his chest, but as

always, curiosity got the best of her. As though drawn by a magnet, her eyes followed the line of silky hair that arrowed down from the mat on his chest. It bisected a hard, flat belly and swirled around his navel before disappearing beneath the brief swath of material riding low on his hips. An impressive bulge stretched the soft cotton.

Her eyes widened. Oh, my. Heat climbed her neck and her chest grew tight.

"Like what you see?"

Her gaze flew upward and her blush deepened. Beneath half-closed lids, his eyes smoldered with laughter and blatant sexual heat.

Fighting the urge to look away, she ignored the pulsing fire in her cheeks and met his look with twinkling eyes. "What I'd like is for you to either go back to bed or put your clothes on. Sweet Mary and Joseph, couldn't you have bought a pair of pajamas while you were in that store yesterday? 'Tis indecent, you are."

Ignoring her thundering heart, she turned and strolled back into the kitchen as though she hadn't a care in the world, opened the refrigerator, stuck her head inside and pretended to scrounge for something for breakfast. She poked through the contents without having any idea of what she was seeing. Her stomach was so aflutter, if she had been starving she couldn't have eaten a bite.

Wyatt grinned appreciatively at her cute little rump as he sidled around her. "I never wear pajamas." Making no effort at all to hide his amusement, he picked up the jeans he'd tossed on the chair the night before and stepped into them. "As a matter of fact, I'm only wearing these briefs out of respect for your modesty. Normally I sleep nude."

The remark, as she was sure he intended, sent a fresh surge of color to her face, but she kept her head buried in the refrigerator long enough to let her cheeks cool and regain her equilibrium.

Straightening with a carton of milk in her hand, she sent him an amused look over the top of the refrigerator door, deliberately letting her gaze linger on his body. "Och, and don't think I don't appreciate it. Enticing as I'm sure your lady friends find your sleeping habits, seeing you naked as a jaybird is a pleasure I'll forego, thank you. The sight might be too much for this old-maid heart of mine to take."

She closed the door and turned. She jumped and let out a little squeak when Wyatt's hands slapped against the refrigerator on either side of her. Penned in by his braced arms, she pressed back against the cool enamel and stared, wide-eyed into his face, just inches from her own.

The look in his eyes made her heart trip. "Honey, believe me, you may be an innocent, but you're no old maid," he murmured in a husky voice that did strange things to her insides. "And I promise you, before this trip is over, you will see me naked. Just as I'll see you. In fact, I plan to kiss every inch of your delectable little body."

Maggie's heart did a dance against her ribs, but her lips curved up in an impudent smile and she rolled her eyes. "Och, would you listen to the conceit of the man?"

"It's not conceit, just a sure thing." He touched her neck with his forefinger where a pulse hammered. "You know it as well as I do. It's just a matter of time."

Not a single sassy comeback came to mind. All Maggie could do was stare into those silver eyes like a deer caught in headlights, while her heart thundered and her lungs struggled for air. Never in her life had she been so totally aware of another human being.

With every painful breath she drew, his scent invaded

her being—clean, musky, uncompromisingly male. The heady aroma made her head swim.

This close, she could see tiny flecks of charcoal in his eyes, each individual black eyelash, feel his breath feathering over her cheek, moist and warm.

His gaze dropped to her mouth. Slowly, he bent his elbows and leaned in closer. Maggie caught her breath and waited. Her eyes drifted shut.

It seemed forever before his mouth touched hers. The kiss, when it came, was soft, a mere feather touch, but she felt it all the way to the soles of her feet. Her toes curled inside her bunny slippers. She leaned back against the refrigerator, her spine flat against the cool enamel, her body on fire.

She expected him to take her into his arms, perhaps even carry her into the bedroom. At that moment she wasn't sure she would have tried to stop him, but she never got the chance to find out. The next instant he straightened and stepped back, leaving her slumped there, weak and shaken and quivering with a yearning so strong she hurt.

The look in his eyes said he knew exactly what he'd done to her. He touched her cheek with his fingertips and smiled. "Soon," he whispered. "Very soon."

Abruptly, he turned away and picked up his shirt. "Give me a minute and I'll cook us some breakfast," he said as though the last few minutes had not happened.

For several seconds after he had disappeared into the bathroom Maggie remained absolutely still, staring at the closed door. "Och, Margaret Mary Muldoon, now see what a fine mess you've gotten yourself into with your cockiness. You should never have let him come with you," she murmured to herself. She raised a trembling hand to her lips. "You're in trouble, my girl," she whispered. "The man is lethal."

It was several seconds before she realized she still had the milk carton in her hand. Muttering a curse, she jerked open the refrigerator and shoved it back inside.

A slight noise in the bathroom threw her into a tizzy and she turned in a circle three times before she finally yanked open the silverware drawer and grabbed a handful of flatware.

When the table was set, she dashed into the bedroom, threw on the first pair of jeans and T-shirt her hand encountered, dashed back to the sitting area, snatched up the rough draft of the Mergatroid and Arbuckle adventure she'd started the night before and parked herself on the sofa.

Wyatt reappeared a short time later, fully dressed, hair combed, clean-shaven and devastating. After one covert glance, she kept her gaze riveted to the manuscript pages.

Normally once Maggie got started on one of her stories she became so engrossed she was oblivious. The sofa could blow up beneath her and she wouldn't notice.

Not that morning. The instant Wyatt stepped from the bathroom, every cell in her body sat up at attention.

Maggie kept her head down and her eyes on the paper, but her nose twitched as the smells of soap and shaving cream reached her. A tingle raced over her skin as though someone had run a feather over it.

Pretending she hadn't noticed him, or that her skin wasn't pebbled with gooseflesh, she gritted her teeth and turned a page. Oh yes, she was definitely in a fix.

Wyatt paused in rolling up the cuffs of his chambray shirt and glanced at the set table, then at Maggie. She sat cross-legged on the sofa, her nose buried in a stack of papers. He assumed she was working on another of her children's books.

She had changed into a pair of jeans and an emerald

green T-shirt with a devilish leprechaun and the words Life's Too Short Not To Be Irish emblazoned in white across the front.

A grin tugged at his mouth. If all the Irish were like Maggie that was probably the truth. He'd never met anyone who relished life more.

"What would you like for breakfast? You've got your choice of bacon and eggs, frozen waffles or cereal."

"Mmm?" She raised her head slowly and blinked, as though pulling herself back from some faraway place. Wyatt sucked in his breath.

He felt as though he'd been kicked in the gut. It didn't seem possible that eyes could be that blue, or a face that innocently lovely.

She had obviously attempted to do something with her hair, but the unruly mane would not be tamed. It billowed around her face and shoulders in a glorious cloud of burnished curls that flamed and sparked like fire in the early-morning sunshine pouring in through the window at her back. He itched to touch those silky strands. He wanted to run his hands through them, feel them slide between his fingers and twine and cling, bury his face in those fragrant curls.

Her feet were bare. So was her face. But then, cosmetics on Maggie would be superfluous, he realized. Her skin was dewy fresh and creamy, her lips and cheeks rosy with healthy color—and perhaps a lingering trace of excitement. He hoped so, anyway.

Everything about her was colorful—emerald shirt, red hair, rosy cheeks and lips, auburn brows and blue, blue eyes.

Dear God. Had he ever truly considered her to be merely cute? It was true, she wasn't beautiful in the accepted sense, but there was an ethereal loveliness about her, an innocence and purity of spirit, that took his breath away.

"What do you want for breakfast?" he asked again, when he realized she was waiting for a reply.

"Oh, anything. It doesn't matter," she answered absently, returning her gaze to the papers she held.

His jaw tightened. It irked him that she seemed to be able to dismiss him so easily from her mind, but he turned to the stove without a word.

When they sat down to eat a few minutes later, Maggie's expression registered surprise at the meal he'd produced. After one bite her eyes lit up. "This is really good."

Wyatt's half smile was wry. "Somehow, coming from a woman who eats pickle and peanut butter sandwiches for breakfast, that compliment doesn't carry a lot of weight. Anyway, it's hard to mess up scrambled eggs and microwave bacon. You should try your hand at it sometime."

"I'll take your word for it," she said with a grin, and popped another bite into her mouth.

For a while they ate in silence, but curiosity got the better of Wyatt. "Tell me, what made you so jubilant this morning?"

"Oh, I just felt energized and happy because my book is going so well. Then when I saw the pink and orange sunrise it made me feel like dancing and singing." She shrugged and stabbed another forkful of eggs. "That's all."

Wyatt digested that as he watched her devour her breakfast. She was truly a creature of impulse. Maggie skipped headlong through life, embracing it with open arms. He had never known anyone like her.

"Tell me about your life in Ireland."

"Och, 'tisn't all that interesting. Mainly, when I wasn't

in school, I spent my time running free about the countryside like a wild animal.''

Wyatt paused in buttering his toast. ''Didn't your guard-
ians worry?''

''Och no. Not as long as the support checks came on
time each month. Of course, they knew I could take care
of myself,'' she added, noticing his expression. ''Truth to
tell, I doubt they even noticed I was gone most of the
time.''

''You mean they only kept you for the money?''

''Now don't go gettin' the wrong idea, Your Nibs. They
weren't bad people…merely poor, and the support money
came in handy, what with having twelve children of their
own. And 'twas a wee tiny cottage they lived in. I always
felt penned in when I had to stay inside with that many
people in so small a space. That was all.''

Wyatt thought about the spacious loft she lived in, and
put two and two together.

Was that why she guarded her freedom so fiercely? Because she'd felt trapped and used in that house?

She narrowed her eyes at him, then laughed. ''Stop trying to psychoanalyze me, Wyatt. I promise you, I don't fit
into any of the profiles that you read about in psychology
class back in college. But just so you know, I like my
freedom because it's my nature to roam.''

''That's not the only reason, though, is it?''

Her smiled faded a bit. She took a sip of coffee and
studied him over the rim of her cup. Elbows propped on
the table, she cradled the cup in both hands and held his
gaze for an interminable time. Wyatt was beginning to
think she wasn't going to answer him, but after a while
she nodded.

''You're right. It isn't. From the time I was a tiny child

until her death, I watched my mother pine away for a man she adored.

"The place John Hightower bought for her was a bonnie cottage, I'll give him that. White it was, with emerald green shutters and doors and roses climbing all around. Och, the roses were glorious. Reds, pinks, yellow, all kinds. My mother spent all her time tending them." Her vivid eyes were slightly out of focus, fixed on a time and place far removed from the present. Wyatt wondered if she realized how thick her brogue had become, or how revealing that was.

"But for my mother the cottage was a prison. She never left it, for fear that he would come and she'd be gone. I did the marketing for her, ran all the errands. She didn't even go to church...although...that was probably due more to shame. She went nowhere, did nothing, had no friends. She had no life beyond the waiting...and the grieving. And all it got her were the crumbs of affection that John Hightower tossed her now and then.

"I made up my mind years ago that I would never let myself be shackled to anyone that way. That I would never let love rob me of my freedom. All my mother's love brought her was pain and betrayal and a lifetime of loneliness and shame. If that's what loves does for you, I want no part of it."

"Maggie," he began hesitantly. "It doesn't have to be that way."

She seemed to snap back to the present and shake off her mood. Sitting up straighter, she sent him a twinkling look and snorted. "I don't believe this. I'm getting advice on love from the likes of you? Have you ever even been in love?"

"Well...no. But there are plenty of successful love

matches around. Just look at your grandparents. They were married for…what? Thirty-five, forty years?''

Maggie nodded. ''Something like that.''

''There. You see. Why, Asa can't even talk about his Jessie without getting choked up.''

For the first time since he'd known her, Maggie looked uncertain. She chewed her lower lip and stared out the window at the activity in the campground, but after a moment she seemed to gather her defenses, and when she looked back at him she was her old cocky self again.

''I'm sure there are a few exceptions, but from what I've seen, love is highly overrated. For most people it usually turns sour. Just look at the divorce rate in this country. I'm sure most of those couples married for love.''

''Come on, Maggie. Sure there are a lot of broken marriages, but the data on divorce is not all that reliable. The numbers are skewed by the people who marry and divorce over and over. They make it seem like every other couple is splitting up, but we both know that's not so.''

What the devil was he doing? He'd become an expert at avoiding marriage, and here he was extolling the institution.

Maggie apparently saw the irony in the situation, too. Her eyes twinkled at him over her coffee cup. ''Och, such sage advice. Does this mean you're contemplating taking the leap into matrimony?''

''No, it does not,'' he said with more force than was necessary, and Maggie grinned. ''But we were talking about you, not me. And I believe the subject was love, not matrimony. I think it would be a mistake for you to cut yourself off from love because of your mother's experience.''

Maggie leaned closer. ''I tell you what, Your Nibs. If

ever meet a man I can't live without, I'll give it a go. But don't hold your breath."

The statement infuriated Wyatt. *If?* What the devil was he, totally resistible? Evidently she thought so. She couldn't have made it plainer that she could get along quite well without him.

They spent the day taking in the rodeo and stock show. Maggie cheered the cowboys on during every event, and she got so excited during the children's calf scramble Wyatt thought she was going to fall right out of the stands. Her enthusiasm and delight in everything charmed him. While touring the stock show she oohed and ahhed over every animal. When she cuddled a newborn lamb he got the strangest sensation in his chest, a warm and fuzzy feeling.

In the early evening they return to the RV. Outside the camper Maggie turned in a circle, her face tipped up to the sinking sun, arms wide. "Hasn't it been a beautiful day?"

"If you say so." It was scorching hot and humid as a steambath, but he wasn't about to do anything to spoil her mood.

"And just look at that sky." She gestured toward the west where silver-lined clouds of orange, pink and mauve billowed just above the horizon. "It's much too nice to go inside. I feel like going for a ride. How about you?"

"A ride on what?"

"My bike." Without waiting for his agreement, she dashed around to the rear of the RV and opened the trailer.

Great, Wyatt thought, following more slowly. He could just see them riding double down the highway on a rickety bicycle. They'd probably die of heat stroke if they didn't get squashed by an eighteen wheeler first.

"Just wait 'till you see it," Maggie called from inside the trailer. "She's a beaut."

I'll bet, Wyatt thought. Cocking one hip, he leaned a shoulder against the rear of the RV, and tried to come up with a legitimate excuse to beg off. The next second Maggie came around the corner of the trailer, rolling the biggest, meanest looking machine he'd ever seen.

Wyatt's jaw dropped. He straightened slowly away from the RV, his muscles tightening one by one. All he could do was stand there and stare. Finally he shook his head and muttered, "I don't believe it."

Maggie beamed, her pixie grin stretching wide. "See. Didn't I tell you she was great?"

"That's a motorcycle," he said in a dazed voice.

"Och, man, 'tisn't *just* a motorcycle. 'Tis a Harley-Davidson. She's got enough horsepower to peel the paving right off the highway."

"Good Lord." Life poured back into Wyatt's body as his heart began to pump like crazy. He walked slowly around the wicked-looking bike. Even idle, it looked like a ferocious black beast, straining to break free and race the wind. "You actually *ride* this thing?" The bike was so monstrous and Maggie so tiny he didn't see how she even held it up.

"Of course. All the time." She gave him an eager look. "You ready to go for a spin? Here, put this on."

Taking his agreement for granted, she grabbed the two helmets strapped to the back of the Harley, tossed one to him, fastened the other one on herself and slung a leg over the saddle with all the confidence of a cowboy mounting a horse. "Well? C'mon. What're you waitin' for? Let's get goin'," she said, giving a little bounce on the seat.

Wyatt eyed the motorcycle, then Maggie. If ever he'd seen a formula for disaster, there it sat. The words "Not on your life'' hovered on his tongue, but the delight and anticipation in her pixie face held them back.

With a sigh, calling himself all manner of fool, he pulled on the helmet and gingerly climbed onto the saddle seat behind her.

His hands settled naturally on either side of her waist, almost spanning its tiny circumference. Their bodies fitted together spoon fashion, his thighs bracketing hers, Maggie's round little derriere snuggled intimately against his crotch. The feel of that firm flesh almost made him forget the trepidation that squeezed his chest.

"You ready?"

"As ready as I'll ever be."

Maggie turned the key in the ignition, kicked the starter, and the bike roared to life with a deep rumble. A few twists of the throttle revved the engine up to a throaty roar that sent a wave of gooseflesh crawling up Wyatt's back and neck and made the hairs on his nape stand on end. His knees pressed in on Maggie's legs, and his grip on her waist tightened.

She glanced over her shoulder, eyes alight. "Okay. Here we go. Hold on," she shouted.

The order was unnecessary. Wyatt's whole body clutched around Maggie. You could not have pried him loose with a crowbar.

She gave the engine a couple more good revs, then poured on the gas. The back wheel spun and gravel spewed. They burned rubber for about twenty feet, then suddenly the bike leapt forward like a wild animal released from a cage.

"Holy—" Wyatt's heart jumped up into his throat as they tore out of the campground and down the drive toward the fairground exit.

There was almost no traffic on the interstate. Maggie

shot out onto the highway without slowing, leaning the bike into the turn at an angle so sharp Wyatt could feel the heat radiating off the paving. He fully expected to go body surfing down the road at any second. Then, miraculously, they were upright again and zooming westward. Ahead there was only open highway and a brilliant sunset.

Maggie let out a whoop and kicked up the throttle, and the Hog almost jumped out from under them. The G-force popped Wyatt's head back, and he held on for dear life.

They flew down the highway. He would have sworn they were going at least a hundred miles an hour, but when he glanced over her shoulder at the speedometer, the needle was sitting steady on sixty-five. Which was plenty fast, he decided. Especially when there was nothing between you and the pavement but a two-wheel vehicle and air.

"Isn't this great?" Maggie yelled over her shoulder.

"Oh, yeah, great," Wyatt replied through gritted teeth, but the words were ripped away by the wind.

Maggie laughed and kicked the throttle up another notch.

They rode west for miles. After a while Wyatt began to realize that Maggie handled the powerful bike with skill and self-assurance and that, though she drove fast, she observed all the rules of the road and did not take risks or cause a hazard for other motorists.

Gradually his heart rate slowed and the tightness in his chest eased, along with his death grip on Maggie, and he began to relax and enjoy the ride.

Without the paralyzing apprehension gripping him, he became aware of other things. The smell of Maggie's perfume wafted to his nose, mixed with the smells of the road—hot asphalt, dust and gas fumes.

Between his legs he felt the low-throated rumble of the Hog's engine vibrating through him, through both of them.

Maggie's tight little bottom jiggled against his manhood with each tiny reverberation. The erotic abrasion was sweet torture, arousing him almost to the point of madness.

Every bump in the paving rubbed their bodies together. He relished the feel of her legs pressed tight against his inner thighs, the heat and rub of her back against his chest.

The wind caught the long hair that had worked its way from beneath her helmet and whipped it across his face. It caught in his mouth and caressed his skin like strands of silk. Wyatt closed his eyes and groaned.

The ride was the most sensual experience of his life, but if Maggie felt anything beyond the exhilaration of speed and freedom it was not apparent. For almost an hour she guided the powerful bike down the highway. Once in a while she pointed out something or made a comment over her shoulder, but mostly she acted as though she'd forgotten he was there.

When the sun sank below the horizon and the sunset began to fade, she turned around and drove back toward the fairground.

It was full dark when they reached the campsite. Wyatt was not anxious to climb off the bike. He didn't want to relinquish the close fit of their bodies, nor was he all that sure that his legs would work, after sitting astride the rumbling motorcycle for over an hour. Most of all, though, his concern stemmed from the state of his arousal.

He needn't have worried. Maggie never even looked his way. The instant he dismounted she gave the Hog some gas and it purred like a lion as she rode it up the ramp and into the trailer at a slow roll.

It seemed to take Maggie forever to stow the bike and lock up. By the time she finally entered the RV, Wyatt had his body under control and had started dinner.

"Mmm, what smells so good?" she asked eagerly.

"Just a ham steak and corn on the cob," he said curtly, and went back to preparing salads, his mouth tight. He whacked up the celery stalks on the cutting board as though they were vicious monsters about to attack him.

Their little jaunt sure as hell hadn't gotten her hot and bothered. He'd just endured over an hour of the most exquisite sensual torture known to man. Even now he had difficulty holding on to his control.

He felt the heat simmering just below the surface, ready to burst into flame at the least provocation. But did Maggie? Oh no. She bounced around the RV with her usual élan, oblivious to the sexual tension humming around them like a swarm of bees.

Out of the corner of his eye, Wyatt watched her move about the RV. Humming a lively Irish ditty, she went into the bedroom and gave her wild hair a quick brushing. She returned and peeked into the microwave at the corn, then gave him a bright smile. "I'll be right back in a minute to set the table," she said, and darted into the bathroom.

When the door shut behind her, Wyatt aimed an annoyed look at it and cleaved a head of lettuce in two with one chop.

Hours later, Maggie lay in the dark, wide awake. No matter how hard she tried, she could not relax. Her body felt as though there was an electric current zinging through it.

She couldn't stand this much longer. She'd barely made it through dinner. It had been all she could do to restrain herself from leaping across the table and attacking Wyatt. Who would have thought that a simple motorcycle ride could be so erotic and arousing? She could still feel Wyatt's body all around hers, the delicious warmth of him.

Maggie groaned and flounced over on her other side. A

second later she rose up and gave her pillow a vicious punch and flopped back down. It didn't help. She was still wide awake as an owl.

She silently recited a string of Gaelic curses. Och, what a fool you are, Margaret Mary Muldoon. What on earth possessed you to think you could share this tiny camper with a sexy hunk like Wyatt and keep your relationship platonic? You'd have a better chance of flying to the moon, you silly creature, you.

The attraction she had felt for him from the first had merely grown stronger by the hour. Sweet Mary and Joseph, everything about the man, every move he made, set her nerve endings aquiver.

There was no help for it. One way or another she was going to have to end this torture, and soon. The way she saw it, she had three choices: she could turn the RV around and hotfoot it back to Houston; she could kick Wyatt out; or…she could give in and do what her body—and yes, dammit, her heart—wanted her to do.

From the front of the camper came the soft rustle of sheets, and the whole rig rocked slightly as Wyatt turned over in bed.

Maggie closed her eyes and groaned.

Chapter Ten

The first flush of dawn lit the eastern horizon when they pulled out of the rodeo campground and took to the highway.

Since they were getting such an early start, Wyatt expected they would cover a lot of ground that day. Slipping off his athletic shoes, he slumped down on his spine in the padded captain's chair. Head back, eyes half-closed, socked feet crossed at the ankles and propped on the dash, his toes wiggling to the beat of Reba McIntyre singing "Fancy," he settled down for a long haul.

They had gone barely three miles when Maggie gave an excited cry and slammed on the brakes.

"What the—" Wyatt slid forward out of the chair. He landed hard on his rump, folded in half, legs, head and arms sticking straight up in the air.

The string of curses that spewed from him turned the air in the cab blue, but Maggie didn't hear them. She swung the lumbering vehicle off the road and brought it to a screeching halt on the shoulder of the highway.

"Look! Oh, look, isn't that a gorgeous sight." Excitement glittered like diamonds in her eyes. Gripping the steering wheel with both hands, she bounced on the seat.

Wedged into the small space on the floor between the seat and the dashboard Wyatt tried to extricate himself, grunting and straining and contorting his body like a pretzel.

"Dammit to hell, woman, what're you trying to do, get us killed! Where did you get your driver's license, anyway? Out of a grab bag?"

He could have saved his breath. "Oh, this is great! This is just great!" Maggie enthused, oblivious to both his plight and his pithy comments. "I've got to try this. If I can get out there before they take off, surely I can find someone who'll be willing to give me a ride," she muttered to herself as she quickly checked the rearview mirrors for traffic and pulled back onto the highway.

"Try what? Get a ride on what?" Wyatt demanded. He managed to untangle himself enough to climb to his knees, but just as he craned his neck to look around she made a sharp left turn that sent him slamming against the door. Before he could recover his balance the rig rattled over a cattle guard and bounced across a rough field.

Still on the floorboard on his knees, Wyatt held on to the arms of the captain's chair for dear life. Maggie drove over the uneven ground so fast his teeth clacked together with each jostle.

The rig had barely come to a complete stop when she jumped out.

"Maggie, come back here! Where are you going?" Wyatt's head swiveled from one window to another, his eyes growing round as he took in the activity in the field all around them. "Aw, damn."

Spread out over several acres, dozens of hot-air balloonists were preparing for lift-off, their brightly colored crafts in various stages of readiness: some fully inflated and straining at the tethers that held them earthbound; some stretched out and lying limp on the ground; others slowly taking shape as the hot air plumped out the panels. All around, the roar of burners filled the air.

Wyatt scrambled up off the floor and rammed his feet into his shoes, cursing and straining to keep his eye on Maggie, all the while yanking up the strings and tying them. The second he was done he bailed out of the cab and took off after her at a dead run.

Maggie's mane of red hair shone like a beacon in the early morning sunshine. Wyatt ran after her, following that bright spot of color bobbing through the crowd.

For a moment he lost sight of her, and his heart took a leap right up into his throat. The damned fool woman. He wouldn't put it past her to try and talk one of the balloonists into letting her try a solo ride.

He slowed his pace and swiveled his head, cursing under his breath. Then suddenly the milling crowd shifted, and he spotted her, talking to a group of men beside the basket of an inflating balloon that had an enormous rainbow on it. Wyatt shook his head. It figured.

"Maggie, what're you doing?"

"Wyatt! Isn't this great? They're having a rally. Oh, this is Dennis Conn. He owns this balloon. And this is Jack and Boyd and Ricky, his ground crew. This is Wyatt. I explained to Dennis that I write children's stories and that I would like to include a balloon ride in one." She flashed a grin, so excited that she did a little jig right there on the spot. "He's agreed to take us up with him. Isn't that terrific?"

"Pleased to meet you." The balloonist stuck out his hand for him to shake, and the other men followed suit. "Like I told Maggie, this isn't a race, so it won't matter if you slow me down. We'll just go up and drift around awhile. We'll be getting started in about ten minutes. You can go ahead and climb into the basket if you want."

"If you don't mind, I need to have a word with Maggie first."

"Wyatt, what are you doing?" she complained when he hustled her away. "I want to get in the basket and watch the lift-off preparations."

He started to tell her to forget it, that she wasn't going joyriding in a balloon, but he remembered in time her reaction when he'd lifted her off the rodeo bull.

"Maggie, listen to me. I think you should give this more thought. People have been killed riding in these things."

"So? People are killed all the time riding in cars."

"It's not the same thing. Can't you just watch from the ground and write about it?"

"Maybe. But I won't. And I don't want to argue about it. Besides, you promised you wouldn't interfere in what I did, remember?"

"I promised to try, but—"

"No. Not another word. The whole point of you coming along on this trip was to prove you could adapt to my way of life." She made a sweeping gesture with her arm. "Well, this is it. I *live* my life. I don't just watch it go by from the sidelines, and I won't allow you or anyone else to tell me, or even suggest, what I can or cannot do. Either accept that, right here, right now, or forget this whole thing and get a flight back to Houston."

Frustration darkened his face and made his whole body

rigid. He opened his mouth, then snapped it shut again and stared over her head at the giant balloons dotted across the open field. The muscles in his cheeks worked, and she knew he was grinding his teeth. His effort at restraint took some of the heat out of her ire.

Maggie sighed and tried a coaxing smile. "C'mon, Wyatt. As risks go this isn't such a big one. People do this all the time. Try it. It'll be fun, you'll see."

He muttered something under his breath, then exhaled a gusty sigh. "All right. I'm probably going to regret this, but let's go."

"You see. Didn't I tell you you'd enjoy it?" Maggie crowed a few hours later, when they climbed back into the RV.

"It was all right," Wyatt conceded reluctantly.

"'All right!' It was terrific. I can hardly wait to put it into a story."

Grinning, Wyatt sprawled on the sofa and watched her. Her eyes sparkled and her cheeks were flushed. She was so exhilarated she was almost bouncing off the walls. "You want me to drive so you can work on your laptop?"

"What? Oh, no thanks. I'm too wired to settle down right now. I need to move." She slipped behind the wheel and started the engine. As the RV began to bump toward the highway she blasted the horn, leaned out the open window and waved. "'Bye, Dennis! Thanks for the ride! 'Bye, Boyd, 'bye, Ricky, 'bye, Jack. I'll see you fellas next time through."

The balloonists shouted back to her, and Maggie laughed and blasted the horn again.

By the time they pulled out onto the highway, Clint Black's mellow baritone was pouring from the stereo speakers, and Maggie was singing along at the top of her lungs and bouncing to the beat.

Wyatt watched her, a bemused smile on his face. He'd never known anyone like Maggie. She held nothing back. Whatever she felt, she let show; whatever she did, she did with gusto, embracing life and all its experiences with open arms. He wondered if she would make love the same way.

He hadn't expected to enjoy the balloon ride. He had gritted his teeth and braced for the worst, possibly even disaster. He had to admit, it had been more than just all right. It had been terrific.

To his surprise, after the first lurch of apprehension when the tethers were released and they began to ascend, he had enjoyed himself tremendously.

It had been incredibly peaceful and lovely, floating along high above the ground in absolute silence, broken only now and then by the roaring hiss of the burner. Everything had taken on a new perspective. The mundane worries and problems of the everyday world had seemed far away. The lulling effect of the leisurely pace made it impossible to dwell on anything but the beauty below and the exhilarating sense of soaring free.

The thought brought a frown to his brow. Was that what Maggie felt every time she plunged headlong into a new experience?

Wyatt considered himself a well-traveled man. He routinely flew to New York, London, Paris, Tokyo, Berlin, all the money capitals of the world, but touring the country in a motor home with a free spirit like Margaret Mary Muldoon turned out to be a novel new experience.

The balloon rally proved to be just the beginning. The days that followed, as they meandered aimlessly through

West Texas, revealed sharply Maggie's restless nature and demonstrated just how much of a creature of impulse and mood she really was.

Whenever she got behind the wheel she crackled with energy and anticipation, eager to be on their way, to see what was over the next hill or around the next bend in the road.

Maggie did not simply travel; she explored, she experienced. If a place looked interesting, whether a town or a stretch of countryside, she stopped and wandered through it. Creeks and rivers beckoned to her to take off her shoes and wade. Meadows of wildflowers had to be smelled and strolled through. Meandering back roads piqued her curiosity, luring her down their dusty paths. Old country stores, abandoned farmhouses and barns, a tree cleaved in two by lightning, a rusty old Model T with a For Sale sign on it, antique stores, small-town cafés, even blatant tourist traps with their outrageous prices and tacky souvenirs—all fascinated her. She even stopped to read the historical markers posted alongside highways.

A native Texan, Wyatt had traveled the state numerous times, both by car and airplane, but seen through Maggie's eyes, everything looked new and different. She had an almost childlike ability to see beauty and magic in even the most ordinary of things.

The lush green, rolling hill country of central Texas, dotted with lakes and picturesque little towns, drew oohs and ahhs from her.

She looked at the rugged land of mesquite and sage around Abilene and imagined the grit and adventure of frontier days.

As they approached the caprock—the escarpment that jutted six to seven hundred feet up out of the gently rolling West Texas ranch land in an unbroken north-south line for two hundred miles—she saw the power and majestic beauty of nature and was awed by it.

Once on top of the caprock, otherwise known as the Llano Estacado, or the Staked Plains of West Texas, instead of tabletop flat farmland stretching out in furrowed rows for mile after monotonous mile, Maggie saw a rich breadbasket, and marveled at the fortitude of the farmers whose countless hours of toil and sweat had produced such a plentiful bounty.

When they entered New Mexico she raved over the expanse of land and sky and the feeling of solitude and spoke with reverence of how humbling and insignificant the vastness of it made her feel.

At first Wyatt was amused by her enthusiasm, even a bit patronizing, but her zeal and unaffected pleasure was contagious. Before long he found himself looking at things differently, doing things he would never have dreamed he'd do in a million years.

However, Wyatt was a businessman, accustomed to the daily thrust and parry of the corporate world, and the habits of a lifetime were not easy to set aside. Thoughts of business nagged at him. At times he questioned his sanity for coming on the trip. Of course, he'd been questioning his sanity ever since he'd met Margaret Mary Muldoon.

He worried about the deals he'd left hanging fire and how they were faring at Sommersby Enterprises without him. The rational part of him knew that they were most likely doing just fine. He had a top-notch staff that he had handpicked. Still…not knowing made him antsy. In those moments he would have traded his twenty-thousand-dollar watch for access to a telephone or fax machine.

Then, in the middle of his fretting, Maggie would laugh or point out something he'd never noticed, and for a while thoughts of the workaday world back in Houston would recede.

Despite his occasional manic twinges about work, gradually, to his surprise, Wyatt realized that he was truly enjoying himself. He also felt more relaxed than he had since taking over the family business after his father had died.

Just after dark their sixth evening of travel, Maggie announced that she was tired and ready to stop for the night and abruptly pulled off the road.

"What, here?" Wyatt protested, looking around at the empty landscape. They were in the middle of nowhere between Clovis and Fort Sumner, New Mexico.

"It's as good as any."

"But I don't see any lights. There's no town around here. No campground."

"So? That's all the better. I like camping alone."

Wyatt gritted his teeth and held on as the RV bumped over a rutted track that passed for a road. He had intended to sneak out after Maggie was asleep and use the telephone at the campground that night and call Eric. So much for that plan.

Maggie brought the rig to a stop at the base of a mesa. After working the kinks out of her body with an allover stretch that raised Wyatt's temperature by several degrees and temporarily wiped his mind clean of everything else, she went about setting up for the night.

For something to do, he stepped outside with her while she set the jacks to level the rig. He offered to help, but she refused, which was just as well since he still hadn't the foggiest idea what to do. In any case, his assistance wasn't needed; Maggie had the routine down to a science. Within minutes she was finished and came to stand beside him on a knoll a little way from the camper.

"It's beautiful, isn't it?" she said in a hushed voice, ollowing the direction of his gaze.

"Yes. And so big. It seems to go on forever."

An almost full moon hung in the sky, lighting up the empty countryside. You could see for miles in every direction. There was not a light or a moving vehicle or any sign of human life anywhere. Only the two of them and he endless land and sky. And the utter solitude.

"Is it always like this?"

"You mean the stillness? Mmm. But things do get lively now and then in the animal kingdom."

As if to verify her statement, something rustled in the brush a few yards away. Wyatt looked up and rubbed the back of his neck. At least a billion stars dotted the sky. Somewhere in the distance coyotes began to yip, and even farther away another pack answered. Off to their right an owl hooted, and a second later they heard a soft swoosh and saw him silhouetted against the moon-washed sky, gliding on silent wings in search of unwary prey.

Maggie had stood like this before, contemplating the awesome mysteries of the desert, but never with another person. Never with a man. She hadn't realized what a difference it would make to share this vista with another, how much richer and more profound the experience would be.

She was acutely aware of Wyatt standing beside her, the closeness of their bodies. If she shifted just slightly their arms would touch.

The night was cool, growing cooler by the minute. In the desert when the sun went down so did the temperature. Along her left side she could feel his heat radiating out, seeping into her, warming her, raising gooseflesh along her skin.

A trembling started deep within her. She hugged her arms close to her body and gazed out at the moonlit mesas

and long, sweeping valleys. Except for the occasional stirrings of the night creatures, all was tranquil and still. They
might have been the only two people in the universe.

Turning her head just slightly, she studied Wyatt. The
sharp clarity of his profile against the night sky made her
heart bump. He was so handsome and so utterly masculine
that merely looking at him made her weak in the knees.
She stared at his chiseled lips, his strong jaw. Was this
man fated to be her lover?

Her reaction to him certainly made that seem a likely
possibility. She had always known that someday, when the
time was right, when it felt right, she would explore that
side of her nature. After all, she was a sexual creature. If
even half of what she'd read and heard on the subject was
true, it was a pleasure like no other, one she'd be a fool
to deny herself.

She'd had an old-fashioned, deeply religious upbringing
in Ireland, and it had continued under Asa's care. The
thought of indulging in sex outside marriage gave her
twinges of guilt, but since she didn't intend to ever marry,
she had no other choice. With her passionate nature it was
unrealistic to expect to live like a nun forever.

Her gaze skimmed over Wyatt again. Moonlight threw
his face into sharp relief, etching the angles and planes
with blue shadows and silvery highlights. According to
Asa, Wyatt was tough and aggressive in business, but he
was honest and ethical. Both characteristics were certainly
in his favor.

Another was he didn't want to get married.

In addition to all that, he attracted her as no one else
ever had. Clearly, if she was going to take a lover, she
could do much worse than this man.

Wyatt turned his head as if he'd sensed her scrutiny and
looked at her, his silvery gaze capturing her blue one with

an intensity that made her chest feel as though it were being squeezed by an iron band.

For the space of three heartbeats he merely stared at her. "Maggie," he murmured. Then, even softer, "Maggie."

He turned and cupped his hands on each side of her neck and lifted her chin with his thumbs. Without conscious thought, Maggie grasped his wrists. They were broad and powerful and warm against her palms. Her fingertips threaded through the crisp hair on the top. She stared at him, unable to breathe, unable to move away. "I want you, Maggie."

His raspy voice stroked over her like a caress. Maggie trembled. She couldn't look away from those mesmerizing eyes.

She could have rebuffed him. She could have made a flippant remark and broken the spell. She did neither.

Perhaps it was the magic of the moment—this place with its awesome beauty, its humbling immenseness. Maybe it was the residual excitement of what had been a perfect day. Or perhaps it was years of suppressed desire catching up with her.

In truth, she was shocked and a little frightened by the raw hunger that gnawed at her. She felt the pull of that need drawing her inexorably toward him, like steel shavings to a magnet. Her hands tightened on his wrists as her body swayed nearer to him.

This was what scared her, what made her hold back—the extreme emotions, this irresistible attraction over which she had no control. As though she had no say in the matter, no will. Maggie liked—no, needed—to feel in control of her life.

"Wyatt, I..." She swallowed hard, and caught her lower lip between her teeth. Caution fought with need, fear with a yearning so strong she ached.

"Say you want me, too, Maggie," he whispered. "God, I need to hear you say it. I see it in your eyes. I can feel it here." The pad of his thumb pressed against the throbbing pulse in her neck. "And here," he added in that soft, caressing voice and laid his hand over her left breast. "But I need the words, Maggie."

Her crazy heart went wild beneath his touch, caroming and booming like a kettle drum. Her knees began to tremble, and she tightened her hold on his wrists.

He wouldn't force her; she could see that in his eyes. She had always known it. If they became lovers it would be her choice.

As long as she didn't let herself get swept away, if she made a conscious decision to do this, then she was still in control, she told herself almost frantically. They could simply enjoy each other for the length of this trip—no ties, no commitments, no emotional attachment. At least...not beyond this potent attraction.

Wyatt watched her, waiting, his eyes willing her to agree, his expression almost fierce with longing. "Say it, Maggie," he urged in a rough whisper. "Say you want me, too."

Maggie stared at him. She saw the hunger, the intensity, the caring in that strong face, in those beautiful eyes, and she knew what her decision would be. What had been a dilemma only moments ago was now clear. She turned her head slightly and snuggled her cheek against his palm. "I want you, Wyatt," she whispered. "Now. Tonight."

She felt his hands tighten around her face. "Ah, Maggie. My sweet Maggie." He dipped his head and took her mouth in a long searing kiss. The caress was so hot, so sensual, she swayed and hung on tighter.

Breaking off the kiss, Wyatt scooped her up in his arms and held her high against his chest. Their faces were mere inches apart, their gazes locked. "You won't regret this. I swear it," he vowed. Then he kissed her again, and with their mouths still fused together he walked toward the camper.

Inside, he carried her into the bedroom and slowly placed her on her feet. Never taking his gaze from her face, he began to unbutton her shirt. Maggie stood still as stone, her breathing shallow, her eyes wide and a little dazed. A pulse fluttered madly at the base of her throat.

"I want you so much," Wyatt murmured in a velvety voice. "I feel as though I've been waiting for you forever." The buttons undone, he gently tugged the tail of her shirt from her jeans and spread the garment wide.

He drew in a sharp breath, and for several seconds he simply looked at her. "God, you're beautiful. So tiny. So perfect." He raised his hand and ran the backs of his knuckles over the pearly flesh that swelled above her ecru lace bra. Maggie shivered. Wyatt smiled.

"You feel like satin," he continued in that same smooth voice. "Soft, warm satin." He watched his dark hand move against her pale flesh, and his pupils expanded until only a thin ring of silver surrounded them.

He pushed the shirt off her shoulders and tossed it aside without looking where it landed. Maggie shivered again.

"Cold?"

"No, I, uh…it's just…this is all new to me. I-I'm not sure what to do."

"Ah, Maggie. Sweet, innocent Maggie," he groaned with something close to reverence. He drew a deep breath and closed his eyes, and she felt a shudder ripple through him.

When it passed, he looked at her with such adoration she felt as though her insides were melting. "Sweetheart, you can't imagine how it makes me feel to know that no other man has touched you. It doesn't make any sense, and I know it's unfair and chauvinistic. Hell, I never cared before how experienced a woman was. I never even gave it a thought. But with you somehow it's different.'' Smiling softly, he smoothed back a curling strand at her temple and gazed at her as though she were the most precious thing on earth.

"There are no rules, sweetheart." Slipping his arms around her, he drew her close and buried his face in the fragrant cloud of hair at the side of her neck. "Just follow…" He strung a line of nibbling kisses down over her shoulder, then reversed the path back up to her ear. "…your instincts."

"But…should I—"

Nimble fingers plucked open the hooks on her bra, and her thought processes stumbled to a halt. A second later the scrap of lace hit the floor and Wyatt's warm hand closed around her left breast. His fingers squeezed gently, lifted, kneaded. Maggie's breath rasped in and out in short pants.

Wyatt pulled her close again, and the slight abrasion of his cotton shirt against her nipples drew a low sound from her that was part sigh and part moan.

"What were you saying?" he whispered in her ear.

"I…um…" Maggie grappled through the fog of passion for a coherent thought. "I…I just wanted…to know if I sh-should…unbutton your shirt?"

She felt him smile against her ear. His tongue traced the tiny swirls while his fingers popped open the snap on her jeans. The zipper slid down with a soft whir.

"Just do what feels right."

What feels right? Maggie clutched his shirt with both hands. She closed her eyes and let her head loll back in languid response to his nibbling caress. Her breath came in shuddering gasps. Sweet Mary and Joseph, everything felt right. Everything felt wonderful.

Not in her wildest fantasies had she dreamed she could feel this way—so awash with pleasure that she ached, so utterly free, so exquisitely alive. It was as though every cell, every molecule in her body had sprung to attention, her senses suddenly fine-tuned, responding with acute sensitivity to every tiny stimulus.

A fire burned low in her belly and radiated outward. Her skin felt hot, her nipples tingly and raw. The brush of his fingertips across the swollen nubs was a sweet agony that wrung a cry from her throat.

Wyatt eased her jeans down over her hips, hooking his thumbs into the tops of her bikini panties on the way and whisking them along, too. Maggie swayed and had to clutch his head for balance, when he dropped to his knees before her and slipped the garments over her feet and off, along with her sandals.

He rose slowly, kissing his way up her legs, pausing on the way to nuzzle the nest of auburn curls at the juncture of her thighs. Maggie made a small sound and fisted her hands in his hair. If there was pain Wyatt paid it no mind. He trailed his open mouth leisurely across her belly, dewing the silky skin with his moist breath. He delved his tongue into her navel then moved up to trace a wet line along the underside of her breast. Maggie cried out and her legs gave way.

Before she could fall, Wyatt surged to his feet and swept her up in his arms. Bracing one knee on the mattress, he laid her down as though she were made of fragile glass. He paused only long enough to examine her flushed face and drop a kiss on her mouth. Then he stood, and with frantic haste he snatched off his clothes, all the while watching her watch him through feverish eyes.

Then he was there, stretching out beside her, pulling her close, and they moaned in unison as they experienced a shock of pleasure as warm flesh met warm flesh.

In a frenzy, hands clutched and stroked, legs entwined, teeth nipped, tongues soothed, mouths rubbed and kissed and explored.

Maggie was lost, awhirl in a maelstrom of sensations, caught in the magnetic pull of passion and want. Rational thought was beyond her. All she could do was give herself over—body, mind and soul—to the irresistible longings that pulled at her. She was so immersed in voluptuous feelings they seemed to run together, one delicious sensation blending into the next, until her whole body pulsed and burned with a need so great she couldn't bear it.

Writhing on the bed, she clutched Wyatt's back and cried out—for what she didn't know.

"Easy, sweetheart. Easy," he murmured, rising above her.

Maggie barely heard him. Driven by instinct, she wrapped her legs around his hips and urged him closer.

"Slow down, my love," Wyatt gasped, trying to hold back. "I don't...want to hurt you."

Maggie was beyond caution, beyond reason. When she felt his hard flesh nudge that intimate part of her that throbbed and burned for him, she instinctively arched upward. Wyatt's control snapped. Braced up on his arms, his head thrown back, he gritted his teeth and sank into her with one silken thrust.

The sudden burst of pain was white hot and startling, pulling a sharp cry from her. Stilling instantly, Wyatt raised up on his arms and looked at her with worried eyes. "Are you all right? I can stop if—"

"No! Don't stop. Please." Already the discomfort was fading to merely a sensation of pressure, and as Wyatt began a tentative rocking movement she felt the pleasure building again, demanding, driving her toward some elusive pinnacle.

In a delirium of pleasure and need and frustration, Maggie clung to Wyatt, meeting each thrust, reaching... reaching...reaching.

Then, suddenly, they seemed to soar into an abyss of purest ecstasy.

Moments later Maggie lay utterly still, her head thrown back, her breathing harsh and rapid as the firestorm of pleasure eased into tiny, pulsing aftershocks. She felt limp as a wet rag and so deliciously sated she could have died at that moment with no regrets. She wasn't sure that she hadn't. Sweet Mary and Joseph. She'd had no idea!

Awash with sweet lassitude, she gazed dreamily at the ceiling and stroked her palms over Wyatt's slick back, a contented smile tugging at the corners of her mouth.

A tiny grunt of displeasure escaped her when he began to rouse himself. Not wanting to relinquish the wondrous feelings that coursed through her, she tightened her arms around him to hold him close, but he ignored her urging and raised up on his elbows. He bracketed her cheeks with his hands. A slight frown puckered his brow, and his silvery eyes held concern as his gaze swept over her face.

"Are you all right?"

She threaded her fingers through his hair and gave him a sultry smile. "Oh, aye. I'm fine."

"Did I hurt you very much?"

"'Twas nothing, and a small price to pay for what came after."

"You're sure?"

"Of course I'm sure. Saints preserve us, if I were any better I couldn't stand it. I didn't know such pleasure existed."

The furrow on his brow eased a bit but he still did not look convinced. "You would tell me, wouldn't you, if—"

"Och, man, why are you making such a fuss?" Out of patience, she shoved at his shoulders, and he rolled off her. Sitting up, she swung her feet to the floor and sent him an exasperated look over her shoulder. "I'm small but I'm not made of spun glass, you know."

Wyatt looked insulted. "You were a virgin," he said huffily. "The first time is never easy. Any man with an ounce of decency feels responsible when he takes a woman's innocence."

His words touched something deep inside Maggie, but the sweet rush of emotion frightened her, and she pushed it aside. "Is that all?" she replied with a roll of her eyes. "Well, there's no need for you to feel responsible or guilty. 'Twas bound to happen sometime. If not with you, then someone else."

Chapter Eleven

Wyatt didn't like that at all.

His eyebrows snapped together. "Thanks a lot. You really know how to make a guy feel special," he snarled at her back.

Maggie leaned over to pick up her T-shirt, and his gaze followed the curved knobby line that marked her spine, all the way down to the shadowy cleft at its base. Distracted, he stared at her delectable bare bottom, his anger momentarily forgotten.

Straightening, she pulled her shirt over her head and rose. The hem barely reached the tops of her thighs. Wyatt's mouth went dry as he watched her stuff her feet into those ridiculous bunny slippers and walk away into the kitchen.

"Well, don't take it personally," she said over her shoulder, going up on tiptoe to pull a glass from the cabinet. "You said yourself, it wasn't normal for a woman to reach my age without any sexual experience. All I meant was, it was just a matter of time.''

Pulling his gaze away from her legs, he shook off his erotic thoughts and sat up, scowling at her through the doorway as she filled the glass with water and drank it. ''So what you're saying is any man would have done. I just happened to get lucky and be here at the right time. Oh yeah, that really makes me feel better.''

Maggie set the glass on the counter and looked back at him. She had been striving to ignore the disturbing feelings that gripped her and keep this light. She'd wanted to make it clear that she did not harbor any foolish notions that what had happened between them would lead anywhere, or that she even wanted it to. She had thought Wyatt would be pleased and relieved. Instead, she could see that he was offended.

No, he was more than offended—he was hurt. He tried to hide the reaction behind anger, but it was there in his voice and in his eyes.

Holy Mary and Joseph, the perversity of men was beyond belief. He'd all but shouted from the rooftops that he wasn't interested in marriage or any kind of permanent relationship, but now his nose was out of joint because *she* wasn't, either. She supposed it was some sort of male ego thing.

Did he think this was easy for her? Her own emotions were skittering all over the place like ball bearings spilled on a marble floor, for pity's sake. One of them had to be sensible. This thing between them—this sweet ache when she looked at him, this tightness in her chest, this crazy, walking-on-air feeling—it was just…just…chemistry. That was all. It would burn itself out soon. It had to.

No matter how he made her feel, a serious relationship was out of the question. She didn't trust love and wanted no part of it. She certainly wasn't foolish enough to let herself fall for a man like Wyatt. Even if he weren't a self-proclaimed, dyed-in-the-wool bachelor, he was too possessive, too protective and controlling. He would smother her.

The only way to handle this was to keep it light and let the infatuation run its course. No strings, no regrets.

Maggie sighed. Except—curse the man—seeing that angry hurt in his eyes twisted her heart.

She walked back into the bedroom. "Aw, c'mon, Wyatt." Standing between his knees, she bracketed his face with her hands and looked deep into his eyes. "'Tis not true, a'tall. You have to know that I'm attracted to you. That I...well...I have feelings for you," she said in a caressing voice. "Strong feelings. Would I have made love with you, after all those years of abstinence, if I didn't? Hmm?"

"I don't know, would you?" he asked testily. "I've seen first hand how curious you are about everything. Maybe you merely wanted to find out what making love was all about?"

She sighed and rolled her eyes. "Well, so what if I did? I still wouldn't have done it if I hadn't been tremendously attracted to you." Tipping her head to one side, she cocked an eyebrow and rubbed his earlobes between her thumbs and forefingers. Her smile was coaxing, her voice soft as velvet. "Bad as I hate to admit it, you're...well...special to me. You have to know that."

"Oh, yeah? How special," he grumbled, and Maggie almost chuckled at his sullen expression. He looked like a sulky little boy.

"Very special." She threaded her fingers through his hair, pulling his head forward until his face was snuggled against her breasts. His breath filtered through the cotton knit and feathered over her skin, warm and moist, sending gooseflesh prickling down her arms. A delicious little shiver rippled through her, and she closed her eyes and smiled. "Very, very special," she whispered.

She loved the feel of him, she discovered, massaging his scalp with a slow, seductive rhythm. And the smell of him. Burying her face against his crown, she inhaled deeply and ran her hands down the back of his head, over his broad shoulders, down his back, exploring the broad muscles that banded it. She luxuriated in the freedom to touch him, delighted in the warmth and firmness of his flesh.

She kissed the top of his head, then his ear.

And the taste of him. Ahh, yes, the taste of him. "You're the only..." The tip of her tongue traced the swirls in his ear, then dipped inside in a quick foray that made him suck in a sharp breath. "...man I've ever..." She gave his lobe a sharp nip. "...wanted." Her tongue lathed the tiny hurt, then her hot breath filled his ear.

Wyatt shuddered and tightened his arms around her.

"Ah, Maggie, Maggie," he groaned against her breasts. He trailed his open mouth up one warm slope. Her nipple puckered and hardened into a tight, almost painful nub as he drew it into his mouth and suckled her through the soft material.

An incoherent sound tore from Maggie. She clutched his hair with both hands, her neck arching back. His hands slid up under the hem of her T-shirt and cupped her buttocks, and every sane thought flew right out of her head.

She became a purely sensual creature, filled with voluptuous feelings of pleasure, giving herself over to them with no thought, no hesitation, just letting the sensations take her.

Instinctively she pressed closer and put her knees on the mattress on either side of his hips, straddling him.

Wyatt made a low, guttural sound. Grasping the hem of the T-shirt with both hands, he whisked it over her head and sent it sailing. He twisted with her, and in an instant she lay on her back with him over her, sprawled between her legs, his hot hands running wild over her body.

"Ah, God, Maggie." He lifted up on his elbows and looked at her. Immediately his hands cupped her breasts and his mouth laid claim to first one, then the other.

Maggie's back arched up off the mattress and her keening whimper filled the tiny room. Her head thrashed from side to side and her hands clutched at him as the drawing pleasure seemed to tug at her womb.

Wyatt teetered on the edge. He was on fire, his control slipping fast. His blood pounded. The need that gripped him was savage, consuming. The feel of that tiny, soft body writhing beneath his was driving him insane. He'd never wanted a woman the way he wanted this one. He hadn't known it was possible to want a woman this much.

"Maggie," he gasped, running his tongue along the underside of her breast. "I think it's…time…for your second…" He stopped, unable to resist pressing a kiss to her midriff, then her belly. "Your second lesson in lovemaking."

"Mmm, I…I think you're…ri-right." With the tip of his tongue, Wyatt drew a wet line on her skin, from her navel to her throat. Maggie lay with her head thrown back, breathing heavily. She moaned and dug her fingernails into his back. "But, Wyatt…there's…just one thing."

"What?" he gasped against her skin.

"I'm still…wearing my bunny slippers."

He raised up partway. A slow, wicked grin curved his mouth. "I know. And it's really turning me on."

* * *

The next morning, lying in bed with Maggie snuggled in his embrace, Wyatt was in a pensive mood as he watched the sunrise through the window. He looked down at the woman in his arms. Damn, it felt good to have her next to him. It was funny. He'd never liked the morning-after scene in the past, but with Maggie it was different.

The thought of having to part with her at all depressed him. If their affair continued, would it be this way every time he left her?

Maggie shifted against him and her eyelashes fluttered against his shoulder. Watching her, he smiled. She came awake slowly, stretching and yawning like a kitten, arousing him instantly. It was amazing, after the night they had just shared, but his hunger for her was as strong as ever. Hell, it was amazing he was even capable of desire.

"Mornin'," she mumbled, blinking sleepily. "Mmm, I feel so delicious." A twinkle lit her eyes, and she ran her hand over his belly. "So do you."

He caught her hand when it began to inch lower. "Now none of that. Behave yourself, woman."

"Why? I'd rather be wicked and wanton. I've discovered I like it." Grinning devilishly, she turned her head and nipped his shoulder.

Wyatt grunted. "I noticed. Nevertheless, it's time to exercise a little restraint. After last night you have got to be sore."

"Mmm, a little. But 'twas worth it." She rose up a bit and leaned over and kissed his belly, then trailed the tip of her tongue around his navel.

Wyatt shuddered. He cupped the back of her head and held her there for a moment, his eyes closed in ecstasy. Then he released her head and dragged her back up into the crook of his arm. "For a woman who was a virgin less than eight hours ago you sure know how to drive a man crazy.''

"I'm a fast learner," she said with a wicked grin.

"I'll say. You— Now cut that out, you little devil."

"Why? Don't you like it?"

"You know damned well I do. Too much. But— Hey, watch it!" Laughing, he wrestled with her to keep her wandering hands under control. "Stop it, Maggie. We're not going to make love again just yet, and that's that. Not until you've had a chance to recover."

"Well, rats. 'Tis a fine lover you're turning out to be. Give a girl a taste of heaven, then snatch it away."

"It's for your own good. I probably ought to be horse-whipped for making love to you so many times last night as it is. Anyway, one of us has to show a little decorum and restraint and since you won't do it…''

"Och, restraint. What a terrible word. I don't believe in it, myself."

"So I've noticed. But this time it's necessary."

"Oh, all right, killjoy." She grabbed a piece of flesh along his ribs and gave it a twist.

"Ow!" He rubbed the tender spot, but his mock scowl bounced off her bare back as she sat up and swung her legs over the side of the bed.

She stretched again, arms over her head, arching her back with such sinuous grace Wyatt almost hauled her back down on the bed with him. Lord but she was so beautifully made—tiny and delicate and perfectly shaped, a masterpiece of womanly curves and creamy skin.

Maggie stood without the least trace of self-consciousness and headed for the bathroom stark naked. "Up and at 'um, Your Nibs. If we're not going to sample any more of those delightful pleasures it's time we hit the road," she said over her shoulder.

Wyatt watched the enticing flex and bunch of her round little bottom, a lecherous smile curving his mouth. "Why? We weren't headed anywhere in particular, anyway."

Maggie stopped at the door to the bathroom and looked back at him. Her expression was one he was beginning to recognize. Her eyes sparkled, the corners of her mouth curved upward and a glow of excitement and anticipation lit her face from within, signaling a return of that insatiable restlessness that drove her.

"Ah, but there's no tellin' what wonderful things are waiting out there. We might miss them if we stay here."

The statement, Wyatt discovered over the next several days, summed up Maggie's philosophy. She rushed at life head-on with her arms open wide. Everything drew her, everything fascinated her. From the tiniest trivial item to the grandest adventure, she embraced it all. Life, to Maggie, was a giant smorgasbord of delights to experience— to taste and touch and smell and hear and behold. To live. She didn't want to miss a single thing or waste a single minute.

At times she seemed not quite real to him, a magical, fey creature, like one of her leprechauns. She was always so joyful, so optimistic and high-spirited, it was as though she wasn't quite tethered to the earth.

As he began to see things through her eyes it amazed him how much he had never noticed before, all that he'd been missing. Maggie showed him how much beauty there was in the world if you only opened your eyes to it. Not just the majestic beauty of the scenery, although they spent plenty of time enthusing over that, too, but minuscule things, ordinary things, like tiny wildflowers growing out of a crevice in a rock or a spiderweb laden with dew and sparkling like diamonds in the early morning sunshine.

She also led him on one adventure after another. Some

were fairly tame and some were hair-raising, some he enjoyed and some scared him spitless, but none were dull.

Some of Maggie's exploits were difficult for Wyatt to swallow, such as parachuting and bungy jumping off a bridge over a mountain gorge. There were times when he had to literally bite his tongue to stop himself from erupting with rage and forbidding her to try a particular activity, but, exercising a supreme effort of will, he managed to control himself. Barely.

As they inched their way through the Southwest, making a meandering loop through New Mexico, Colorado, Utah and Arizona, they also went hang gliding, white-water rafting, took a ride in a glider plane, went off-road driving in the San Juan Mountains, tried their hand at river fly-fishing, kayaked down a raging river and bicycled over a mountain pass.

And between it all, snug in the tiny bedroom of the camper, they made love. Fantastic love. Hot, sweaty, breath-stealing love. Carefree love spiced with boisterous play and laughter. Sweet, slow, magical love that made their hearts pound and their bodies sing and filled them with such joy and pleasure it was almost pain. During those times the world was well lost to them. Maggie's restless nature at last found peace, and for the first time that he could remember, Wyatt forgot about business and responsibilities and simply relaxed.

Alone in their own little world inside the tiny camper they concentrated solely on each other. Without either of them noticing, in many ways, day by day, they grew closer.

Like lovers everywhere, each developed an easy acceptance of the other's personal habits and foibles and personality quirks. They grew comfortable with each other's bodies and relished the familiarity that developed between them, the freedom to touch and caress at will, to relax and be themselves.

In the past Wyatt had always shied away from getting too familiar with the women in his life. He hadn't ever wanted a comfortable "fit like a glove" relationship. Nor had he wanted to know about a lover's family or personal things about her past history. They were merely two people who enjoyed each other for a while then went on their separate ways, the proverbial two ships that passed in the night. True, that passing sometimes lasted months, on one occasion even a couple of years, but he'd always known that they would eventually part.

Yet, in the aftermath of their lovemaking, when Maggie's defenses were completely shattered, Wyatt found himself gently probing for information about her past.

There were gaps in her story that worried him. The need to know everything about her, every single event that had shaped her life and made this tiny, fascinating creature the woman she was, nagged at him like a persistent itch.

"Maggie?" Wyatt trailed his fingertips up and down her bare arm from wrist to shoulders, in a slow, hypnotic rhythm.

Shifting slightly, Maggie sighed and snuggled her cheek more firmly against his bare chest, wrinkling her nose when the curly hairs tickled. "Hmm?"

"These relatives you lived with in Ireland, how long did you say you were with them?"

"I told you, four years."

"Oh yeah." His fingertips skimmed down her arm, circled the small knobby bone at her wrist and traced a path upward again. "Were you happy there?"

"Happy?" She repeated the word, testing it as though she wasn't quite sure of its meaning. After a moment he felt her shrug. "I was okay. Mainly I was marking time."

"Why? What were you waiting for?"

"Och, to grow up, naturally. So I could leave and be on my own."

His fingers paused at her shoulder to thread through the cloud of curls that tumbled there. He watched, fascinated, as the bright locks twined around his fingers and clung as though they had a life of their own. He loved her wild hair. It was as vibrant and alive as the rest of her. For several minutes he said nothing, just toyed with her hair and thought.

"Maggie?" he said finally.

"Hmm?"

"Did they abuse you?"

"What?" She jerked up and braced herself on one elbow and stared at him, her blue eyes round as saucers. "Sweet Mary and Joseph, what brought that on?"

"Did they?"

"Cousin Seamus? Mercy, no. There was never a more peaceful man born. He wouldn't hurt a fly." She didn't bother to tell him that most of the time, when her mother's cousin wasn't working in the peat bogs, he was too far gone in his cups to even notice her.

Of course, that wife of his, Noreen, wasn't above taking a swing at her now and then, but Maggie had been too nimble for the harridan and had managed to dodge most of her blows. Noreen had wanted the money that John Hightower had sent, but not his bastard.

"Did his wife ever abuse you?" Wyatt persisted, as though he'd read her thoughts.

"Wyatt—"

"Did she?"

The look in his eyes told her he would not let the matter drop until he'd gotten an answer. Maggie sighed. "Oh, all right. If you must know, she smacked me around a few times.'' She told him of Noreen's resentment toward her, of her bad temper and hostile attacks. "But I was quick on my feet. I dodged most of the blows.''

"Most of them?'' His eyes narrowed ominously. Maggie shivered and quickly sought to pour oil on troubled waters.

"Och, man, you're making too much of it. 'Twasn't really abuse. Noreen was just bad-tempered, 'tis all. She treated her own children the same way. Anyway, I spent most of my time away from the house. Ran wild through the hills, I did. Mind you, some of the local folks complained to Father McGinnis—said I was a regular little savage. Anyway, I was gone from the house so much, Noreen didn't get many chances to smack me.''

She put her head back on Wyatt's chest and snuggled against him. His arm tightened around her, but his body remained stiff, his jaw clenched. He felt her small, soft breasts pressing against his side, the delicateness of her bones, and the thought of someone hitting her made him feel murderous.

Maggie had never before allowed anyone to get as close to her emotionally as Wyatt had. The bond between them had occurred so naturally, so easily, she had not noticed at first. She was surprised at how wonderful it felt to be close to another person, but it also made her nervous, and she instinctively set limits, put up barriers.

She was perfectly willing to talk with Wyatt about anything and everything—as long as the conversation did not get too personal. She made love with him, she revealed her faults to him, admitted her shortcomings. She allowed him to see her at her worst and her best, and everything in between. In their day-to-day living and loving she was completely uninhibited and open.

Yet there was a part of her she kept hidden away.

She was not at all forthcoming about her hopes and dreams or her innermost feelings. Whenever she noticed their conversation veering in that direction she made a funny quip and deftly changed the subject.

Maggie was every bit as curious about Wyatt as he was about her, but she ruthlessly stifled that inquisitiveness. The less they knew about each other the easier their parting would be, she reasoned.

Wyatt noticed her reticence and guessed its cause. It bothered him that she was already anticipating their parting. Dammit! They'd just become lovers, for Pete's sake! He knew that her reserve was a means of self-protection, but still it irritated him. For the first time in his life he wanted to bare his soul to a woman and share his feelings, and she shut him out.

Despite his pique, Wyatt held his peace. He had already learned that you couldn't push Maggie. What scraps of information he'd pried out of her were gleaned through subtle probing and trickery. Besides, things were going so well between them that he didn't want to rock the boat, so he kept quiet.

Instead, he volunteered information about himself.

He told her about his boyhood, about what social butterflies his parents had been, how their entire lives had been one big whirl of parties and dinners and fun seeking: skiing in Switzerland, sailing the Mediterranean on friends' yachts, opening nights and charity galas, flitting off to all the "in" spots at the drop of a hat.

He told her how, in their absence, he had grown close to his grandfather, Winston Sommersby. The old man had bitterly regretted spoiling his son, and had resolved not to repeat the same mistake with Wyatt. He had taken the boy in tow and with gruff affection and pride, had instilled in him the values of hard work and honor and shouldering your responsibilities.

"'You've got a good head on your shoulders. Use it for something other than a knob to hang a hat on,' he used to say," Wyatt recalled. Lying naked after a glorious bout of lovemaking, with Maggie cuddled, warm and pliant, against his side, he chuckled at the memory. "By the time I was eight he had me reading financial reports and keeping daily tabs on the stock market. By age ten I was analyzing trends and giving him my opinions and recommendations. By the time I went off to college I understood every facet of the business."

"Mmm. If you ask me, it sounds like your grandfather was a greedy old slave driver. All that money, an' him always wantin' more. And forcing a little boy to be just like him. 'Tis shameful."

Wyatt laughed. "There was no force involved. I loved every minute of it. And as for the other, what you don't understand is, in business, if you don't grow you stagnate, and when that happens you become ripe pickings for the competition. Like it or not, it's a dog-eat-dog world out there."

"Humph! Well, I, for one, don't like it."

"I know. And that's your right, but it's a good thing that some of us do. Sommersby Enterprises provide thousands of jobs for people. It's also a good thing my grandfather had the foresight to train me."

Wyatt shared with her how appalled and disgusted he'd felt when he'd discovered the mess his ineffectual father had made of the family business during the short time he'd held the reins. Sommersby Enterprises had been teetering on the brink of bankruptcy when Wyatt took over, and it had taken him years to undo the damage and put them back in the black.

Wyatt also told Maggie his most secret thoughts, his aspirations and disappointments, things he'd never breathed to another soul, not even his grandfather. He told her about Blue Hills, his thoroughbred farm outside of Brenham, and how much it meant to him, how he hoped to retire there someday.

She never questioned him nor pried, nor did she comment when he left the door open for her to do so, but he knew she took it all in. She listened with avid attention to every word.

One thing they never discussed was the future or where their relationship was heading, or even if they would have a relationship once their odyssey was over.

Wyatt had no intention of giving Maggie up. He simply didn't know how to define what their relationship would be. Nor could he tell from her silence how she felt about the matter. Since she had so adamantly rejected his first offer and showed no signs of wanting to discuss their future, he kept quiet on the subject.

He told himself that her silence did not necessarily mean anything. Maggie never even discussed what they were going to do the next day. When a whim struck, she simply went where it led her, no matter the time of day or night or the circumstances.

Once Wyatt was jerked awake at two in the morning to James Brown screaming, "Eeeeooooww! I feel good!" As the father of soul's band pounded out the incessantly upbeat rhythm at a decibel level that could be heard half a mile away, the RV rolled out of camp with Maggie bouncing in time to the beat on the driver's seat.

Another time, with no warning, she pulled over to the side of the road in the middle of the day, crashed facedown on the bed and slept for twelve straight hours.

Wyatt got used to Maggie's bouts of inspiration, when

she bounded out of bed at all hours of the night to write or sketch. The clickety-click of the computer keyboard in the wee hours became as commonplace to him as the cicada's whir. Soon he could sleep through her obsessive pounding.

When working, Maggie's concentration was so great she would go all day without eating if he didn't shove food under her nose. At other times she could stuff herself from dawn till dark, then wake up in the middle of the night so ravenous she devoured everything in the refrigerator.

Wyatt had never known anyone like her. She was witty, clever, inquisitive to a degree he'd never encountered before, good-natured, hardworking, entertaining, unpredictable, at times utterly maddening, but always, *always,* endlessly fascinating.

The longer he was with her, the more the thought of parting from her disturbed him. He could no longer imagine his life without Maggie in it.

Maggie felt the same way about Wyatt, and that scared her silly.

She tried to ignore those feelings and not think about what they meant, or about what would happen when they returned to Houston. Most of the time she was successful, but now and then, usually when she found herself alone, the disturbing questions crowded in on her and she could not shut them off.

The day that Wyatt took the Harley and rode into Ouray, Colorado, the town nearest to their campsite, the disturbing thoughts would not leave her alone.

She sat huddled on the sofa, her arms locked around her updrawn legs, her chin propped on her knees, staring out the large picture window.

They were camped in one of her favorite places on earth, high in the mountains between Ouray and Silverton. Because it was so high and so difficult to reach, few people used the campsite. The night before, when she and Wyatt arrived, only one other campsite was occupied, and today they had the place all to themselves.

The scene outside the large window over the sofa was spectacular. A river so clear you could see every pebble and rock along its bed tumbled and gurgled down a canyon not twenty feet away from the RV's door. Majestic mountains surrounded the camp. High above timberline, their snowcapped peaks glittered in the sun. Puffy, pink-tinged clouds drifted in a sky so blue it hurt your eyes to look at it. There in the high country a few aspen trees were beginning to turn, their quaking leaves shimmering in the slight breeze like gold spangles on a flapper's dress. Maggie saw none of it.

She had been a fool to think she could have an affair and remain detached. The proof was this reluctance to go home.

It was time. Past time. They had been on the road for almost four weeks. She had all she needed to complete her next book. She should turn her rig around first thing in the morning and head back for Houston.

She pressed her lips together and blinked rapidly. It was the smart thing to do. She knew that. But the thought made her feel as though there was a cannon ball sitting on her chest.

She tried to tell herself the reason she put off going home was because she didn't want to lose the bet with Wyatt.

She had to admit he had surprised her. When they'd made their bet, she would have given ten-to-one odds that he would not last a week away from his company. He had not only stuck it out, after a rocky start, he had adjusted well and joined right in. He even seemed to be enjoying himself.

Her mouth twisted. Of course, it didn't hurt that they had become lovers.

No, that wasn't exactly fair. She had known weeks ago that he had proven his point. She should have accepted defeat gracefully and turned around then.

Maggie sighed. So who was she kidding? That stupid bet wasn't the reason she was prolonging this trip. Face it. You're dragging your feet because you dread saying goodbye to Wyatt.

She didn't regret what had happened between them. Not for a minute. Wyatt was a sensual and sensitive lover, and she would always be grateful that he had been the one to introduce her to those intimate pleasures. However, no matter how much she desired him, she could not be his mistress.

Nor did she delude herself into thinking that she could retain her independence and at the same time continue their intimate relationship. With another man, that might be possible, but not with Wyatt. It was his nature to take charge, to possess, and she could not tolerate that. It was pointless to even try.

That meant they would have to say goodbye.

The admission made her chest constrict. Maggie gritted her teeth and put her forehead on her knees. Dammit! It wasn't suppose to hurt like this. Wyatt had many fine qualities. In many ways she admired him. He was honest and hardworking and intelligent, capable of a surprising tenderness and sensitivity. She was not only attracted to him physically, she truly liked him. And, of course, she enjoyed their lovemaking. But he was all wrong for—

A distant, deep rumbling broke her chain of thought. Her head came up and she frowned. What in the world?

The sound was getting closer.

Unfolding her legs, she stood up and went to the door and scanned the surrounding area. As it drew closer the rumble turned into a roar. She looked at the rutted track they had followed to this clearing, just as a pack of grungy, leather-clad motorcyclists crested the rise.

Leading the pack was a huge, tough-looking character in a chain-draped, black leather vest. His dirty hair hung to his waist and was held in placed by a rolled bandanna tied around his head. An even dirtier beard straggled down over his barrel chest, which was bare except for the vest. One bulging biceps sported a metal-studded leather arm band, the other a tattoo of a skull with a knife sticking out of it. He looked as though he would kill his mother if she crossed him.

The roaring motorcycles circled the RV twice before their leader came to a stop in front of the door in which Maggie stood. Slowly, his lecherous gaze traced over her, taking in everything from her toes to her crown. His mouth curled in a lopsided smile that didn't reach his eyes.

"Well, well, well. Lookie what we got here."

Chapter Twelve

"Dammit, Wyatt, when are you coming home? This isn't amusing anymore."

"I told you, Eric, I don't know. It's up to Maggie."

Wyatt heard an audible sigh from the other end of the telephone line. It was followed by several seconds of silence. He got the definite impression his brother was mentally counting to ten.

"This isn't at all like you, Wyatt. You've never let anything interfere with business before. You've never even taken a vacation, for Pete's sake. Now all of the sudden you've chucked your responsibilities to run around the country in a motor home with a woman whom, quite frankly, I consider to be a bit flaky. Have you completely lost your mind?"

"My mind is quite sound. And for your information, so is Maggie's."

Eric did not miss the anger in Wyatt's voice. When he

spoke again his tone was apologetic. "Sorry. I didn't mean that in an insulting way. I like Maggie. I really do. However, you do have to admit she is, well…different."

"As compared to what?"

"Well…us. And our friends and associates. She deliberately thumbs her nose at all our crowd. With her background, you'd think she would jump at the opportunity to belong, but she makes no effort whatsoever to fit in."

Wyatt dipped his head forward and rubbed the back of his neck. Hell. His brother sounded like a grade A snob. Had he himself appeared that way to Maggie when they first met? "You're right. And quite frankly, I consider that a plus."

"I see," Eric said, but it was clear that he did not see at all. He cleared his throat and started again. "Wyatt, I realize that Maggie is a novelty to you, but this really has gone on long enough. I was pleased at first that you were taking time off, and I'll admit I was happy to have a chance to prove I could pull my weight in the company, but it's time for you to come home."

"Is there a problem that I don't know about?"

"No. Not exactly. But the way the stock market is fluctuating makes me nervous. I'm not as good at reading trends as you are. And most analysts think we're heading for another big crash. I just think you should be here."

"You'll do fine. Our investments are rock solid. Unless there's a general crash, we can pretty much ride out a slump."

He knew his attitude shocked Eric. It came as a surprise to him as well. As little as six weeks ago he would have lost no time in racing back to Houston to take charge. Now, strangely, the possibility that their stocks might drop a few points just didn't seem all that earth-shattering.

"Also, I think you should know, I heard a rumor that

Asa is talking to attorneys and financial experts about possibly letting BargainMart go public.''

That got his attention. Wyatt abandoned his relaxed stance, his spine straightening. "What? Who told you that?"

"I heard it from several sources. Joe Tate, for one."

"Have you asked Asa about it?"

"Yes, but he just smiled and gave me a noncommittal answer. He did give me a message for you, though. He said to tell you that he's upping his offer five percent, if you're interested. Do you know what he's talking about?"

Five percent! Damn. That put Asa's wedding gift up to fifteen percent of the BargainMart stock. Twenty-five percent if the options were exercised.

Wyatt sighed and pulled his palm down over his face. That wily old fox. He sure as hell knew how to play hardball. If word got out, men would be beating down Maggie's door to marry her and get control of that much BargainMart stock. "Yeah, I know what he's talking about. Don't worry about it. It's not important."

"So, are you coming home? If Asa does move to go public with BargainMart you really should be here."

"He won't. Regardless of what you've heard, trust me, Asa will hold on to that company until his last breath. The old buzzard probably started that rumor himself."

"Why would he do that?"

To test the waters. To stir up interest. Hell, maybe the old man was doing it just to toy with him, Wyatt thought. To Eric he merely said, "With Asa, who knows?"

They talked for a while longer. Eric continued to try to convince Wyatt to come home, but he remained adamant. He did promise, however, to keep abreast of the stock market figures and contact Eric if he noticed anything that called for them to take action.

After hanging up, Wyatt picked up some toothpaste and shaving cream and a few other personal items, which, ostensibly, had been his reason for coming to Ouray in the first place.

When he left the little pharmacy, he took his time. Carrying his plastic bag of toiletries slung over his shoulder, he strolled down the town's main street, stopping now and then to look in store windows, admiring the abundance of flowers that were everywhere: overflowing hanging baskets and old barrels; bursting from window boxes; planted around the bases of trees and lampposts. In front of one store an old horse trough from the previous century contained a riot of blooms.

Smiling to himself, he breathed deeply of the clean mountain air and scanned the surrounding scenery. Ouray sat in a narrow valley. All around the town, mountains rose almost straight up, like enormous castle walls. It was easy to see why it was called the Switzerland of the United States.

It occurred to Wyatt that the tourist crowd had thinned out over the past few days. Most of the small, picturesque towns they'd visited in Colorado had been overflowing with vacationers. It was early September now, though, and young families with children had returned home to get ready for the start of school. The tourists that remained were of the older variety, pensioners enjoying their golden years after a lifetime of hard work.

A smile tugged at the corners of Wyatt's mouth as he watched a silver-haired couple meandering down the street in front of him, holding hands. They had a look about them that said they'd been together for many years, a closeness and easy intimacy that was as comfortable as an old pair of slippers.

The couple stopped to admire a barrel of flowers beside

a shop door, and the old man picked a petunia and handed it to his wife, kissing her papery cheek. Placing a gnarled hand on his arm, she went up on tiptoe and returned the favor, then looped her arm through his and leaned her head on his shoulder as they went on their way.

Inexplicably, Wyatt's throat tightened. How would it feel, he wondered, to share a love so strong it spanned decades? To always have that special someone you could depend on through thick and thin, someone who cared about you above all others, who would always be there, loving you and supporting you, no matter what?

He gave a self-deprecating little chuckle when he realized the drift his thoughts had taken. That such a thing would occur to him at all was yet another indication of how much being with Maggie had changed his outlook.

A month ago if anyone had told him that he would be entertaining such introspective thoughts or that he would derive pleasure out of simply strolling through a quaint old town, soaking up its unique ambience and admiring the scenery, he would have told them they were dreaming. If they had predicted that big business and the art of the deal would cease to be the end-all and be-all of his existence, he'd have sworn they were certifiable. But, to his chagrin, he realized it was true.

Of course, there was no danger of him chucking his business and responsibilities permanently. He enjoyed what he did and he believed it was important and meaningful, but thanks to Maggie, he saw life from a slightly different perspective now.

By stepping off the fast track for a while and slowing his pace, he could see things clearer, feel things more acutely, appreciate life and all its small blessings as he never had before. It was liberating and exhilarating, and at the same time it imbued him with an incredible feeling of peace and contentment. No wonder Maggie was so addicted to her vagabond life-style.

He hadn't felt this relaxed since…since… Hell, he'd never felt this relaxed. Wyatt smiled to himself. It had taken a sprite like Maggie to teach him that life was about more than just work.

Wyatt had parked the Harley in front of a restaurant. The tantalizing aromas that wafted from the open doors as he approached the bike reminded him that it had been a long time since he'd eaten anything but his own cooking. It had been hours since breakfast, and it would take him almost an hour to get back to camp. He thought about it a moment, then stowed his purchases in the saddlebags and went inside.

He enjoyed a simple but delicious home-style meal of chicken and dumplings, whipped potatoes, homegrown squash and tomatoes and biscuits. Afterward, over several leisurely cups of coffee, he read the *Wall Street Journal.*

When, over an hour later, he went to the cash register to pay for his lunch, the man behind the counter glanced out the window at the Harley. "That your motorcycle out there?"

"It belongs to a friend of mine," Wyatt said, handing the man a twenty.

"Hmm. You're not part of that motorcycle gang, are you?"

"What motorcycle gang?"

"The one that rode through town earlier, right after you came in. You must've been in the men's room when they went through, otherwise you couldn't of missed 'um. Make more noise than the Third Army, all them blasted machines roaring at once."

Wyatt looked out the window, frowning. "Which way were they headed?"

"South. They come through every year about this time, on their way to Ignacio for the Iron Horse Motorcycle Rally." The restaurant owner shook his head. "Just glad they don't stop here overnight. Most of the bikers that come for the rally are decent folks, but not that bunch. They're bad news, that lot. Real bad news. I'd as soon tangle with a grizzly as that leader of theirs. He's meaner than a rabid dog."

A knot began to form in Wyatt's gut. "I suppose they'll ride straight through to Ignacio, right?"

"Maybe, maybe not. The rally doesn't start for three days. Sometimes they camp out up in the National Forest between here and Silverton for a night or two before they move on. Hey, mister! Where're you going? Wait a minute, you forgot your change!"

"Keep it," Wyatt yelled back, slinging his leg over the seat of the Harley. He turned the key, kick started the engine and took off, burning rubber for twenty feet.

He roared through town with no regard for the local speed limit. Heart pounding, he took the steep, hair-pin curved climb out of town as fast as he dared, passing cars and old people in their motor homes as though they were standing still.

This was crazy, he told himself. He was no doubt over-reacting and was going to feel like a fool when he reached the camp. It was early yet. Those bikers were probably riding straight through. Even if they did decide to camp out overnight, the forest was enormous. There were hundreds of places to make camp without getting anywhere near Maggie.

He gritted his teeth and sped up another five miles an hour.

If only his friends could see him now, he mused with self-deprecating irony, leaning into a curve. Wyatt Som-

mersby, international businessman, discriminating sophis-
ticate and scion of an old, respected and wealthy family,
riding a Harley-Davidson hell-bent for leather to protect a
madcap imp from a motorcycle gang. He gave a sharp bark
of laughter and shook his head. They'd never believe it.
He didn't believe it.

He took a sharp U curve at a dangerous speed, almost
laying the cycle on its side. Coming into the straightaway,
he poured on the gas.

Luckily, there were few vehicles on the road. For the
next three-quarters of an hour he drove like a maniac. The
Harley purred between his legs and took the mountain
passes with power to spare. Throughout the whole trip Wyatt told himself he was worrying for nothing, but by the
time he turned onto the dirt track that led to the campsite,
his heart was racing and the knot in his chest had doubled
in size. The instant he saw the numerous tread marks in
the road his worst fears were realized.

Terror filled him. He kicked the engine up another notch
and raced up the track through the trees.

He was braced for raucous noise and mayhem. When
the Harley roared into the clearing moments later the scene
that greeted him was so unexpected he almost wrecked the
cycle.

Motorcycles were parked all around the clearing surrounding the RV. A few of the gang members, including
some rough-looking females, were resting on their bikes.
Others stood aimlessly about, smoking and shooting the
breeze, but most were gathered around the aluminum camp
table set up under the RV awning.

His noisy arrival drew everyone's attention. Heads swiveled and leather-clad bikers sprang to attention. Most of
the men assumed menacing stances, but Wyatt ignored

them. Through the crowd of black leather jackets around the table, he'd caught a glimpse of bright red hair.

Sending dirt and gravel spraying, he brought the bike to a halt in a sideways slide, bailed off and strode across the clearing to the table.

An unsanitary looking creature with long hair and multiple tattoos stepped into Wyatt's path. He bared fuzzy, snuff-stained teeth and growled like an animal.

"Get out of my way, punk," Wyatt growled right back, and shoved the guy aside without breaking stride.

The other bikers glared at him with suspicion and menace, but the look at his eyes cleared a path through the motley bunch like Moses parting the Red Sea. The last gang member stepped aside, giving him a clear view of the table. Wyatt jerked to a halt and stared.

Seated around the camp table playing cards were four of the foulest, raunchiest, meanest looking men Wyatt had ever clapped eyes on—and Maggie.

She looked like a pint-size Mississippi riverboat gambler. A small mountain of red, blue and white poker chips were stacked in front of her. Clamped between her teeth was a thin cigar. Her shirt sleeves were pushed up and held in place by what looked like frilly pink garters. She even had on a green sunshade headband.

With the stogie still clamped between her teeth, she grinned around it and winked at him. "Hi there, lover. How's it goin'?"

Wyatt goggled. For a fraction of a second his mouth dropped. *How's it going?* That was it? After he'd risked life, limb and property to race back here and save her from a gang of cutthroats, she sat there calm as you please, playing cards, and all she had to say to him was *How's it going?*

On a gut level he knew that the wisest approach in a

dicey situation was to remain calm and authoritative, but fear, frustration and anger boiled up and reached flash point.

"What in the name of almighty hell do you think you're doing?" he erupted in a roar.

Maggie took the cigar out of her mouth and gave him an exasperated look. "What does it look like? We're playing poker."

"This you're old man?" the gruesome looking specimen sitting next to Maggie snarled, eyeing Wyatt through narrowed eyes.

"Yeah, that's him," she acknowledged in a bored voice. Glancing at Wyatt, she gestured toward the vile creature and said, "This is King Kong. They call him Kong for short. He's the leader of the Black Devils."

It didn't take a genius to figure out how he'd come by his moniker. The man was built like a gorilla. He had biceps the size of small trees and a hairy chest at least a yard wide. Since he wore only jeans and a leather vest covered with steel studs and chains, both physical attributes were prominently displayed. His dirty red beard hung in scraggly strings to the middle of his chest. One cheek sported a tattoo of a tarantula. A two-inch-long safety pin pierced the other.

The guy sitting next to him was equally repulsive. Dirty blond hair, held in place by a dirtier bandanna, hung in limp strings past his shoulders. An ugly red scar slashed diagonally across his sullen, pockmarked face, bisecting one eyebrow. He wore a black leather eye patch over one eye. The other one stared at Wyatt, filled with aggression that bordered on hatred.

If looks and the stench they gave off were any indication, neither One-eye nor Kong nor any of their cohorts had bathed in weeks.

The other two men seated at the table were equally grungy and loathsome but instinctively Wyatt knew that Kong and the one-eyed man were the biggest threat.

Narrowing his eyes into slits, Kong looked Wyatt over as though trying to decide whether to break him into two pieces or three. "Humph, he don't look like much to me. A fine chick like you needs a real man. Someone like me or Snake here," he said, jerking his head toward the one-eyed man. "If I didn't already have me an old lady I'd take you on, but Sheba would pull your hair out if she thought you was moving in on her man. Wouldn't ya, doll?" he said, tipping his head back and flashing a yellow-toothed smile at the female standing behind him with her hands on his shoulders.

"Damned straight," Sheba snarled at Maggie, and gave her gum an extra loud pop for emphasis.

One corner of Wyatt's mouth curled. What a charming example of femininity. Sheba had purple hair, black eyeliner that looked as though it hadn't been removed in a week, and makeup so thick it had to have been applied with a trowel. Beneath her black leather jacket she wore a red lace bra and a spandex miniskirt that barely covered her undies—if she had on undies. Judging by the rest of her, Wyatt wasn't at all sure that she would bother with such a nicety.

The woman looked as though she was about a half a second from going for Maggie's eyes with claws unsheathed. And the little imp, damn her, didn't appear in the least concerned.

"Dammit, Maggie, don't you know—"

"Hey! Hotshot! Back off!" Kong rose halfway out of the chair, his tree-trunk biceps bulging, nostrils flaring with challenge. His little piggy eyes shot fire. "You heard Irish. We're playing cards here, so bug off."

Beside him, One-eye jumped up, too, teeth bared. "You want me to clean his clock, Kong?"

"You and who else, scum bag?" Wyatt said, bristling as he stepped forward.

"Whoa! Whoa!" Maggie jumped up and placed both palms flat on Wyatt's chest to hold him back. "Let's call time-out for five minutes, Kong," she said quickly over her shoulder to the hulking biker. "I need to talk to my old man. Okay?"

Kong frowned, but not even a lower life form such as he could resist her pixie smile. "Okay, Irish. For you, five minutes," he granted grudgingly. "But get him in line or I'll let Snake here cut out his liver."

Wyatt saw red. "Maggie, get out of my wa—"

She gave him a shove and a hard look. "Inside," she hissed. "Now." Then, lowering her voice to an urgent murmur, "Wyatt, *please*. If you care anything at all about me, do as I say. I'm begging you. Please."

Muscles worked along Wyatt's clenched jaws. His gaze darted back and forth between Maggie's pleading expression and the hulking Neanderthals. Snake stood in a half crouch watching him with an evil grin and look of unholy anticipation glittering in his lone reptilian eye. It was clear, even through Wyatt's haze of anger, that the biker was spoiling for a chance to fight.

Wyatt's self-control was strained to the limit. Against her palms, Maggie could feel the angry tension in him. His whole body quivered with it.

Breathing hard, he looked down at Maggie again. She pressed harder against his chest and gave him a speaking look, jerking her head toward the camper. After a brief hesitation, Wyatt made a sound of protest, but to her immense relief he stomped to the door and snatched it open.

He swung on Maggie the instant she closed them inside,

but before he could light into her she planted her fists on her hips and launched an attack of her own.

"Would you be tellin' me just what you thought you were doing out there?"

"*Me?* I was trying to protect you from that riffraff. What in bloody hell were *you* doing?"

She rolled her eyes and looked heavenward as though seeking guidance from a higher power. "Och, would you listen to the man. Now he thinks he's the Terminator.

"Protect me, is it," she scoffed, ignoring his question. With every word her brogue became broader and her agitation grew. "An' how, pray tell, would you be after doing that?"

Wyatt looked insulted. "I'm not a helpless wimp, you know. At Harvard I was on the boxing team."

"Ah, well, the boxing team, is it. That's different then." The pithy sarcasm in her voice made Wyatt's spine stiffen, but she gave him no chance to retort.

"Sweet Mary and Joseph, are you daft, man?" She exploded. "While you're out there dancin' around with you oh-so-proper Marquis of Queensberry Rules, Snake will be fightin' low-down and dirty. The man'll gut you like a fish."

"Thanks a lot. Your faith in me is overwhelming."

"Och, now I've wounded his male pride," she said with utter disgust, speaking to the ceiling again. "Mother Mary and Joseph! We haven't the time for that foolish macho nonsense, man! Saints preserve us, don't you get it? Even if by some miracle you did manage to beat Snake, there's thirty others waitin' in line to take his place. Would you be plannin' to take them all on, then?"

Wyatt's jaw took on a sullen set. "Well, I have to do something. Dammit, Maggie, we're sitting on a powder keg here. I don't think you know what you're dealing with.

Have you any idea how dangerous those creeps are? Or what could happen to you?''

"Of course I do. I wasn't born under a cabbage, you know. And until you came blaring in here acting all macho and proprietary I had the situation under control. So just back off and let me handle it.''

"How? By playing poker with those animals? You call that handling the situation?''

"Yes. At least the game is diverting them from more violent pastimes—like ripping your head off.''

He couldn't argue with that, though it was clear from the muscles working in his face that he'd like nothing more. "I still don't like it,'' he retorted finally.

"You don't have to like it. Just bite your tongue and play along, and I think I can get them to leave. Unless, of course, you've a better idea.''

She had the satisfaction of seeing Wyatt's lips thin into a hard line. His silvery eyes glittered with frustration. He knew she was right. In a fight, he'd never win against such odds.

Taking his grim silence for agreement, she gave a sharp nod. "All right then. For the rest of the afternoon, just keep quiet and let me handle things. Better yet, why don't you stay in here.''

"Oh, no. Not on your life. If you think I'm going to let you go out there and face that bunch alone, think again.''

Maggie sighed. She should have known. "All right. All right. You can come with me, but for mercy's sake, keep your mouth shut.'' She paused with her hand on the doorknob and looked back at him. Narrowing her eyes, she shook a finger under his nose. "Now you mind what I say. You keep your tongue behind your teeth. 'Tis not a single word I'll be wantin' to hear out of you. If you so much as clear your throat too loud, I swear I'll let Snake and Kong tear you limb from gizzard. I mean it.''

"All right, I got the message," he muttered.

When they stepped outside, Kong and Snake sneered at Wyatt and muttered a few uncomplimentary and vulgar comments about his manhood. Maggie felt him tense. She held her breath, but he kept his word and ignored the jibes.

Ever since the Black Devils had ridden into camp she'd been afraid for him. She had hoped to get rid of the gang before Wyatt returned, but fate was not that merciful. For all his fine manners and urban sophistication, she had known that he would spring to her defense and stir up a hornets' nest. He hadn't disappointed her, more's the pity.

Men, she thought with disgust, taking her seat at the table. The ornery creatures and their damnable pride created most of the havoc in the world.

As for herself, she wasn't all that concerned. She had always been able to talk her way out of tight spots. Spin a few tales, strike the right note, and even the most savage beast could be lulled into docility by a glib tongue—at least temporarily.

Fear for Wyatt had the hair on her nape standing on end, and her stomach felt as though it contained a swarm of butterflies, but she picked up her cards as though she hadn't a care in the world. She smiled at Kong and the others and rubbed her hands together eagerly. "Well now, gentlemen, shall we be gettin' on with it?" she said, cool as can be. "We have a side bet to settle, I believe."

Sneering, Kong turned his chair backward, straddled it and picked up his hand. "This shouldn't take long. Never saw a chick yet who knew beans about poker."

"You got that right," Snake agreed. "Anyways, I got me the winning hand right here," he said, patting his vest pocket. "This is one bet I'm gonna enjoy collecting."

"Whooee! It sounds like ole Snake's got plans for Irish!" Kong whooped, slapping the one-eyed creep on the back. The others resumed their places amid laughter and ribald comments.

Snake pulled out his cards and laid them facedown on the table without so much as glancing at them. Tapping the hand with a dirty finger, he leered at Maggie and tossed five blue chips into the pot. "Dealer bets fifty."

"A side bet?" Wyatt hissed in Maggie's ear. "You never said anything about a side bet."

She slanted him a warning look over her shoulder. "Shh! I told you to be quiet. If you're after gettin' out of this with your hide whole, then I'll be needin' me concentration."

Before he could retort, she fanned out her cards, looked them over and refolded them. Coolly, she took five blue chips from her stack and pushed them into the center of the table. "I'll see your fifty, and…" She pushed out another five chips. "I'll raise you fifty." Bold as brass, she looked straight at Snake and flashed a cocky grin.

Standing behind Maggie, Wyatt watched as she took hand after hand. He wanted to snatched her up and shake her and demand to know the terms of her bet with these loathsome creatures, but he didn't dare do anything to distract her from the game. Especially since he had a gut feeling a great deal was riding on the outcome.

The next hour was torture for him. He should have known that Maggie would play poker the same way she did everything else—with reckless abandon and panache and the boldness of a shyster preacher at a tent revival.

He had to admit, for the most part she had phenomenal luck with cards. Consistently she was either dealt a winning hand or she drew exactly the cards she needed. The occasional bust hand was no obstacle for Maggie, either.

With amazement and horror, he watched her bluff her way to a win with a pair of deuces. And Wyatt's heart nearly stopped when she drew to an inside straight and made it. He wondered if the words *caution* or *conservative* were even in Maggie's vocabulary.

After what seemed like forever Maggie had most of the chips in front of her and everyone had dropped out of the game but her and Snake. She dealt them both five cards, then picked up hers. The bottom one was the seven of clubs. Slowly she fanned out the rest with her thumb. The jack of diamonds appeared next, followed by the seven of diamonds and the four of spades. Sweating bullets, Wyatt held his breath.

Air escaped his lungs in a long hiss as the seven of hearts emerged from behind the four.

Three of a kind. Not a bad hand. Not the best in the world, but a possible winner. Hope fluttered in his chest until he glanced across the table at Snake.

The man fancied himself a card shark, but every thought registered on his face. At that moment the biker was staring at his hand with his one good eye about to bug right out of his head. He practically vibrated with suppressed excitement.

This time he did not even try for a poker face. Smug triumph radiated from him as he looked up at Maggie. "I'll play these."

If his supreme confidence rattled her it didn't show. "Dealer takes two," she said calmly, discarding the jack and the four from her hand and dealing herself two more cards.

She added them to the three she held and picked up all five. Wyatt shifted his weight from one foot to the other, his heart pounding as he craned his neck to see over her shoulder. She fanned out the three sevens. The ten of clubs came next. Then, with excruciating slowness, the seven of spades.

Wyatt had to grit his teeth to keep from shouting. Four of a kind! The luck of the Irish had shone on Margaret Mary Muldoon again. Unless Snake held a higher four, the hand and the game was Maggie's.

"I bet fifty." Snake shoved his chips into the center of the table and took a swig of beer. After a loud belch, he wiped his mouth with the back of his hand and looked around at his buddies with a gloating sneer.

Uneasiness crept into Wyatt's chest. Holy hell, what if this cretin really could beat her? What had Maggie bet?

She smiled. "I tell you what, Snake. I'm getting tired. So why don't we make this interesting and play winner take all. I'll bet all I have against what you've got."

Snake's greedy little eye zeroed in on the stacks of chips in front of Maggie. She had easily five times what he had. "You serious?"

"Perfectly."

He chuckled, a raspy sound that had Wyatt's stomach doing flip-flops.

The smug look Snake sent Kong and the other gang members reeked contempt. "I always did say women was only fit for one thing." A chorus of snickers and raucous comments erupted all around.

Snake shoved his winnings to the middle of the table. "Read 'um and weep, woman," he jeered, and slapped down his hand, faceup. "I got me a flush."

"Hmm. So you do. Very nice." Maggie smiled sweetly and laid her hand down. "But I'm afraid four of a kind beats it."

Snake's face fell. His slack-jawed look would have been humorous if it hadn't been for the sudden leap of rage in his eyes when he looked from the cards to Maggie. "Why you—"

Kong clamped a meaty hand on Snake's shoulder and grabbed a fistful of leather jacket, lifting him out of his chair. "Can it, Snake. You lost. Irish won. That's the end of it."

"But—"

Kong bared his teeth. "I *said* let it go. We don't renege on a gambling bet. She won, and that means we ride. That was our deal. Now shut up and get on your bike." He shook the smaller man as though he were a dog and shoved him toward where some members of the gang were already mounting their Harleys. Stumbling away, Snake shot several sullen glances over his shoulder, but he went.

Kong turned and gave Maggie a long look. Wyatt stiffened, his hands curling into fists at his sides. "You're one helluva woman, Irish."

Within minutes the entire gang was saddled up and rolling out of the clearing, the roar of the cycles reverberating through the forest. When the last taillight disappeared down the dirt track through the trees, and the horrendous rumble of thirty motorcycles began to fade into the distance, Maggie turned toward the RV.

Wyatt snagged her hand and jerked her to a stop. "Uh-uh. Oh, no you don't. I want to know about that side bet you had with those creeps."

Maggie shrugged. "Just that if I won they'd leave the clearing and not give us any trouble. And they did."

"And if you had lost?"

"Then I would join their gang."

"*What?* Are you crazy? Good God! What if you'd lost?"

"Oh, there was no chance of that," Maggie said airily. "I cheated."

"What?" he squawked again. "You *cheated?* You actually had the brass to cheat those thugs?"

"Oh, don't look so shocked. You didn't think I would risk actually having to live with that bunch of social misfits, did you? And get passed from one woman abuser to another? Not me. Anyway, Snake and Kong were cheating, too. I'm just better at it, is all."

Maggie grinned and lifted Wyatt's sagging jaw with an upward jab of her forefinger, her blue eyes twinkling. "Watch it, Your Nibs, or you'll be catching flies."

He shook his head. Gradually, however, his dazed expression gave way to a slow grin that spread across his face like blinding sunshine after a storm. Throwing his head back, he let loose with a hearty laugh, followed by a very un-Wyatt-like whoop.

"Ah, Maggie, my love, you're fantastic." He snatched her up in his arms and swung her around three times, nearly squeezing the life out of her. "God, I love you!"

Chapter Thirteen

He hadn't meant it. Wyatt Sommersby in love? And with her, no less? Och, what a foolish notion.

Maggie tapped her fingers on the steering wheel and worried the inside of her lip. She cast a covert glance at Wyatt. Of course he hadn't meant it. It had just been one of those things that people say when they're in a jubilant mood. That was all. 'Twas certainly nothing for her to worry about.

She cast another glance his way and exhaled a deep breath, her tense shoulders relaxing a bit. Och, 'tis a fine mountain you're making out of a teeny molehill, my girl, she told herself bracingly. Since tossing out the startling remark, Wyatt had not mentioned it again, nor, apparently, had he given it another thought.

The only thing on his mind at the moment seemed to be making sure they weren't being followed. He stared out the window, his gaze fixed on the side mirror and the road behind them.

Following the Black Devils' departure, after swinging her around and kissing her soundly, he had abruptly released her and insisted that they break camp and leave at once.

"We need to get as far away as we can, as fast as we can," he had urged. "Those guys aren't rocket scientists, but eventually they'll figure out that the only way you could have beaten them when they were cheating was if you were cheating, too, and they just might come after your hide. Even if they don't, I don't trust that Snake not to sneak away from the others and double back. You did some serious damage to his machismo, beating him that way. Besides, the slime ball's got the hots for you."

"Eeeeooouu. Don't even *say* that." Maggie had made a face and shuddered, but the revolting thought had been enough to send her flying around the camp. In record time they were on the road, heading in the opposite direction the Black Devils had taken.

"I know you don't like commercial campgrounds, but I think it would be a good idea if we stayed in Grand Junction tonight," Wyatt said, drawing her attention again. "I think we should stay close to a city with a sizable police force we can call on. Also, it will make it more difficult for them to find us."

"You really think that's necessary? There's been no sign of them."

He pulled his gaze from the side mirror and gave her a reassuring smile. "Probably not, but just to be on the safe side, I think we should." Winking, he reached across and touched her arm with his fingertips. The tiny contact sent fire zinging up her arm. "Humor me on this, sweetheart."

Normally Maggie's love of freedom would have

prompted her to dismiss the suggestion with a laugh, but the softness of his voice and the concern in his eyes stirred a confusing welter of emotions in her chest. For no good reason that she could figure out, her eyes grew misty and she could not speak around the achy tightness in her throat. She answered with a nod and drove on in silence, blinking furiously.

She felt Wyatt's gaze but she kept her eyes on the road.

"Are you all right? I'll drive if you want."

"No, I'm fine. Why wouldn't I be?"

Actually, she was a bundle of nerves. She had been ever since those hoodlums had come roaring into camp scaring the daylights out of her. Wyatt's careless declaration hadn't helped any, either. She'd sooner cut out her tongue than admit as much to him, however.

Though there had been times over the past few weeks when she could tell he had wanted to object to some of the things she had insisted on trying, overall he'd been, if not exactly approving, at least tolerant. The last thing she wanted now was to trigger a lecture on the dangers of a lone female traveling around the country unprotected.

They reached the campground on the outskirts of Grand Junction a little before nine that evening. Wyatt had learned how to set up the RV, and between them he and Maggie finished the job in minutes. The instant they stepped inside and locked the door, he surprised her by snatching her into his arms.

He wrapped one arm around her, holding her to him like a vise. His other hand cupped the back of her head and pressed her face against his chest. "Oh, God, Maggie," he said in a hoarse voice. "I was so scared those gorillas were going to hurt you."

Releasing her head, he put his fingers under her chin and tipped her face up. The look in his eyes made her breath catch and her heart stutter. He searched her features, one by one, settling at last on her mouth. His head began a slow descent, and his eyelids drifted downward. She could feel the flutter of his breath against her skin. The feathery touch was warm and moist and incredibly erotic. Maggie shivered helplessly. ''I couldn't bear it if anything happened to you,'' he whispered against her trembling lips an instant before his mouth claimed them.

Maggie's nerves were sizzling, and the heated kiss was like striking a match to tinder. She threw herself against his chest with something close to desperation, wrapping her arms around his neck and holding on with all her might.

A sound rumbled from Wyatt's throat, something between a groan and laughter. Without breaking the kiss, he lifted her clear of the floor and carried her into the bedroom.

He fell with her across the bed, and they rolled together, clutching and grasping at each other like greedy children. Within seconds, buttons, zippers and recalcitrant hooks were dealt with and clothes went flying. Foreplay and tenderness were not options. They were wound too tight, their need for each other was too urgent. The fear and tension that had gripped them for hours demanded release. Now.

They kissed and rolled together on the bed, and when Wyatt rose above her, Maggie opened to him eagerly, in a move as smooth and natural as life itself. And as their bodies merged their sighs blended together.

In the sweet aftermath, Maggie lay in Wyatt's arms, sated and content and filled with a delicious lassitude, the tension of the past hours vanquished.

She rubbed the sole of one foot up and down his shin bone, sighing into his chest hairs, a tiny, self-satisfied smile curving her lips. If she had only known how glorious lovemaking was she would have indulged years ago. Her smug smile faded and a tiny frown line creased between her eyebrows. Except, she had an uneasy feeling that it wouldn't be the same with anyone but Wyatt. That was not a comforting thought.

Absently, his hand massaged her shoulders and back. Maggie dismissed the disquieting thoughts and gave herself over to the tactile pleasure of his touch. Making a purring sound, she stretched, arching her back like a cat.

"Maggie."

"Hmm?"

"I meant it, you know."

"Meant what?" she mumbled sleepily.

"I love you."

It took a couple of seconds for the words to register on her drowsy brain. When they did she was sure she hadn't heard him right. "What?" She braced up on her elbow and blinked.

"I said, I love you."

The words pierced straight to Maggie's heart, bringing an odd mixture of joy, pain and panic. However, other than an infinitesimal widening of her eyes, she managed to keep her expression calm—just barely. Wyatt watched her, those sharp, silvery eyes studying ever nuance of her expression.

"No you don't." Maggie sat up on her haunches. Panic gained ascendancy and welled up inside her, but she fought to control it. Shaking her head, she gave a nervous little laugh. "Don't be silly. Of course you don't."

Trying to act unconcerned, she scooted backward across the mattress and scrambled off the bed. She kept her back to him and tossed the huge football jersey over her head and stuffed her feet into her bunny slippers.

Normally, she was not in the least self-conscious around Wyatt, but now she felt somehow exposed. She moved over to the small dresser and picked up her brush and began a furious attack on her hair, her heart thundering. Sweet Mary and Joseph, she couldn't deal with this.

She could feel him watching her, waiting. Maggie groped for something to say, some flippant remark that would turn the whole thing into a joke, but she came up empty.

The silence stretched out, grew thicker, tauter. She prayed he would laugh and say she was right, that he was just kidding, or at the very least say that he had merely been carried away by the emotion of the moment—anything to shatter the awful tension.

Wyatt remained stubbornly silent.

Her gaze accidentally clashed with his in the mirror. She attempted to hide her panic behind a saucy grin. It turned out stiff and a little weak around the edges, and she knew by his steady stare that he saw right through her charade. Still, she brazened it out.

"C'mon, Your Nibs," she told his reflection. "You can't expect me to believe you're serious. Why, practically from the first you warned me you weren't the marrying kind."

"That was then and this is now. A lot has changed since we met."

"Not a'tall. Look, we've had a lovely interlude, and it's only natural that we have warm feelings for each other, but…well…I think you're confusing that for love."

"I'm thirty-six years old, Maggie, not a randy teenager. I know what I'm feeling. I've never felt this way about any woman before, and I don't expect to ever feel this way again. I love you, sweetheart. And I want to marry you."

"*Marry!*"

She whirled around, her eyes wide. Her knees seemed to turn to water. Clamping both hands over her mouth, she sank down on the edge of the bed and stared at him. "You really mean it," she murmured against her fingers.

"That's what I've been trying to tell you."

"But you *can't* love me!"

She wailed the protest in an instant of pure panic. Grimacing, she quickly reined in her rioting emotions, falling back on her normal defence of amused nonchalance.

"Wyatt, be serious," she chided, forcing a chuckle. "Saints above, we've nothing in common. I'm totally unsuited to be Mrs. Wyatt Sommersby. Never this side of heaven would I fit into your life-style. Och! If I said yes, you'd be regrettin' it within six months, an' that's a fact. 'Tis crazy you are for even thinkin' such a thing." Smiling saucily, she leaned over and patted his cheek. "But don't be thinkin' I'm not flattered."

"It's true you're not at all the kind of woman I would have ever expected to fall for. You're maddeningly independent, reckless, restless, irreverent and at times a royal pain in the posterior."

Maggie felt a spurt of affront, but she quelled it and forced another laugh. "There you are, then."

"But none of that matters. Because, Margaret Mary, I adore you. You make me happier than I've ever been in my life. When I'm with you I feel freer, more relaxed and at ease than I ever have. You're funny and smart and sweet, though I know you won't admit to the last.

"You make me laugh and you make me want to tear my hair out at times. Most likely you'll drive me crazy, but I've come to realize that I'd rather be crazy with you than miserable without you. I love you, Maggie, and you can deny it until you're blue in the face, but that won't change a thing. What's more, you love me, too."

"What!" She laughed. It was that or panic. "I do no such thing." Bounding up, she headed for the kitchen with as much sangfroid as she could muster, shaking her head and chuckling. "I'm sorry, Wyatt, but this is really too funny for wor—"

"Stop it, Maggie. Stop it right now."

She hadn't realized that Wyatt had followed her until he grabbed her arm and spun her around. He grasped her shoulders and held her in place, and she found herself staring into a pair of silver eyes that glittered like hot ice. Her facade of amusement vanished in an instant.

He stood before her naked and supremely unconcerned, a potent male in a towering rage. Anger blazed from him. His nostrils quivered with it and she could see a vein pulsing in his temple.

"That's your answer to everything, isn't it?" he snarled. "Laugh it off, treat everything as a joke. That way you won't have to deal with anything of substance. You talk about experiencing life and living it to the fullest, but that's all a sham. You run around trying new things, meeting new people, taking chances, and you call it living, but what you're really doing is running away."

"That's not true!"

"Oh, it's true, all right. You take physical risks, but when it comes to emotions you're a coward, Margaret Mary. You hide behind laughter and treat everything like a lark. It's a way of holding other people at arm's length so they never get too close. That way you never have to deal with true emotions.

"Think about it, Maggie. You make hundreds of acquaintances but you never stick around long enough to become involved in anyone's life, not even members of your family. That way you don't take the chance of getting hurt.

"Well, let me tell you something, sweetheart, that's what living is all about. It's not about jumping out of airplanes or riding wild bulls or facing down man-eating sharks. It's about love and hate, and jealousy and anger and sorrow. It's about opening your heart to someone. And yes, running the risk of getting it broken and experiencing pain. But at least if that happens you *feel* something. You know you're alive.

"You know what I think? I think you're terrified because of what happened to your mother. You're afraid if you allow yourself to care deeply—like your mother did—it might restrict your precious freedom and you might end up getting hurt."

"And so what if I am?" Maggie shouted, her brogue thickening with every word. "I've a right to be wary. I watched me mother pine away for a man who brought her shame and in return gave her the crumbs of his life. He broke her heart, he did, and ruined her life. I'll not be lettin' anyone do that to me."

"It doesn't have to be that way. Maggie, you can't just turn your back on love because of what happened to someone else."

"I never said I loved you."

"But you do."

Her pixie face tightened and took on a mulish set. She fixed her gaze over his shoulder and refused to answer.

"Dammit, Maggie! I know you love me. I see it in your eyes when we make love. Whether you know it or not it's evident in everything you do, every touch, every look you give me. But you won't admit it, not even to yourself, but not because you've gained some profound wisdom from your mother's experience. You're smart enough to know that not all relationships are like that. No, it's because you're afraid to really take a chance. You're a coward, Margaret Mary.''

''Oh, that's what you think, is it?'' she snapped, incensed. ''Well, you don't know what you're talking about, you big loobie, you. I don't love because I don't choose to love. But I can tell you this. If I did choose to love a man it wouldn't be an arrogant, overbearing, possessive, domineering lout the likes of you, Wyatt Sommersby. Now let me go!''

Twisting free of his grip, she stalked into the bedroom and slammed the door so hard the RV rocked like a ship in stormy seas. Mere seconds later the door flew open again, and a barrage of Wyatt's clothes and belongings came flying out. A shirt and a pair of jockey shorts hit him right in the face and clung. While he was still blinded he caught a pillow in the midsection.

''I'll be headin' home at first light. I intend to drive straight through, so be ready to take your turn behind the wheel.''

Wyatt peeled the articles of clothing off his face and threw them on the floor with the rest of his things. ''Maggie, will you calm down and be reasonable. If you think you can just run back to Houston and pretend that none of this happened—that *we* never happened—you can forget it. I don't give up that easily. Dammit, Maggie, we have to talk about this.''

For an answer she slammed the door and locked it with a decisive click.

No amount of reason or anger or pleas budged Maggie. For hours Wyatt tried them all, but from the other side of the locked door came only stony silence. Around one in the morning he gave up in disgust and climbed into the high bunk above the cab. It was clear that, short of kicking the door down, he wasn't going to see Maggie again that night.

Angry and frustrated, Wyatt tossed and turned for over an hour before finally falling asleep. It seemed as though he'd barely closed his eyes when he awoke to the sound of the RV engine starting.

"What the—" He raised his head and his bleary eyes darted around. It was still dark outside, for pity's sake. He glanced at his watch and groaned. It wasn't even four o'clock.

"Maggie, for love of— It's still the middle of the night. What're— Ahhhhh!" He barely had time to brace his arms and legs and save himself from being tumbled to the floor before she drove the RV out of the campground.

The camper's sway reduced dramatically when she pulled out onto the highway. Wyatt felt like hell and could have slept for at least ten more hours, but he dragged himself out of bed. He pulled on a pair of jeans and raked both hands through his hair. He could've used a shave, he realized, pulling his palms down over his sandpapery face, but he didn't want to wait that long to speak to Maggie.

Slipping into a shirt, he pulled back the privacy curtain between the cab and the rest of the RV. "Good morning."

He stepped between the seats and sat down in the captain's chair on the passenger's side and swiveled it around to face her. Several seconds ticked by, but she remained mum, her gaze fixed on the road. She did not acknowledge his presence by so much as a blink.

Wyatt sighed and rubbed his red-rimmed eyes with his thumb and forefinger. "C'mon, sweetheart, talk to me," he exhorted in a weary voice.

Silence.

"Maggie, this is crazy. We're not settling anything this way."

She cut him a sideways glance. "There's nothing to settle."

Encouraged by the terse statement, Wyatt tried to draw her into a discussion, but she refused to say another word. Finally, exasperated, he gave up, shucked his jeans and shirt and crawled back into the upper bunk.

So it went all the way to Texas. Except to toss him the keys and mutter a terse "You drive" now and then, she acted as though he weren't there. Ignoring his offers to cook, she grabbed sandwiches and coffee from service stations when they stopped for gas and ate them alone. Wyatt began to despair of her ever speaking to him again. The closer they got to Houston, the more concerned he became.

Around five the next morning Wyatt sat behind the wheel, cruising east out of Giddings on Highway 290, worrying over the problem in his mind. Ahead, the pale light of dawn edged the gently rolling hills along the horizon. A mile or so in the distance he could see an eighteen wheeler making the pull up a hill, but otherwise there wasn't another vehicle in sight.

Wyatt shifted in his seat and flexed his shoulders. He was in the middle of a stretch when, out of nowhere, a Texas Highway Patrol car came up behind the RV, red lights whirling. The officer gave his siren a tap, and it snarled like a dyspeptic electronic cat. Wyatt glanced at his speedometer and frowned. He was going exactly fifty-five.

"What is it? What's wrong?" Maggie demanded from the rear of the RV. Holding on to the furniture for balance, she staggered to the front and plopped down in the passenger chair beside him. Yawning, she looked all around at the fading darkness. Sleep marks creased her right cheek and her glorious mane of hair stuck out in all directions.

"I don't know," Wyatt replied, pulling over to the

shoulder of the highway. He brought the rig to a halt and switched off the engine. In the side mirror, he watched the patrolman get out of his car and walk toward them, carrying his clipboard. "It looks like we're about to find out, though."

"Morning, sir. Ma'am." The clean-cut young highway patrolman looked past Wyatt to Maggie. "Would you be Miss Margaret Mary Muldoon?"

"Why…yes I am. How did you kno—"

"We were given your license number and asked to be on the lookout for you, ma'am. There's some sort of emergency in your family."

"Emergency?" She stared at him dumbstruck. "Who? What?"

"I don't know, ma'am. I'm just suppose to tell you to call home as soon as possible."

"Oh. Yes…of course…yes. I will, officer. Right away. Th-thank you."

"No problem. Burton is just a mile or so down the road. If you can't find a telephone there I'm sure you can in Brenham." He touched the brim of his hat. "Good luck, ma'am."

"Thanks, Officer," Wyatt called as he started the RV. He glanced at Maggie and leaned over and patted her arm. "Hang on, sweetheart. I'll get you to a telephone before you know it."

Whether she heard him or not he didn't know. She sat like a ramrod in the passenger seat, staring straight ahead, her hands clasped tightly in her lap.

Wyatt frowned and stepped on the gas. Dammit, if she hadn't drowned his cellular phone she could make that call right now, without the delay of driving to the next town. Wisely, he kept that thought to himself.

The air in the cab pulsed with a sense of urgency and

dread. Gripping the steering wheel tight, he drove as fast as he dared. Maggie didn't say a word, or even move, and her silence added to the invisible tension. He glanced her way.

"Are you all right?"

"I'm fine," she said too quickly. "I'm sure this is nothing. Probably just Daphne going to extremes over something, as usual. She gets hysterical over the least little thing. Or this could just be Asa's way of getting my attention. It's been a few days since I called him."

"You're probably right. I'm sure it's nothing to worry about," Wyatt reassured her, but he noticed how she twisted her fingers together in a ceaseless wringing motion. "We'll call and probably find out that you've missed the Junior League Fashion Show or something equally earth-shattering."

She glanced his way and attempted a chuckle, but the sound came out rusty and strained. After that, neither spoke.

Maggie spent the next ten minutes telling herself she wasn't worried. It was probably just as she'd told Wyatt—no more than a tempest in a teacup.

In Burton they located a bank of telephones outside a convenience store that hadn't yet opened for the day. While Maggie made the call, Wyatt leaned against the wall beside her, trying to look unconcerned.

Maggie's independent spirit demanded that she tell him it wasn't necessary for him to hover over her, that she wasn't going to fall apart no matter what news she heard, but she couldn't quite bring herself to shoo him away. His mere presence, so strong and stalwart and quietly capable, was somehow reassuring.

Which made no sense at all, she silently scolded herself

while she punched out Asa's telephone number. If she received bad news what possible help could Wyatt be?

The telephone rang seven times before it was picked up with a sleepy "Hightower residence."

"Mrs. O'Leary. It's Maggie."

Every vestige of sleep fled the housekeeper's voice. "Maggie Muldoon, you naughty girl, you. Where the devil have you been? We've had the constables out lookin' for you these past three days."

"So I just learned. What is it? What's the problem?"

Wyatt's gaze never left Maggie while she listened to Mrs. O'Leary's reply. Within seconds he knew that something was terribly wrong. He watched the blood drain out of Maggie's face, saw the shock flash in her eyes. He straightened away from the wall and stepped forward, putting his hand on her arm. "What is it? What's wrong?"

He could tell that Maggie hadn't heard him. "Asa?" she whispered.

Faintly he could hear Mrs. O'Leary's voice coming through the receiver, but he couldn't quite make out her words. He didn't have to. Maggie's face told him that whatever had happened was bad.

Her chin began to quiver and tears filled her eyes. Wyatt felt a fierce protectiveness well up inside him. He had an almost overpowering urge to jerk that receiver out of the telephone and snatch her close, shield her from whatever terrible news Mrs. O'Leary was passing on.

Maggie nodded and choked out, "Yes. Yes of course. I'll be there as soon as I can."

She started to hang up, but Mrs. O'Leary stopped her.

"What?" Maggie snapped, frowning. She shifted from one foot to the other, impatient to be on her way.

Wyatt watched another wave of shock wash over her

face and ground his teeth. He'd never felt so helpless in his life.

She closed her eyes and pressed her lips together tightly. Finally she exhaled a long sigh. "I see. Well…thank you for telling me, Mrs. O'Leary. Now, would you be a dear and call Daphne for me. Tell her I'm on my way."

Maggie hung up the receiver, but her hand remained on it. She stared blindly at the black box as though in a trance.

"Maggie, talk to me." Wyatt grasped her upper arms and turned her to face him. "What's happened?"

She looked up into Wyatt's anxious face. Gradually her shocked look cleared and her lower lip began to tremble. "It's Asa. He's…he's had a heart attack."

Chapter Fourteen

They burst through the front doors of St. Luke's Hospital at a dead run. They would have been there sooner had they not hit the early-morning traffic rush on the edge of town. Wyatt had broken every speed law between Burton and Houston.

As they dodged through the people and potted plants in the lobby, he cast anxious glances Maggie's way. She was so pale the freckles across her nose stood out like splatters of paint.

During the entire two hours it had taken to reach the hospital she had not said more than a half dozen words, and then only when he asked a direct question.

After she had told him about Asa he had wrapped his arms around her and held her close. She had accepted the comfort for only a few moments before breaking away and attempting to slip back behind that facade of insouciance she used as a shield against the world.

"Och, would you look at me. Gettin' into a tizzie over what is probably nothing," she'd said with a chuckle and an airy wave of her hand. "Asa's healthy as a horse, for pity's sake. He'll pull through this with no problem a'tall. By now he's no doubt bellowing the house down an' harassin' the poor nurses to bring him his cigars and brandy."

The fluttery, almost manic attempt at lighthearted unconcern had rung false, even to Maggie's ears, and after that she had fallen into a stoic silence that worried Wyatt. It wasn't natural or healthy to deny feelings the way Maggie did.

A quick stop by the receptionist's desk revealed that Asa was still in the ICU, a bit of news that caused Maggie's face to whiten even more.

Daphne, Eric and Corinne were standing in the hallway outside the ICU waiting room when they arrived on the floor. The minute Maggie and Wyatt stepped off the elevator her sister pounced.

"It's about time you got here. Where have you been? Granpère has been asking for you ever since he regained consciousness two days ago. While you were out running around, God knows where, our grandfather has been hovering between life and death. You haven't even bothered to call in days. How could you be so thoughtless? So—"

"I don't think attacking Maggie is going to help the situation."

The warning in Wyatt's voice was unmistakable. So was his cold look and the subtle move that simultaneously drew Maggie closer to his side and put him between the two women. One glance into those icy eyes sent alarm flashing across Daphne's face and silenced her tongue. Without realizing it, she took a quick step backward.

"Where is Tyson?" Maggie asked, looking around.

"He just went home to get some sleep," Corinne replied. "We felt that at least one family member should be here at all times and the dear boy's been taking the night shift."

Wyatt turned his attention to his brother. "How is Asa?"

"Holding his own," Eric replied solemnly. "Although the doctor has warned that he's not out of the woods yet. I'm sure it will help his spirits to know that Maggie has arrived." Eric shot back his cuff and checked his watch. "Visiting period starts any minute. They only let two in at a time. Daphne and Corinne were getting ready to go in, but now that Maggie's here I'm sure it would be best if she went in with Daphne. You don't mind, do you, Corinne?"

"No. Of course not. Perhaps poor Asa will finally be able to rest once he sees Maggie." Corinne's voice oozed gentle concern, but beneath the distressed tones Maggie heard the subtle criticism aimed her way. The lump of suffocating guilt that had sat on her chest all morning grew heavier.

"Maggie and I will go in together," Wyatt stated.

Daphne and her mother gasped at his audacity. Eric raised his eyebrows but remained silent.

"Really, Mr. Sommersby." Corinne gave a fluttery little laugh. "I appreciate that you want to see Asa. Really, I do. However, at a time like this I think he would want to see both of his granddaughters."

"Asa will be more than pleased to see me, I assure you." His tone and his expression warned that the matter was not open for discussion.

"Well…I…that is…uh…" Corinne wrung her hands and glanced at her daughter for support, but Daphne looked as uncomfortable as her mother.

Wyatt was being deliberately highhanded and intimidating. Under normal circumstances Maggie would not have tolerated such behavior, but she was too grateful to him to object. She simply could not deal with Daphne and Corinne at the moment.

The door to the ICU opened and a nurse stepped outside and announced visiting time. Without so much as a look at the two flustered women, Wyatt ushered Maggie inside.

Terror seized her the instant she saw Asa. Horrible, cold terror that clawed at her like icy talons.

His eyes were closed and they appeared to be sunken in his head, the crepey lids wrinkled and so thin they were almost translucent. His skin had a gray tinge and his once magnificent shock of silver hair lay limp and lifeless against the pillow. It seemed to Maggie that he had shrunk. The grandfather she knew was big and robust, but the man lying in the bed was shriveled and gaunt and terribly frail.

A frightening tangle of tubes and wires appeared to be hooked up to every part of his body. Above the bed, a wall of monitors beeped and flashed incessantly. The air in the small glass cubicle reeked of medication and disinfection, making Maggie's stomach churn.

Hesitantly, she laid her hand on her grandfather's arm and murmured, "Asa, are you awake?"

His crepey eyelids fluttered, then lifted. "Maggie?" He blinked several times. "Well it's about time," he grumbled, but the statement did not carry the sting it had when her sister had made it.

Slowly his hand turned over and grasped hers. Maggie squeezed the gnarled old hand tight. "How are you feeling?"

"I've been better," he murmured. He looked from Maggie to Wyatt, and his eyes narrowed. "So...you've had your way with my granddaughter, I see."

"Asa!" Maggie's face flamed.

"We're lovers, yes," Wyatt replied without a twitch of embarrassment or apology. "But it was a mutual decision."

"Humph! A likely story." Scowling, Asa raised a bony finger and shook it at Wyatt. "You do realize you'll have to marry her now. If I have to, I'll get out my shotgun," he threatened weakly. "Soon as I get out of this cursed place." He closed his eyes, breathing as though he'd just run a mile, and Maggie's terror escalated. She squeezed his hand tighter.

"Asa, you old bear, don't be silly—"

"I've already asked her to marry me."

"Wy-att!" Maggie shot him a horrified look of censure. It bounced right off him without the least effect.

"Have you now? Well, good. Good. At least you're an honorable man. When's the wedding?"

"She refused me."

The old man's eyes flashed to his granddaughter. "You did what?"

"Now, Asa, you mustn't upset yourself."

"Upset *myself!* You're the one upsetting me. You listen to me, girl. I've been patient with you, but it's time—"

A coughing spasm stopped him. The wheezy sounds terrified Maggie. As he struggled to overcome the strangling coughs his face turned red, then pasty, and the monitors over the bed went wild. Maggie sent Wyatt a desperate look. "Call the nurse! *Do* something!"

"No...don't. I'm...all right," Asa gasped as Wyatt turned to leave, but a nurse came bustling in, anyway.

"Here, now, what's this?" She shooed Wyatt aside and lifted Asa's head, at the same time checking the monitors' fluctuations. When he had the coughing fit under control she gave him a sip of water, checked his color and his pupils, then bustled out again.

Asa drew several labored breaths, relaxed against the pillow and closed his eyes. The monitors settled back down to their monotonous rhythmic beeping.

After several tense moments he opened his eyes and looked at Maggie. "As I was saying, up until now I was willing to wait and let you come to grips with whatever problem it is you have with marriage and commitment, but I don't have time for that anymore. This little episode with my ticker has made me realize that I've got to get my affairs in order. When I go, I want to know that my business is left in good hands and that my heirs' interests are protected."

"Asa, don't talk that way," Maggie insisted with a nervous chuckle. "You're going to pull through this just fine. Why, you'll be around for decades yet."

"Maybe. Maybe not. But I won't rest easy until I get everything settled. That's why I'm leaving control of BargainMart to you."

"What?" Maggie gaped at him, flabbergasted. "Me? Asa, you have to be kidding." She struggled to keep her voice light and amused so as not to upset him again, but panic was rising inside her like gorge. "I don't know anything about running a business. I wouldn't know where to start."

"Humph. You could learn if you wanted to. You're the smart one, Maggie. You can do anything you set your mind to." He sighed heavily. "But I know how much you like your freedom. That's why I think you should marry Wyatt."

Maggie's heart skipped a beat. She experienced the most peculiar sensation—like a tiny explosion in her chest. Strangely, it was made up of equal parts terror and joy.

"He's the perfect man for you. He'll not only love you,

he'll look after the business for you. I can't think of anyone I'd rather have at the helm.''

''Thank you. Coming from you, that's a tremendous compliment,'' Wyatt said, but Asa's suggestion produced a startled laugh from Maggie.

''I don't believe this. You expect me to marry Wyatt so he can run your company?''

''Why not? It's not as though you don't love the man,'' Asa shot back with a touch of his old irascibility.

The last thing Maggie wanted was to antagonize him or upset him in any way, but amazingly, the prospect of doing battle seemed to fire him with energy. Color touched his cheeks and his eyes glinted.

''And don't try to tell me you don't love him. You can lie to yourself but not to me. You wouldn't have slept with him otherwise. I know you, Maggie girl. Better than you think.'' Asa paused, and for an instant his eyes went dreamy and a tender smile curved his lips. His voice dropped to a husky pitch. ''You're just like your grandmother. I had to win my Jessie's heart before she would let me touch her.''

''But, Asa—''

''I have friends down at City Hall,'' Wyatt interjected. ''With their help we could cut through the red tape and get a license in a matter of hours. We could rustle up a minister and have the ceremony right here before the day is over.''

''Wyatt, you stay out of this.''

''Nonsense. The lad has a stake in this, too.'' Asa beamed approval at the younger man. ''You know, that's not a bad idea, my boy. Not bad at all.''

''I thought you'd like it.'' Wyatt looked smug as a cat lapping cream. Maggie could have cheerfully throttled him.

"Now just a darn minute, you two. There is *not* going to be a wedding. And for your information, Asa Hightower, I am not in love with anyone. I refuse to fall in that trap. So you can just forget this crazy scheme."

Asa shook his head and gave her a pitying look. "Maggie, girl, you're my only hope. I'm depending on you."

"But why me?"

"Because you're the one with backbone and brains. Daphne is a good girl, but when it comes to business or handling money she's got the common sense of a flea. All Tyson thinks about is slopping paint around and calling it art. Left to those two, the company would go under in a year, tops. Financially, your sister would be totally dependent on Eric, assuming he still wanted to marry her, and Tyson would starve to death in a damned garret somewhere."

"Then leave the company to Daph and let Eric oversee it."

"I've considered that, but to be honest, I don't think the boy's got what it takes for the job. No offense intended," he added in an aside to Wyatt.

"None taken. I agree with you. Eric means well, but he's too much like our father to keep his nose to the grindstone for long. The social whirl is more to his liking."

Asa's grip on Maggie's hand tightened. "All I'm asking is that you marry a man you obviously care about. It that so terrible?"

Marry. The very word sent a cold chill through her. A vision of her mother flashed through her mind—a slender, flamed-haired woman with tragic eyes, day after day, year after year, waiting—always waiting—for John Hightower, her talent going to waste, her beauty fading. A hundred or more times each day Colleen Muldoon had gone to the window and pulled back the lace curtain to check the road for some sign of him. While working in the garden she had glanced over her shoulder constantly, the desperate hope in her eyes always fading to disappointment.

Of course, her mother had not married John, but her deep love had bound her to him just as surely as holy vows, imprisoning her in that lonely cottage with no life, no hope for a future.

Maggie wanted to be with Wyatt. She couldn't deny that. What they had together was too wonderful to give up. Not just yet at any rate. But marriage?

Her chest became so tight she could barely breathe. She felt trapped, as though the glass walls of the tiny cubicle were closing in on her. Slowly she shook her head, her eyes frantic. "No...I...I can't do it. I can't...I...I *won't*—"

"Maggie, you know I'm right about your sister and brother. Before you make your decision, ask yourself one question. Could you live with yourself if Daphne and Tyson ended up with nothing?"

"That's not fair," Maggie gasped. She no longer even tried to disguise the panic in her voice. "That's...that's emotional blackmail." She backed away from the bed, still shaking her head. "It's not fair!" she wailed and spun on her heel and fled like a wild thing.

"Maggie, come back!" Wyatt took a step after her, but Asa put a restraining hand on his arm.

"No. Let her go, boy. She needs some time alone. And you and I need to talk."

"But she's upset and not thinking rationally. In that state anything could happen to her."

"True. But you've got to let Maggie be Maggie, and that means giving her space."

Wyatt's hands clenched at his sides. Planting his fists

on his hips, he threw his head back and cursed roundly at the ceiling.

"I know exactly how you feel, son. Believe me. I went through the same kind of hell when I was courting her grandmother. As one who's been there, let me give you a word of advice, don't try to hold on to Maggie too tightly. You'll only drive her away."

"What the hell am I suppose to do? Just let her slip away from me? Dammit, I love her. I want to marry her and spend the rest of my life with her. I want to shower her with love and give her the world on a plate and protect her from harm. The way she acts, you'd think I wanted to throw her in prison."

"What you have to remember is, Maggie is a free spirit. My Jessie was, too. When we first met, in my need to claim her as my own, I almost drove her away. Luckily for me I learned in time that it is possible to keep a wild bird in a gilded cage, but only if the door is always open.

"That's why, when I proposed to Jessie, I gifted her with a warehouse—so she would always have the means to live independently if she chose to leave me. That warehouse was Jessie's open door. She left it to Maggie because she recognized her own restless spirit in the girl."

Wyatt stared at the old man. "You gave the woman you loved the means to *leave* you?"

Asa nodded. "The only way to keep a wild creature is to set it free and hope it comes back to you on its own. That warehouse was the most valuable piece of property I owned at the time and I had struggled like hell to get it." Asa's mouth twitched. "I called it the bride price.

"You and I, we're a lot alike, my boy. We like to own things, to hold on to them. Possess them. But with Jessie I had to make myself let go. It was scary, I'll admit. Especially in the beginning. But it worked. She never left.

Not once in forty-two years. I think just knowing that she could was all the freedom she needed.''

Wyatt ground his teeth. He raked a hand through his hair and brought it down the back of his neck to knead the tight muscles there. The advice was hard to swallow. Intellectually he knew that Asa was right, but every instinct he possessed demanded that he bind Maggie to him so tight she could never get away.

''Take my advice. Give Maggie your own bride price. It'll go a long way toward easing her fear of being trapped. Besides, she's going to need it now that her warehouse is gone.''

Wyatt's head snapped up. ''Gone? What're you talking about?''

''Didn't she tell you? It burned to the ground three nights ago.''

''Good Lord. No, she didn't say a word.''

''The building was insured, but not for enough to rebuild. Of course, she still has the land, but property in that neighborhood is hard to unload.''

Wyatt barely heard him. His face set, he headed for the door. ''I'd better go find her, talk to her.''

''Oh, and Wyatt.'' Wyatt turned and waited, an impatient look on his face. ''In case you're interested, my offer of fifteen percent of BargainMart stock is still good. I'll give it to you as soon as the marriage certificate is signed.''

''Keep your damned stock,'' he snapped. ''That's not why I want to marry Maggie.''

He stormed out of the cubicle. Through the glass wall, Asa watched him stride through the ICU and disappear through the outer door. He closed his eyes, and a slow smile lifted the corners of his mouth.

Wyatt found Maggie in the park not far from the hospital. He had the keys to the RV in his pocket, so he'd figured she had to be around somewhere, and with Maggie an open space was the always the best bet.

She sat on the grass, absolutely still, her arms wrapped around her updrawn legs, staring straight ahead at nothing. Except to glance at him out of the corner of her eye when he sat down beside her, she didn't move a muscle or acknowledge his presence in any way.

"Are you okay?" he asked gently.

Maggie dipped her chin in a nod so slight he might have missed it had he not been watching her. She stared straight ahead at the manmade lake a few yards away, but he doubted that she saw the ducks swimming or the people in peddle boats gliding across the water.

Bracing himself on one hand, Wyatt draped his other arm over his updrawn knee and waited. A child's laughter floated to them across the water. In a nearby patch of clover, a bee buzzed. The mingled smells of hotdogs and popcorn wafted to them from the vendor's stand at the end of the lake. Overhead, pine boughs swayed and whispered in the light breeze, dropping a gentle shower of needles over them. Maggie paid them no mind.

"I thought I had done a pretty good job of keeping my distance," she murmured finally. "I thought I wasn't deeply attached to any of them—not Daph nor Tyson nor Corinne. Not even Asa. I thought I could go my own way and not be particularly affected by what happened to them. But I was wrong," Maggie murmured dully. "I don't want to care, but I don't seem to have a choice."

"Yeah, I know what you mean," Wyatt agreed quietly. "Family is family, and you love them no matter what."

Another silence stretched out. Finally, in the same wooden voice, she continued. "Asa is right about Daphne and Tyson, you know. They would never make it on their own." She sighed heavily. "He was right about me, too.

No matter how much I may want to, I can't turn my back on them.''

She turned her head and looked at Wyatt, and her heart gave a little bump. He was so beautiful, with his silvery eyes and that wonderful masculine face. Just looking at him, feeling his nearness, made her body hum. Thinking of the closeness they had shared these past weeks, the beauty and soul-shattering pleasure of their lovemaking, filled her with choking emotions. The thought of losing him made her physically ill. How was it possible to want someone so much and yet be terrified of having him?

Wyatt plucked a pine needle out of her curly mane and absently twirled it between his thumb and forefinger. "Why didn't you tell me about your warehouse burning?"

"So you heard about that."

"Asa told me. I'm sorry, Maggie. I know it meant a lot to you, especially since it was a gift from your grandmother."

Maggie looked back at the lake and shrugged. "After what happened to Asa, it just didn't seem important." The warehouse was more than just a gift from her grandmother; it was her independence. Her children's books were earning fairly well, but her royalties were not enough for her to live on—not yet, anyway. The money the warehouse brought in supplemented her income and allowed her to live free as a bird and roam the country as she pleased—dependent on no one, obligated to no one.

On a remote level she knew that later she would grieve the loss of her home and practically all she owned, but right now she had too much else to deal with.

"What you said before about not being able to turn your back on your family…does that mean you will marry me?"

Closing her eyes, Maggie hugged her legs tighter and

pressed her lips together. She was so confused. A part of her wanted to marry him. There was no point in denying it. It gave her a warm feeling to think of waking up beside Wyatt every morning, of growing old with him. But she was so afraid—afraid of losing her freedom, afraid of losing herself.

Still, she could not live with herself if she deserted Daphne and Tyson. Neither of them had a clue what it meant to work for a living. So what choice did she have? Learn to run the BargainMart chain?

She cringed at the thought. Asa had always loved the thrust and parry of big business, had seemed to be energized by the long hours, the constant decision making, the responsibilities. To Maggie it sounded like a life sentence in hell.

Steeling herself, she turned her head and looked at Wyatt again. "It would appear that I have little choice."

Wyatt snorted. "That wasn't exactly the most enthusiastic response to a proposal of marriage that I've ever heard." He reached out and cupped her face in his hand and smiled ruefully. "But...I love you too much and want you in my life too much to let a little thing like a bruised ego get in the way. Where you're concerned I don't seem to have any pride, because I'll take you any way I can get you."

His eyes looked deep into hers, and the love and warmth she saw in those silvery depths sent a confusing welter of emotion rushing up into her chest. "You won't be sorry, Maggie. I swear I'll do my damnedest to give you the freedom you need. I can't promise I'll always be happy or comfortable with the things you do, but I'll try accept them. I adore you, Maggie, and I want you to be happy."

The sincerity in his eyes, in his voice, tugged at her

heart. Her throat grew so tight she could not swallow, and her chin began to wobble.

Noticing the tiny movement, Wyatt smiled tenderly. Slowly, softly, his thumb rubbed back and forth across her lower lip. "I don't ever want you to feel trapped in this marriage, sweetheart. I know that someday, hopefully in the distant future, you will inherit a sizable fortune from Asa, but in the meantime I want you to be financially independent. As my wedding gift, I'm giving you Blue Hills. I'll have my attorney draw up the transfer of title today."

Maggie gaped at him. "But…you love that farm. Blue Hills is your most prized possession."

"Yes. It is. Which is why I'm giving it to you, so you'll know that I'm serious. If our marriage ever becomes intolerable, you will have the means to walk away."

Something inside her cracked and gave way. Her chin wobbled even more and tears filled her eyes. "Oh, Wyatt," she whispered in an unsteady voice. "Are you sure you want to do this? You deserve so much more. You deserve someone who will love you back, without reservation."

"You do love me, Maggie." His smile was both tender and sad. "You just haven't accepted it yet. But you will. You'll see."

Chapter Fifteen

Over the next few months Wyatt's confidence slipped several notches. By Christmas he was even beginning to call himself an arrogant fool for ever thinking that once they were married Maggie would accept that she loved him. With Maggie, nothing was that easy.

Sitting slouched in an overstuffed chair in Asa's living room, he held a mug of steaming coffee cupped between his hands and brooded. In the corner, the gigantic Christmas tree that Maggie had insisted upon twinkled, its base bare now and a little forlorn looking. At the crack of dawn his wife had rousted everyone from their warm beds to open gifts.

The ritual had been nothing like the polite exchange of presents his parents had overseen on Christmas morning when he and Eric had been boys. Maggie had torn into the gaily wrapped packages like a three-year-old and had encouraged everyone else to do the same. Her enthusiasm had been contagious, and before they knew it they were all wading in, laughing and exclaiming over their loot and exchanging noisy, good-natured taunts. Even Corinne had unbent enough to join in the mayhem with enthusiasm. Within moments, the living room, looking as though a bomb had hit it, had been knee-deep in shredded paper, empty boxes and ribbons.

A reluctant smile tugged at Wyatt's mouth at the memory, and at that of his wife's reaction to his gifts. Maggie had been just as pleased with the fuzzy bear-paw slippers, complete with two-inch-long claws that clacked on the floor with each step, as she had been with the diamond earrings.

"Ah-ha! Gotcha!" Maggie whooped, drawing Wyatt's attention back to the present. Grinning triumphantly, she jumped three of her grandfather's checkers and plucked them off the board.

Asa glared and growled, "That was pure luck, so don't go getting a big head, Missy. This game's not over yet."

"Good as," Maggie taunted, grinning.

Wyatt shook his head. His wife was irrepressible, and Asa loved it. So, for that matter, did he.

Wyatt's eyes lingered on the old man. Asa looked his old, robust self again. Ever since the wedding, which had been performed at his bedside, his recovery had been nothing short of miraculous. He had been released from the hospital a little over a week later and was now back at work on a limited basis. If Asa kept on the way he was going he'd be around for another thirty years or more.

From the kitchen came the delicious aromas of roasting turkey and dressing, sweet potatoes, rolls and pecan pie. Eric and Tyson were glued to the football game blaring from the television, and Daphne, Corinne and Great-Aunt Edwina sat on the sofa discussing the details of Eric and

Daphne's wedding, which was set for the second week in June.

Listening to them, Wyatt was profoundly grateful that he and Maggie had not been subjected to such an ordeal—mainly because he had no doubt that she would have cracked under the strain and run for the hills. As it had been, she'd been jumpy as a cat, and he'd sweated out those few hours it had taken to make the hurried arrangements.

Wyatt tried to work up an interest in the football game, but his gaze, like his thoughts, kept returning to his wife. Maggie sat at a table before the roaring fire in the hearth, playing checkers with Asa and laughing at his testy grumbling, teasing him as though she hadn't a care in the world.

And why should she have? Wyatt thought sourly. From her perspective, their marriage was a rollicking success. They got along well, they enjoyed each other's company, and their love life was fantastic.

For a woman who had remained chaste until the age of twenty-six, Maggie was a delightfully sensual creature. As with everything she did, she approached lovemaking with wholehearted enthusiasm. Open and spontaneous, she followed her instincts and gave herself over to the pleasurable sensations with no inhibitions, no reservations, alternately submissive and aggressive as the emotion of the moment moved her. She was a constant delight. Sex with Maggie was the hottest, most arousing and erotic, most loving he had ever experienced.

Out of bed she pleased him just as much. She was bright and inquisitive and funny and fun to be with. Life was never dull with Maggie around. Thanks to her, he had learned to slow down and relax and appreciate little things and enjoy life as he never had before. The month-long trip in the RV, which he had been so sure he would abhor, had

not only been enjoyable, it had taught him that Sommersby
Enterprises could manage to creak along without him now
and then.

His gaze traced Maggie's profile, and he felt that familiar sweet pressure in his chest. It still amazed Wyatt
that he, a man who had always scorned marriage, who had
cringed at the thought of spending the rest of his life with
one woman, was so completely, irrevocably enthralled by
the tiny sprite he had married.

He missed her when he was at the office, and trips out
of town were pure misery. At odd times he caught himself
thinking about her, and he couldn't wait to come home to
her at the end of a day. Maggie saw the amusing side of
everything and laughed at the world and its silliness. No
matter how trying a day he'd had or what crisis he faced,
she never failed to cheer him. He was happier than he'd
ever been, happier than he'd ever imagined it was possible
to be.

Yet one thing was missing—those three little words that
he wanted so desperately to hear.

He still believed—no, dammit, he *knew*—that Maggie
loved him. Whether or not she would ever admit that was
another matter.

Dammit! he thought, scowling at her over his mug as
she gleefully jumped two more of her grandfather's checkers. A woman didn't respond to a man the way she did to
him unless she loved him. She was, without a doubt, the
most stubborn, pigheaded, obstinate female he had ever
encountered. It had been over three months since their
wedding, but the minx had yet to voice a single word of
love, not even in the hottest moments of passion.

"I win! I win!" Maggie crowed, sweeping the last of
Asa's checkers from the board.

"Only because I let you," he grumbled. "I didn't want you to get discouraged and quit."

"Let me, my foot! I won with skill, cunning and superior play," she said, with her nose in the air.

"Oh, yeah. Well, we'll just see who wins the next game."

Asa had barely begun setting up the board again when Mrs. O'Leary appeared at the door of the living room. Her cheeks were rosy from cooking, her plump body encased in a voluminous white apron. "Dinner is ready, Mr. Hightower. If you'll be good enough to take your seats in the dining room I'll be after servin' it."

The Christmas dinner was as different from that the Sommersbys had shared in the past as the gift exchange had been. Usually Wyatt's parents had taken him and Eric to dinner at the country club or one of Houston's posh restaurants.

Asa, however, for all his wealth and social aspirations, had never abandoned his simple family values. Formalities, such as which fork to use and what was considered proper dinner conversation and etiquette, were less important than the sense of belonging and conviviality that dominated the Hightower feast. Wyatt suspected that was one of the reasons Asa had never been fully accepted by Houston's social elite. As he listened to the laughter and good-natured banter swirling around the table, he was glad.

The meal was sumptuous and plentiful. Wyatt watched with amazement as his tiny wife tucked away more food than a lumberjack. Where did she put it all? When busy with whatever had her attention at the moment, she could go days without eating, but when the opportunity presented itself she gorged herself like a bear preparing for hibernation.

By the time they reached the coffee and dessert course

Wyatt was feeling sated and mellow, his earlier discontent all but forgotten. Then Maggie dropped her bombshell.

"Och! I won't be able to eat for a week," she groaned, patting her tummy. "'Tis a good thing I start fire fighters' school next week."

Wyatt's head snapped up. "You do what?"

"I start fire fighter training. Don't be lookin' so surprised. I told you that in my next book Mergatroid and Arbuckle join the National Forest Service and become fire fighters, and that I'd be going out on a research trip soon."

"You'll have to excuse me. Somehow I didn't connect that with my wife going out in the woods and risking her life fighting a forest fire. How stupid of me."

"The training minimizes the risks. Besides, I'll just be an observer and I'll be out there with the elite in the business." Excitement sparkled in her eyes as her gaze swept over the others. She didn't seem to notice their stunned expressions. "They're called Hot Shots, and they go all over the country fighting fires in the National Parks. Sometimes they have to parachute into remote mountain terrain."

A muscle twitched along Wyatt's jaw. He started silently counting to ten.

Asa scowled. "Didn't a bunch of that outfit die last year fighting a fire up in the Rockies?"

"Well…yes, but—"

"All right. That's it," Wyatt snapped, giving up at six. He pointed his finger at Maggie and snarled through clenched teeth, "You are *not* going. Do you understand me? I won't have you risking your life that way. I've watched you jump out of airplanes and off bridges and turn yourself upside down in a kayak and pull a dozen other crazy stunts, and I've held my tongue. But not this time. I won't allow you to do this, Maggie."

"*You* won't *allow?*" She laughed. He couldn't believe it. She actually chuckled out loud. That was the trouble with Maggie; it was difficult to argue with someone who took so few things seriously.

"I'm sorry you don't approve, Your Nibs, but you really don't have any say in the matter. Just because we're married doesn't mean you can tell me what I can and cannot do. We had an agreement. You were going to accept what I did without interfering. Remember?" she said with a coaxing smile.

"Within reason, yes. But this is insane."

"According to you. I don't happen to think so."

"That's it? You're going? No matter how I feel?"

Giving him a regretful look, she shrugged. "I'm afraid so."

"Fine." Wyatt shot to his feet, slapped his napkin on the table and stormed out without another word.

"Stubborn man," Maggie mumbled. Folding her forearms on the top rail of the corral, she propped her chin on her hands and watched Wyatt lead Hot Streak, Asa's prize Arabian stallion, from the barn to where Philip Townsend waited astride King Tut, his Appaloosa.

"Well, you can't blame him," her grandfather said. Asa leaned an elbow on the top rail beside her and watched the two men. "Philip did goad him into racing with all that talk about being able to outride and outjump any rider around. You can't expect a man to just ignore a challenge like that."

Maggie grunted. Her comment had had nothing to do with the race, but if Asa wanted to think so, that was fine with her.

"And you can't blame him for being upset with you,

either, Missy. The man's got a perfect right to object to you risking your neck. He loves you.''

Maggie barely stifled a groan. She should have known that nothing got past Asa. "We had an agreement.''

"Agreement, bah! It's basic instinct for a man to protect the woman he loves, even from herself.''

The comment pricked at Maggie, but she pushed the uneasy feeling aside. She had come to accept that Wyatt truly did love her, but that didn't give him the right to interfere in her life.

Ignoring her grandfather's pointed look, she watched her husband swing into the saddle. Hot Streak did a sidestepping dance, bobbing his head, but Wyatt quickly controlled him.

This tension between them was intolerable. In the three months of their marriage they'd had a few minor disagreements, but he'd never really been furious with her before. She'd had no idea how miserable it would make her feel. Since storming out of the house the day before, he had barely said three words to her. She had tried in every way she could to cajole him out of his anger, but he had remained stiff and distant.

Philip's arrival this morning hadn't helped ease the situation. He and Wyatt bristled like two pit bulls whenever they encountered each other.

Wyatt was convinced that Philip was in love with her, and nothing she could say would change his mind. He resented him hanging around all the time. Never mind that Asa had allowed Philip to board his horse at the farm for years, her husband believed he came to see her.

Philip was no better. He had not been pleased to learn of her marriage, and he seemed bent on needling Wyatt every chance he got.

Today was no exception. His bragging had bordered on

insult, and the race that was about to take place plus a ridiculous amount of money wagered, was the result.

Men, Maggie thought with disgust. They acted like overgrown boys, always trying to outdo one another.

"Okay, Asa, we're all set," Philip called from atop his prancing horse. "We'll race from here down to the creek, around that stand of oaks on the other side, and back. First one to pass the water trough over there is the winner. You give us the signal to start."

"Will do." Stepping up onto the bottom rail of the fence, Asa raised a starter pistol over his head. "Okay, look alive. This is it. Get ready! Get set! Go!"

Even though she was braced for it, Maggie started when Asa fired the gun. So did the horses. They leapt forward as though poked with an electric prod and took off for the creek at breakneck speed, their lean, graceful bodies stretching out, straining, reaching. Thundering hooves shook the ground and kicked up clods of dirt as their riders crouched low over their backs, exhorting them on to even greater speed.

"Look at 'um go!" Asa whooped.

Maggie rolled her eyes. "Honestly. I swear, you're as bad as they are. Why are men so competitive?" she grumbled, but her heart began to pound as she watched the two riders race away. She gripped the board rail so tight her fingers whitened. Straining forward, she silently urged Wyatt on.

They hit the creek side by side, sending water spraying upward in silver arcs. Up the opposite bank they went. For a few seconds they disappeared behind the stand of huge oaks. Then they burst into the open again and came pounding back, splashing back across the shallow creek, up the bank, then pouring on the speed in the straightaway.

Both men had shed their jackets for the ride. Somewhere

along the way Wyatt had lost his hat, and the wind plastered his black hair against his head and molded his shirt to his powerful chest.

Hot Streak slowly pulled ahead, at first by a nose, then by half a length, a length. As the riders thundered closer, Maggie saw that the remote anger that had marked Wyatt's expression for the past twenty-four hours was gone. His face wore a look of fierce exultation as he and Hot Streak flew past the horse trough a length and a half ahead of Philip.

Maggie turned to watch him as he raced by. She expected him to rein in as Philip was doing, but Wyatt urged the horse on even faster.

"What is he doing? Oh, no! Sweet Mary and Joseph! He's going to try to jump the fence!"

"Has the boy lost his mind?" Asa barked. "That fence is too high to jump."

"Wyatt, stop! Stop!" Maggie turned to her grandfather and grabbed his arm. "Do something, Asa. Stop him. He's going to kill himself!"

"It's too late, child," Asa said, never taking his eyes off the horse and rider.

Maggie whirled and clamped her hands over her mouth, her eyes filled with horror as horse and rider neared the fence.

It seemed to happen in excruciatingly slow motion—she saw Hot Streak's hindquarters bunch, saw his rear hooves set, the powerful muscles spring, the sleek body stretch out, Wyatt crouch low over that graceful arched neck. Then, as one, they were sailing up…up…up…

Hot Streak cleared the fence but stumbled on the landing, and Wyatt went flying over the horse's head.

"*Wy-att!*"

Maggie was running before he hit the ground. She ran

so fast her feet barely skimmed the ground, her heart banging against her ribs. She strained for all she was worth, sobbing and gasping. She didn't feel the stitch in her side or the burning in her lungs. Her entire being was focused on the inert form lying in the pasture beyond the fence.

She hit the fence going flat-out, leapt up on the bottom rung and vaulted over in one continuous motion.

Wyatt lay flat on his back, one arm flung above his head. Before she reached him Maggie saw that his entire body was shaking as though in convulsion. "Wyatt! Oh, blessed Mary. Darling, are you all right," she cried, dropping to her knees beside him. Her hands flew over him—his face, his chest, over his concave belly, his sex, down his long, sturdy legs, and back up—frantically searching for an injury. "Please. Oh, please, be okay. You've got to be okay," she sobbed hysterically. "You've got to. I can't lose you. I can't!"

Philip came thundering up on King Tut and Asa arrived on foot not far behind.

"Is he all right?"

"Don't move him. Something might be broken."

Maggie was oblivious to both men. Fear had her by the throat. She stroked Wyatt's hair away from his face and patted his cheek but his eyes remained closed and the horrible shaking continued. Distraught, she put her ear to his chest. His heart beat strong and sure. Then she heard the other sound, a low rumble rising from deep within his chest.

She jerked her head up and gaped. "You're *laughing!* You're not hurt at all!"

She sat back on her heels. She was so furious the top of her head felt as though it were about to blow off. Wyatt writhed on the ground, shaking, unable to speak. Finally, catching the breath that had been knocked out of him, his silent mirth erupted in full-bodied laughter.

Rich guffaws rumbled from his chest, and tears squeezed from the corners of his eyes. Maggie ground her teeth.

After a while, his laughter subsided and he sat up. Wiping his streaming eyes with the back of his hand, he gasped, "Oh, man, that was some ride." Still chuckling, he lowered his hand and grinned at Maggie. "Did you see Hot Streak take that fence?"

"You...you louse," she snarled. "You despicable, sorry, misbegotten, low-down son of a lop-eared jackass!"

Both of Wyatt's eyebrows shot skyward. "Is something wrong?"

That was too much. She drew back her hand and slapped his face with all her might—so hard her hand stung and his head snapped to the side. Then she burst into tears, jumped to her feet and bolted for the house.

She didn't stop running until she reached her room and fell facedown across the bed, sobbing.

That was how Asa found her ten minutes later.

"Here now, child, don't carry on so." He sat down on the bed and pulled her into his arms, and as she burrowed her face against his chest he held her close and stroked the back of her head. "It isn't the end of the world, you know. Hush up that crying now," he ordered with gruff tenderness.

"I can't," she wailed. "I...I don't even kn-know why I'm cr-crying. Or...or why I'm s-so upset."

"Ah, well, that's easy. You're in love."

The words zinged straight to Maggie's heart like an arrow shot from a bow. She went utterly still in Asa's arms.

"Well now," Asa said with satisfaction, and she could hear the smile in his voice. "At least you have the good sense not to deny it.'' He stroked her back and rubbed his chin against the top of her hair. ''Don't you see, child? You watched the man you love take a terrible risk, and it ended in a fall. The danged fool could have killed himself or been severely injured. It's perfectly natural for you to be upset.''

Pushing free of his embrace, Maggie stared at her grandfather. Her heart contracted painfully and her eyes widened. Sweet Mary and Joseph. He was right. She loved Wyatt.

When she had seen him go flying over that horse's head, she had experienced fear like nothing she had ever known. In that split second when she'd thought that he might die she had wondered how she could possibly go on without him. Her heart had felt as though it had been cleaved in two.

''Now maybe you can understand your husband a little better,'' Asa said, giving her a pointed look.

She sucked in a sharp breath and clamped a hand over her mouth. ''Oh, Dear Lord,'' she gasped against her palm. Was this what Wyatt went through every time she tried something dangerous? Did he feel this suffocating fear? This horrible icy sensation in the pit of his stomach? This utter helplessness?

Maggie closed her eyes and groaned. ''No wonder he gets so upset with me.''

''Exactly.''

Her eyes popped open. ''How could this have happened? I tried so hard not to love him. I don't *want* to love him.''

Asa's mouth quirked at the petulant wail. ''Ah, Maggie girl, there's no escape from the silken ties of love. Not if you've got a heart.'' He reached out and stroked her cheek. ''And you, child, have the biggest heart of anyone I know.

"Don't fight it, Maggie. Enjoy it. Love doesn't have to hurt. It can be the most wonderful adventure you'll ever have if you'll just give it a chance."

Looking into those wise old eyes, Maggie's heart expanded with the first stirrings of hope. Emotion welled up inside her, creating a painful pressure in her chest and flooding her with a deep yearning she was powerless to ignore. Her eyes grew moist, and she placed her hand over Asa's and held it against her cheek. "I...I want to, but...I'm not sure I know how."

"You can start by finding that husband of yours and telling him what you feel," Asa pronounced gruffly.

"But—"

"No *buts*. Just do it." Standing abruptly, he pulled her to her feet, pointed her toward the door and gave her a little shove. A few feet away Maggie hesitated and shot him an anxious glance over her shoulder. "Go. Go," Asa growled.

Maggie went.

She found Wyatt in the barn giving Hot Streak a currying. Maggie approached the stall with trepidation. She hadn't felt this unsure of herself since she was fourteen, when she had entered Asa's magnificent home for the first time, clutching her meager belongings and wondering how she would ever fit in.

Wyatt spotted her, and the brush stilled against Hot Streak's flank. He didn't speak, but merely watched her over the stallion's back as she entered the stall. He looked so stern and unyielding, she almost lost her courage and turned around to flee. The stallion shamelessly nudged her for attention, and she obliged by scratching his forehead.

"You okay now?" Wyatt asked and resumed stroking the brush over the stallion's sleek hindquarter.

"Yes." Maggie kept her gaze fixed on Hot Streak. "I, uh…I'm sorry I hit you."

"Um."

She waited, but it was soon apparent the noncommittal reply was all she was going to get out of him. He went on with his task, running the brush over the Arabian's back with long, rhythmic strokes.

Maggie sighed. He wasn't making this easy for her. "I learned something today," she murmured after a lengthy silence. She forced herself to look at him, and when their gazes met, Wyatt raised one eyebrow.

"Oh? What's that?"

"That…" Maggie paused and licked her lips. "Well…that the heart seems to have a mind of its own."

The brush stilled and his eyes flashed to hers, but he merely waited.

"When…when you, uh…care about someone, you want to keep them safe from harm and close by your side. It's, uh, instinctive, I guess."

"What're you saying, Maggie?"

She looked into that beloved face, so taut with hope, and her heart fluttered. Set free at last, love welled up inside her in a hot tide, overflowing her heart, warming her, filling her with a pleasure so sweet it was almost pain. Tears filled her eyes, and her chin quivered. Emotions clogged her throat, but she forced herself to speak around the aching tightness. "I love you, Wyatt."

He stilled, but something flared in his silvery eyes, something so hot and intense it took her breath away.

Never taking his gaze from her, he tossed the brush over his shoulder. It hit the wall of the next stall with a loud clatter as he stalked around the horse's rear. Without breaking stride, he swept her up in his arms, kicked open the half door and carried her from the stall and into an empty one across the aisle.

Maggie's exultant laugh rang out as he tossed her onto the pile of fresh straw and followed her down. The sound became a moan of pleasure as his mouth closed over hers in a rapacious kiss that sent her temperature soaring.

"Say it again," he demanded, when they were forced to come up for air.

Laughing, Maggie clutched his hair with both hands and brought his head down for another hard quick kiss. "I love you," she said, and brought his head down again. "I love you. I love you. I love you," she vowed over and over between lusty, open-mouthed kisses.

When she finally released him, he raised up on one arm and looked down at her. His face was flushed with passion and his eyes burned. "I'll never get tired of hearing that," he vowed in a raspy growl. "Never."

Then they were rolling together, frantic and wild. Clothes were discarded in manic haste, and soon there was only warm skin to warm skin. There was no need or desire for foreplay. Their emotions were too high, their yearning for each other too great. Their coming together was swift and urgent and so beautiful their hearts soared as one. There, in the quiet barn, with the fecund smells of animals and straw all around them, they loved each other with a depth of emotion that melded their souls.

Neither was conscious of the prickly straw poking their flesh nor the December chill of the barn. For long, heady moments the only sounds were the creaking of the loose loft door overhead, the contented munching of the horses in their stalls and the low moans and sighs of the entwined lovers.

With emotions so high fulfillment came quickly, and soon their cries of joy echoed through the cavernous barn.

Then there was only their stertorous breathing and the hush of contentment.

Exhausted, utterly replete, they lay entwined for a long time, both loath to relinquish the wonderful closeness. Absently Maggie stroked Wyatt's sweat-slicked back and gazed through half-opened eyes at the massive beams high overhead, saturated with a feeling of joy and peace and perfect freedom. What a fool she had been to let her mother's experience deprive her of this happiness for so long. It hadn't been love that had ruined Colleen Muldoon's life, but loving the wrong man.

She closed her eyes and tightened her arms around Wyatt, smiling against his shoulder.

"What?" he mumbled sleepily.

Maggie chuckled and nipped his earlobe, and Wyatt grunted. "Oh, nothing. I was just thinking. This loving and being loved really isn't so bad after all."

* * * * *

Dear Reader,

For me, a lot of the fun of writing comes from stepping into another's shoes. After all, what little girl hasn't imagined herself as Cinderella? Or my favorite, Beauty contending with the Beast. So…what if I were an heiress…and lived a very restricted and lonely life through no fault of my own…and what if my beloved uncle were trying to kill me? Is there anyone I can trust?

When Jessica hired Brody as her bodyguard, she found that person. He was the strong, silent type, totally dedicated to his job, a man she could trust with her fortune and her life.

And her heart? Well, that makes the story more complicated.

And much more fun as I watch these two struggle with strong emotions and an equally strong attraction. Give them good reasons to guard their innermost feelings, put them on an isolated ranch, stir well and wait to see what develops….

Laurie Paige

HUSBAND:
BOUGHT AND PAID FOR

Laurie Paige

Chapter One

Jessica Lockhart rested her forehead against the wall-to-wall-plate-glass window and stared at the Chicago traffic on the street forty-five stories below. She sighed. Her breath appeared briefly on the cool pane as a circle of moisture. The glass echoed the sigh back to her so that she heard the sound at the same instant.

The city was busy on this chilling March night.

Headlights swept a path through the dark for the vehicles that rushed along the streets as if they were strange insects, each scurrying to do their important deeds before dawn broke. She glanced at her watch. Almost two.

She stood on an observation platform that was part of a skywalk overlooking an atrium two floors below. Through the hazy glow of light reflecting from the window, she could see the fig trees swaying with the stir of warm air from the registers. The image of her bodyguard was also reflected in the window.

Brody Smith. Private Investigator. Partner in a small security agency that handled special cases and only by referral. Thanks to a large inheritance, her trustees could afford the best for her.

The thought sounded cynical, even to her. Money was supposed to make life easier. And it did. She wasn't stupid when it came to economics. But it was also a burden.

She watched as Brody glanced around the area. His dark gaze lingered on her. He was probably wondering how much longer she was going to stand there staring out at the night.

The atrium skywalk was her favorite spot to contemplate life. It suited her, this high and lonely place.

In the glass, his image stood, then stretched. He rotated his shoulders as if they were stiff. He was a tall, lean man with black hair and eyes so dark they, too, seemed black. He rarely smiled, but when he did, it changed his rough features in a manner that was startling.

Not that he became handsome. He'd lived a hard life. It showed in a nose that had been broken—twice, he'd said with that cynical, so-what? smile he used when she pried into his personal life. Along his right temple, the flesh was puckered into a narrow scar an inch long. A bullet that someone had tried to put his name on, he'd told her.

The scar gave him a somewhat forbidding look. It told the observer that here was a man who wasn't afraid of life.

By contrast, his smiles, when they came, were sudden and breath-catching. He had beautiful teeth, perfectly straight and very white against his swarthy skin. He'd come by them naturally. She'd had to pay a fortune for her straight smile.

She sighed again, knowing it was time to go home for the night. Home was her grandfather's estate an hour's drive from downtown, where she'd lived for the past six months. She turned slowly, regretting the intrusion of reality. "Shall we go?"

"When you're ready."

No emotion stirred the rich timbre of his voice, neither impatience nor irritation. She wondered what would stir him.

Perhaps if she made a pass? No, he'd give her that dead-level stare as if he hadn't a clue to what she meant. Neither anger nor passion would light his eyes.

That was no particular obstacle to her plans.

She faced the window again. Putting her palms against the pane, she felt the cold seep into her hands. An urge to strike the glass came over her. She hit it with the heel of her fist, but not terribly hard. The blow was intended to state her defiance, not to inflict damage. The strength of the tempered glass was greater than any brute force she could muster.

There were times of late that she'd thought of herself as a bird in a glass cage, beating her wings uselessly against a fate she couldn't change.

"If I marry," she said, "that would solve all my problems, wouldn't it?"

In the night-framed window, she saw his gaze swing to her as if it were a heat-seeking missile locking on target.

"That depends on the guy you marry."

She ignored the sardonic twist to the words. "I meant as far as the inheritance goes. I'd be free of my mother's will."

The private investigator strode the perimeter of the observation platform, his gaze alert for the slightest sign of danger. The trustees thought someone was trying to kill her. Actually they thought her uncle was the culprit. He would inherit her trust fund if she died without heirs.

"Only if you stay married for one year."

"Yes. A year. That's not so much out of a person's life. Not when you look at how long people live nowadays."

He gave a noncommittal, "Huh."

She faced him again. "After one year, I'd be free to leave the money to anyone I wanted. Or to a charity."

"At thirty-five, you'll inherit without having to marry," he reminded her. He watched her with the wary expression of a man who had braved danger often in his life and knew its signs well.

"That's years from now. I want to be free."

He nodded his head, an almost imperceptible movement, and his eyes narrowed. He wasn't going to help her out.

"I've been living with a bodyguard for almost a year. To face nine more years of it..." She shook her head in refusal.

"Someone tried to kill you," he reminded her.

"The police think they were accidents." She was grasping at straws.

"How many of these accidents have you had?" he questioned, goading her into remembering the strange occurrences in her life since she'd turned twenty-five and could presumably take control of her inheritance by staying married for one year. If she died before that event took place or before she turned thirty-five, her uncle stood to gain everything.

"Shortly after my birthday, my brakes failed. The fluid had leaked out. Fortunately I always step on the brake pedal when I start the car. It went down to the floor, so I knew I had no brakes. The mechanic found the line might have been cut."

She fell silent, remembering that the police had been called in to investigate. They'd found an ID medallion belonging to her uncle's gardener, who had mysteriously disappeared, near where she'd been parked. But there hadn't been anything that could prove her uncle's guilt—or innocence. Uncle Jesse had accused her grandfather of trying to frame him. There was no love lost between the two men.

Nor had there been between her mother and her grandfather—stepgrandfather, actually. Her mother had left the older man out of her will. She and Uncle Jesse had never accepted him in their real father's place.

However, he was the only grandfather Jessica had ever known. He'd taken her in as a twelve-year-old orphan and raised her. For that she would always be grateful. He was also one of her trustees since Mr. Parker of the original three had died.

"And after that?" Brody prodded.

"Someone forced me off the road one snowy night. I thought the driver was the gardener. Since then I've tried two security agencies, neither very satisfactory." A chill crept around her heart as she told of the mishaps.

"You rebelled last month and fired the last guy."

"It was a she. I caught her going through the clothes in my bureau. She was nosy and intrusive."

"During your bid for freedom, the steering came loose in your car, which is less than a year old. You were lucky to be able to stop before you hit a concrete embankment. Your uncle's fingerprints were on the car. You said you'd talked to him at a charity ball and he'd leaned against your car."

"He did."

She gripped the railing. It was daunting to realize her relative might be plotting to kill her. "A friend's husband recommended you. He said you would ferret out the truth if it was possible to do so. You've been here three weeks without results. The other agencies didn't find anything in eight months. I've thought of another solution, an easier one." Her smile was brittle. "I simply need to marry."

"For one year."

She met his dark, moody gaze and directed a challenge to him. "Don't you think I can make it through a year?"

"No."

The blunt reply sent a wave of heat through her. Anger warred with humiliation. "I didn't realize your opinion of me was quite so low."

He shrugged. "Don't ask if you don't want an answer."

"I'll remember that in the future." She clutched her tiny evening bag against her chest and headed for the elevator door.

Brody fell into step beside her. She walked faster. He kept up effortlessly.

At the elevator, he punched in the code. The door slid open. He checked it before letting her enter.

She stepped in and pulled the silver fox—a remade jacket from one of her grandmother's coats—close around her, burying her nose in it so he wouldn't see the color in her cheeks.

In the parking garage, he checked the car out as carefully as the elevator although the longtime family driver was inside and had been there since they'd arrived an hour ago.

Guilt for keeping them out so late added to her inner turmoil. However, she'd needed the quiet. As chairperson of a charity ball, she'd spent most of the evening in a crowd, Brody's disapproving presence always at her side. A friend had flirted shamelessly with him every chance she got. Brody had paid absolutely no attention.

That's when Jessica had gotten her brilliant idea. Brody was in his early thirties. The fact that he wasn't married and seemed quite free to follow her around and investigate her life and friends suggested to her that he might be willing to go along with the idea of marriage.

When they were well on their way to the country house, she drew a deep breath and plunged in. "Would you be willing to marry me for a year?"

He gazed at her for what seemed to be ages. "No."

She'd thought she was prepared for a denial, but still she was surprised when tears stung her eyes. "I'd pay you well. Your regular salary plus a bonus equal to the same amount."

"No."

She forced herself to look upon the proposal as a business deal, which it was, not as a personal matter between them, which it wasn't. "All right," she said, injecting a smidgen of resigned humor in the words. "I'll double your salary. And the bonus. Isn't that enough for one year of your time?"

"It isn't the money."

"Then what is it?"

"I don't want the entanglements that marriage brings."

"It isn't as if it would be a real marriage. You'd make a lot of money and I...maybe I would have a life."

"You don't now?"

She glared at him. "No. Not with you around."

"This to the guy she just asked to marry her," he murmured, one dark eyebrow lifting as he mocked her suggestion.

"Since I turned twenty-five and someone decided to play tricks with my life, I've not had one. Until I marry, the trustees insist that I keep you on. Or, if not you, another just like you," she added glumly. She gazed out the windows as snow began to fall. More and more, the luxury in which she lived seemed like a cage, gilded, yes, but a cage nevertheless.

"Nice that you can distinguish between us."

This time she heard the slice of humor served with the cynicism. "Sorry, I didn't mean to be insulting."

Ironically Brody was the one person she did trust. She did it instinctively. He seemed to know exactly what he was doing and why. At times, she'd found his presence comforting.

But the fact was she hadn't had a moment alone in ages. Never alone, but always lonely. Oh, stop feeling sorry for yourself, she mentally chided.

"I'm serious about marriage, Brody. That would solve the problem since the trustees won't let me give any money to Uncle Jesse. One year of marriage and they're out of the picture."

"Will you give your inheritance to your uncle?" Brody asked on a curious note.

"I don't know," she said honestly. "I loved him when I was a child. When he came to visit, we had a great time. My mother thought he was wonderful, but he wasn't very good at holding a job. She used to give him money. It made my grandfather angry. I remember they quarreled about it once when he invited us home for Christmas. He said my uncle was no good. That made my mother furious and we left."

"But you were sent to live with your grandfather when your mother died?" Brody knew the facts of her life, but he sometimes asked questions as if not clear on a particular point.

Jessica nodded. "My mother set up the trust fund with the law firm and the bank, but she didn't say where I was to live. I guess she didn't expect to get cancer and die in eight months. There was a custody hearing, then I came here to live. My uncle had charm but not much else. He'd made a lot of bad investments."

"Did he say that?" Brody asked.

"No. Grandfather told me."

"Your uncle seems to live well."

Her hackles rose. She was defensive about her uncle. He had a different life-style, but she found it hard to believe he would try to harm her. "He's found his niche."

"And a partner who's quite wealthy."

A chill went down her spine. Brody's voice was deep, with ominous undertones that conveyed an intimate knowledge of the sinister side of life. She peered at him, trying to guess his meaning from his expression. Naturally she couldn't.

"Are you insinuating Uncle Jesse's partner has something to worry about?"

"I never insinuate."

The flat statement stilled further arguments from her. Brody didn't trust anyone. That much was clear. She touched the car window and felt the coldness creeping near, one thin slice of glass away. A shiver ran over her.

"Are you cold?" he asked, his hand already on the controls.

She shook her head and dropped her hand to her lap. "Sometimes the cold seems to be waiting," she said. "Like the Snow Queen, if it touches a person, it turns one's heart to ice."

"Poor little rich girl."

She clenched her cold hands on her purse and managed a laugh. "Not at all. I only have to find a husband. Then all my troubles will be over. And you'll be out of a cushy job."

Brody walked the perimeter of the terrace that surrounded the country estate. All the security devices were on and working properly. He moved his shoulders, irritated at the tightness across his back and up his neck.

Tension.

A certain amount was good. A man had to stay alert. But this wasn't that kind of strain.

A cynical smile flitted over his mouth. He knew what the problem was, had known the moment he walked into the office where the attorney, a longtime friend, had introduced Brody to Jessica Lacey Lockhart, and his sense of caution and preservation had gone at once on red-alert.

He knew danger when it came at him with a curvy body, wind-tossed, sun-streaked hair and a smile that belied the trace of vulnerability in gray eyes as translucent as rain. He'd taken the case, against his better judgment, but he'd taken it.

Now—marriage.

He should have cut and run when he'd still had the chance, that first moment in the law office. Now he couldn't. It was a failing of his—this concern for the underdog, for anyone not quite dealt a fair hand.

Jessica fell into that category. She paid a price for her privileged life.

He stretched and rubbed the back of his neck with one hand. A yearning to be in Colorado, riding his land, breathing the cold mountain air, swept over him. A man felt free there, not constrained by the constant press of humanity found in the city.

Walking around the corner of the century-old brick mansion, he checked the digital readout on the security monitor, clicked off the LED display and replaced the device in his jacket pocket. He paused and looked at the light falling from a bedroom window.

Jessica's room.

For a moment, he wondered if she'd experience the sense of freedom he did on the ranch he'd bought with his life savings and visited whenever he could. With his office in Denver and his work taking him all over the States, he didn't get there as often as he'd like.

That would change soon. The ranch was breaking even, sometimes making a small profit, and he nearly had enough money to retire from active cases. He could run the agency from the ranch for him and his partner. They could take in an associate in his place. The money Jessica had mentioned would be enough to do it.

He gave a start of surprise. He was considering her offer. He was really considering her offer.

Was he out of his ever-loving mind?

A movement in her room drew his attention. He quickly checked the open slope of lawn that ran to the perimeter fence. No signs of an interloper. At the ranch, other than a coyote or an occasional mountain lion, he could go days without seeing another living soul. He liked it that way.

When he turned back to the French doors, he saw Jessica standing there, her expression pensive as she gazed out at the night. She wore a white, silky-looking nightgown with a lacy robe over it. Her short curly hair, backlighted by the bedside lamp, formed a halo around her head.

She looked like an angel, but he knew that someday she would be some man's downfall. He wasn't going to be that man.

When he moved from the shadows into the light, she drew back, a hand to her breast, then relaxed when she saw who it was.

They watched each other through the glass for a long ten seconds, then she flicked the dead bolt and opened the door.

"All quiet in the OK Corral, Sheriff?" she asked, one slender eyebrow arched slightly.

"Yeah." He checked the room, then let his gaze drift slowly over her. She was a curvy woman with a small waist, but flaring hips and full breasts. The innocence in her eyes didn't go with that body that was nothing but temptation in the flesh.

He glanced down. That's when he noticed her feet were bare. Her toes were the daintiest things he'd ever seen, rounded and pink with pale polish on the manicured nails.

He got an ache in certain places that wouldn't quit. He gave an irritated snort at his eager response to a woman who saw him only as a way out of her predicament. He quickly checked to make sure he didn't shock her with his body's flagrant behavior.

When he looked up, it was in time to catch her gaze following his. Her eyelashes flickered before she raised her gaze upward again.

"I was wondering earlier what it would take to stir you," she said in a husky murmur.

She had an eyebrow with an attitude. It lifted slightly in mocking humor at his discomfort. His response to her was obvious behind the fly of the jeans he'd changed to before making his nightly rounds of the security system.

He gestured with one hand. "Night. A bedroom. A woman ready for bed. That's about what it takes for any man." He managed to keep his voice from dropping to a register of hoarse desire, although his blood pulsed with it.

Her scent pervaded the room. She smelled sexy—of perfume and powder and a woman's secret spice. His nostrils flared as he dragged air into his lungs.

For two cents, he'd sweep her into his arms and they'd both land in that prissy white bed with its jumble of pillows covered in delicate eyelet lace pillowcases and matching sheets.

Yeah, that would be a real smart thing to do.

"Change your mind about the money?" she asked.

It took him an instant to figure out what she was talking about. "The marriage proposition," he confirmed.

"Yes."

"No way am I going to be suckered into that noose." He stuck his fingers into his back pockets with the intention of keeping them there.

A tide of pink crept up her neck and settled in her cheeks, but her smile was as cool as an icicle. "Too bad."

"What's wrong with one of those society guys at the ball tonight?"

"I don't trust them."

Her eyes issued a challenge that for a moment he wanted to accept. He controlled himself with an effort. "The implication being that I'm honorable and all that. Sorry, but that form of manipulation won't work, either."

He couldn't help but think of a form that would. All she had to do was step close and press those high, bouncy breasts against him and he'd probably roll over and let her walk on him if she wanted to.

Jessica shook her head in exasperation. Brody weighed every word she said, then used it against her. Odd, to be so trustyworthy himself, yet not to trust anyone else. Psychology class had taught her that most people suspected others of their own sins. Not Brody. He trusted no one on general principle.

"If an appeal to your better instincts won't work, what will?" she asked boldly. She liked the idea of solving her problem with Brody. As her husband, he could continue his job of protecting her at a darned good wage, then after a year…

A year of being married to Brody. It occurred to her to wonder just what else he would expect as her husband. And what she would be willing to give.

Sex?

Would she be willing to exchange her body for the security of marriage to him? Women had done so since Day One for the same or less. She instinctively knew she would get much more than security from him. Brody would know how to please a woman. He was too virile, too much a man not to be considerate of his partner. He'd see that his woman was satisfied before seeking his own total pleasure.

A delicate heat infused her skin as if someone had turned a furnace on inside her. She held his gaze with an effort and stood her ground as he moved closer.

He reached out and ran a finger along the lacy edge of her peignoir. "What do you call this?" he asked on a deep note.

An electrical shock ran through her, dropping deep into an abyss of need she'd rarely allowed to surface. She found herself wondering about his kiss and how it would feel, and exactly how he would touch a woman in passion.

She knew he was aroused. It wasn't something he could hide in those jeans that fit like skin and with a short jacket over them. Gazing into his dark eyes, she saw other passions as fleeting as a mist in sunshine. He was a man of caution.

"A peignoir," she said flippantly, pushing his hand aside.

"A temptation," he said, correcting her. "One I don't intend to try." He spun and headed for the door.

"Coward," she said softly.

He stopped but stayed with his back to her. "Or maybe I'm just not that desperate yet." He walked out.

When he stood on the other side of the door, she watched him, puzzled. He rattled the door. Oh. She went over and snapped the dead bolt into place. He tried the knob, nodded and disappeared into the darkness.

Jessica sank into her favorite chair. Weakness rushed

over her as if she'd faced down a terrible danger. Her head ached above her eyes and at the back of her neck. She rubbed her temples absently.

She went through all the men friends she had. There weren't many. Her grandfather had sent her to an all-girls prep school in Virginia. She still wrote to a couple of girl-friends from those days. At her grandfather's urging, she'd attended her grandmother's alma mater, an all-female college back east.

When she'd mentioned joining the Peace Corps after college, her trustees had been horrified. Surprisingly her grandfather had taken her side when she'd wanted to go to other countries and teach health classes as part of a foundation grant sponsored by a missionary couple. The four young women who had volunteered had been strictly chaperoned. After three years, she'd come down with a new strain of malaria and returned home.

She realized she'd hardly been in Chicago long enough to meet any adults her age, much less form lasting friend-ships, until this past year.

Her acquaintances now were mostly the bankers and at-torneys who handled her trust and directed the atrium building and other properties, which were part of her hold-ings. She knew lots of people from her charity work, but none as close friends.

She'd had one near-serious relationship: a young doctor on an intern program. He'd quarreled with a resident phy-sician and been dismissed in disgrace. He'd left the area.

Having a bodyguard cast a pall on any relationship. Brody, with his dark scowls and sharp scrutiny, would make the devil himself run for cover. If he wouldn't marry her, not even for money, who would?

Brody paced his unlit room, feeling as if he were a caged panther who needed to prowl. He still felt a sense of shock that Jessica Lockhart, heiress, had suggested marriage.

To him. Brody Smith, the kid that nobody had wanted. His own mother had deserted him when he'd been fourteen.

I love you, hon, but I got to go. Bill wants me to come with him, but there's no room for you. You're big for your age. You'll do fine.

She'd given him a twenty-dollar bill and put him on a bus to a small town where a distant relative was to take him in. He'd arrived there two years later, older and a lot wiser for his time on the road. His foster sister, an orphan whose parents had been killed in an auto accident, had already been in residence at his great-aunt's house. He'd never seen his mother again. She'd died in a fiery crash a few months after sending him on his way.

Aunt Essie was dead now, too. Carly was married to a rancher in California. Things hadn't been easy for her. She'd trusted one man who had turned out to be a liar. But the second one had been okay, in spite of an earlier divorce. He'd checked out the guy himself.

Unable to stand the confines of the room, he went outside and surveyed the perimeter of the house once more. The landscape was coldly beautiful under the glow of the winter moon that had risen and now hung low on the horizon.

On the eastern side of the house, Jessica's bedroom was dark. She'd gone to bed.

At once a picture of her in the bed came to him. White on white, her gown against the sheets. Her tousled curls, artfully streaked at the best shop—he knew because he went there with her, although they'd tried to make him wait outside—would be spread in disarray over the pillow...

He grimaced as pleasure-pain danced through him, filling him with needs that drove him on his restless, nocturnal meandering. He frowned at the dark doors, then realized someone was staring back at him.

Jessica. Standing there in her white gown, looking like a fairy princess come to life. Her outrageous request hummed through his mind. He obviously was a man who looked as if he could be bought.

Maybe he could.

He went to the door. The dead bolt snicked open. He went inside. "I'll do it."

"Thank you," she said quietly. "You won't regret it."

He doubted that. "There's a condition."

She stiffened fractionally, then nodded.

"We have to live at my ranch for the year."

"Live...at your ranch," she repeated as if trying to comprehend a strange language.

"That's the condition."

The moonlight picked up the flash of her teeth as she smiled, then she laughed, a soft relieved flutter of merriment in the moon-glazed night.

"Well, what's your answer?" he demanded. Her laughter invaded his blood, causing it to froth and pop like champagne bubbling through his veins.

"I'll do it." She laughed again.

He wondered if he'd lost his mind.

Chapter Two

Jessica moved without thinking. She closed the two steps between them and caught him by the shoulders. The next thing she knew, her hands were pinned over her head and she was flat against the wall. Brody held her captive between the wall and the warm cage of his body.

She blinked up at him in stunned surprise. She sensed the moment his reaction to her sudden move changed to one of sensual arousal. He released her and backed up.

"Sorry. You took me by surprise," he said gruffly.

"Me, too."

They stood there, only inches apart, their breaths quick and audible in the dark room. Awareness sizzled in the air between them. A strange lethargy filled her at the same time a whirlwind took control of her body. She swayed slightly and put out her hands for balance.

Brody steadied her with a hand on her arm. His fingertips brushed her breast as he did. She gasped. The whirlwind became a roar of wild yearning, bursting from some-place deeply hidden in the nooks and crannies of her soul.

"Brody?" she whispered, filled with wonder at the sensations that arced and glittered between them, surprised and enchanted as a sweet softness stole over her. She laid a hand on his chest.

His hands grasped her upper arms, and he held her when she would have moved into the warm shelter of his body. A low murmur of protest pushed its way from her throat.

"Don't," he said. His tone was harsh, like rocks being forced through a crusher.

"I'm sorry." She didn't know why she was apologizing. Her voice was husky with the desire that flooded her. They were a mere five feet from her bed, its whiteness a foil to the darkness that quivered and stirred with restless energy all around them.

It was strange…to find passion when she least expected it, to know it was there for them to share… She shivered as the magic washed over her, enchanting, beguiling, beckoning them to follow its sweet, wild call…

Brody muttered an expletive and thrust himself away. "You've bought yourself a husband, Ms. Lockhart, not a toy to be turned on at your bidding."

Brought abruptly back to earth, she watched while he locked the outside doors and left her room by the hall door. When he was gone, she wrapped her arms over her chest and felt the cold seep in. If it touched her heart, she would surely die.

Jessica heard Brody's deep voice conversing with her grandfather before she entered the breakfast room. She slowed, reluctant to face him. Chiding her sudden attack of nerves, she strode into the room with her head high.

Brody's eyes were on the door when she walked

through. Although she wore ballet slippers and made no discernible sound as she walked, he'd somehow known she was there. His eyes swept over her as if surveying a mine field where hidden explosives lurked in every inch.

She felt as self-conscious as she had when at fourteen her breasts had swelled from bud to full bloom almost overnight. She smoothed the vibrant pink sweater over her hips and wished she'd worn a blouse instead of the clinging silk knit.

"Good morning, Jessica," her grandfather said in his usual somber way.

"Good morning." She gave Brody a cool glance. "Good morning, Brody." She selected toast and a poached egg.

"Coffee or tea?" Brody asked. He appeared beside her.

"Coffee."

He poured her a cup, then refilled his own and her grandfather's. They returned to the table. She ate while the men resumed their conversation about the storm that was supposed to hit that night. When there was a lull, she put down her fork.

Waiting until her grandfather had taken a sip of coffee and replaced the cup in the saucer, she asked, "Did Brody mention our news?"

A beat of silence followed the question.

"What news is that?" the older man asked. His dark eyebrows rose fractionally.

Jessica thought he was an incredibly handsome man to be sixty-six years old. Physically he looked twenty years younger. His hair was smooth and thick and pure silver. His high forehead gave him a patrician air.

Ronald Leary had been ten years younger than her grandmother, and everyone had been scandalized at the marriage of the wealthy widow to the younger attorney in her deceased husband's firm twenty-five years ago. However, he'd been a good husband, and the marriage had been stable.

As far as Jessica was concerned, he was her grandfather. He'd been there when her beloved grandmother had died, then her father, and finally her mother. If her life as the only child in his house during vacations from boarding school had been lonely, it wasn't his fault. He'd done his best for her.

Once he'd railed against her mother and the foolish conditions of the will. Jessica, shocked and hurt, had defended her mother. Seeing that he'd hurt Jessica with his harsh words, he'd never mentioned it again. For all those reasons and more, she felt a fierce loyalty toward him.

"Brody and I are to be married."

Her grandfather froze. He flushed deep red. A blood vessel enlarged and throbbed at each side of his neck. He laid a fisted hand on the table at each side of his plate. He leaned forward in the chair, his eyes on Brody.

"Pack up and get out," he said.

"Grandfather," she protested, shocked at this turn of events. "What are you saying?"

"How much will it cost to get rid of you?" he demanded of Brody, ignoring her.

Jessica had never heard him sound so harsh and contemptuous in her life. He looked ready to leap from his chair and kill Brody on the spot.

Brody leaned back in his chair as if thinking about it. "You don't have enough money," he finally said.

Jessica gasped. Brody flicked a glance her way, then studied her grandfather with insolent poise.

Her grandfather's flush deepened, and she worried about a stroke. "Please," she said, laying a hand on his sleeve.

He shook her off. "Be damned to that fancy lawyer who

recommended you. I knew you were a fortune hunter the moment I saw you.''

Brody's lips tilted up at the corners in that maddening little grin that wasn't a smile.

''Stop it,'' Jessica said, butting in to head off the escalating tension. She may as well have spit into the wind for all the good it did her. The men continued to scrutinize each other, her grandfather angry, Brody as cool as silk.

''Did you seduce her?'' her grandfather continued, his eyes narrowing. ''Is she pregnant?''

Brody didn't answer. Instead he gave the older man a stare that would have withered a strangler fig in ten seconds flat.

She stood up. That finally got their attention. ''I am not going to sit here and be insulted and ignored. When either or both of you are ready to listen, I'll tell you my plans.''

With her back ramrod straight, she sailed out of the dining room. Her legs trembled as she rushed down the hall. She was shocked at her grandfather's accusation. She knew he was protective and all that, but to accuse Brody…

Pregnant, indeed. In her room, she curled into her favorite chair and propped her elbow on the padded arm. She covered her eyes with her hand. So much for her big announcement.

The door opened. She wasn't startled when Brody walked in unannounced. She kept a wary eye on him.

''When do you want to set the date?'' he asked. He shoved his hands into his pockets and leaned against the door. They could have been discussing an appointment for the dentist.

''As soon as possible.''

He nodded. ''I can be packed and ready to leave in an hour. We can marry in Denver and get to the ranch before the blizzard breaks.'' He smiled. It transformed his face into a work of near beauty, but not quite. He was a man who'd lived hard in the world, too hard for something so simple as beauty.

She laid a hand over her aching heart. "It's Saturday."

His smile chilled. "We can fly to Vegas for the ceremony, then head out. I assume we aren't planning on having a society wedding with all the trimmings?"

"No."

"Good. How soon can you be ready to go?"

"An hour." She rose. There was one thing she wanted to know. "Uh, about the marriage. What besides the money are you expecting from it?"

He reached for the doorknob. "No entanglements," he said in a low, ominous tone, his face darkening.

That, she assumed, meant no intimacy. To her chagrin, she didn't know if she was hurt or relieved. She recalled his warmth surrounding her when he'd held her pinned to the wall. Winters were long and cold in Colorado, she'd heard.

She nodded.

He continued to gaze at her, his eyes like deep, dark pits filled with danger and secrets too dire for her to know. A shiver plunged down her spine. For a moment, she knew real fear. It rushed over her, causing her to draw back. Then she relaxed.

Brody was danger personified, but she trusted him with her life. She didn't know why.

Finally, with a satisfied air, he walked out.

As if freed from a spell, she dashed to her closet and set out her luggage. In fifty-one minutes, she had her clothes rolled and packed with underwear, gloves and scarves tucked into the middle the way she'd learned at school. She closed and locked the last piece, then opened the door to wait for Brody.

He appeared as the clock struck the hour. His dark eyes took in her three pieces of luggage and the weekend case that held her makeup and toiletries. He nodded, as grim as a funeral attendee. Their wedding generated no joy for him.

Her grandfather met them in the foyer. "You're foolish to do this," he said. His color was nearly normal, except for the twin flags of anger that highlighted his cheekbones.

"I have to." She realized she did.

He touched her shoulder, a thing he rarely did. Expressions of affection didn't come easily to him. She hugged him, feeling the fierceness of love churn in her, then stepped back before she embarrassed both of them with tears.

"The car is here," Brody said. His hand propelled her toward the door.

She looked back as they left the house. Her grandfather stood where she'd left him, his hands clenched into fists. The harshness of his expression frightened her. Hatred gleamed in his eyes as he stared at Brody.

It was an inauspicious note on which to begin a new life.

In the car, Brody handed her a handkerchief without speaking. She wiped her eyes, leaving a dark smudge of mascara on the white cotton. Brody took the handkerchief and stuck it into his pocket when she finished.

The wind at the airport chilled her to the bone. While Brody checked their bags, the driver paused by her. "We'll miss you, Miss Jessica, the missus and I." He tipped his hat and left them. She watched the taillights disappear.

A hand touched her shoulder. "It's time."

She looked up, her thoughts in a whirl. She wanted to chase after the car and return home where she knew who she was and what would happen the next day and the next…

Brody's midnight gaze shot questions at her. She realized he thought she would change her mind, that he'd expected it all along. She lifted her chin.

"Yes. I'm ready."

The wind shifted and hit them full force. The shiny strands of Brody's hair caught the sun as they lifted and settled across his forehead. His breath huffed out frostily, as if he sighed.

He slipped an arm around her shoulders. "Come," he said. The tone was oddly gentle.

Brody slipped the ring on his bride's icy finger. She'd seemed in a daze since they'd left her home that morning. It was early afternoon. Flying west, they'd gained an hour.

They signed the papers that made them officially husband and wife. Leaving the wedding parlor, they walked out into seventy-degree heat. "Do you want to spend the night and fly in tomorrow?"

She shook her head.

The cab was waiting. They returned to the airport. In an hour, they were on their way north. They landed in Denver well before dark. His sports utility vehicle, with its necessary four-wheel drive, was at his office. They took a cab downtown.

"Is it far?" she asked, practically her first sentence in the past six hours.

"An hour's drive." He helped the driver move their bags from the cab to the rear of the sports ute.

After the cab left, he frowned at his wife. She stood there in the lengthening shadows of the parking lot, her gaze on the lofty white peaks that formed a backdrop to Denver's skyscrapers.

Her gray eyes reflected the lavender shades of twilight. He recognized sadness and a longing for things he couldn't describe in those translucent depths. She squared her shoulders as if facing off against the world. "Shall we go?"

He was reminded of the boy he'd once been, lost and abandoned and frightened…and determined that no one would know it. He cleared his throat. "Yeah."

"Tell me about your ranch. Is that where you live when you're not out solving cases?" she asked when they were on their way out of town.

The highway was clear. He punched on the cruise control. The act of driving gave him something to concentrate on and he regained his equilibrium. Jessica Lockhart…Smith, he corrected, wasn't anything like the boy he'd once been.

She'd simply seen a way out of her dilemma and had grabbed it. For himself, he'd get a nice bundle of cash out of the deal. That's all he wanted and was as far as he'd involve himself. Except for keeping her safe for the year.

Jessica had trouble keeping her eyes open. They were passing through a small town tucked up in a mountain valley above Denver. The town drifted behind them. The road narrowed into a winding county highway. She didn't know where they were. She realized she didn't care. Being with Brody was enough at the moment. She felt safe…

"We're here."

She sat up and peered through the deep twilight. A ranch house was barely visible among a stand of tall trees. It appeared to be made of timber and stone. "Is this your home?"

"Yes." He shoved open the door. Cold air rushed into the sports ute. Brody handed her the weekend case when she hopped out to help him with the luggage. "I'll get the rest."

She followed him up the snow-dusted flagstones to the house. Shivers raced along her back. Her legs trembled. She couldn't decide what she was afraid of.

Not Brody. That much she knew.

Inside, he set her luggage in a stone foyer, then turned the thermostat up. She heard the stir of air, then felt it cascade onto her shoulders from a vent overhead. Her mouth dried up like a desert lake when he started forward again.

He handled her three large cases with ease, reminding her of how strong he was. He led her to a bedroom tucked under the stairs. A sturdy oak bed angled out from the corner rather than being set against the wall. A cedar chest was conveniently located at the foot of the bed. A rocking chair and table occupied another corner. A corner cabinet was filled with books and a dried arrangement of leaves and grasses in a huge snifter.

"The bathroom is through that door," Brody informed her. "There's a walk-in closet here." He placed her luggage in front of the chest, then opened doors.

The bed was larger than standard. She thought of them in it, of his arms around her, holding her close. No one had hugged her since her mother had died.

"Is this your room?" she asked, letting herself look at him, this silent, scowling man who was her husband.

Husband.

The word astonished her. An unbearable lightness stole over her, a mist of longing for the life that eluded her.

"It's yours." He strode to the door. "For a year." He walked out without a backward glance.

She sat on the bed and rubbed a hand over the old-fashioned quilt. She wondered if she dared invite him to share it. With that thought haunting her, she unpacked her nightgown, washed up and went to sleep almost immediately.

The blizzard had struck during the night, silently dumping its load of snow over the landscape while she slept. She dressed in wool slacks and an oversize sweater of Nordic design in blue and white. In thick sports socks, she padded into the main quarters of the ranch house.

The living room and kitchen were modern in creature comforts, but rustic in tone. The outer wall was made from twelve-inch logs that were square cut, the caulking painted white. A stone fireplace separated the living room from the kitchen-family room. She walked into the kitchen.

A half pot of coffee awaited her on the kitchen counter. She poured a cup and glanced out the window.

Her heart skipped around in her chest when she spotted a bundled figure out in a paddock. The errant organ righted itself with a dull thud when she realized the man wasn't Brody, but someone shorter and thinner. The man was checking the sheep in the pasture.

Laughter bubbled out of her when she spotted the llamas on the far side of the barn. They were watching the man with expressions of avid curiosity. Occasionally they glanced at each other and nodded as if approving his actions.

She ate two pieces of toast with peanut butter and jelly before donning boots and the fox fur and heading outside.

Standing at the end of the porch leading off from the kitchen, her breath caught at the beauty around her. The sky was the incredible blue of postcards, the snow so white it hurt her eyes. A row of jagged mountain peaks rose to the north of the house, awesome in their grandeur.

Closer to the house was a ridge of rimrock that slanted

upward at a thirty degree angle, ending in a fifty-foot cliff. When the snow cleared, she'd hike up there.

From the porch, tracks sank deep into the fresh snow. Brody. She wondered how long he'd been up and where he was.

After another minute of indecision, she plunged into the snow, stretching her steps to match his. Although he was a bit under six feet tall, he had a long stride. She had to leap from one print to another. All went well for about half the distance to the barn, then she caught her toe on an unseen object and fell facedown into a fluffy drift.

She floundered helplessly in the soft, dry powder. The more she fought to sit up, the deeper she sank. When she opened her eyes, she could see nothing but snow. It surrounded her, filling her mouth and nose, stinging her eyes as she tried to fight her way out. It pressed upon her from top and bottom, from every side as well.

When she realized she couldn't tell which way was up, panic set in. She quickly quelled it. Lying still, she cleared a space in front of her nose with her gloved hand. The snow caved in. She cupped both hands in front of her face to maintain a breathing hole.

Her breath sounded loud in the confined space, and the air seemed thin. If only she'd yelled a greeting to the shepherd, he might have come to her aid. As it was, no one knew she was in trouble. She might be trapped until the snow melted.

Stop it, she chided her runaway imagination. She surely wasn't going to suffocate right there in the yard, less than a hundred feet from the house. She merely had to get her bearings.

When she'd fallen, she'd gone in headfirst. She was pretty sure she'd slithered down an embankment of some kind, but not a terribly deep one. She'd once read that if she was caught in an avalanche, she should swim. It seemed silly, but she'd try it.

With the weight of the snow all around her, she found she couldn't swim, but she could make a crawling motion rather like a clumsy frog. Dizziness washed over her. The panic edged closer.

She paused and listened. The silence was absolute. Being under the snow was like being underwater. The snow crept around her face and down her neck. The cold seeped into her. It was, she found, very peaceful—

Something grasped her foot in talons of iron. She started, then struggled for all she was worth against the monster that was dragging her deeper into the snow. Panic took over.

The next moment was a confused swirl of snow and fox fur as her coat slid past her. *Avalanche.* She flailed as hard as she could. Swim, she ordered her frozen limbs.

"Be still, dammit," a growly masculine voice ordered.

Suddenly the world reappeared through a haze of fur and falling snow, blinding sunlight and dark eyes that snapped with fury. Brody let go her leg and caught her under her arms. The world whirled again, then righted itself as Brody stood and she was set on her feet.

Rough hands brushed snow off her face and settled her coat over her body after giving it a good shake.

She laid her hands on his arms to steady herself. She grinned, knowing she looked foolish, but unable to help it. "Good morning," she said.

"Have you lost your mind? Only fools wander around in the snow when they don't know the lay of the land."

"I guess that puts me in my place." She grinned some more, so happy to see him she wanted to give him a kiss. In fact, that sounded like a fine idea. She grabbed the lapels of his plaid wool jacket and planted one on his jaw, missing his mouth by a quarter inch. When she would have tried again, he held her off.

"I wanted to thank you," she explained. "I thought I was going to suffocate."

He was unrelenting. "You should have." He looped an arm around her and propelled her to the porch. He lifted her easily and set her down on the top step. "Stay inside. I don't have time to chase after you like a Saint Bernard dashing to the rescue every time you get a fool notion in your head."

"Have you had breakfast?"

The change of subject caused him to blink. "No."

"That's why you're so grouchy," she concluded. "I was coming to ask what time you'd be at the house. Do you like eggs *en papillote?*"

"No."

"You don't know what they are. You'll love them. I can make gravy, too."

"I won't be coming in. Don and I have work to do."

"Don?"

"Don Adono. He works for me."

"The shepherd I saw in the pasture earlier?"

"Yeah. Lucky for you he saw you fall in the dip. A creek runs through here in the spring." He gestured to the place where she'd fallen in.

"Why didn't you fall?"

"I knew it was there. I jumped across."

"No wonder that step was so long. I was wondering how to manage it when I stumbled over something."

"There're rocks along the sides of the creek. Stay put." He walked off.

"Wait. When will you be in?"

He turned and watched her for a long second. She put a hand up to her hair self-consciously and felt the snow clinging to the strands. She noticed the snow on him. If she had as much snow on her as he had on him, and she was sure she did, they must look like the fabled abominable snowmen in person.

She leaned forward and brushed the snow off his lapels. "I thought I was in an avalanche. When you yanked me out by my ankle," she added at his ominous frown. "I thought…well, never mind… Thanks for coming to the rescue." She patted him on the cheek. "Breakfast in half an hour."

Leaving him standing on the steps, she retreated gracefully into the house, then flew around hanging up her coat and tugging off her boots. She quickly combed her hair into order with her fingers and shook off the last of the snow.

Her cheeks flamed with cold and excitement. She paused to look at the plain gold band on her left hand. This was her first morning as a wife. And what a start.

With a laugh, she checked out the refrigerator and pantry. She decided on sausage and eggs scrambled with green peppers and onions, cottage-fried potatoes and hot flour tortillas. With a jar of salsa to go with the meal, she had it ready in thirty minutes. Forty-five minutes later, she admitted Brody wasn't going to come in.

She propped her chin on her hands and thought the situation over. She wanted to make this year easy on both of them. She'd be a wife if it killed her…or him.

Chapter Three

The door opened. Jessica watched in pleased surprise as a bulky figure entered the kitchen. Another, smaller male followed Brody inside. The men took off their gloves, coats and hats, then washed up at the utility sink in the corner. Brody didn't offer to introduce her or the other man.

She had a hard time tearing her gaze from her husband. He was dressed in jeans and a flannel shirt. He wore blue waffle-knit underwear, visible at the neck, under the flannel. A glow produced by the cold permeated his dusky skin. The freshness of the outdoors clung to his broad shoulders. She'd never seen him look so vibrant, so alive and virile. She swallowed and forced her attention to the older man.

"Good morning. You must be Don Adono. Brody has spoken of you. I'm Jessica." She glanced at Brody, then tilted her chin up. "Jessica Smith, Brody's wife."

The shepherd was one of those men whose age was impossible to determine. His days in the sun had given him a weather-beaten appearance, but his wiry frame and movements indicated strength and agility. His hair had some gray sprinkled through it, but not copiously. He was close to her grandfather's age, she decided, going by the lines on his face.

"Pleased to meet you," the shepherd replied with old-fashioned courtesy. He smiled and bobbed his head.

Hmm, her husband could take some lessons in manners from his hired hand. He had yet to offer her a greeting.

"Thank you. I'll get your breakfast. Do be seated, gentlemen." She glanced at Brody when he came to the table.

His expression was not encouraging. He took a chair and watched without a word while she took the bowls from the oven and placed them on stone squares she'd found on a shelf. The squares must have been left over from those in the entry hall since they were the same design.

She tried not to watch him as if she were a neophyte trying to please her master while he sampled her cooking. Instead she rolled a tortilla around the scrambled eggs and spooned some salsa over it. Don put everything, including the sausage and potatoes, inside the tortilla, wrapped it up and, holding it in his hands, ate it with quick, neat bites. Brody did the same.

After finishing, Jessica watched in amazement as the men ate three servings each, cleaning out every bowl. She thought they would have eaten more if she'd prepared it.

"Verra good," Don said, displaying a slight accent.

She asked him where he was from originally.

"I was born here, but my parents were Basque."

"How interesting. Were they from the French or Spanish side of the mountains?"

"Spanish."

Brody's eyes flicked to her in surprise when, in Spanish, she asked Don what other languages he spoke. She and the shepherd discussed the Basque region and the number of Basque families now living in the States. Don had relatives in California, a sister and her husband plus two nieces and three nephews. His two brothers and their wives and children lived on the family ranch in southern Colorado.

She switched back to English so Brody wouldn't feel left out. "I always wanted brothers and sisters. I felt I'd missed so much by not having a large family. Did you feel that way?" she asked her husband.

"No."

The blunt answer momentarily halted the conversation. "But you had a foster sister, didn't you? That must have been nice. Does she have a family?"

He nodded, then sipped his coffee. The furnace clicked off. The silence eddied around them. Deciding to use it to advantage, she smiled sweetly and waited.

"Carly lives on a ranch in northern California," he finally said. "Her husband has a son by a former marriage who lives with them. They're expecting a child later this year."

Jessica thought of having children. Hers and Brody's? He'd probably have a coronary if she mentioned wanting a child. But a baby... The idea grabbed her and wouldn't let go. She wondered what kind of father he'd make.

Was there nurturing or tenderness in this tough hombre she'd married? She doubted she would ever know. That caused an odd hurting twist inside. She pushed aside the useless thoughts.

"Could I speak to you?" she asked politely when the men rose to leave.

He scowled impatiently. "I'll meet you at the stable," he told the shepherd.

After the older man left, Jessica refilled hers and Brody's coffee cups, then resumed her seat. "I need to know the setup here. Shall I do the cooking and take care of the house while you do outside chores, or do you prefer another arrangement?"

Something like amazement stormed through his dark eyes, then his mouth moved slightly in a cynical snarl. "What do you know about taking care of a house?"

"I can do it." She waited.

He studied her for a tense thirty seconds. "I have a woman from a neighboring ranch come in twice a month. She cleans, changes the beds and washes the clothes. Don and I do our own cooking and cleaning in the meantime."

She nodded. "I'll do the cooking and keep the place picked up during the week. Do you need me to do anything outside?"

"Like what?"

"I can ride. I've been on a cattle drive—"

"At a dude ranch, on vacation?"

She quelled her rising temper at his contemptuous manner. "I spent several summers with a friend whose family owned a ranch. A working ranch," she added for good measure. "I can pull calves, brand, open gates, whatever is necessary."

"I'm impressed." He stood and put his hat, gloves and coat on. "Just stay out of the way and out of trouble. I don't have time to watch you every second. The ewes will start dropping their lambs any day. Blizzards are one of their favorite times. Like most females, they like to make life as hard as possible."

She flung her napkin on her plate and stood, the chair screeching on the vinyl-coated wood flooring. "You're getting paid a damn good salary and bonus to watch me every second."

The next thing she knew, he was in her face, a handful of sweater gathered into a big fist that rested under her chin. "I'll make sure you're safe," he told her with an icy snarl, "but nobody owns me. You got that?"

She returned his hateful stare without a blink. "Loud and clear. If we're going to make it through a year without serious words between us, we'd better come to some agreement about what we expect from each other."

He relaxed his hold and stepped away. "I expect you to do what I tell you. I expect you to stay out of the way and not interfere with work the way you did today."

"Stay out of the way. Don't interfere." She crossed her arms and tapped her fingers. "I can handle that." She paused for emphasis. "But don't tell me what to do, Brody."

"I knew there was a reason I shouldn't take on this job. Are we going to fight over every single thing?"

"I don't know. Are we?" She sent the verbal ball back to his court.

His eyes narrowed, but that was all the emotion he displayed. He walked out, giving the door a solid slam behind him. She watched him cross the yard and jump the gully she'd fallen into. Someday she'd find out what, besides passion, lay beneath that tough exterior.

Jessica yawned, then stared at the ceiling. The bed was warm. She hated to get up. She wasn't a morning person, but she'd learned to rise early during her years abroad. Now she woke up at six even though she'd stayed awake reading until midnight the previous evening.

She'd left a pot of stew on the stove and gone to her room at ten. Brody hadn't come in until very late. She wondered if he'd watched from the barn until she'd turned off the light in her bedroom. She'd heard him upstairs in the shower soon after he'd arrived. Later, she'd listened as he came down the stairs and entered the kitchen. He'd paused outside her door before going to his room for the night.

Don Adono had a house of his own. She'd seen him go to it and lights come on when she'd been peeling vegetables for the stew. She wondered if Brody had eaten lunch at Don's house.

She sighed and watched the snow hit the windows of the cozy bedroom. They hadn't had but one day's respite from the blizzard. The news last night had included a weather alert. The state police had asked that everyone keep off the roads until the storm let up and they could clear the highways.

The wind whistled around the eaves of the snug house. March was supposed to be windy, but it was the last day of the month. In like a lion, out like a lamb. That was the saying.

Brody roared like a lion…well, he acted fierce, but maybe his heart was gentle. If anyone could reach it.

She blinked the sleep from her eyes, startled at the direction of her thoughts. She had only a year. That probably wasn't enough time to dig through the layers of granite Brody had encased himself in.

Sluggish, she pushed the covers off and shivered as the cooler air of the room hit her. Maybe she should start sleeping in a sweat suit. She hurried to the shower.

When she entered the kitchen, she gave a start at finding Brody at the table, a coffee cup in his hand. He was scowling at the blizzard howling outside the window.

The temperature on the back porch was eighteen degrees, a drop of ten degrees from the night before. "Cold," she commented. "What are your plans for the day?"

"Staying warm and hoping the sheep don't drop any more lambs until the storm is over." He gave her one cursory glance, then went back to eyeing the storm.

"Do they usually have them in March?"

"Only if there's a blizzard." He sounded as if he thought the ewes planned the births to inconvenience him.

She smiled at his exasperation. It almost made him seem human. "Did you get the pregnant ewes in the barn?"

"Hardly. We have a thousand head."

"Oh. Are all of them expecting?"

"About eighty percent."

"I noticed a dozen llamas in one paddock. Are they expecting, too?"

"Three of the older females are."

"What are you doing with them?"

He turned his dark gaze on her, causing little tendrils of electricity to arc through her. "I'm thinking of establishing a herd for wool."

She nodded in understanding. "I've heard their fur is some of the warmest in the world. Are you going to have ski clothes made from the wool?"

"No, work clothes for ranchers who have to drag lambs out of blizzards to keep them from freezing to death."

"That makes sense," she said agreeably. She mixed up a batch of biscuits and put them in the oven. "Do you like fried eggs?" She cracked one into the pan for herself. When he didn't answer, she gave him an inquiring glance.

Brody thought his blood was going to boil. Jessica wasn't wearing a bra under the sweat suit. Her breasts bounced in an unbounded way with each move she made. She had to know she was driving him crazy. He needed to touch her, to know the smooth heat of her skin once more…

He cursed silently and gripped the cup with an unsteady hand. He and Don had been up half the night taking care of lambs and ewes, now he had to face *her* when he was tired and his defenses were down.

He risked a glance at her perfectly shaped rear as she bent over to check the biscuits. She'd made the damn things from scratch. He'd seen it with his own eyes. He hadn't known she knew which end of a skillet went on the stove.

Muscles rippled jauntily at him when she straightened. He wanted to walk over to her and take her right there, maybe sitting on the counter, his body snug in hers…

He suppressed a groan and forced his attention back to the storm. He tried to figure out why he'd thought it was a good idea to get her here before the storm broke. Oh, yeah, so nothing would happen to her if her brakes went out on a slick road back at her home. The storm was supposed to blanket the entire northern part of the country.

Gazing out the window, he thought nature was doing its best to comply with the weather forecast. He rubbed a weary hand over his face.

"Breakfast."

Something wonderful wafted below his nose. He removed his hand and stared at eggs cooked to perfection, two slices of ham browned just right, biscuits that looked as if they'd float right off the plate and a steaming bowl of gravy.

If that wasn't enough to drive a man wild, her scent floated around him as she reached past him to refresh his coffee cup. She used lavender-scented soap and shampoo, he recalled, that matched her perfume.

"Look," he said, almost in desperation. "You don't have to do the housewife act."

"Why not?" She sounded insolent.

"Because you're not a wife." He tried to lighten up. "I don't want to get used to this, then have it stop when you get tired of playing house."

"I am your wife." She gave him a level perusal, then went to the phone. "Shall I call Don and see if he wants to come over?"

"He's already eaten by now."

She nodded and prepared a plate for herself. When she joined him at the table, he realized she wore thick socks but no shoes. It made her seem more approachable, more like plain Jessica Smith and not Jessica Lacey Lockhart of the Virginia Laceys and the Chicago Lockharts.

The food was perfect, but he couldn't concentrate on it. He was too aware of the woman next to him and the fact...the awesome fact...that she was his wife.

For one year.

That was something else he didn't intend to forget. He wasn't going to get used to having her around. *I love you, hon, but I got to go.* He knew about women. His own mom hadn't been able to stick around.

He'd learned early, after his father had left them, then his mother had opted out, not to trust anyone with his whole heart. It only got in the way when it was time to move on.

He broke open a biscuit and watched the steam rise and disappear. He ladled gravy over the halves, then took a bite. Ambrosia. It was the best meal he'd ever eaten. Except for the stew and hot bread ready in the oven when he got in late last night. That had warmed his insides as no fire ever could.

Something else that could warm a man was a passionate woman waiting for him in bed.

Frowning at the woman who quietly ate her breakfast as she contemplated the snow that fell steadily outside the windows, he felt danger closing in. A man could get in over his head before he knew it with a woman like her.

On the surface, she seemed to be the answer to a lonely man's dreams. He knew her for the socialite she was. Charity work was a way for rich people to feel good about themselves, meet for lunch at expensive restaurants and get their pictures in the paper. He'd seen it all before.

He'd almost fallen for one of his client's daughters. Until he'd mentioned marriage in a casual way. She'd made it plain he was great for fun and games, but not up to her social register when it came to bloodlines.

He could handle that as long as he knew where he stood.

The trouble with Jessica was he didn't know any such thing. She didn't act the way she was supposed to. He'd thought she'd want to head right back to Chicago when she saw his home and the wilderness surrounding the ranch. She hadn't said a word about the isolation or lack of servants. Instead she'd pitched in without being asked. It made him uneasy.

"Why the big frown? Aren't the eggs to your liking?"

He refocused his thoughts. "They're fine." He paused. "The biscuits are good, too. Everything is."

"But?"

"I just wonder how long it's going to last." He gave her an assessing glance. She'd last a week at the outside.

"For a year?" she suggested, that one slender brow, the one with an attitude, going up slightly, mocking his doubts.

Mocking? No, by damn, she was challenging him.

"We'll see," he said.

She smiled and didn't say a word.

* * *

Brody hit the window frame with the flat of his hand. The blizzard showed no signs of abating. The weather had been fitful for five days with no clearing in sight. It was one of the worst storms in recorded history. One side of the cabin was buried in drifts to the porch rafters.

From the second-floor bedroom where he was sleeping—or not sleeping, as the case may be—he could see Don dropping hay off the flatbed for the cattle.

They'd spent the morning collecting ewes and lambs and bringing them in to the inner paddock. They'd built a storm shelter with bales of hay set at ninety-degree angles to the barn and used the tractor scoop to keep the area relatively clear of snow. He wondered how many lambs and calves he'd lose this year.

His salary and bonus would cover the loss. He frowned. Jessica's money. He hadn't gotten to the bank to deposit the check for the first month yet.

Going to his desk, he looked at the amount and her signature at the bottom. The other trustees had been dismayed when she'd called and told them she was married. When the storm was over, he planned to forward a certified copy of their marriage license so they and her grandfather would know the marriage was for real.

He'd wondered if either of the three could be in on the attempts on her life when he'd taken the case. A discreet check had disclosed no skulduggery. An audit of the books had proven her money was wisely invested and carefully guarded.

Still, he had a gut feeling that all was not as it appeared on the surface. As Jessica's husband, he had more leeway to follow his instincts. He'd hired his own investigator to check into a few details he was interested in.

Her uncle, for one. The man seemed to have recouped

his losses from prior bad investments and appeared to be doing well.

Brody had learned never to go by appearances.

Then there was the grandfather. The old man had nearly had apoplexy when he'd learned of the marriage. Strange that all his attention had been focused on the groom and not the bride. Odd, too, was the fact that her grandfather had managed to isolate a woman of her charm from most eligible males, thus ensuring her single state. Were the two men conspiring to keep her fortune for themselves?

A grim smile crimped the corners of his mouth. Little did they know, to paraphrase an old novel he'd once read, that the marriage could be annulled quite honestly and legally.

A tightening in his nether regions reminded him that this chaste state of affairs was not to his body's liking. Damn, he was having erotic dreams every night as if he were a pubescent teenager with hormone surges.

From his open door, he detected signs of life below. Turning from the storm, he went downstairs to see what his wife would cook for breakfast this morning. Yesterday it had been whole-wheat pancakes, so delicate he'd hardly had to chew.

Don had taken to coming over and having the midday meal with them. Jessica always sent him home with enough food for his supper, too. She'd cooked a roast on Monday and prepared different dishes from it all week. When the housekeeper hadn't been able to get over, she'd cleaned house, too.

However, she'd asked before going into his room. Feeling guilty, he'd cleaned it himself and washed the sheets and the stack of towels accumulating in the bathroom. She'd made up the bed with fresh sheets, though, and left a lingering trace of her lavender-based perfume to haunt him every minute he was there.

Entering the kitchen, he saw Jessica with a cookbook in hand, leafing through the recipes. "Run out of ideas?"

She glanced up, her gray eyes as beautiful as a cat's, hazy with the misty translucence of rain seen across a great distance.

They unnerved him, those eyes. They seemed to gaze at some point far beyond the horizon, seeking things that no mere mortal could see. Sometimes he wanted to ask what she sought when she stood gazing out the window at the mountains.

He didn't. She'd probably think he was a fool.

"No, just browsing."

"What smells so good?"

"Oatmeal."

"Oh."

Her smile switched from warm and sexy to teasing. "Yes, Oliver, you may have a second bowl."

"Of oatmeal? No, thanks."

"You'll eat those words. Don is going to join us. I thought you both could use something that would warm you up and stick to your ribs after being out in that weather."

"It's zero today," he commented, recalling the harsh bite of the cold through thermal underwear, jeans and waterproof pants.

She made clicking sounds of disapproval and proceeded to set the table. His mouth actually watered when she set a bowl of the porridge in front of him. It smelled of cinnamon and spices he couldn't identify. Butter floated on top along with caramelized brown sugar. A loaf of cinnamon bread came out of the oven. She wrapped it in a towel and set it in a wooden bowl before placing it and a bread knife on the table.

"Eat up before it gets cold," she advised. She poured a pitcher of milk and brought it to him.

The scent of lavender wafted around him along with the cinnamon and oatmeal. Her hip brushed his arm as she set the small pitcher down. Without thinking, he reached out.

His hand settled on her waist and slid along the enticing curve of her hip. He was aware of her in every clamoring cell of his body. He needed more than food for sustenance.

She put a hand on his shoulder as if she needed support, then she slipped her fingers under his hair, which had grown to collar length, and caressed the back of his neck.

Heat like a flash fever ran through him.

When she made no move to run from him, he let his hand glide along her thigh. Again she wore a sweat suit, this time in a forest green with leaves embroidered on the front. Again she wore no bra, but he'd felt the line of her underwear high on her leg. He moved his hand under the shirt and up to her back.

As smooth as silk, with no strap crossing the slender expanse of her rib cage.

He swallowed. His mouth dried up as if dusted with bonemeal. He couldn't dislodge the knot that had formed in his throat. Or the ridge that bloomed in the sweats he'd changed into when he'd returned to the house.

Glancing up, he found her gaze on his arousal. Her face took on a thoughtful mien. He wondered how far she'd let him go before she demanded he stop.

"I had wondered if sex was to be a part of our bargain," she said, her voice as soft as a whisper.

It shocked him into action. He jerked his hand away from her warmth and out of her shirt. He couldn't believe he'd lost himself that way, forgetting everything but the feel of her.

"No." His voice came out a growl of anger.

"I think…" She gazed past him out the window, then back at him. "I think I wouldn't mind."

Blood surged through him in so many places at once, he couldn't respond for a second. When he could get his bearings in a world gone crazy, it was too late. Don was on the porch, stomping snow off his boots before he came in.

Jessica went to the counter and poured another cup of coffee. "I was afraid we were going to have to come rescue you. You must be frozen by now."

The old shepherd grinned in his bashful way as he hung up his outer clothing, then took the place set for him.

Brody realized his seemingly guileless wife had enchanted his hired hand just as much as she had him a moment ago. He'd be on his guard against such foolishness in the future.

After the delicious meal, he and Don went out to check the ewes once more. They cleared snow and left it piled up for a windbreak against the fence. Any protection was better than none from the fierce wind that beat down from the northwest.

It was four o'clock and already as dark as twilight when he entered the house again. A fire crackled in the stone fireplace in the living room. His wife was asleep on the sofa.

He sat on the floor and removed his insulated boots, then set them on the hearth to dry. He stretched his toes toward the flames. Ah, that felt good. It was the first time his feet had been warm in hours.

He leaned against the sofa. Behind him, Jessica turned

to her side. Her hand dangled over his shoulder. He risked a glance at her. Sound asleep.

Stuffing a floor pillow behind him, he let his head rest on the sofa. In a minute, he felt a caress on his neck.

She continued to rub lightly along his neck and collarbone until he sighed and closed his eyes. He didn't know when her hand stilled. He went to sleep.

Jessica woke reluctantly. Her dream was of summer fields dotted with wildflowers and shady pine woods. She breathed deeply and inhaled the scent of balsam and subtle spice. Instinctively she pushed closer to the wonderful aroma and felt crisp strands of hair shift over her face.

Opening her eyes, she realized it was Brody's hair that had made her dream of piney woods and fields of fresh flowers. He smelled of shampoo and aftershave and an enticing masculine warmth that sent waves of heat shimmering through her.

She snuggled closer and let herself drift, a strange happiness suffusing her. Or maybe it was contentment. Whatever it was, she'd never felt it before.

With careful movements, she smoothed the strands of black hair off his forehead. He had nicely shaped ears, set close to his head, the rim a smooth arch ending in a thin lobe. She drew a finger around the edge and noticed he'd once had his left earlobe pierced.

That small fact seemed intimate, as if she'd discovered a wonderful secret about him that only she knew. If they had been really married, as in heart and soul married, what hopes and wishes would they confide in the quiet of their bedroom, perhaps after making love?

She would never know those things with Brody, not in their year together. During the few weeks he'd taken over her life, she'd learned practically nothing of his. She'd been stunned that he'd made living at the ranch a condition of the marriage.

However, she could see why he had wanted to come home. It was the most beautiful place she'd ever been. There was something wild but peaceful about the mountains and this secure valley tucked in a fold between the hills. It made her heart soar, and for the first time as an adult, she felt a freedom she'd never had.

Brody had given this gift to her, this freedom to soar—

He turned his head, and she realized he was awake. In the dying embers of the fire, with no lights on in the house, his eyes seemed fathomless. They invited her to come to him...

A sensation rather like pain arced through her breasts. Her nipples beaded beneath the fleeced cotton of her sweat top.

She stopped stroking the silky strands of his hair and dropped her hand to the sofa, self-conscious at being caught touching him. He'd made it plain he was off limits.

He pushed himself to a sitting position and tossed the floor pillow aside. Electric currents ran over her nerves. He was watching her with such an odd expression, one almost of dislike, but with an intensity that drew her in like a netted butterfly. She couldn't look away.

Slowly his head came down. She realized he was going to kiss her. Her pulse pounded wildly, and her breath became trapped in her throat. She swallowed painfully.

Brody tilted his head slightly to the side, questioning her and what was happening. She didn't look away.

Letting his mouth settle lightly on hers, he flicked out his tongue and followed the outline of her lips. He'd been wanting to do that for days, he vaguely realized. He also knew his guard was down. He didn't care.

Her lips moved under his, and he felt her draw in a shaky breath before she pressed forward ever so little, enough to indicate she wanted more. Elation swept through him like champagne on an empty stomach.

He touched her shoulder. Part of him marveled at the delicacy of bone and tissue that composed this woman.

His wife.

The title still seemed odd to him, as odd as the one of husband. He couldn't relate it to himself or marriage to them.

Something savage rose up to remind him it wasn't a marriage in any sense of the word. He'd been a convenience to an heiress, a means to an end with her freedom from a will that had put her in danger the ultimate goal. He'd better remember that.

Her tongue touched his. He stiffened as fire shot through him in places he'd thought had shriveled and died years ago. Her touch brought them to painful, throbbing life.

"Brody," she whispered, an urgent sound of need that burned all thoughts from his head. She pressed against him.

Those breasts, those wonderful bouncy breasts that had teased and irritated him for weeks, knocked the breath out of him with just a touch. Closing his eyes to reason and self-preservation, he gathered her in and kissed her as if there was no tomorrow.

His hands, freed of restraint, slipped under the forest green top and stroked over skin so satiny smooth, it was like touching warm butter. Making a space between them, he glided up her rib cage and found the treasure.

Holding her was like holding a moonbeam that had come to life. She was life and heat and every whimsy he'd ever had. When her breast beaded under his touch, he groaned and pulled back slightly. He had to see her, to enjoy fully this feast of the senses…now…before he woke…

Jessica almost sobbed as pleasure spiraled deep into the center of her being. Being kissed and held and caressed by Brody was the most wonderful thing she'd ever experienced. When he pushed her top up and his mouth closed over her breast, she almost cried out.

His tongue circled the engorged tip. His hands roamed over her at will. She slipped her hands under his sweats and caressed the smooth skin of his back. A shudder went through him.

He jerked his head up. "What the hell are we doing?"

"Making love?" she ventured, all her certainty fleeing as a dark scowl settled over his face.

"Entanglements," he stated. He pushed her hands off him and stood. "I'm not one of your toys, Jessica, to be picked up or laid aside at your pleasure. If you play the seductress, you'll pay the consequences."

She smoothed her top down. "What are they?"

He glared at her as if she'd cheated on some rules that only he knew. Then he walked out.

She heard his feet hitting the steps up to his room, then the firm closing of the door. She lay there and thought about being his wife while the fire in the hearth and the passion inside her slowly turned to ash.

Chapter Four

Jessica jumped when the phone rang. Other than a couple of calls from her trustees after she'd informed them of her marriage, no one had called. She knew Brody had a phone in his bedroom office with a private line and that he used it to communicate with his office in Denver.

A few times during the week, she'd heard the high-pitched tones of a modem as he sent or received messages. At odd hours, she'd heard the *clackety-clack* of his fax machine, as if someone rushed out messages no matter what the hour in their time zone. Once she'd heard the noise at five in the morning.

She reached the wall telephone next to the planning center in the kitchen just as it shrilled a third time. "Hello," she said, holding the receiver between her chin and shoulder while she put on a fresh pot of coffee.

The static hum of the line greeted her. "Hello?" she tried again, a bit louder. The line went dead. She hung up, then clicked the coffeemaker on. Sitting on the high kitchen stool, she gazed outside.

No signs of her husband this bright, sunshiny morning.

Overnight the weather had changed. The wind that had been blowing steadily from the northwest for a week now swept toward them from gentler climes due west. It delivered on the promise of spring that March had failed to produce.

Upstairs, Jessica heard the phone in Brody's office ring. It was abruptly cut off on the fourth ring. The answering machine had picked up. A few seconds after that, the wall phone rang again, startling her.

"Hello," she said in a cooler tone than the first time she'd answered. She had a hunch it was the same person who'd just called the office phone and gotten the machine.

"Who is this?" a female voice demanded.

"Who are you trying to reach?"

There was a beat of silence. "Brody."

"He isn't available. May I take a message?" For some reason, Jessica was surprised that a woman had the ranch number. She'd somehow formed the ridiculous notion that Brody had never had a woman there. Furthermore, the knowledge that he surely had stirred up some rather clamoring emotions in her that she would prefer not to explore.

"He is staying at the ranch then?"

"Yes." Jessica wondered where else this person thought he might stay. In town, she answered her own question. He had an office there. Maybe he had an apartment, too. After all, it was a good hour's commute from the ranch to the city.

"And you are?"

Jessica didn't know whether to be amused or exasperated at the blatant probing of the other female. She seemed to think Jessica was intruding or something. Well, there was a way to squelch that suspicion.

"Brody's wife." There, let her think about that.

"What!"

The shriek nearly made Jessica drop the phone. She clutched it firmly. As calm as a cat, she reiterated her position.

"You can't be," the caller declared. "He would never…without telling a soul…yes, he would. Tell him I'm going to kill him when I see him. And I'll see him as soon as the roads are clear."

"I beg your pardon?" Jessica was alarmed. She had a thing or two to say to Brody about women who thought they could drop in whenever they pleased.

"Tell him…never mind." There was another pause. "So, when did the nuptials take place? And where?"

Jessica used her best boarding school tone—cool, snobby and condescending. "Las Vegas. A week—"

The words had hardly left her lips when the woman shrieked again. "That louse. To marry without calling, without letting anyone know…oh, I'll have his ears for this." By now, the amazed disbelief had changed to mirth. The woman was laughing.

Jessica thought Brody's friend was a bit bonkers.

"When did you say you got married?"

"Saturday, a week ago yesterday."

"A week. Oh, I'm going to feed him to the buzzards. I'll never forgive him. What's your name, by the way?"

"Jessica. Jessica Smith." It was the second time she'd said it. Another ten thousand and she might begin to believe it.

"Brody's been on a case in Chicago for the month, and I know he wasn't dating anyone in Denver when he left. Did you meet in Vegas? Are you a showgirl?"

"No. Brody and I met in Chicago," Jessica admitted. Her old school chum had recommended an attorney who knew a private investigator who was very good. She'd met Brody at the law office and hired him over her grandfather's protests.

However, she wasn't going to blurt out the truth about their rushed marriage arrangement, not even to her best friend, much less this nosy stranger.

"Hmm."

Jessica was silent. She could hear another voice in the background. A man's deep tones.

"I've got to go," whatever-her-name-was informed her. "I'll see you soon." It was a promise...or a threat. "Bye."

"Wait. Your name—" But the telephone was dead. Jessica hung up, feeling rather disoriented by the strange conversation.

The oven buzzer went off before she could sort out her feelings. She removed two loaves of cinnamon bread, Brody's favorite, and a cookie sheet of cheese and sausage biscuits that traveled well and were good for a quick snack.

Brody stepped up on the back porch. She recognized the sounds he made—the long stride, then the stomping of snow and mud off his boots before he entered the kitchen. He came inside a second later, stopping by the door to tug his boots off.

"That smells good. I could eat a whole loaf by myself. What are those things?" He pointed to the cookie sheet as he slung his coat onto a wooden peg.

"Cheese and sausage biscuits. I thought you and Don might like to take some with you to the barn when you miss lunch."

"Thanks." He gave her one of his veiled glances. Sometimes she wanted to ask what dire crime he suspected her of committing when he did that, but she held her tongue.

"Your girlfriend called," she said instead.

She busied herself by placing the cinnamon loaves on the cooling rack with a lot more care than needed. Her heart jumped nervously around her chest while she waited for a reaction.

Brody snorted in amusement. "Yeah? Which one?" He came over to the counter and snatched one of the hot cheese biscuits, tossing it from hand to hand while it cooled.

"She didn't leave her name." She took a breath. "I think we'd better talk about…other women."

He hooked the stool with his toe and dragged it closer. Seated, he broke the biscuit open and took a bite. "This is really good."

She gave him a tight smile. He always acted totally surprised when her cooking came out all right. "I took a summer course in *cordon-bleu* cooking at an academy one year."

"Why would a rich girl need to learn to cook?"

"The same reason we learned how to keep house—so we could direct our cooks and maids in the proper method, of course." She gave him the most supercilious smile she could muster. It had no effect that she could discern.

He studied her while he chewed and swallowed the last bite of biscuit and reached for another. "Sorry, didn't mean to ruffle your feathers."

"You needn't apologize." She scooped a spatula under the biscuits, removing them from the cookie sheet to the cooling racks. "Your girlfriend took it hard that you'd married without telling her. Perhaps you'd better explain the situation to her. She plans to come up as soon as the weather clears."

He groaned audibly. "That could only be one person."

She drew a steadying breath. "While our marriage may be a bit...unusual, I won't...I'd prefer..." She laid the oven mitt aside and faced him grimly. "You'll have to tell your girlfriends that you're out of circulation. For a year."

There, she'd said all she had to say on the subject.

Brody's mouth crimped at the corners. The lines bracketing his sensuous lips deepened. He burst into laughter.

She thought of helping his girlfriend kill him. She thought of doing it herself. She hoped he choked on the third biscuit he was eating. She poured two cups of coffee while he contained himself.

He reached out when she came near and caught her under the chin. His thumb brushed over her lower lip seductively, back and forth, softly, gently, as if he were soothing her. When she would have pulled away, insulted by his attitude, he ran his fingers behind her neck and under her hair, holding her fast. He gazed into her eyes as if trying to read her mind.

"Would you rather we made our marriage usual?"

She refused to back down from his sardonic scrutiny. She shrugged. "I'm not as afraid of entanglements as you are."

His expression darkened into a scowl. "Because it's easy to get rid of them if they get in your way? Hire a lawyer and wipe the slate clean. Is that your philosophy on marriage?"

"I don't have a philosophy regarding marriage," she stated. "I've never given it much thought. Until this past month," she added truthfully.

He let her go so abruptly her head snapped back. She hadn't realized she'd been straining against his hold until then. He walked over to the door and picked up a boot.

"Until you came up with a scheme to gain control of

your money and buy your freedom at the same time," he said on a hard note. "I once heard that marriage is never free. It always costs, whether to get in it or to get out of it."

She watched while he jerked his insulated boots on over the thick, wool socks. "Has that been your experience?" she asked, curiosity overcoming her sense of self-preservation.

"This is my first experience with wedded bliss." His smile mocked the description.

"Mine, too," she reminded him, comprehending the irony of the situation. Their make-believe marriage was already entangled in more problems than the average for-real one. "I suppose we'll find out the costs during the coming year."

"And during the divorce settlement." He gave her a look she couldn't decipher, but one that somehow contained a challenge. "You forgot to demand a prenuptial agreement."

"It never occurred to me we'd need one," she said slowly, mulling over the implications. She gave him a cheeky glance. "I trust you to keep to the terms of our bargain."

His lips tightened into thin lines. "Don't ever trust anyone. That's the first rule."

His tone was so harsh, she couldn't let his statement pass. "That's a terrible way to live. It would be too horrible never to trust another person. You'd have to forever be on guard because you thought someone was going to cheat you or—"

"Or kill you?" he supplied, bringing her up short as she recalled exactly why she'd thought marriage to him would solve all her problems.

"Money." She sighed. "The root of all evil."

"No." He fastened his boots and reached for his coat. "The *love* of money. That's what the saying actually is." He grabbed an old and battered Stetson from a peg and headed back outside, buttoning his coat as he crossed the wooden planking.

It wasn't until he was gone that she realized he'd never told her that he'd call and tell the prying female not to visit. Jessica clamped her lips firmly together. She was not a jealous wife...

Was she?

No, she wasn't, she decided. But she wasn't going to put up with any philandering, either. Brody could curb his randy male instincts for a year.

Or he could come to her.

Her heart went into overdrive at the thought. She couldn't decide if she would accept him or haughtily tell him to get lost.

If she told Brody to get lost, he'd probably laugh. She hadn't exactly turned a cold shoulder to his caresses. He'd been the one to stop before things went too far.

She should probably be grateful that he kept his distance. Common sense forced her to admit he was right—the fewer entanglements, the easier life would be when the time came for them to go their separate ways.

For some reason, she found that depressing. Maybe she hadn't given much thought to marriage, but she had ideals. She believed it should last for a lifetime.

Pacing restlessly from window to window, she decided she had to work off some energy. The wind had stopped blowing across the narrow valley, and the snow wasn't falling although the clouds still hovered ominously overhead. She would go see what was happening in the barn.

Ten minutes later, dressed in an old ski parka and snow boots, she headed across the path through the crusty snow.

At the steep gulley, she found the snow had been packed into a foot bridge of sorts with a bale of straw on either side for supports.

Hmm, it looked as if Brody had expected her to come traipsing over for a visit. Or maybe she was ascribing kinder thoughts to him than he deserved.

She smiled as a surge of something strangely akin to affection for her curmudgeon of a husband filled her. Maybe she would dig through the stone surrounding his heart before the year was up and find out what made him tick.

The barn was warm and surprisingly antiseptic she discovered upon entering. The concrete floor was covered with clean straw in each stall that held a mother and baby. She found Don in one of them with two lambs. He was feeding them from a nipple attached to a bucket.

"Oh, aren't they darling," she murmured. "May I come in?"

He nodded, his shy smile flashing before he concentrated on his chore once more. He held one bucket out to her. Taking it, she felt the pull of the lamb on the nipple as it fed hungrily.

"Where's their mother?"

He shook his head, and his smile turned sad.

"She didn't make it?"

"She was old, that one, but a good mother."

They were silent while the two babies finished their meal. For the next hour, Jessica helped the shepherd with the other orphans until they came to the last stall. "Oh, this one is so tiny. We'd better feed it double."

"That one's for the bone pile," Brody spoke behind her.

She glanced around and knew he'd been watching her for a while. A shiver chased down her spine. Her husband looked ruggedly masculine in a suede cloth shirt with a teal green turtleneck under it. His words finally registered.

"For the…oh. What's wrong with it?" When she leaned over the low fence, the lamb raised its head and bleated at her, the sound so low, she could barely hear it. She scratched around its head. It tried to suck her fingers.

"It's too weak."

"I'll take care of it," she volunteered. She knew she was being sentimental, but she couldn't stand by and let it die without trying to save it. "Tell me what to do."

For a moment, she thought he was going to refuse, then, giving his head a little shake, he showed her how to mix up the powdered nutrient. Instead of putting it in a bucket, he fetched a baby bottle from a supply room and filled it. The nipple had a big hole punched into it.

She took the bottle and slipped into the stall. Lifting the lamb into her arms as if he were a baby, she rubbed its mouth with the nipple. Milk dribbled down its chin. She kept trying, but to no avail.

"It won't swallow," she said.

Brody nearly groaned when Jessica looked at him, her eyes liquid with worry. She held the premature lamb as if it were a human baby, cradled to her breast, while she tried to feed it.

"A lamb doesn't feed on its back. Set it on its feet and hold the bottle where its mother's belly would be."

Instead of taking umbrage at his sardonic tone, she did exactly as instructed. The lamb still didn't get the hang of it. She looked at him again, clearly expecting him to come up with another suggestion.

"Rub his throat."

She stroked under its neck while she rubbed the nipple across its mouth. "Why won't he eat? He sucked at my fingers earlier."

"Wet your fingers with the milk, then see if he will suck."

After letting a stream of milk run down her fingers, she pressed her fingertips against the lamb's mouth, then ran one finger inside his lips. The newborn gave a tentative lick, then sucked weakly at her finger.

Jessica laughed and looked at him, her eyes alight with shared triumph.

It did strange things to Brody's insides. He ignored the sensation. "He probably won't last the day. He's pretty far gone due to dehydration."

"Why didn't you put him on a ewe that lost her baby?" she asked softly before going back to making little crooning noises to the lamb.

"None of them would take him."

"Poor baby," she soothed as if the lamb understood every word. "No one wanted a runt. I'll take care of you."

Brody snorted. She'd last about fifteen minutes.

Brody hung up the phone in exasperation. His foster sister, Carly, was determined to visit and meet his wife. Her husband was on a fishing trip with his brother and his son, and she was restless. She was also nearly six months pregnant.

He rubbed his eyes wearily as he padded downstairs to break the news to Jessica. He wondered what his bride would think of having company.

As usual, she was in the kitchen. She seemed to like cooking and taking care of the place. Odd, he'd never have pictured her as domestic from her life in Chicago.

"We have a problem," he announced.

Jessica glanced at him, then concentrated on the concoction in the pot. "Which one is it this time?" The eyebrow with the attitude arched in amusement.

He was forced to admit she was right—their problems seemed to hit several levels. "The caller earlier today was my sister. She's decided to pay us a visit."

"Oh, how nice. I've wondered about your family."

"Not so nice. Where will we put her? She's almost six months pregnant, by the way."

Jessica shook some chili powder into the mixture, stirred and tasted. "Here, see what you think." She held the spoon out to him.

He grabbed it with an impatient frown. She often asked his opinion on her cooking, a first in his experience. His mother had rarely cooked and Aunt Essie had her own ideas in the kitchen. He tasted the chili. "Fine. About Carly—"

"Where does she usually sleep when she comes here?"

"The guest room." He ran a hand through his hair and remembered Jessica's delicate touch stroking through the strands or rubbing his neck... He cursed silently as his thoughts steamed up.

"Well?" She evidently didn't see the problem.

"That's where you are," he snapped. "There are only two bedrooms here, in case you hadn't noticed," he added on a sarcastic note.

"Yes, I have. We'll give her the guest room. I can sleep on the sofa—"

"The hell with that."

One slender eyebrow tilted upward. "I suppose we could share your room. Do you snore?"

"I don't know. What the hell does that matter?" He paced the narrow area between counters. Her scent tantalized him each time he passed her.

"I've heard several friends complain that their husbands' snoring kept them awake. Once I'm asleep, though,

I rarely wake until morning. Since you usually go to bed after I do, it shouldn't be a—''

"That is not the problem!" he roared.

"What is?" She stopped stirring and looked directly at him.

"Sharing a bed." Just saying it aloud started things happening in his body that he couldn't control.

She gave him a slow once-over, smiled as if she found his predicament vastly amusing, then went back to stirring. "Ah, yes, I see."

He considered breaking the wooden spoon in half, but managed to control himself by dint of willpower. She'd drive him crazy before a month was out, much less a year.

"You have a small sofa in your office. I could use it."

"Carly would ferret that fact out on the first day."

"Oh," Jessica murmured. She followed the word with a wicked little laugh. "You don't want her to know our marriage isn't, ah, usual. Is that it?"

He glared at her.

Jessica was enchanted that Brody cared about his sister knowing the circumstances of their union. "I'm surprised it matters to you."

"It doesn't," he denied, a bit too quickly. "I was thinking of you, that you might be embarrassed."

"Why not tell her the truth—that it's a marriage of mutual benefit and will be annulled in a year."

She was seized and spun around.

"There won't be an annulment," he told her. "Not at the rate we're going."

His breath smelled faintly of the brandy he'd had when he came in from the barn. He'd joined her in front of the fire to warm up before he went to his room to shower. He hadn't kissed her again, but she'd thought about it. If he had...if they'd made love there...but of course he hadn't.

"You have too much control to become entangled," she reminded him, keeping a cool tone in spite of his nearness.

He surprised her with a low curse. "No man has that much control when sharing a bed with a woman, especially if—" He broke off as if he'd said too much.

"If she's his wife." She finished the sentence for him. She couldn't help but grin.

"If she's as beautiful and tempting as you are." He corrected her on a harsh note.

She opened her eyes wide. "Compliments, Brody? Be careful, else I'll think you're trying to *lure* me into bed."

"This isn't a joke." He let her go and resumed pacing.

She stopped her teasing. "How long will she be here?"

"A long weekend, she said. This Thursday until Monday."

"Okay. We can surely share a bed four nights without mishap. I'll behave if you will." She tossed him a challenging glance.

"There's no other way. Carly will badger us to death if she suspects anything out of the ordinary."

"So we want to convince her our marriage is... ordinary?"

"Yes."

She nearly laughed at his desperate manner. This was a Brody she didn't know, one who was concerned about another's opinion of their marriage. Why should he care if his sister knew he'd married for money? So what? It was a good deal for both of them. "You want to pour some milk?"

Don supplied her with fresh milk each morning from a cow he'd gentled. She poured the cream off and fed it to the barn cats, thus making nonfat milk for her and Brody. If he was used to whole milk, he didn't say anything.

Distracted, Brody performed the task while she took up

bowls of chili for them. She set the food and crackers on two colorful plastic trays she'd found in the pantry. "I thought we would eat at the sofa tonight. There's a special I wanted to catch on TV."

He placed the glasses on the trays. She carried one to the living room. He followed behind her with the other.

When they were settled, she flicked the television on with the remote control. "I'll move my clothes to your room on Wednesday, okay?"

Brody stopped with the spoon halfway to his mouth. "Yes," he agreed after the pause became too long. There was no way around it. He thought of the coming weekend with his irreverent sister and his sassy wife in the same house.

God help him.

Jessica surveyed the room. She'd changed the sheets and hung up fresh towels in the bathroom. All was ready—oops, her book. She picked up the paperback on the night table and tucked it under her arm. After throwing the used sheets into the washer, she turned it on, then went upstairs.

Hesitating beside the king-size bed, she wondered which side Brody slept on. Shrugging, she chose a side and put her book on the wall shelf above it.

She studied the titles in the bookcase over the bed. Spy adventures predominated, but there was a surprising number of bestsellers and mainstream titles, too. The nonfiction works included historicals and first-person accounts of dangerous periods in history. There were none of the historical romances that she loved, though.

Glancing at the alarm clock, she exclaimed and rushed to the kitchen. The cherry pies were ready to come out of the oven.

An hour later, she prowled from window to window.

The road held only one set of tire tracks where Brody had left for the Denver airport to pick up his sister.

The trip was his first off the ranch since they'd arrived. It gave her a satisfied feeling to be so independent. With a freezer in the storage room off the kitchen, they could live quite comfortably on their mountain without a trip to town for weeks at a time.

With canned, frozen and dried fruits and vegetables along with bags of rice and beans, plus all the beef they wanted, she could make a variety of dishes. She mentally reviewed her menus for the duration of the sister's stay.

Sitting on the stool so she could see the road, she admitted she was nervous about Carly's impression of her. With a laugh, she realized she felt like a bride meeting the groom's family for the first time. She hoped the sister wasn't as hard to please as Brody was.

Suspicious man. He eyed everything she did or offered to do with a gleam of deep-seated cynicism in his gaze. He hadn't let her help once with the lambs or calves that were appearing quite regularly in the broad pastures.

If the weather continued warming, she was going to explore the place whether he liked it or not.

The whine of the truck engine set her heart to beating like mad. She spied the flash of blue through the trees before the vehicle broke into the clearing near the house. Brody followed the driveway and parked near the decking extending outward from the back porch. A woman peered at the house, spotted Jessica and waved.

Jessica drew a deep breath and rushed to the back door. She held it open while Brody helped his sister down from the truck and onto the porch. While he fetched luggage, Carly rushed eagerly forward.

"So you're Jessica," she cried and gave her a bear hug

as if the two women were sisters who hadn't visited in a while.

Jessica wasn't sure what she'd expected, but it wasn't this vivacious female with long black hair and eyes as dark as midnight. As Brody had said, Carly was nearly six months pregnant and showed it.

Brody came in with one medium bag and a small case. He took them to the guest room without a word. Jessica's throat went dry at the thought of the coming night.

"Let me take your coat," she said.

"Thank you. It's wonderful to meet you. I've wondered about the woman who would sweep Brody off his feet and make him eat his words about never marrying. You're as beautiful as I knew you would be."

"I'm hardly beautiful—"

"Oh, yes, you are," Carly declared with a delightful laugh. "How do you like the ranch? Do you mind the isolation? Or have you had time to get used to it? After all, you are still on your honeymoon." She cast a reproachful glance on her brother when he came into the kitchen.

"I love it here," Jessica said, hanging the parka on a hook near the door. "The isolation doesn't bother me at all, but I'm glad the snow is melting. I'm dying to explore. So far Brody hasn't let me outside the house."

Carly burst out laughing at this confession.

Realizing how it had sounded—as if Brody kept her chained to the bed or something—Jessica experienced an onrush of blood to her face. Risking a glance at Brody, she saw he, too, was rather pink in the ears.

"Well, well, well," murmured his sister. She plopped herself on the kitchen stool. "Tell me everything. Start from the moment you met."

Before Jessica could explain, Brody spoke up. "There's little to tell. We met through mutual friends—"

"When?" Carly demanded.

"Last month." Brody gave her a superior smile. "So it wasn't as sudden as you think."

"You had a case in Chicago a month ago."

"I was it," Jessica announced. "Brody was checking into some problems for me regarding my mother's will."

Carly smiled slyly. "I made up all kinds of exciting stories on the way here about you being an heiress in danger and Brody marrying you to protect you…oh-oh, I think I'm on to something by the looks on both your faces."

Brody threw up his hands. "You've figured out most of it."

His sister looked disappointed. "So it isn't a real marriage?"

"Yes—" said Jessica.

"No—" said Brody.

Jessica glared at Brody. He was making her look like a fool. After all, he was the one who hadn't wanted his family to know the truth.

"Well, which is it?" Carly asked.

"We're married," Brody said. "That's real enough." His smile was feral. "But who knows how long it will last?"

"Years and years," Jessica told him. "I don't believe in divorce. Didn't I mention that?"

"No." He headed for the door with a scowl on his face. "I'll put the truck up, then I have to help Don with the chores."

A blast of cold air hit them with his departure.

"Prickly, isn't he?"

Jessica smiled weakly at Carly's amusement. "He

hasn't had much sleep since we arrived…'' She realized how that sounded. ''The blizzard and…and everything.''

''I understand.''

Jessica met Carly's eyes. They burst out laughing.

Carly stood and linked her arm in Jessica's. ''So, sister, why don't you tell me all about it? The truth this time, if you don't mind.''

They talked the rest of the afternoon. By the time Brody came in for the supper Jessica had prepared, they were chatting like long-lost friends.

''Brody,'' Carly sang out when he entered the house, ''you've found yourself a jewel. Jessica is definitely a keeper.''

Jessica met his dark gaze and smiled modestly. ''Your sister should have been in business with you. She wrung a full confession out of me this afternoon.''

''Everything?'' he asked warily.

''About why we married.'' Jessica flashed him a warning with a very direct gaze. She hadn't confessed that they weren't sleeping together. His sister took it for granted that they did.

He relaxed and smiled. ''Ah, yes.''

Carly frowned. ''You will be careful, won't you? Both of you? I hate to think you might be in danger.''

''The marriage solved that,'' Jessica assured her.

''Unless the person kills both of you.'' Carly looked from one to the other.

Jessica felt a painful constriction in her chest. She hadn't thought about Brody being hurt. He seemed invincible, but he wasn't. She looked at him with guilt-stricken eyes.

''No one will hurt either of us,'' he said. He gazed into her eyes. ''That's a promise.''

Chapter Five

"The evening went well, didn't it?" Jessica asked when she and Brody were in his...their...room with the door closed.

"You and Carly hit it off" was his noncommittal response.

"She's delightful."

He sat in a chair and yanked off his socks, then went to a bureau and removed a pair of pajamas. They appeared to be new. She wondered if he usually slept nude.

Of course he did.

Sensations poured over her as if she'd suddenly stepped under a waterfall. Ignoring them, she went to the dresser, which Brody had graciously given up for her use, and retrieved her nightgown. She hesitated.

"You may use the bathroom first," he said.

She hurried through her routine and returned to the bedroom. "Oh," she gasped, stopping dead in the doorway.

Brody had removed his clothing. He pulled up the pj bottoms and tied the drawstring at the waist. "Sorry, I didn't mean to startle you. I received a fax and read it before changing."

"That's okay."

His image burned itself into her brain—the broad chest with its thick triangle of hair, the muscular torso and narrow hips...the manly staff that had started to swell and rise when he saw her standing there gawking at his masculine beauty. Wildfire blazed to life all over her.

She went over and picked up her book. "I think I'll read a while," she mumbled, keeping her eyes carefully on the page.

Brody cursed the entire time he brushed his teeth and prepared for bed. There was no way he was going to sleep with Jessica in the same bed...not with her wearing that silky outfit she slept in.

The lace was cleverly sewn to conceal without totally hiding her lush body. Those high, bouncy breasts were gently cupped in satin with a lace overlay. He could discern the jutting nipple under the blue frothy material.

Or maybe that was his imagination. Who was he kidding, anyway? It didn't matter what she wore or how much of her he could see. He'd want her if she was dressed in flannel from neck to toes.

Entanglements, he reminded himself. He didn't intend to get in over his head nor to lose his head over her. She was just a woman. She'd be gone soon enough.

Taking a calming breath, he entered the bedroom and nearly forgot his pep talk. Jessica sat with her feet curled under her, her nose in a book. The light picked out the blond highlights in her shiny, light brown hair. The strands shimmered as if painted with gold. He knew how soft each lock was and that it was naturally curly.

"Will the light bother you if I read a bit longer?"

He shook his head. She smiled at him, then went back to reading. He drifted into the adjoining alcove that formed his office and looked over a couple of reports from the agency, but his mind wasn't on them.

He'd stopped in the small town that served the area on his way to Denver that morning and deposited her check. The act had felt like a commitment on his part. Up until that moment, the thought had been in the back of his mind that he could simply hand the money back and walk away. Okay, maybe not that simple, but close.

The situation was becoming more complicated by the second. He rubbed a hand over his face and decided to face the music, or rather, the bed and, he feared, a sleepless night.

He crawled under the covers and switched off the light on his side. A minute crept by, slower than any snail he'd ever seen. He laid an arm over his eyes to block out the light. Another minute. He turned to his left side, away from her.

"I'm keeping you awake," she said. "I'll come to bed."

He suppressed a groan.

The bed moved slightly as she slipped beneath the covers. The room went dark with a *click* of the light pull. He heard her sigh as she settled down to sleep.

After an agonizing period of lying perfectly still, he quietly raised up and peered at the clock. It had been only twenty minutes since the light went out.

"Do we need to talk?" Jessica asked.

"No."

"This isn't going to work." The light snapped on. "I'll sleep in your office—"

"No, you won't."

"But Brody, you aren't sleeping."

"Neither are you."

She laughed. It sounded a bit shaky. "Well, I've never tried to sleep with a man before."

"Never?" He couldn't believe the implications. He sat up and pushed his pillow between him and the headboard.

"Never." She sighed and sat up, too. "When would I have had the chance? I taught health classes to disadvantaged women while I was in Africa. This past year, I could hardly ask the guard to wait outside while my date and I…uh…"

"I get the picture." He did, in spades. Images leapt into his mental vision—Jessica with her hair spread across a pillow, her eyes closed in ecstasy while he did all the things he'd dreamed of doing to her.

"We are married—"

He threw the covers off. "God spare me from curious virgins," he muttered, removing himself from the temptation that was growing by the second.

She laughed. He glared at her.

"I think it's more than curiosity. You're very attractive in a growly kind of way."

"Yeah," he admitted. "There're sparks between us. Proximity will do that. Sorry, but I'm not going to satisfy your personal need to know what you're missing."

"Afraid?"

"Scared to death." He gave her what he hoped was a cynical smile and beat a retreat before he did the things he'd only dreamed about for weeks.

Grabbing his pillow, he retrieved a blanket from the top shelf of the closet and went into the alcove. He tossed the items on the small sofa and closed the French doors between the rooms. He jerked the blinds down to block the light from the bedroom and shook out the blanket.

It was going to be a long night.

Jessica woke to the sounds of the shower. She wondered what Brody would do if she joined him. A delicious sense of languor seeped into her. She stretched and yawned. Surprisingly she'd slept better last night than she had in months...since the last strange accident had happened to her.

She gazed out at the dawn just beginning to light the sky and gild the mountains. She liked it here. The solitude was peaceful. Solitude? They had a guest. She'd better see about breakfast.

Flinging back the covers, she rolled out of the sack and went into the bathroom. "Is your sister an early riser?" she asked Brody.

He stood with a towel around his middle. A razor was in his hand. His face was half covered in lather. "She used to be."

She waited to see how he went about shaving. He scowled at her in the mirror. She smiled back.

With a little grunt of exasperation, he went on with the chore. She brushed her teeth at the twin sink, fascinated with this bit of male routine. It felt so very intimate to share the bathroom with a man. "My father used to let me watch him shave when I was little."

He acknowledged this information with a grunt.

"Did you watch your father?"

"My father ran out on us when I was five."

"That's a terrible thing to do. My father died when I was six. A three-car pileup. It was odd. One moment he was there, the next he was gone. It must have been that way for you, too."

Sorrow for both of them rushed over her. He washed the remaining dollops of lather off his face and dried off.

She moved closer and leaned against the edge of the counter.

"I used to check to see if my dad had missed any patches." She lifted her hand to Brody's face.

He stepped back. "I'm not your father."

"I never thought you were."

They watched each other warily. His eyes contained a warning. She ignored it and laid her fingers along his jaw.

"Smooth."

He hooked the hand towel behind her head and pulled her close. "Don't try any of your sexy games with me. They might work on your society boyfriends, but you're liable to find out more than you want if you try them with me." He let her go. "Don't push me too far. If you do, I can't promise to be gentle with you."

It was a warning more potent than the shaking of a rattlesnake's tail. He stared at her with frustration raging in his eyes, then he turned and walked out, slamming the door behind him.

She dropped her hand, feeling a little sad, a little sorry for herself. Yeah, poor little rich girl, she chided her image in the steamy mirror.

Brody was gone when she returned to the bedroom. She dressed and made the bed before she left. He had already straightened the office and opened the doors.

She squared her shoulders and went to face him and his sister with a calm air. Composure could demoralize the enemy as well as a mortar shell.

Walking down the stairs, she wondered when she and Brody had declared war.

War it was, Jessica decided after Brody left the house that morning. He'd ordered her and Carly to stay inside.

"Let's take a walk," Carly said as soon as the dishes

were done. She peered out the window. "I want to get out."

Jessica did, too. "I have an extra pair of snow boots, if you need them." She pulled a pair out of the hall closet. "I think we're close to the same size." Carly was a couple of inches taller than she was, but otherwise they seemed a match.

"I brought mine, but thanks."

They put on warm clothing and ambled out into the sun. The snow was still deep under the trees, but was mostly melted from the open ground. Water rushed down the gully, forming a small, but noisy creek across the back-yard.

"Let's hike up the hill," Carly said as she pointed out the one Jessica had wanted to explore.

"Are you up to it?" Jessica didn't want anything to happen to Brody's sister. That he cared deeply for her was clear to Jessica. It opened a new side to her husband that was very appealing. There was gentleness in him, belying the gruff exterior he showed to the world.

A shiver ran over her as she wondered what it would be like to be loved by this man.

"Sure. I'm pregnant, not disabled."

Letting Carly set the pace, Jessica climbed the rock ridge overlooking the house and home paddocks with her new friend and sister-in-law.

"Oh, the view," she exclaimed, standing on the rocky cliff.

"Magnificent. It's much more awesome than the view from our ranch in California. The mountains are gentler there." Carly cast a sly look at Jessica. "But then, so is my husband."

Jessica didn't know how to respond, so she kept silent.

Carly touched her arm. "No matter why you married,

there's something between you and Brody. Don't let him close you out.'' She laughed softly. ''There. I've said my piece. I'll not embarrass you by mentioning it again. But I do think you're going to be good for him.''

''Why doesn't he trust anyone?''

''Too many people ran out on him when he was young. He learned never to share his whole self, only bits and pieces. Except with my stepson. He's good with children.''

''I see.''

''He'd never run out on his child,'' Carly added.

Jessica didn't think he'd want a child with her. That would be an entanglement of the highest order. She envisioned a little boy with that stubborn look Brody assumed when she pushed too hard into his personal life.

Down in the pasture, she saw Brody come out of the barn on a tractor. Using a forklift attachment, he stacked the bales of straw used as a snow break on a wagon and took them to the barn. Later, he came out without his coat. His shirtsleeves were rolled up. He looked toward the house, then disappeared again. When he drove the tractor and wagon out of the building, the bales had been unloaded.

Carly gave a piercing whistle. Brody stopped the tractor and glanced around. Carly whistled again. She waved both arms over her head to attract his attention.

Jessica knew the exact moment he spotted them. The tension radiated from him as if it were the static hum of electricity from a high-voltage wire. She saw him take in the area where they stood, then his gaze swept the woods and the trail behind them. He waved only after he was sure they were safe.

The hair rose on the back of her neck. She glanced toward the trail, then the woods. It was one thing to put herself in danger. It was another to involve Carly.

Or even Brody. Thinking of him hurt…or dying…did odd, painful things to her.

"Look, there's a deer," Carly said, spying one in the trees behind the outcropping of rock.

Jessica scrutinized the path into the woods. The snow was still too deep to wade through, and she saw no tracks to indicate someone had attempted it. However, the woods were dense and shadowed. A person could hide in them undetected unless he moved. The brightness went out of the day.

"We'd better head back," she said.

"Wait. Here comes Brody. He might like to see the view."

Jessica saw her husband coming up the ridge, his coat slung over one shoulder. His long stride covered the ground at twice the rate she and Carly had climbed. His gaze constantly shifted over the terrain, taking in every rock and crevice.

"Hi," she called when he approached them. "You didn't tell me how beautiful the view was from here."

Anything to distract him from the lecture she was sure he was going to deliver. She didn't want Carly to worry about danger in her condition. She glanced meaningfully at Carly, then back to him. He got the message, but the anger still blazed in his eyes as he checked the woods as she had done.

He relaxed a bit. But not entirely. She figured she was still in for a dressing-down when they were alone.

"You two going to stay up here all day?" he asked. "It's almost lunch, and I'm starving."

"Ah, the way to a man's heart," Carly quipped. "I'll make sandwiches—"

"I'll do it," Jessica insisted. "You must rest."

"I'm not tired at all."

"I'd feel better if you sat," Jessica declared. She laughed when Carly made a wry face. "I've not had any experience with delivering babies."

"Brody has."

Jessica was astounded. She looked at her husband, who was scowling at his sister as if she'd given away the family secrets. "Whose? Why?"

"He's a volunteer fireman for the county," Carly continued when he didn't offer the information. "A couple of years ago there was a forest fire in the area. A man and his wife were trapped at a camping site when the fire burned along the only road out. They had a cell phone, and the husband reported the woman had gone into labor."

Jessica met Brody's gaze. She remembered him saying that females always picked the worst times. Of course that had been in relation to the ewes having their lambs during the blizzard, but the situation with the pregnant woman fit perfectly.

Carly went on with her story. "The husband panicked. Brody volunteered to be airlifted in—"

"To go behind the fire line?" Jessica asked. "You could have been trapped."

Brody shrugged. "It was my job."

Just as it was his job to protect her. That's what she paid him for, Jessica reminded herself. The worry in his eyes was for his sister, not *her*. She was his client.

"He delivered the baby, moved the couple and the child to a trench surrounded by rock and covered them with a safety blanket. With the fire coming toward him, he climbed the highest rock and directed the helicopter pilots in dropping water and fire retardant over the area. The governor gave him a medal," Carly concluded with unconcealed pride.

Jessica didn't try to hide the admiration she felt. She

reached up and rubbed her hand along his strong jaw. "My hero," she said softly, teasing but meaning it, too.

He scowled at both women. They laughed.

"Let's go," he ordered. He told Jessica to lead the way, put Carly in the middle and followed the two women.

At the house, he left them and returned to the tractor and wagon. Jessica watched him drive across the pasture and stop by the covered bales of hay stacked by the fence while she washed her hands at the sink.

"You're in love with him," Carly declared.

Jessica jerked around, startled. "No, I—" She pressed her lips together, not sure what to say.

"Yes, you are." She nodded her head positively. "I can't tell you how relieved I am. Brody needs to be loved. He won't admit it, of course. You'll have to convince him."

"Right, and pigs will fly."

"Seduce him," Carly advised.

Jessica shook her head. "I don't think I can."

"He's fighting it," Carly agreed, "but Aunt Essie used to say there's nothing a smart woman can't do if she sets her mind to it."

"That was the woman who took you and Brody in, wasn't it?"

"Yes. Would you like to know about our life with her?" Jessica nodded.

Until Brody and Don came in for lunch, Jessica listened while Carly told her about the life of two youngsters that nobody wanted except an old woman who'd taken them in and loved them until the wounds of life had healed.

"But the scars are still there," Jessica murmured.

"And the defenses," Carly added. "To get to Brody, you'll have to get past a wall of doubt and distrust."

"What if I don't?"

"It will be a terrible waste." Hearing a car engine outside, Carly went to the door. "Here are the men. Oh, no, I can't believe it." She tore out the door at a run.

Jessica arrived at the door in time to see Carly enveloped in a bear hug by a tall, blond-haired guy dressed in jeans and a fleece-lined jacket.

"Ty," Carly was saying. "Oh, darling." They kissed deeply, passionately.

"I take it you two know each other." Jessica took Carly's coat to her.

"This is my husband, Ty Macklin. This is Jessica, Brody's wife," Carly introduced them. "What are you doing here?"

"Looking for my missing wife."

"Where's Jonathan?"

"Staying with Shane and Tina and helping with Ian. Their son," he added in an aside to Jessica.

She nodded. "Have you had lunch? We're about to eat."

"I'm starved. That airplane food wouldn't fill a hollow leg, much less a grown man...or a pregnant lady." He looped an arm around his wife and patted her tummy. "Where's Brody?"

"Uh, he should be in any moment." Jessica ushered them into the house and made four more sandwiches. She emptied a bag of chips into a bowl and set it on the table.

When Brody arrived, dinner, as they called the noon meal on the ranch, was ready. Jessica noted Brody greeted his brother-in-law with respect and friendship. She also realized he'd known who had arrived and when. He kept a sharp eye on the house.

He wanted to know where his nephew was and was obviously disappointed that he wasn't with his father.

"He has school," Ty explained.

While Brody washed up, Jessica and Carly poured coffee, iced tea and sodas. The talk was lively and interesting around the table as the three of them caught up on family news. Jessica, seated opposite Brody, smiled happily.

"Brody married Jessica and brought her here to protect her," Carly explained the marriage to her husband when he teased Brody about the sudden nuptials. "Isn't that romantic?"

Her husband looked a question at Brody, who nodded, admitting it was true.

Jessica glanced up to find his dark gaze on her, his expression unreadable. "We have to stick it out a year, then I'll be free of my mother's will. And Brody will be rid of me," she added with a laugh that caught at her throat.

"Maybe he'll decide to keep you," Carly suggested with a hard look at her brother.

"Maybe," he agreed in a lazy drawl that drew a laugh from his brother-in-law.

Jessica's heart skipped a couple of beats.

"I'm thinking of throwing you back," Ty told his wife. "Or chaining you in the house if you ever take off again while I'm gone."

"I called you on the cell phone," she reminded him, not the least daunted by his threat.

Jessica was fascinated by the playful jousting between husband and wife. That they were mad about each other was evident. She thought of Brody loving her that way. The thought produced shock waves of longing in her.

An image of his strong, muscular body as he'd put on his pj bottoms came to her. She wanted to be enfolded in his warmth again, the way he'd held her pinned to the wall in her bedroom that time. Only she wanted to be in bed…with him holding her that way.

A knot of desire pulsed in her throat. She wanted her

husband, really wanted him, not out of curiosity, not even because of the flames he set within her. She wanted *him.*

She wanted him to kiss her and make love to her without reservation. She wanted passion and fire with him. All the things she'd read about in books and poems, she wanted.

With him.

Chapter Six

By the time supper was over, Carly and Ty had brought Brody up-to-date on family doings. Jessica listened with rapt attention as Carly teased her foster brother about hiding his bride away on the ranch.

Much more surprising was the fact that Brody took the ribbing in stride, a tolerant smile on his sensuous lips the whole time, and returned it in kind. "Don might quit if I let her off the ranch. He says her cooking is better than mine," he informed his sister.

"She's much too nice for you to keep her to yourself," Carly insisted with a mischievous grin. "So when are you going to bring her for a visit? Jonathan wants to meet his new aunt."

Jonathan was Ty's son from his first marriage. He and Carly were very close, it appeared.

"When I'm sure it's safe," Brody replied.

That brought a sober element into the evening. Jessica

felt the weight of responsibility for introducing danger to others. Until her year was up, she was a menace to whoever associated with her. Especially her husband.

"We shouldn't have married," she said aloud. "I didn't think... I considered only my own freedom. I didn't think about danger to others...to you and perhaps Don."

"That's why I get paid big bucks." His sardonic smile indicated his disregard for danger. Not that he didn't know it existed, but he wasn't afraid of it.

"It must be tough to live with a threat hanging over you all the time," Carly murmured in sympathy.

Jessica mulled the past year over before she spoke. "It isn't, not really. I try to be careful, of course, but I refuse to let it rule my life. And it helps having Brody on my side," she added with a laugh. "He's better than a whole pack of watchdogs."

"Keeps a close eye on you, huh?" Ty inquired with a gleam in his gorgeous blue eyes. "Husbands tend to be a bit like that. We like to know where our women are and what they're up to."

He gave Carly a stern perusal that earned him a quick hug from her.

"Jessica isn't convinced she's in danger," Brody mentioned. "She thinks her close calls were accidents."

"Not really, but there have been only two real incidents."

"Maybe someone is being extremely cautious."

She didn't have any argument to that. "Well, I'm going to write a will and leave everything to charity. That should take care of the problem."

"But what about your mother's will?" Carly asked.

"I talked to my attorney. Now that I've fulfilled the first part of it, even if the marriage doesn't last, I can probably get the rest set aside. If something should happen to me during the year, it wouldn't be my fault, so my will would stand.''

"Nothing will happen to you," Brody said abruptly.

He looked so fierce Jessica was momentarily put off balance. She slipped her hand into his and squeezed it in gratitude. He tightened his grasp when she would have pulled away and continued to hold her hand in his.

He rubbed his thumb along her knuckles, apparently unconscious of his actions while he talked to Ty about cattle prices. But she wasn't. She felt the tough calluses in his palm, the rough place where a cut healed on his thumb.

A storm of longing ran through her. Emotions she couldn't identify clamored in her chest. She wanted...she wanted... She didn't know what she wanted.

At last he let her go to replenish their coffee cups. She served the last of the cherry pie she'd made the day before.

At ten, Carly decided to say good-night. She admitted she may have overdone it with the hard climb up the ridge coming on top of the trip. Her husband watched her with a trace of worry in his gaze as she left the family room.

Jessica stood. "I'd better go, too. Breakfast comes early on a ranch, although Brody doesn't wake me when he first gets up," she hastened to add in case he thought she was complaining.

She went upstairs and prepared for bed, her thoughts on the visiting couple. She wondered if Brody would ever look at her the way Ty looked at Carly, as if his world revolved around her.

Remembering she hadn't readied the coffeepot and turned on the automatic timer, she returned to the kitchen.

"Is it the uncle?" she heard Ty ask in a musing tone. "He has the most logical motive, but..."

"The obvious isn't always the way of things," Brody finished during the pause that followed.

Jessica froze on the bottom step. They were discussing her. She waited to hear Brody's thoughts.

"You've had the uncle thoroughly checked out?"

"Yes."

"And?"

"His investments are sound. Apparently he's recovered from his past losses. That puts a different spin on the situation."

"Meaning?"

"He has enough money for a comfortable life. Why risk the fortune you have for one you probably wouldn't get to collect, especially now that Jessica is married?"

"Some people become obsessed with money. They want theirs and anyone else's they can get. It's more than greed. It becomes the focus of their lives."

"The love of money," Brody muttered. "Like the love of a woman, it has led to the downfall of many a man."

"Unless it's the right woman," Ty suggested wryly. "Then life can be pretty nice. You'll find out when you get this case solved and have time to think of...other things."

"Huh," Brody said.

"Any suspicious activity since you and Jessica married and moved to the ranch?"

"There were tracks on an old logging road coming in the back way. The driver got stuck. It was probably a hunter."

Jessica heard movement and realized too late that Brody was heading for the kitchen. She turned to flee up the stairs, but light flooded the area before she could escape. Brody stopped at the counter and narrowed his eyes.

"Can't sleep?" he asked.

"I forgot to put the coffee on and set the timer."

"I'll do it."

She nodded. "Thanks. When did you find the tracks?" she asked, worried about him.

"Yesterday. I check the perimeter of the property every day. Don't worry. If anyone comes this way, I'll know it."

"I'm not worried." She realized she wasn't. Not for herself. "Don't confront anyone you find on the ranch, okay? Call the sheriff and report it."

He tilted his head slightly and studied her. "A deputy sheriff lives a few miles down the road to town. I brought him up-to-date on our problem. He knows to watch out for strangers in these parts."

"Good." She gave him a relieved smile and headed back up to bed. When she looked back, Brody was still watching her. Her nerves tingled at the fierce, protective expression he wore.

She climbed into bed, feeling safe and maybe just a little bit cherished. A ridiculous notion, that. But it made her feel warm all over. She fell asleep at once.

Brody closed the door behind him and gazed toward the bed. His wife slept peacefully, looking like an angel in her blue gown. The lacy robe was laid over a chair. The nightlight cast a soft glow over the room. His body stirred hungrily.

After going into the bathroom, he shucked his clothes, pulled on the pajama bottoms and brushed his teeth. Finished he returned to the bedroom. Again he was captured by the innocent picture his wife made while she slept.

In a just world, it would be hard to imagine anyone wanting to hurt her. But the world wasn't just. He'd found that out a long time ago. Jessica was learning that lesson, too. Slowly. She still didn't quite believe someone would harm her.

No one would while there was breath in his body. He'd make sure of it. A fierceness rose in him, urgent and lethal.

He frowned at the reaction. Emotion wasn't good. It clouded a man's mind and interfered with his judgment. He had to stay cool and in control. It was what he was paid for.

Except when he lost his head over his sexy wife.

So okay, he'd be on guard from now on. No more episodes like that one on the sofa.

Instead of making his bed in the office, he calmly appraised the king-size one. There was enough room in it for them to sleep without touching. He was tired. Sleeping with a crimp in his neck and his feet hanging off the end of the sofa wasn't all that comfortable. He could handle a couple of nights in the same bed. Without thinking further on it, he slipped under the covers.

After snapping off the light, he settled down with a sigh. The extra-firm mattress felt good. He planned to be up and out before Jessica woke in the morning. She'd never know he'd been there. He'd keep his distance…

Brody woke with a satiny strand of hair tickling his chin. Jessica snuggled against him as if they'd been sleeping together for years. "Cold," she mumbled.

He raised his head cautiously and surveyed the bed. The cover was mostly on his side. He must have pulled it away from her during the night. She'd followed it, trying to stay warm.

She shifted again, pressing closer. Her leg slid over his and nestled between his thighs. Her arm crept over his chest.

Sensation hit him, awakening the hunger and filling him with needs he didn't want to acknowledge. His skin suddenly felt too tight to contain his body.

Her leg moved over him restlessly. He smoothed the curls that brushed his chin and tried to figure out what to do.

Getting the hell out of bed was probably the wisest course. Before he could ease away, she stirred again, causing an answering stir in his nether regions. He was hard and pulsing with eagerness to claim her.

Her lips brushed against his chest. She kissed him.

His breath strangled in his throat. She was asleep. She didn't know what she was doing. But he did. He lifted her arm, intent on getting out of bed at once.

"Don't go," she murmured. Her lips nibbled at his chest.

He was close to exploding. "You don't know what you're doing to me—" He stopped when she raised her head and gazed into his eyes. "The devil," he said.

She knew exactly what she was doing. The knowledge was there in her eyes. She watched him without blinking, a challenge in those rain-swept depths. When she smiled, her expression teased, daring him to take what she was offering.

Sweat broke out in a fine sheen all over him. He ought to teach her a lesson that would send her scurrying to the sofa in the future.

With a rough growl, he rolled her onto her back and pressed his greater bulk over her. He took her mouth in a punishing kiss that spoke of the days and nights of frustration she'd caused him. He caught a handful of hair in one hand and dragged the gown off her shoulder with the other.

"Mmm," she crooned when he cupped her breast in his hand, taking possession of the pert globe that had tantalized him for weeks. He left her mouth and tongued the tip of her breast into a rigid pebble.

It took only a second to bare the other side. He circled it with his tongue until she writhed under him, setting off fires he wasn't sure he could control.

"So you want to play games," he taunted, pinning her arms over her head and stretching his full length over her, taking his weight on his elbows.

"No. I want this to be real. Make love to me, Brody."

He sucked a shuddering breath into his lungs and tried to clear the whirling haze of passion from his mind. There were damn good reasons why he shouldn't be doing this. He couldn't think of a one.

"Are you protected?" he finally asked, which wasn't what he meant to say at all. With her hot, silky softness under him, he couldn't think straight.

"I'm not on the pill or anything." She slipped her hand free and stroked across his chest, stirring up a storm inside him with her caresses. "It doesn't matter."

"It doesn't matter that you might get pregnant?" He fought and won a small battle not to kiss her again.

"I think I'd like a child." She smiled.

"What about the kid?" he demanded, sense returning with a stomach-dropping plunge as if they'd tumbled over a cliff. "What happens when you decide you don't want him anymore?"

"Is that what your mother did? She just decided one day she didn't want you and left?"

He scowled at the inquisitive woman who looked at him as if she understood every blow life had dealt him. "She met a man who didn't want a teenage son around. She sent me to live with a relative."

"Your great-aunt. Carly told me of your life with her. She must have been a special person."

Briefly a picture of his years on his aunt's small farm returned to him—morning chores and all the pancakes he could eat every Sunday, movies on Friday night, the first time he'd driven a tractor, prom night and the money to rent a tux like the other boys, burning fall leaves and roasting hot dogs over them, returning from a stint in the air force in time for the funeral.

"I didn't mean to make you sad," Jessica said. She touched the twin frown lines between his brows.

His body still covered hers, but the torrent of desire had ebbed. She thought of trying to revive it, but this wasn't the time. She instinctively knew Brody needed to learn to trust her.

"You didn't," he told her, swinging away and sitting up on the side of the bed.

"We could have our own family," she suggested, planting the seed in his mind, hoping it would take root as it had in hers. She liked the idea more and more.

He caught her wrist when she would have laid a hand on his arm. "No way. Kids deserve more than being the result of a whim conceived during a passionate moment."

"I agree." She sat up and drew her knees against her chest. "I'd like at least two. That would make a nice family. We could visit—"

A knock cut off the rest of her statement. Carly spoke from outside the door. "Are you two awake?"

Brody strode to the door and opened it. "What's wrong?"

"Nothing." Carly glanced at Jessica, her gaze taking in the tumbled bed where two people had obviously slept. She gave them a brilliant smile. "It's late. I hope you don't mind that I fixed breakfast. I tend to become ill if I don't eat soon after I wake up."

Jessica glanced at the clock. Almost eight. That was late for Brody. He was usually up before six. She lowered her gaze demurely when her husband flicked a frowning glance her way as if it were her fault he'd been detained. She hid a smile.

Brody nodded. "We'll be down in a moment."

Jessica was already up and reaching for her sweat suit by the time he closed the door. They dressed in silence, took turns in the bathroom, then hurried downstairs.

After the meal, the four of them went outside for a tour of the ranch. Jessica and Carly fed the lambs while Don checked over the sheep. Ty saddled up and moved part of the cows and their calves to a different pasture with Brody. They put mineral blocks in the fields for the cattle.

With the coming of night, Jessica found herself more and more jittery. She didn't know what would happen between her and Brody when they retired to their room. She'd always tried to play fair with people, and it bothered her that she was actually thinking of trying to tempt Brody into forgetting his vow against entanglements. She wanted him to make love to her. Beyond that, she didn't let herself think at all.

The two couples played bridge after supper. Jessica and Ty beat the brother and sister team with a final grand slam.

"You're a crafty player," Brody told Jessica. There was a smile in his voice and admiration in his gaze.

"Just good cards."

Carly linked hands with Ty. "Tomorrow Brody and I will beat the socks off you two. Right now, I'm for bed." She patted back a huge yawn.

After they said good-night and went to their room, Jessica prepared the coffeemaker and turned on the timer for the next morning. Brody checked the doors. "I'll be up in a bit," he said when she waited for him.

In bed fifteen minutes later, her fingers trembled as she turned the page in her book. She realized she didn't recall one word of the page she'd just read. Laying the book aside, she waited for Brody to appear. A half hour crept by.

Finally she slipped into her robe and slippers and went to see about him. He was standing in the dark, staring out at the night. She joined him by the window.

"What is it?"

"Nothing," he said. His tone was repressive.

"Aren't you coming to bed?"

He snorted. "Why? I wouldn't sleep."

"You seemed to sleep okay last night...if your snoring was anything to go by. Of course I've not had a lot of experience with such things," she concluded with demure innocence.

"Really rattling the rafters, was I?"

She relaxed at the amusement in his tone. "Mmm, I don't know. I was asleep, too."

He laughed, but the sound was harsh, startling her. "Are you inviting me to your bed?"

Her breath caught. "Our bed," she said, correcting him. "You've been busy all day. Aren't you tired?"

"Not tired enough," he said enigmatically. He touched her chin, lifting her face so he could study it in the pale glow of the moon. "I wonder why I thought I could resist you."

"Why do you have to?" she immediately countered.

"Entanglements. Lives can become entangled in a year and difficult to sort out. I don't intend for that to happen, no matter what happens between us. Do you understand?"

"Yes. You make yourself perfectly clear." She retreated to the bedroom. Its silence echoed the chill in her heart. The coldness was getting closer. She shook her head at her musing. Taking a pillow and blanket, she made her bed in the office.

It was a long time later that Brody came upstairs. She

wished he'd come and scoop her into his arms and carry her to their bed and keep her warm all through the night.

Ty was in the kitchen, a cup of coffee in hand when she quietly descended. Brody had been up and gone when she woke that morning.

The television in the adjoining family room was on. The newscaster finished one report, then launched into a description of two burglary convicts who had escaped from a jail in Oregon.

"That's Shane's territory," Ty said. Shane was his brother, the sheriff of the county where the escape took place.

"Do we need to get back?" Carly asked, clipping her hair back as she entered the kitchen from the guest room.

"Maybe. I'll call and see what's happening," he said in answer to his wife's question. "The convicts have headed into the mountains. Shane will need trackers."

He went to call his brother. Carly explained the situation to Brody when he came in.

"Do you want my help?" Brody asked when Ty returned.

"No. We'll have dogs and men who know the area. You'd better continue with your plans."

Jessica cast a quick glance Brody's way, but his expression told her nothing. They ate the breakfast Jessica quickly prepared, then Jessica hugged her new family before they left for Denver and the airport there.

When she and Brody stopped waving and returned inside, she turned to him. "What plans?"

He didn't pretend to misunderstand her. "To catch the person who wants you dead."

"How are you planning to do that?"

"By being here." He gestured at the ranch and the surrounding territory. "He'll have to come to us. The later it gets, the more chances he'll have to take."

"To do me in before the year is up."

"Right."

She sighed and pushed a strand of hair away from her face. "I thought my troubles would be over if I married."

His cynical smile told her she should have known better.

"Life is never simple," she concluded. "You could be killed along with me."

Brody shrugged. "I could be, but I don't plan on it."

She wasn't amused by his confident statement. "I don't want you hurt because of me."

He frowned the way he did when he was thinking things through. "I won't get hurt. Neither will you. I told you I'd take care of you. I will."

With that, he left her and went about the chores that never let up on a ranch. She returned to the house and started on the dishes, her mind awash with worry in spite of his reassurance.

Brody dismounted and left the gelding ground-hitched while he scouted the area. Dropping to his haunches, he studied the ground along the bank. The ford was the only place the creek could be crossed in a vehicle along this entire backstretch of the ranch. The land rose abruptly into mountainous country beyond this point.

Someone had been through here again. The rain Wednesday had washed out the older tracks he'd found last week.

He studied the tire tread, noting a V-shaped cut along one edge that would make it easier to identify the tracks if he found them on other parts of the ranch. He saw where the vehicle had stopped on this side of the creek and turned around.

Remounting, he crossed the fast-flowing stream, high from spring runoff, and checked the other side. No tread there, but someone had stood on the bank and surveyed the area. Then the person had walked up the old logging road to a high point and looked over the land from there.

Brody stood on the same spot, his eyes narrowed behind his sunglasses. Yeah, this was a good spot. From here, he could see Don moving the sheep up the narrow valley to the high pastures where they would stay the summer. The summer cabin was clearly visible from here. An observer could watch the comings and goings of anyone in the two-room cabin, which had only a front door, with impunity.

He used a twig to blot out his own tracks and returned to his horse. Mounting, he laid down a false trail as if a group of horsemen had crossed here and ridden into the woods. He circled around and left the area by another trail.

Riding cross-country, he returned to the ranch house. It took an hour's hard ride. But it would take longer for a vehicle to cover the rutted, rocky logging road from the creek to where the rough track meandered over the ridge above the ranch house.

Stopping on the rimrock, he watched the activity below. The two college students who helped with the cattle in the summer were branding calves and attaching pesticide tags to their ears before moving them to higher ground.

Another figure emerged from the barn. He felt a painful tightening all the way down to his toes. Jessica.

The lamb she'd adopted frolicked behind her, following along as if he were a puppy at her heels. When the lamb grew into a yearling, it would become a pest. Too big to be a pet, it would continue to act like one unless he intervened. He'd separate the two the same as Don separated the ewes from the lambs when it was time.

Time. He could hardly believe three weeks had passed since their marriage. Three weeks of wedded bliss.

Ha.

Jessica had moved back to the guest room as soon as Carly and Ty drove out of the yard. She'd been rather quiet since then. He found himself worrying about her at odd moments while he did the never-ending chores and kept up his surveillance of the ranch. Carly had called to report the escaped men had been captured and all was well with them.

He wished he could say the same for himself and Jessica. It was getting harder to share the house with her. Every night he tossed and turned, haunted by the memory of that one night she'd slept with him.

Shaking his head in disgust at his inability to root the feel of her out of his dreams, he guided the gelding down the steep slope. After setting the horse free in the paddock, he went to the house. Jessica smiled at him from the stove where she stirred something that smelled good.

His pulse leapt as he gazed at her. She was a continual surprise to him. He still couldn't believe the way she'd taken over the cooking and the house. She cared for the orphaned lamb and helped with the chores day after day, her humor intact. It didn't add up. There had to be a catch somewhere, the fatal flaw that would prove it was all an act.

But his doubts didn't stop the rush of eagerness that had him hurrying to remove his boots and get closer to her.

"You went for a long ride," she murmured before tasting the contents of the pot.

"Checking fences."

"What did you find?"

"The usual. What are you cooking?"

"Chicken and dumplings. Do you like them?"

"Yeah. They're one of my favorites."

The only ones he'd eaten was at the diner in town where the dumplings were doughy strips in a thick broth. Jessica's broth was thick, but the dumplings were round. He took the spoon from her and chased one around the pot. When he fished it out and bit into it, he nearly swooned.

"That's the best thing I ever ate," he said without thinking. He was hesitant to offer her compliments. He didn't want to encourage her. She already drove him crazy with her nesting activities. Next thing he knew, she'd be wanting to change the furniture or curtains or something.

"So what kind of tracks did you find?" she asked.

He nearly dropped the spoon. When he looked into her eyes, he realized she'd been testing him. His start of surprise had given him away. "How did you know about those?"

"A calculated guess. Were they similar to the ones you found on the logging road?"

Brody recalled the night he'd caught her eavesdropping on the stairs. "No, but I found a track with a plug gone on the front tire of the vehicle. Someone stopped at the creek turnoff recently. It might have been a couple who parked last night for a little moonlight and romance."

She didn't pick up on his quip about a romantic couple. Instead twin lines appeared between her eyes as she frowned. "Brody, I never meant to put you in danger when I suggested marriage. I didn't think—"

"I charge a fair amount to put myself in danger for my clients." He interrupted her apology. "That's what you pay me to do. It's part of the job, just as it was before the marriage."

"Part of the job," she repeated, thinking it over.

"That's right. This is just a job, nothing more." His heart pounded crazily against his ribs, startling him. It exposed the lie in what he'd just said. Protecting Jessica had been more than a job from the first minute.

"You know," she said slowly, "it occurs to me that I don't have to live with you. I merely have to stay married for the year. My mother's will said nothing about living together."

"It's rather difficult to have a marriage otherwise, isn't it?" he countered.

"I could move somewhere else...where no one knows me. As Mrs. Smith, I'd be incognito, so to speak."

Anger erupted in him. "Any woman using my name and claiming to be my wife will live where I can keep an eye on her. You leave here and you'll find our marriage annulled before you hit the state line."

"But Brody, it would be safer for you—"

"And that's that," he added for good measure, stopping her concerned protests.

She looked into his eyes, her own troubled and guilt-ridden. "I've never been anything but trouble to the people I lo—the people I'm kin to, either by blood or marriage."

He caught the change in wording, but didn't pursue it. "Poor little rich girl," he scoffed.

Her eyes flickered with sadness, but she gave him a saucy grin. "Rich is the operative word. One year and I won't have to put up with your insults. Is Don coming in for lunch?"

"No. He's moving sheep. He and I will take turns keeping an eye on them until his nephew arrives when school is out."

"I see." She set the table. "If you could do anything you wanted, what would you do?" She gave him an earnest glance before turning off the heat under the dumpling pot and laying the spoon aside. She put the pot on a trivet on the table and indicated he should take his seat.

"Live at the ranch most of the time. I can run the office easily enough from here." He washed up at the sink before sitting in his usual chair.

"How long would you be satisfied to rusticate?"

He turned the question on her. "Are you bored with ranch life? You still have over eleven months to go."

"No, I'm not bored," she was quick to deny. "You seem too active to drive a few cattle and sheep to pasture for the rest of your life."

"It's the life I like."

"Because you don't have to deal with people?"

"Something like that," he agreed.

The truth was, he was restless. He wasn't sure if it was due to having to deal with Jessica living in the same house day after day or to the lack of action. Since waking up with her in his arms, he'd felt the emptiness closing in.

He liked it that way, he reminded himself ruthlessly. Eleven months and she'd be gone. Maybe he should let her go before it was too late. Too late for what? He didn't want to think about that. He ate and left the house as quickly as he could. To linger was foolish.

Chapter Seven

Jessica listened to the hum of the vacuum cleaner in Brody's bedroom. A totally unwarranted wave of jealousy had overcome her when the woman who cleaned for him finally made it to the ranch.

The housekeeper was maybe all of twenty-two. She had long brown hair, blue eyes with lashes to die for and a sweet smile. She was married to a cowboy who worked over on a big ranch east of them. Thank goodness. Or else Jessica might have felt compelled to fire her on the spot.

Jealousy. It wasn't a pretty emotion.

The first Jessica had known the other woman had arrived was when she'd heard Brody's quiet laughter in the kitchen. Curious, she'd hurried from her room. She'd found him chatting with a young, spritely female who moved familiarly around the kitchen as if she belonged there. Brody had introduced his housekeeper before heading outside again.

He was going to the cabin to deliver supplies to Don. He wasn't sure what time he'd be home, he'd told her earlier that morning when they'd had breakfast. He'd left her without a backward glance and was outside loading an old pickup truck for the drive up the mountain.

Jessica sighed gustily. Her feelings for her stubborn husband were confusing to say the least. One minute she wanted to kiss him until they both melted from the heat; the next, she wanted to pound his hard head with a brick.

After pulling on a jacket, she drifted outside. The wind brought the scent of the pines and firs that grew in profusion along the shanks of the mountains, of the awakening earth that was softening from the melting snow, of the springtime and its promise of life and warmth and all good things. She breathed deeply, hungrily, feeling that promise fill her body.

Longing, harsh and urgent, trilled like a band of bagpipes through her, its rhythms strange and haunting and lonely.

She walked to the rail fence near where he worked. "I'd like to ride along with you. I've never been to the higher pastures."

He scowled at her request.

"Would that be all right?" she persisted in the face of his obdurate silence. He'd been cold and distant since his sister and her husband had left.

"I suppose."

"You're lucky I don't have a brick handy," she said in a perfectly calm manner.

That caught his attention. "What in hell is that supposed to mean?" he demanded.

Jessica clenched her hands on the bed of the pickup. With his housekeeper, he could chat and laugh. With his wife, he could only scowl and curse. "Whatever you want it to," she retorted, giving him back glare for glare.

She turned and watched the llamas as they grazed in the lush new grass of the pasture. One of them stuck his head over the fence and gazed at her from limpid brown eyes, his long lashes fluttering in the breeze. His lips puckered as if inviting her closer for a kiss. Well, the animal was certainly more tempting than her moody husband.

Brody moved so fast she didn't have time to react. His big hands caught her shoulders and whirled her around. "Don't touch me," she ordered haughtily, the restless anger overcoming her better judgment.

Splat.

A blob of green spit landed on her white shirt. She stared at it in disbelief. She jerked her gaze upward.

"Don't look at me," her husband said in evident amusement. "I didn't do it. Oh-oh."

Splat.

He moved them in time. The second missive landed on the fender of the pickup and slithered down.

Jessica's mouth dropped open. "The llama spit on me?"

The llama gazed at her over the fence railing. He fluttered his eyelashes at her, his expression pleasantly satisfied with his feat.

She could feel the moisture soak right through her bra and on her breast. "Yuck."

Brody shook out his handkerchief. "Sorry, I forgot to warn you about our friend here." He rubbed at the spot.

White-hot heat spread in ever-increasing circles as he cleaned her shirt. Although he held the material taut with one hand, he rubbed against her breast with each stroke of his handkerchief. When she stole a glance at him, there was laughter in his eyes.

"Have you ever had llama stew?" she asked with vengeance gleaming foremost in her mind.

Brody could contain it no longer. He burst out laughing. His city wife had looked so shocked, then indignant when she'd realized what the llama had done.

"I think I can safely say I've been dissed." She gave him a wry grimace and reached for the handkerchief.

"I'll do it," he volunteered. "Mind if I use some spit? It'll take the stain out."

"Feel free," she said in a resigned tone.

He subdued the smile that tickled the corner of his mouth and moistened the handkerchief. Rubbing at the green stain, he felt the amusement fade, to be replaced by feelings far stronger and more tempestuous than laughter.

Her nipple tucked into a tight little bud that brought back the memory of exactly how it had felt when he'd kissed her there and run his tongue over the intriguing tip. His own body contracted, then expanded with a painful surge as desire flooded him. He stopped rubbing and let his hand stay where it was.

She looked at him again, then lifted her hands and laid them on his chest. Her lashes drifted downward. He recognized the signs of arousal in her, the muted excitement as passion began to build. He started rubbing again, around and around the full globe of her breast. He knew he should back off, get the hell out of there, but he stayed.

Jessica arched her back, wanting more. "Brody," she murmured. Her lungs ached as she tried to draw a breath. She moved forward, stretching upward at the same time.

His mouth met hers in a kiss of searing hunger. She opened her mouth and felt him sweep inside, his tongue stroking hers in a fashion so erotic it made her knees weak. She flicked her tongue against his, then joined in the intimate caresses.

When her legs could bear her weight no longer, she leaned against him. Arms as strong as a mountain ash wrapped around her, nearly lifting her off her feet. She was crushed to his powerful frame. His strength shocked her, yet she sensed that the mighty flex of his muscles that so awed her was a bid for control on his part.

Brody fought his own need to hold her even tighter. He took two steps and lifted her to the tailgate of the rusty truck. He pushed his way between her thighs. A roar invaded his head as he felt her heat through the layers of their jeans. Her hips rolled against him, caressing the hard ridge and fueling the fire in him into a roiling inferno.

Without thinking, he leaned over her, pressing her against the bed of the truck, her head pillowed on a five-pound sack of rice. She shifted restlessly beneath him, deep in the sensual abandon of a woman lost in ecstasy. He raised one knee and rested it beside her thigh on the tailgate, letting her take some of his weight. With each movement of her hips, she caressed him.

He pushed closer and heard her give a breathless moan. She opened her thighs and wrapped her legs around his hips. He moved against her, oblivious to anything but the intense pleasure they shared. She moved from side to side, driving him crazy with the feel of her lush breasts against his chest. With one hand, he freed the fastenings on her shirt, then his. He pushed her bra out of the way.

"Ahh," he groaned when her breasts hit his bare flesh. It was the sweetest torture he'd ever experienced. He dipped his head and caught the taut nipple between his teeth. Holding it gently, he stroked his tongue over it again and again.

She cried out and her hips bucked against him. Heat exploded in every part of his body. When she laid her hands on each side of his face, he let her guide his mouth back to hers while she pressed upward, those unbound breasts like brands against his skin. Her arms encircled his shoulders and whimpering sounds escaped her as he kissed along her neck.

Some wiser part of him, knowing it couldn't wrest control from the wild passion that clamored through his body, issued quiet warnings about consequences and a future he couldn't foresee. He knew he should stop, but he couldn't. God help him, he couldn't give her up…

The sounds of an engine cranking, dying, then cranking again brought him out of the sensual trance. He looked up in time to see the housekeeper drive off in her ten-year-old compact.

She tooted the horn and waved as she hurtled down the driveway at her usual dust-stirring speed. He realized she couldn't see Jessica lying half clothed on the bed of the truck and was grateful for small favors.

After the housekeeper was gone, he lowered his leg and stepped back. Jessica opened her eyes and gave him a smoldering look that had his heart racing again. He shook his head, denying the need to sink into her hot, silky depths and find the release he so desperately needed.

"I've got work to do," he reminded her harshly.

The hazy translucence disappeared from her eyes. He saw her throat move as she swallowed. She rose to a sitting position and glanced around the quadrangle between the house and outbuildings as if orienting herself in a strange land. She shivered and wrapped her arms across herself.

"Get back to the house," he ordered, gruffer than he meant to be. "The wind has a nip to it. A storm is supposed to come in tonight. I need to get the supplies to Don."

She nodded and slid off the truck. Without looking at him, she adjusted her bra and fastened her shirt, then she walked to the ranch house and went inside without once looking back. Her back was straight and rigid.

He checked the supplies, then threw a few bales of straw into the truck. Straw came in handy for lots of purposes. He at once pictured Jessica lying in a bed of the stuff, her arms outstretched in welcome, inviting him inside...

With a curse, he leapt into the truck and took off.

Jessica put the magazine on modern ranching aside when she heard the truck arrive and went to the window. Brody was back. No, it was Don. Curious, she grabbed a jacket and went outside.

"Hi, where's Brody?" she called, jumping down from the porch and running across the stable yard.

Don's answer was barely audible. "At the high cabin."

She realized he had laryngitis. When he was racked by a rattling cough for several seconds, she worried about his health. "You need to go to the doctor. You might have pneumonia."

The shepherd nodded. "That's why Brody sent me in. He said you were to come to him and bring the lamb. I'll help you load him."

"No, I can manage. You take care of that bug. How do I get to this cabin?"

"Take the county road to the creek, then turn left. You can ford the creek there, then continue up the logging road."

She watched the older man anxiously until he was safely in the sports ute and on his way to the small mountain town twenty miles down the road. Then she opened the gate and whistled for Ram, short for rambunctious.

The lamb bleated and ran toward her at full speed. She dodged the woolly head when he tried to butt her. Hmm, maybe she should tie a rope on him in case he decided to jump out of the truck. She headed for the barn.

Whump.

Her legs went out from under her as Ram lived up to his name and butted her in the back of the knees. She sat down in a shallow puddle.

"I should have named you Goat," she muttered, lifting herself from the mud. She wiped her hands on her ruined jeans and grabbed the lamb before he thought of a new trick. She cleaned its tiny feet on her shirt and shoved him in the cab of the truck.

With a beat of excitement, she raced into the house, threw her soiled clothing into the washer and showered as fast as she could. She put perfume at her wrists and elbows and behind her ears, then, feeling wicked, dabbed it at other strategic spots.

Dressed in floral bikini briefs and a matching bra, she hummed to herself as she prepared to go to her husband. Her hands trembled as she zipped fresh jeans over the briefs, then pulled on a long-sleeve velour top of ruby red. She debated between her gown and sweat suit, then decided she would be practical. And she could use the sweat suit as a change of clothing just in case Ram sneaked up on her again.

Carrying the ham and lima beans she'd prepared for their dinner, she returned to the truck. Ram had chewed up a newspaper and scattered it across the seat. She put the food in the back, folded the newspaper and climbed in. With a turn of the switch, they were off.

She drove carefully along the county road, afraid that she'd miss the turnoff…no, here was the creek and the dirt road was on the other side of the bridge to the left as Don had said.

Feeling lighter with each mile, she made the turn, found

the ford and crossed it slowly, her heart pounding as the water formed a muddy wake to each side of the front bumper. Once she cleared that hurdle, her confidence increased as she made her way up the winding track, going higher into the mountains with each hairpin turn.

At last the terrain opened into a narrow valley. The creek meandered through the center of it. Off to one side, set among fresh-leaved aspens, was the cabin. Her heart nearly crashed through her rib cage with its hard beat.

Brody crossed the meadow and opened the truck door when she stopped by the tiny cottage.

"Hi." Her voice was husky, sexy. She cleared it.

"Who's your passenger?" he inquired in his usual sardonic manner with her.

"Just someone I picked up on the road." She jumped down. Ram landed at her heels, then tried to butt Brody before dashing off to taste a patch of wildflowers near the cabin.

"I brought lunch." She lifted the plastic-covered bowls from the bed of the truck.

Brody took the heaviest container from her and led the way inside. Jessica took in the cabin at a glance. It was composed of two rooms—the living-dining room, which they were in and a bedroom visible through a doorway. There was no door on the frame. There were two cots for sleeping with a table between them. A clock ticked on the table.

"Plates are behind the curtain," he told her. "I'll take care of your pet."

She pressed a hand to her heart. "What…what are you going to do?"

"Put him in with the flock. It's time he learned he's a sheep, not a lapdog." Brody's gaze sharpened when she sighed in relief. "What did you think I was going to do, make mincemeat out of him?"

"I wasn't sure." She gave him a brilliant smile. "I'm glad we're not going to have to fight about it."

His snort clearly said he didn't consider her much of an opponent. Obstinate man.

She followed him outside and watched as Brody tucked the frisky lamb under one arm and carried him to the edge of the flock. She watched in amazement as he squirted glue on the lamb's back and stuck a wad of wool on it. He then put the lamb next to one of the ewes munching on the spring grass and rubbed the ewe with a piece of material.

The lamb bleated and butted against the ewe the way he did when he wanted food. The ewe looked around in surprise. Her nose twitched as she caught a whiff of this rambunctious interloper. She smelled the lamb cautiously, then moved away when he searched around her belly. The lamb followed.

"What did you do?" Jessica asked Brody when he returned to her side.

He smiled. "Rubbed the ewe with your scent and glued a dab of the ewe's wool to the lamb to confuse her."

"Will she take him as her own?"

"Not really, but she'll probably let him stay near. The others will smell her on him and let him stay with the flock."

"Oh." She laughed as Ram tried once more to find the bucket with the teat on the ewe that smelled like Jessica. "What did you use that had my scent on it?"

He hesitated, then confessed. "I used some of your perfume on a handkerchief."

She realized he'd gone into her bathroom to find her perfume without her seeing him. "My best perfume used on a sheep."

He grinned when he saw she didn't really mind.

She took the handkerchief from him. It had dark smudges on it. She recalled his giving her one to use when she'd become teary-eyed at leaving Chicago. He'd kept it all this time. Not that it meant anything...

Stuffing the hankie into her pocket, she couldn't help the smile that insisted on forming. "Smart man," she said.

Brody cut her a glance from the corner of his eye and was relieved to see the laughter gleaming from hers. "Yeah, that's what I thought you would say."

The thing he couldn't say to his sweet wife was what it had done to him every time he caught a whiff of the handkerchief. Nor could he tell her he'd been aware of her lavender scent for weeks and couldn't stop wondering exactly where she spritzed the floral perfume after she took her bath.

He focused on the lamb again. He'd been trying for a week to think of a way to move the lamb into the flock where it could be with its own kind, rather than with humans. It had taken to raising a ruckus whenever Jessica was out of sight. When he'd mentioned the problem to Don, the shepherd had told him he needed something with her scent and explained how to use it so the lamb would stay with one of the ewes.

When Brody had seen her lace bikinis in the laundry basket that morning, a plan had come to mind. However, he hadn't counted on the consequences. With her perfume wafting around him at every turn, he'd been in a state of semiarousal for hours, then to have her come out to the truck and want to trail along with him...

No way. He'd left the ranch in a cloud of dust, anxious to get away before he made a complete fool of himself. He couldn't believe he'd nearly taken her right there on the pickup, in sight of the housekeeper or cowboys...or the person who was trying to get rid of her.

That was really what had brought him to his senses. It had reminded him of the fact he was a hired gun, one year of his time bought and paid for so she could be free.

Anyway, he'd forgotten the blasted lamb. It was only after he'd realized Don had more than a spring cold that he'd decided to let her come up and bring her pet. He needed her at the cabin so he could keep an eye on her since he would have to stay with the flock. He heaved a desperate sigh. It was going to be another of those long nights.

Her laughter drew him like a moth to light. She was watching her pet annoy every sheep in his vicinity. Ram was feeling frolicsome. Finally another lamb joined him in dodging around the ewes. The two ran like crazy, then gave a leap into the air as if jumping through an invisible hoop. They continued in this vein for several minutes before flopping to the ground, worn-out from their exertion.

He shook his head in exasperation.

"Watch it. You're about to smile," she quipped. "Ready for lunch, I mean, dinner?" Without waiting for a reply, she linked her arm in his and started for the cabin.

Brody sensed her warmth all the way down his side. He could feel changes taking place inside, a softening totally at odds with the hunger that had him hard and aching. There were things a man could get used to in a year: a neat home, good food, a woman in the house...

He pulled free and stepped away from the temptation of her lavender-scented femininity.

Jessica sensed Brody's withdrawal as if a winter wind blew down her collar. She fought a feeling of rejection and lost. Anger followed closely behind.

Leading the way, she sailed into the cabin in a fine temper. She searched behind a curtain along one wall and found shelves with dishes, food and a few pans and skillets. After setting out plates and forks, she uncovered the ham-and-bean dish, plunked a spoon into it and another in the dish of vinegar slaw. She sat in one of the two folding chairs at the card table that served the cabin as a dining suite.

Brody opened the last bowl and found corn bread sticks, crisp and still warm from the oven. "This is a feast," he commented appreciatively.

She didn't respond.

"I don't have any tea, but the mountain water is better than the finest champagne. Would you like a glass?"

"Please." She kept her eyes on her plate while he pumped two glasses of water from an old-fashioned hand pump beside the stainless-steel bowl that served as a sink. When he was seated opposite her, she picked up her fork and began eating.

Her gaze kept drifting to the open doorway of the bedroom and the twin cots that lined the walls. She could move a cot to the living room if she shoved the table and chairs against the wall. At least she'd be in a different room.

But why should she? Brody was her husband. If he didn't like sleeping in the room with her, let *him* move out.

He went outside after the meal and checked the sheep. Two dogs circled the flock with him, both border collies. Ram gamboled along with them. One of the dogs nipped at his heels to keep him with the flock. The lamb cowered, shocked at this unfriendly act, then raced back to the tolerant ewe he'd decided represented safety.

Jessica, watching from a dusty window, smiled and finished washing the dishes. She settled on a stump in the front to watch the sheep and more particularly her husband as he checked the animals over. The sun warmed her through the red velour, making her sleepy. Her thoughts roamed without control.

She liked sharing life at the ranch with Brody. Basically he was easy to please. He never said yea nor nay about her activities around the house, but let her do as she wished. She cooked and cleaned and sometimes rearranged the cabinets to please herself. He and Don ate everything she cooked with a gratifying pleasure in the food and complimented her on her efforts. She realized she was content.

Almost.

There were things to be ironed out between her and her husband if their time together was to run smoothly. She sighed, thinking of when she would have to leave.

The thought depressed her. She didn't want to go. Brody was the one person in all the world that she trusted.

A painful contraction squeezed the air out of her chest. She pressed a hand to her heart and drew in a shaky breath. Of the people she'd loved, only her grandfather and Uncle Jesse were left. She was estranged from both of them, albeit for different reasons.

Her gaze followed Brody's powerful form as he moved among the flock. His life had been harder than hers but similar in that the people he'd loved and trusted had left him, too, his parents for their own selfish reasons, his aunt Essie because of death. Now he didn't let himself trust anyone.

But in a year anything could happen.

She was reminded of a parable about a thief who'd promised the emperor he could teach a horse to sing if he'd let him live another year. When asked why he'd promised such a foolish thing, he'd replied, "Anything may happen in a year. The horse may die, the emperor may change his mind, I may be pardoned...or the horse may learn to sing.''

At midafternoon, she went inside and rummaged through the shelves for the cookies she'd seen earlier. She prepared lemonade from a mix and took the treat outside.

''Brody,'' she called, cupping her hands around her mouth. ''Snack time.''

He lifted his head. For a long moment he stared at her across the narrow green pasture, then he nodded. He finished his inspection of a lamb's hind leg, then came to the cabin. He washed up at a stand outside the cabin and sat on a rock near the stump where she perched.

''I found lemonade mix in the pantry, so I assume you like it,'' she said, smiling at him.

He didn't return the courtesy. Instead he surveyed the meadow and the woods behind them and the mountains beyond that.

''Have you seen anything suspicious?'' she asked.

''No.''

''Is something wrong?''

''Not a thing.'' Brody noticed the way her mouth pruned up at his short answer. He recalled how it had felt pressing kisses all over his chest and making him ache with hunger—

''Why are you so grim?''

He shot her a glance, then went back to studying the terrain. ''Why are you so smiley?'' he countered.

She finished off a devil's food cookie and brushed the crumbs off her fingers. ''Well, the sun is shining. It's the first day of May and spring seems to be truly here, I'm with a handsome man...'' She cast him an oblique glance as if to see how he took this blatant compliment.

He snorted derisively.

"Oh, you've been called handsome before and by better women than me, I take it?"

He wolfed down a third cookie and tried not to notice the slender eyebrow with the attitude lofted in challenge.

He couldn't figure his sexy-as-hell wife out at all. She'd gotten mad about something when she'd come out to the truck that morning, but when the llama had spit on her, she'd laughed, then she'd taken his kisses and given them back to him so hot and so hard he'd nearly gone into cardiac arrest before he wrestled half their clothes off so he could feel her skin on his.

Now she was teasing him or some damn thing. He wasn't sure if she was joking or leading up to a tirade. Over what, he hadn't a clue.

Women. A man never knew where he stood with 'em.

Except he had some good ideas. Experience had taught him not to take how they acted or what they said as the gospel truth.

"What's your point?" he asked, too impatient for guessing games and the little innuendoes that women seemed to like.

"My point," she mused. She bit into a second cookie, leaving crumbs at the corners of her mouth. She neatly wiped them away with the tip of her tongue.

He nearly groaned aloud. He wanted to lick them off for her, then stay and taste her for a good long while, then he'd leisurely roam down her neck and throat to those bouncy breasts that were confined in a bra again. He felt a rebellious need to set them free, as if they were unfairly imprisoned...

Honest to Pete, he couldn't believe the ridiculous notions he was getting just sitting there eating a cookie with her.

"I was jealous this morning," she stated.

He was so startled by this piece of news his jaw unhinged and sagged for a second before he could snap it closed.

"You laughed and chatted with your housekeeper. I heard you from my room. But you're always grim with me, except when the llama spit. But even when you grab me and kiss me—"

"I don't remember any protest from you about the grabbing and kissing part," he reminded her self-righteously.

"Well, I don't object, not exactly, but I'd like to be, oh, I don't know, courted, maybe."

The word almost blew him away. He'd have fallen off the rock if he hadn't had both feet firmly on the ground. What the hell was she talking about, courting?

"*You* were the one who wanted marriage. If anyone is supposed to do any courting, I'd think it would be you." He was already hard just thinking about it, her kissing and stroking him, maybe rubbing his back when he was real tired. "If you want me in your bed, you'll have to be more direct," he advised and drained the cool glass of lemonade, "but it's an entanglement I don't recommend. If you're getting bored, I'll remind you that you were the one who thought you could hold out a year. If you can't…" He let the thought trail off and shrugged.

He set the glass on the washstand and headed for the fields before he begged for a demonstration of her technique.

She said something behind his back, but he couldn't make it out. It sounded like, "And maybe the horse will learn to sing," but of course, that didn't make any sense.

Chapter Eight

Jessica watched the awesome display of lightning from the small window set in the west wall of the front room. The one other window in the room was on the opposite side. The bedroom had two similar windows, one in each side wall. For light and cross-ventilation, she assumed.

The cabin wasn't elegant, but it was adequate. Electricity had been added at a later date than the original construction. A single bulb dangled from a wire attached to a ceramic base. The wire ran across the ceiling to a hole drilled in the thick pine wall. Another wire entered the bedroom from a hole drilled through the windowsill. The bedside lamp was plugged into the socket screwed onto the wall.

In the rapidly fading twilight, she could see veils of rain sweeping down the mountainside, but the storm hadn't reached the valley yet. The air was cold now.

"The storm will hit here soon." Brody sat at the table,

a book on forensic anthropology in his hands. He closed the tome and stood.

She watched him stretch his powerful frame and raise his arms toward the ceiling. He looked like one of those half-god, half-mortal beings from mythology, as awesome in his power as the storm outside. She wouldn't have been surprised if he'd called lightning bolts from the heavens by a single gesture.

The light flickered. He reached up and clicked off the bulb, then stood behind her, watching the storm.

"There'll be hail tonight," he said.

"Will the sheep be okay?"

"They wear wool jackets."

She glanced over her shoulder in time to catch the flash of his teeth as he smiled. "Ram is smaller than the others." She worried about the runt who thought he was master of all he surveyed, due, no doubt, to her preferential attention.

"The dogs will keep him with the flock, and the ewe will let him huddle against her. Sheep bunch up during a storm. Unless they're spooked by a lightning strike."

"Will they stampede?" she asked, remembering a scene from a Thomas Hardy book in which the hero's flock had run off a cliff and died, thus taking his entire livelihood with them.

"Not likely. There's no place to run. The mountains are too steep for them to go far. That only leaves the valley. It narrows down this way, making it easy to head 'em off."

"I could help." She smiled at the snort of amusement at her offer. She'd expected it. She was coming to know her husband. He took nothing at face value and trusted no one. Including his wife...most especially his wife.

Light exploded as lightning sizzled as if it were a magnesium strip. The thunderclap followed immediately, booming right over the cabin. The sound ricocheted from peak to peak, drowning out the keening of the wind and the approaching rain. She flinched as Brody cursed.

His hands settled on her shoulders. He leaned forward and peered out the window. She squinted her eyes but couldn't see a thing in the stygian darkness. Another brilliant flash lit up the meadow, limning the sheep in an eerie glow.

The seconds after the flash died and the crack of thunder had rolled into a distant rumble, she could still see the flock, milling and churning the meadow as the sheep ran first one way, then another.

Brody cursed a streak, then released her. She heard the click but no light appeared. He muttered another expletive. A flashlight came on. She saw him pull on waterproof pants and a slicker over a jacket, then he was out the door and gone.

She felt her way to the bedroom door and explored along the wall where Brody had stood. She encountered another slicker. The pants were way too large and a hindrance. She forgot about them and pulled the slicker on. She headed for the pickup.

Inside the cab, she felt behind the seat for the old parka she'd thrown back there before she'd started out. She climbed inside and removed the slicker, then bundled up in the parka and rain gear before venturing out to help Brody.

During the next brilliant flash, she saw him step in front of a renegade bunch and turn them back into the mill. Above the storm she heard him call to the dogs, "Jojo, Curly, circle 'em up." She saw him make a wide sweeping circle with his arm while he kept the sheep around him moving in a circle.

To her left she spied another bunch making a break

toward the lower end of the valley. She ran as hard as she could and waved her arms like a windmill gone berserk. The lead ewe veered off but eluded her.

One of the border collies came to her aid. He turned the ewe while she managed to shoo the others into the flock. Between the two humans and the dogs, they kept the frightened sheep from stampeding down the valley.

"Let's get them into the draw. It'll protect them from the wind and lightning," Brody shouted at her.

"Right." She had no idea where the draw was, but she followed him and did what he did, keeping the sheep bunched and moving at a slow, steady pace to the west side of the valley.

After a period of time—she had no idea how long; it seemed they'd been battling the elements for ages—she felt the downward slope of the land. The intermittent flashes of lightning showed her the way. Brody's flashlight guided her the rest of the time.

"Okay, circle them up," she heard Brody shout.

The collies went to work circling the flock, keeping them tightly grouped. Jessica stumbled over a rock. She tried to push herself upright, but her foot slipped in the mud. She used one of Brody's favorite curses.

She saw the flashlight swing her way, then Brody's deep voice cautioning her to be careful. He came toward her.

Reaching up to brush a wet tendril of hair from her eyes with the back of her hand, she heard a crack, then saw the flash of lightning. It registered in her brain that the order was backward. The lightning was supposed to come first, then the thunder.

The limned outline of wind-whipped trees and rough terrain imposed by the lightning lingered in her eyes, giving her time to interpret it. When she did, she let out a yelp of fear and anger. A man stood on a high slope above the valley. He had a rifle. It was pointed their way. At Brody.

With a burst of adrenaline, she threw herself up and at him, scrambling in the mud and slick grass, running in what seemed to be slow motion forever before she reached him.

"Brody, a gun," she cried, flinging herself at him and bringing them both down in a tangle of arms and legs.

"Dammit all," he growled. "What the hell are you doing?"

He tried to free himself from her grappling arms, but she held on, shielding him from the gunman while she pulled the flashlight against her abdomen, shutting off its stream of light.

"Turn off the light," she shouted. "There's a man with a gun on the ridge above us."

She felt his quick jerk of surprise, then the light went dark. One arm hooked around her waist and flipped them over so he was on top of her.

"Keep still," she heard him say close to her ear.

She felt him reach between them and do something, then he flipped his slicker off and tossed it behind the rock she'd fallen over. In the next flash of lightning, she could see it lying in a heap. Brody covered her, pulling her slicker in against her sides and hiding it as much as he could. She realized the bright yellow could be seen easily in each flash of light.

"Get the slicker off," Brody ordered.

She did it as quickly as possible. He tossed it on top of his and pushed the pile into a hollow behind the rock.

His hand reached around her neck and pulled her close, his body half shielding her from the pounding rain. "We're going to make a run for the cabin. Between lightning flashes. When the lightning comes, hit the ground and lie still for a couple of seconds. Got that?''

''Yes.'' Her teeth were starting to chatter. The icy rain slid down the neck of her parka. Tiny balls of hail hit and stuck in her hair.

''Let's go.'' Brody held her hand, and they ran like marathoners up the side of the draw. ''Down.''

She hit the ground. He fell on top of her, covering her with his broad body. Lightning sizzled across the sky like droplets off a hot skillet. The thunder followed in a deafening clap. The storm whirled all around them as if they were trapped in the hot cloud instead of on the land.

''Run,'' Brody said. He yanked her to her feet.

She flew across the meadow with him. The next flash caught them in the open. She couldn't tell if the noise she heard was thunder, gunshots or the wild roar of her blood through her ears. Never had she felt so scared...or so elated.

Brody practically tackled her, bringing them down in a puddle of dank water and churned up earth. He rolled on top of her when she landed with a splash, her back to the damp.

The rain turned completely to hail. It hit all around them and on them, making little pinging sounds like a child hitting the tinny notes of a toy piano.

Jessica felt the balls of ice grow larger, their force painful against her hands, which were holding tight to Brody's back. His head was over hers, blocking the hailstones, protecting her. Wet drops fell from his hair onto her face.

Without thinking, she kissed his lean cheek. Scattered thoughts coalesced into one clear notion—if they were to die, she wanted them to go together.

''This is a strange time to start courting,'' he told her in a gruff whisper next to her ear.

"Well, I had this irresistible urge," she said, unable to keep the amusement at bay. The whole situation was comical, them wet, lying in a mud puddle, hail pounding them. "The lightning has stopped. Shall we make a run for it?"

"Right."

They were up and away on the next heartbeat. Brody kept her in front of him. She hit the cabin door and opened it with one yank, or else they would have crashed right through.

Brody tumbled in after her and kicked the door closed with one solid lick. He snapped the lock, then dropped a two-by-four beam across two hooks on either side of the frame. She hadn't realized what they were for.

"Get out of those wet clothes," he ordered, turning from his task. Lightning turned the inside of the cabin a luminous green.

"Are you trying to get me naked?" she retorted. Her teeth still had a tendency to chatter, but the elation lingered. Her blood was warm from the run and the excitement.

"You wish," he responded to her jest. "Can you find your way to the bedroom in the dark?"

"Yes. Why don't we try the light?"

"Because I don't want the gunman to know for sure where we are. If there was a gunman."

"There was." She envisioned the images she'd seen. The wind had been wild just then, whipping the trees and bushes into a frenzy. "I think."

She groped her way into the bedroom and found her knapsack. She pulled out her sweat suit, glad that she'd thought of bringing it, and quickly stripped out of her wet clothes. When she attempted to step into her fleecy pants, she had to take a hop on one foot to retain her balance.

Her bare rear hit another, one much harder and leaner, one that radiated heat all over her. She stopped dead still.

Brody cursed.

"Don't," she whispered, suddenly wanting him with a longing that was indescribable. She ached in places she didn't know she had. She trembled and went hot, then cold. She dropped the sweat-suit pants and turned blindly.

His chest was bare and just as warm as his backside. She moved instinctively to it. Her breasts hit the solid wall of his flesh. The wiry hairs tickled her nipples, which were already erect from the cold. The contact excited her as his mouth had done in the past.

"Brody," she whispered, loving the sound of his name.

He groaned audibly, then his arms came around her. A rod, thick, hot and probing, touched her, then lay between them like a smooth log as he crushed her against him.

She ran her hands over his muscular back, awed by the perfection of the human body, by the way they fit together, by the wild incandescence in her blood. A sense of unleashed power, like that of the storm, broke over her. She lifted her face toward his.

Somehow, in the total darkness, his mouth found hers.

The kiss was hard, hot, wild, wicked, provocative, pleasing and finally, infinitely wonderful.

She'd never known anything like it in all her days. Or nights. Or hopes. Or dreams.

His hard staff throbbed between them. She shifted a little and touched it. Brody sucked in a harsh breath. She paused. He thrust his hips forward. She took that as an invitation.

Closing her hand around the warm, living flesh, she moved experimentally and heard him catch his breath, then let it out slowly, as if his control was near the snapping point. She'd never touched a man like this, and the experience thrilled her.

This was Brody, her husband. It was his body she touched, this special masculine part that was made-to-order for her femininity. Between them, they could give life to the seed inside her and grow a child.

Brody slid his hands down her spine, then clasped her buttocks. He kneaded the firm, smooth mounds until the flesh was warm, then rubbed up and down. He let his thumbs explore the dip between the mounds and felt her gasp of surprise as he drew a caress over sensitive nerve endings. There were many erotic spots on the body. As if he were a kid in a candy store, he wanted to try them all at once with her.

The only thing that slowed him down was the knowledge that she was a virgin. He didn't know how much petting she'd done with her dates, but he didn't want to shock her.

When she trembled against him, he took a careful step forward and found his cot. The sleeping bag was already open on it. He clasped her under her hips and across her back and laid her down.

"Hmm," she murmured, "this feels like a warm cloud."

"The best polyester filling money can buy," he assured her, hardly aware of what he was saying. The hot beat of hunger was on him. He knew what he was doing—oh, yes, forever after this night he would never be able to lie to himself and say he was out of his head because of the excitement of the storm. He wouldn't be able to justify it on grounds of the possible danger they had escaped if there had really been a man with a gun.

No, he knew what he was doing. And he was going to

do it anyway. He'd fight the devil himself to have her this once. For this night, his beautiful wife would be his.

He kneed her thighs apart and practically dived between them. He stretched his body over hers, taking his weight on one elbow while sliding his hand behind her neck and tangling his fingers in her wet hair. With his free hand, he raked over her shoulder and found her breast.

Perfection. She was perfection everywhere he touched— smooth and sensuous and curvy. Her skin was cool from the icy rain, but she rapidly warmed as he caressed her with his entire body.

It was the beginning of complete possession.

His or hers?

At the moment, it didn't matter. Nothing did but the exquisite feel of her body against his.

She made murmuring sounds close to his ear. His heart stood still, then nearly beat its way out of his chest when he realized she was urging him on with her little keening cries.

Jessica ran her hands over Brody, her eyes closed as if she savored a particularly delicious morsel and wanted to experience its flavor without any distraction. His flesh was warm and very smooth on his back and buttocks.

Feeling brave, she ran a thumb down the newly discovered erotic spot between his rock-hard buns and felt him buck against her. It took her breath away to realize she could affect him this way, to know she had power over him in some small way.

Maybe not so small, she corrected when she felt the throb of his body against her thigh.

A sensation, as if static lightning sizzled all around them, made every nerve in her body jingle with anticipation. She'd never felt so uncertain and yet so sure of what she was doing in her life. This was her husband, and she wanted him.

"Oh, Brody," she whispered, "yes. Yes."

He knew he wasn't going to be content with a quick joining. It wasn't enough, not after all the nights of restless tossing. He wanted the full feast, from appetizer to dessert.

Sipping at her lips was like tasting champagne. The bubbles were going straight to his head. A mist coated his thinking processes, obscuring reason and all the dangers he knew he should consider...but wasn't.

When she moved her hips against him, he nearly lost it and plunged into her sweet womanly depths without thought of her. He held on until he could reassert control. Sweat and heat replaced the damp and chill of the storm.

He slid against her, then eased to one side. He let his hand drift from her breasts—reluctantly, but there were other treasures to explore—and follow the line of her ribs. He moved down the dip of her tummy and paused where her hipbone pushed against her skin.

Her lips meandered over his neck and throat. He felt her tongue glide along his collarbone, leaving a trail of fire. He took a breath and continued with his own findings.

The thatch of curly hair at the jointure of her legs held his attention for long, passion-hazed minutes. The Venus mound was gently rounded, delineated by the hardness of bone beneath the soft skin. Then he had to move on.

She tensed when he slipped his hand between her legs. He stroked lightly until her hands moved over him again and her legs relaxed. She drew an audible breath.

When he carefully dipped inside, he was elated. She was ready for him, wet and hot and yielding.

Jessica almost screamed with pleasure. What Brody was doing to her was mind-boggling. She was aware of her body in ways she'd never been before. Not only that, but it seemed as if another part of her had taken control, a part that was wild and primitive and very determined to have its way. She could no longer think. Sensation after sensation rolled over her.

Brody's mouth came down on hers, taking her with a force that was new, but not frightening...at least, no more than the totality of what was happening between them. His tongue swept inside and thrust with insistent passion against hers.

She realized he was doing the same thing with his finger, moving gently in and out. A remaining bit of inhibition brought embarrassment at the obvious response of her body to his touch as the lubricant slicked his finger so that he could slide easily into her. She felt a pulling sensation, but no pain.

She turned her face and murmured his name.

"It's natural," he told her, seemingly able to read her mind. "Don't be embarrassed. You don't know what it does to a man to know his woman is ready for him. Besides, turnabout is fair play. I can't hide what my body does when you drive me wild, either."

She felt rather than saw his smile as he kissed along her cheek. His tongue ran a lazy foray over her earlobe and— another sensitive spot, she discovered—down the side of her neck.

So was the underside of her chin. He kissed down to her breasts, then roamed around them, sucking and kissing all over before taking a taut nipple in his mouth. Everywhere he touched stirred the fires that consumed her. She moved restlessly and again felt the throb against her thigh.

Emboldened by his words, she reached down and gathered the hard length in her hand. He didn't move away. She guided him toward the ache within herself that demanded relief and rubbed back and forth, spreading the moisture over the tip of his phallus. He let a breath out in a whoosh and sucked air in as if he were a drowning man. She instinctively knew it was a bid for control on his part.

"You're driving me right toward the brink," he warned in a guttural tone, but he still didn't move away or stop her.

A sense of freedom erupted from deep within. Brody would let her experiment all she wanted. She explored this newfound sense of privilege with greater confidence.

His hips began to roll with her movements although he returned his attentions to her breasts. She couldn't believe all that was happening between them. Fire and need joined and flowed to the point where they were intimately touching.

He groaned and pulled away from her hand, then slipped further down her body, his mouth running wetly over her pausing to encircle then dip into her belly button. Another erotic spot.

Finally he continued his journey.

Her breath strangled in her throat when he nuzzled into the curly nest at the apex of her legs. She suddenly knew what he was going to do and was flooded with shock and anticipation.

"Brody," she said.

"Shh," he soothed her. "It's all right. Let me…"

She clamped her teeth into her lower lip to keep from crying out when he found the sensitive nub and ran his tongue over it. She clutched handfuls of the sleeping bag and held on as desire rioted through her. She wasn't sure what she was supposed to do.

"Relax and enjoy it," Brody advised, his tone hoarse and strained. "Relax and let yourself go."

"I can't," she whimpered. "Something is so tight.. inside me. I think…I'm going to come apart."

"Yes," he urged, his mouth hot and magic against her.

She surged upward and released the cover. She ran her fingers into his hair and pressed him closer as tension coiled tighter and tighter. She moaned. She cried. She screamed. And finally she discovered it wasn't a matter of letting go. It was a matter of shattering. She did. Loudly. Urgently.

Brody thought he was going to come apart with her as she writhed under him. He held her hips in his hands and helped her move in a smoother rhythm so that the climax would be complete. Her little exclamations of "oh, oh, oh," were almost continuous now and her movements were less frantic. Finally she sighed and slumped down on the cot, her energy spent.

He raised himself over her and nudged her legs further apart. He had no protection, nothing to defend himself against deeper involvement and the entanglements he dreaded, but at the moment none of that mattered. Maybe tomorrow the regrets would come, or if there was a child, but for now...

She was still hot and moist and now, very relaxed. He held himself in position and started the journey inside. She moved a little. He paused, then realized she was trying to accommodate his entry.

He pushed harder. He couldn't detect the intact membrane—his body felt only its own hot, wild pleasure at this moment—but he knew it was there. He would hurt her, but he couldn't stop. Lord help him, he couldn't turn back now, not unless she said no.

She didn't.

Making soft sounds of encouragement, she began to rub his arms and shoulders. She caressed his neck, then slid down his chest and along his sides to his hips. To his surprise, she tugged at him, wanting him to move faster.

Taking a breath, he pushed forward. She sighed, then stretched her legs farther apart and rubbed one foot against the side of his calf as she bent her knee and drew her leg up. It gave him better access to those sweet depths.

By dint of will, he kept from plunging in like a stallion on a rampage and made the journey very slowly, very carefully. At last the trip was made. He was as far into her as he could get. Pressing, he felt the delicate feminine mound against the apex of his legs. Their bodies were meshed completely.

"I wasn't positive it would fit," she murmured with a shaky laugh when he rested, his head beside hers on the pillow, his breath coming in shallow draughts.

He felt he'd run a mile straight uphill. His control was as shaky as her laughter. "I knew it would be like this."

"How?"

"Heaven." He flexed and withdrew, then began the mind-blowing descent all over again. He felt her hold her breath, then exhale when he rested again. Her hips moved a fraction.

Pride made him want to shout in delight. He'd pleasured his woman so much her first time that she wanted him again. He didn't think she was aware of it yet. She was still coming down mentally, but her body was starting to soar again.

He covered her face with kisses before taking her mouth and letting her feel his hunger through the thrusting of his tongue. He could taste the sweet dew of her passion and knew she would, too, when her tongue slid over his.

She explored this new knowledge tentatively. He held still and let her dip into his mouth, knowing her experience with all the facets of making love increased with each moment.

"You taste of me," she finally said.

"Someday you'll do that for me," he told her, planting the seeds of more exploration between them for the future. He knew they could never go back to their chaste life. Not now. The passion was too explosive for either of them to withdraw.

He moved his hand between them and rubbed steadily until she began her little moans and cries all over. When he knew he wasn't going to hold on another second, she went perfectly still, then tumbled over the edge. He paused, then thrust heavily, his control gone, as the most powerful climax of his life rolled over him like a wild storm tide. He threw back his head and emitted a guttural cry of release and triumph, as primal as life itself.

Chapter Nine

What does one say to a naked man?

Jessica circled the pads of her fingers on Brody's skin at his side and thought of what she'd like to say. An expression of gratitude didn't seem adequate for all that she'd experienced.

Since he seemed to have felt everything she did, maybe no comment was necessary. "The afterglow is just like in books I've read," she murmured. "Like floating. Like dreaming, only you know you're awake."

"Are you going to sleep?" he asked in a throaty murmur. He moved off her, severing the contact, and lay beside her.

She turned toward him, her forehead against his chest. "Not yet. Are you?"

"No." His lips caressed her temple.

There were other words she didn't dare say or even admit to herself. He'd warned her about entanglements often enough. She held those words inside, afraid to acknowledge them. But she knew what they were.

She felt him move. He groped on the floor and came up with his shorts. "Open," he said, nudging her thigh.

Startled, she obeyed and felt him tuck the cotton between her legs. Warm fuzzies flowed over her at his care. "You're wonderful," she told him, hearing the contentment in her voice. "Everything was wonderful."

"Everything?"

"Yes." The burning sensation had been a fleeting thing, then she'd been aware of a fullness that was new and different but not terribly uncomfortable. When he'd stroked her again, she'd nearly fainted. The climax had been even more powerful than the first time. "I had no idea..."

"None?" He lifted himself to an elbow and began touching her breasts.

She heard the laughter in his voice. Brody, the taciturn, the grim, was being playful. "Not in my wildest dreams."

He kissed the side of her mouth and tickled the corner with his tongue. "So now you know."

"Yes. Show me again." She lifted her face so he could fully reach her lips. He accepted the invitation.

If someone had held a gun to her head and demanded she explain the difference between this kiss and all the others they'd shared up to this point, she wouldn't have been able to.

It was different, she would have said.

That was the sum of her conscious knowledge. The rest was a deep, primitive feeling that blended with the hunger and need he induced in her, plus the vague longing she'd had for other things in her life. With Brody, she'd found them.

The cabin was cold, but on that narrow cot, wrapped in Brody's arms, she didn't need the sleeping bag to keep her warm. With him holding her, she was warm all the way to the center of her heart.

As his kisses became deeper, the warmth became heat, and the heat became a fire that consumed her every thought. The world collapsed to this place, this time and the joining of their bodies into the wild cadence of passion once again.

The storm passed. The clouds parted and disclosed the bright face of the moon. She didn't heed any of that. Her world was here, with this man.

Brody couldn't have faced down a tame cat at that moment. He'd never experienced anything so deep, so draining. He knew he should move, that his weight was too much for her slender build, but he couldn't. Right where he was, that was where he wanted to stay. He pressed his face into the pillow and breathed deeply as his body's need for oxygen caught up with the demands he'd placed on it during the past minutes. The scent of lavender filled his senses, making him dizzy again.

When he finally lifted his head and rolled to the side of her, he saw the flash of her smile in the pale play of moonlight across their bed. He wanted to step into that smile and stay there the same as he wanted to stay inside her even though his body was spent. She touched something inside him—this woman who was worlds above him in wealth and breeding—that made him want to linger and bask in her good will. He wanted her cries of ecstasy, her smiles of joy...

He frowned. Such thoughts were folly. He had to stay in control. A simple reminder that he'd been bought and paid for, as a bodyguard, not a husband, did the trick. And he sure as hell wasn't going to be a plaything for any woman, especially his very rich, very passionate wife.

However, he also knew that passion, like a magic genie

once unleashed, was hard to get back in the bottle. Maybe impossible.

"You'd better get on your cot," he said. "There's a clean sleeping bag—"

Her arms tightened around him. "You're not kicking me out in the cold now that you've had your way with me, so forget it," she told him in no uncertain terms. But there was laughter in her voice. He could hear it as if it were the tinkling of fairy bells far away, enticing mortals to join them.

He struggled between what he should do—get the hell out of the bed—and what he wanted to do—stay with her and make love all night. When she threw a leg over his, rested her arm over his middle and snuggled her nose into the groove of his neck, he lost the battle.

Grimly he pulled the cover over them and settled beside her on the narrow cot. He wouldn't sleep a wink the whole night…no way…not with her breast poking his side and that curly patch of hair against his thigh, reminding him of the pleasure to be shared…he should get up…but the cot was comfortable…he should sleep on the other one…but this one was warm…so very warm.…

Jessica woke when Brody stirred. She opened her eyes and gazed into his. His expression was guarded. She hesitated, then, unable to stop herself, she squeezed him and planted several kisses on his darkly furred chest. The curly hairs tickled her nose. She laughed and chased the tickle away by rubbing her nose on him.

"If you'll let me up, I'll stoke the stove and start the coffee," he said in a sleep-roughened voice. He cleared his throat a couple of times.

"Um, I might keep you here all day," she playfully retorted and nipped at the prickly hairs with her lips.

He tensed all the way down his length, then in spite of his distant attitude, she felt his body begin to rise and harden.

"Well, at least one part of you can't resist me." She raised on one elbow and gave a definitely triumphant smile.

"Don't let it go to your head," he suggested in a repressive manner. "That happens to a man when he's in bed with a woman. Any man. Any woman," he added for good measure.

Nothing he said could suppress the sense of well-being and confidence she felt. "But never to me."

She stretched luxuriously, careful not to fall off the cot. She'd never slept this close to another human that she could recall. She felt wonderfully rested, albeit a tiny bit stiff.

New exercise, new muscles, she recalled her PE teacher's advice if the girls complained of being sore when the basketball season started each year. She laughed softly. New muscles indeed. She caressed his growing tumescence.

He swung out of bed. She ogled his masculine form as he pulled on the cold, damp jeans he'd worn the previous day, then giggled at his grimace and the chill-bumps that raced up his body. "The bed is warm," she suggested seductively.

Before tending to the fire in the wood-burning stove, he surveyed the outside from all the windows. Seemingly satisfied that all was well, he shook out the ash box under the stove, added kindling inside, squirted it with kerosene and struck a big wooden match on the top of the stove.

The kerosene caught with a *whoosh*, igniting the kindling. He added bigger pieces of wood. In a few minutes, the fire was crackling brightly. He turned on a burner of a two-position electric hot plate and put on a pot of coffee. In a minute, it added its merry perking to the ambience.

While the cabin was warming, he pumped a basin of water and, to her surprise, hung a blanket between the rooms before washing up. Brody, shy? When he quit splashing and took the blanket down, he padded into the bedroom, opened a trunk in the corner and pulled out clean clothes.

Her breath became tangled in her throat, and for a second she couldn't get it to go in or out. He was arrogantly, flagrantly and so very handsomely nude.

He dressed quickly, then took their damp clothing and hung the pieces on hooks near the stove.

Jessica plumped the pillow up and lay with her hands under her head, watching through the doorway as Brody did the domestic chores. He searched in the pantry and came up with corned beef hash, eggs and bread.

"Are you going to stay in bed grinning all day?" he asked when she made no move to get up.

She batted her lashes at him, exulting in a sense of certainty and…and *power* she'd never before experienced.

Her past dealings with people were influenced by the deaths of her grandmother and parents, the reserve of her grandfather and the uncertainty concerning her uncle's intentions toward her, all combining to make her wary of others.

There had followed her years in boarding school and college, where she'd been just another quiet, hardworking student. It wasn't until she met Brody that she'd begun to feel secure with another person. Before last night, she'd never had this sense of intimacy with anyone.

"Breakfast in bed would be nice. It's warm here." She gave him a deliberately sultry glance.

He snorted a "huh" and continued to prepare the meal.

She heard some banging around, then he returned to the bedroom. He placed the stainless-steel basin on the trunk along with a sliver of soap, a towel and a washcloth.

"You'd better use it while it's hot," he suggested and retreated to the other room. He put the blanket back in place.

Jessica was amazed at his consideration. She jumped out of bed, winced, then moved a bit slower. She washed in the warm water, dug her toothbrush from the knapsack, used it and put on her sweat suit and a clean pair of socks. After running a brush through her tangled curls, she carried the basin into the other room. "What do I do with this?"

"Pour it down the drain."

She looked around in confusion.

He took it from her, opened the front door and tossed the water outside.

Putting her hands on her hips, she studied him. "Yes," she concluded, "there is a gleam in those dark, mysterious eyes. Mr. Smith is pleased with his little joke on his city slicker wife."

Wife. Saying the word out loud sent a tingle through every nerve in her body. She was well and truly that.

He cast her an oblique glance, but went on stirring the corned beef hash. Her stomach growled impatiently. She realized she was starved.

"I suppose the bathroom facilities are also outside?"

He dumped the browned hash on a plate, then cracked four eggs into the skillet. "Around back."

She sighed and put on her shoes. The sneakers and the parka were still damp, but she bravely faced the chill morning air and found the outhouse as promised, set back in the trees a hundred feet behind the cabin.

"A day of firsts," she mentioned when she returned. "My first trip to an outhouse—which is quite different from those portable toilets at the national parks, I might add—and my first morning to wake in bed with a man.''

He gave another snort and took up the eggs. The bread was toasting on the woodstove. He forked two slices on one plate and four on another.

She joined him at the card table. He split the eggs and hash between them. She pushed one egg and half the hash back on his plate. He set two mugs of coffee and a jar of jelly on the table. Breakfast was ready. She took her seat. He took his.

"Wait. My mother always said you should start the day off with a kiss."

The black slashes that were his eyebrows jerked upward in surprise, then down in a warning scowl. She smiled, not quite so confident as she'd been upon waking. He didn't seem to feel the same sense of connection that she felt.

"Or we could just shake hands," she added brightly. She picked up the coffee cup and noticed a tremor in her fingers.

"And come out fighting?" he asked with a cynical twist.

She frowned, perplexed at his question, then realized that her words combined with his were those of a referee before a boxing match. "I didn't know we were at war."

Brody noticed the diminishing perkiness in Jessica's behavior and felt guilt spread over his conscience as if it were a rash.

Damn. He had known life was going to get complicated with her around. After last night, it was going to be one giant serving of trouble. He shouldn't have… It was too late for regret. The deed was done.

Sucking in a deep breath, he leaned across the table, hooked a hand behind her neck and gave her a kiss that curled his toes. He let her go, picked up his fork and gave her an inquiring glance. "Now can we eat?" he asked in mock-patient tones.

She nodded her head. When she set her cup down, she was smiling again. He was relieved.

That worried him, too.

God, he'd drive himself crazy if he predicated everything he did upon her feelings and moods first. His job was to protect her. He needed a clear head for that. That was what he had to remember when hormones threatened to overcome sense.

As had happened last night.

"Jessica, about last night." He waited until she looked up. The wariness was back in her eyes. He hesitated, swallowed, then tried again. "It was the best I've ever known."

He couldn't believe he'd said that. He'd meant to caution her about their circumstances and keeping their heads and all that. Last night had been a...a... He couldn't bring himself to call it a mistake. It was the most powerful sensation he'd ever experienced.

"Thank you, Brody. It was that way for me, too."

He made his smile droll. "Well, considering it was your first experience, that goes without saying."

She laughed again, that magical sound that made him think of fairy dells and such nonsense. He sighed. Last night was definitely going to make his job that much harder.

His job wasn't all that was hard. He shifted uncomfortably on the chair. Between cold logic and a hot libido, he waged a silent tug-of-war to keep from stripping his sexy, passionate wife and taking her back to bed for an hour or so.

He stuffed his mouth full of eggs and corned beef before he lost another battle of the bulge...so to speak. He groaned at the stupid pun and ate faster. He needed to get outside. There was work to be done.

"What do we do today?" she asked as if reading his mind. She counted the chores. "Check on the sheep, of course. I wonder how poor Ram made it through the night. Then we need to call and find out how Don is feeling and see how the new hands fared during the storm. What's after that?"

"I'm going to have a look on the ridge. I'll see if I can spot any tracks."

"Good idea. I'm not certain what I saw. I mean, with the wind whipping the trees and bushes around and it being so dark, maybe I saw something that wasn't there, like taking one of those inkblot tests. Different people see different things, don't they?"

"Yeah."

With their chores set out for the day, Jessica ate quickly and finished the same time as Brody. She felt her jeans drying by the stove and found them damp but not terribly so. She washed the dishes while he checked his clothes and banked the embers in the stove.

When they were ready to leave, he told her, "I want you to stay here today, Keep the door locked and don't let anyone in."

"No. I'm going with you."

"Jessica—"

"And that's that," she added, throwing words he'd used to her in his face.

"It's too dangerous. You get me...distracted."

Her smoky gray eyes roamed down his body. She crossed her arms over her chest and gave him glare for glare.

Heat shifted into his groin. "Hell," he said, not feeling up to an argument. "Get your coat and let's go."

She nodded and was gracious enough not to gloat. She grabbed the old parka off its hook and was ready in a split second. Without having to fix her hair and makeup and all the other things a woman did before she left the house. The fastest female he'd ever met. He shook his head in wonder.

Yeah, his rich, city slicker wife surprised him in more ways than one. The trouble was, he was beginning to like them all.

Jessica fended off Ram who was joyously trying to leap all over her. She held the bucket to him and let him suck the milk supplement until his tummy stuck out to each side. "Glutton," she murmured, scratching his ears.

She looked up to find Brody watching them with an intensity that warmed and thrilled her. She wished she could tell what he was thinking. Not tender thoughts of love, she concluded when he frowned and went back to his task.

He was studying the ground near their slickers. The spot where they'd lain in the mud with the hail pelting them, his body over hers, protective and provocative.

She sighed, thinking of the night spent in his arms. When Ram finished, she shooed him off, rinsed the bucket and put it in the shed next to the cabin.

"Ready?" Brody asked.

She nodded. They climbed in the truck and headed down the valley. He stopped before they crossed the creek and turned onto the paved road. She was shocked when he removed a handgun from the glove box and tucked it in his pants, his shirt hiding the weapon from view. She followed him up the hill.

"Stay behind me and do what I tell you," he ordered.

"All right."

He cast her a skeptical glance, as if he doubted he could depend on her. She'd show him.

She followed him up the slope without saying a word. She scanned the ground when he did. All she saw were runnels from the heavy rains. Any tracks would have been washed out.

At the top of the hill, she exclaimed aloud. She had an absolutely clear view of the cabin and the valley. She could see the sheep and the two collies guarding them. She even picked out Ram and his playmate annoying the patient old ewe who let him stay close. Then she watched Brody.

He searched the ground as if he were a squirrel looking for a nut he'd buried in the vicinity but couldn't remember exactly where. Finally he gave a little grunt of satisfaction and picked up an object. She moved closer.

"What is it?"

"A spent casing."

She stared at the remains. "Someone was shooting at us. I'd hoped I'd imagined it."

"He wasn't trying to kill us," Brody told her. "He was firing rock salt."

That information meant nothing to her.

"He was trying to stampede the sheep by shooting pellets of salt at them."

"Why?"

"That's a good question," he muttered, his gaze roaming over the valley while he thought. "Whoever it was didn't want his shots to be detected."

"So it wouldn't look like murder?" she asked, realizing all the grim possibilities. She'd almost convinced herself that her trustees and grandfather had been paranoid about her getting killed. Being with Brody at the ranch had induced a false sense of security.

"Yeah." He laughed cynically. "Maybe the hired gun thought the lightning would get us or the sheep would trample us to death in a stampede."

"What hired gun?"

Brody gave her one of his calculating perusals before answering. "You don't think whoever wants you out of the way is going to do the dirty work himself, do you?"

She shook her head solemnly.

Her husband looked around a bit more. "There's nothing here. Let's go home."

At the paved road, Brody cursed and braked to a jarring halt. He was out of the truck in a flash. Jessica, her heart in her throat, watched as he bent over some clearly defined tracks of mud where another vehicle had left the same dirt road and headed for town. The tracks disappeared in a short distance, otherwise they could have followed the culprit to his door.

Brody returned, his expression grim. A chill touched her neck. She laid her hand on his thigh, needing his warmth to ward off the cold that threatened her heart. After a second, he put his hand over hers, his broad palm covering hers completely. She realized he did it to comfort her.

He headed for Don's house as soon as he pulled into the ranch yard and killed the engine. Jessica jumped down and followed. "I want to see how Don feels," she stated defensively when her husband frowned at her.

Don was better. He had three bottles of pills to ensure it, he told them. He'd also made a big pot of mutton chunks and vegetables to keep his strength up. One of the students had brought him a batch of cookies from the bakery in town.

"Send them up to keep an eye on the sheep when they come back to the house. There won't be any trouble, but I want someone up there tonight."

After she and Brody were on their way to town, she asked, "How do you know there won't be trouble to-night?"

"The guy knows what he's doing."

"A professional." The thought was depressing. Someone hated her enough to send a hired gun after her.

"A skilled amateur," he said, correcting her.

"I'm nothing but trouble to everyone."

"Don't start feeling sorry for yourself."

Anger rose like bile in her throat. "I want to know who it is. I want this to end. I want a life," she concluded on a quieter, sadder note.

"Poor little rich girl." But there was understanding in the glance he flicked her way before turning his attention to the traffic on the busy main street of the town.

Jessica trailed after Brody to the bank. She realized she had very little money in her purse. Not that she'd used any since she'd arrived, but there were some personal items that she needed before they returned to the ranch.

"I'd better open an account," she told Brody. "I'll need funds if I'm to stay here for a year."

"It isn't necessary. You're my wife."

To her amazement, he escorted her to the teller window, told the woman who she was and that was that. The friendly teller let her cash a check without a qualm. "It's a pleasure to meet the woman who finally roped this maverick in," she said, then laughed at Brody's scowl. "Don't give him any slack," she advised.

"She'd better not give me any sass."

Jessica huffed indignantly. She'd been as good as gold that morning, following his instructions to the tee.

He cast her an oblique look, then ruffled her hair and laughed. Her heart puddled in her toes. He was so incredibly handsome when he smiled.

"I'm going to dedicate my life to giving him a hard time," she confided to the teller. "How do I arrange to move my accounts here?"

"Fill out this form and take it to the manager. She's in her office now. Just go on in when you're ready." The teller handed her a form and pointed out the young woman in a corner office.

Brody walked across the room with her when she finished the form, but stopped outside the office. Jessica took his hand and pulled him inside. She had no secrets from him. None at all.

A smile tickled the corners of her mouth. Brody knew her as no other human did. Passion was a very intimate act.

The newly discovered jealousy rose as she thought of other women who knew his body as well as she did, perhaps better.

"Good morning," the manager greeted them. "Mr. Smith, isn't it?" She looked a question at Jessica.

"This is my wife, Jessica. She wants to open an account."

"Of course. Please be seated. Would you like some coffee or tea?" She was Miss Cordiality.

Jessica wondered if she would have gotten the same treatment if she'd been alone. She realized the jealousy was showing again. She might have bought his services, but she didn't own Brody. No woman ever would.

When they left the bank, he asked, "Do you think you'll be here long enough to spend that amount?"

She stopped. "What do you mean?"

"I'm pretty sure we'll have your case solved before long. You'll be free to do whatever you want. You'll have the freedom you said you wanted."

"How? Did you see something? Who—" She stopped abruptly, not sure she wanted to know.

"I don't know who...yet."

That ominous pause told Jessica he had a good hunch, though. The cold formed an icy patch on her heart. Her uncle must need money again.

"Hey, Nick," Brody called suddenly. "Wait up."

A man dressed in the uniform of a deputy sheriff turned toward them. He waited until they caught up with him. He and Brody shook hands, then hit each other on the shoulder the way men do when they're glad to see each other.

When Brody introduced her as his wife, the deputy didn't hide his surprise. "Congratulations, Smith, you got yourself a beauty."

"Yeah, the pick of the litter," Brody agreed.

Jessica hit him in the ribs with her elbow. He saw it coming and deflected the blow, then held her hand in his, right there on the street in plain view of the town. A flush of pride and pleasure rushed over her, and she was warm again.

"How about lunch?" Brody asked. "I want to talk to you about a little problem."

"Sure. Is it the same problem you mentioned a couple of weeks ago?"

"Right."

Jessica realized the deputy knew about her. "Oh, are you the one who lives down the road? Brody said there was a deputy close by."

Nick Dorelli admitted he was the one. He led the way into a small deli. When they were settled in a booth, Brody leaned close and told him about the storm last night as well as the shots and the tracks they'd seen on the road.

"A V-shaped cut on the front passenger tire, huh?" The officer got out a notebook and wrote the information down.

"I'll keep an eye out." He put the notebook away. "Say, how's my favorite llama doing?"

"My wife has threatened to make llama stew out of my prize breeding stud," Brody complained.

Nick burst into laughter. "Ah-ha, got you with the old green spit trick, did he?"

"Right on my clean shirt," she confessed. Heat seared her breast as she recalled Brody's touch there as he cleaned it off.

Her eyes met his. He remembered, too. And what followed afterward. And last night. A tremor raked through her and her smile became tremulous. She wished they were alone.

Flames danced in his dark eyes, and she knew he was thinking the same thing. She looked down at the table. It was odd to be so in tune with a person, to know his thoughts, to know he knew hers. Did making love do that to a couple?

She met the deputy's eyes, which were as dark as Brody's, and saw his admiration. She realized he approved of her.

After the meal, she picked up her purse and stood. "I have a few items I need to pick up. Where's the nearest drugstore?"

"Around the corner and two doors down." Nick pointed out the window in the direction she should go.

She looked a question at Brody.

"I'll meet you at the store in fifteen minutes."

"Fine. I'm delighted to have met you," she told the deputy, then hurried on her way. She had a feeling Brody was going to talk to Nick and tell him things he didn't tell her. Her husband could be quite maddening when he chose.

Which was most of the time.

* * *

As soon as Jessica left the restaurant, Brody and the deputy discussed the storm and its happenings in greater detail. Brody leaned forward and spoke quietly. "I think the idea was to get rid of me. The perp didn't expect Jessica to come out in the storm, too. I found the gun casing on the ridge. It was hidden but not so it wouldn't be found."

"Sounds like a frame-up," Nick observed.

"Right," Brody agreed. "Now who would want to get rid of me and Jessica and blame it on someone else?"

"The next of kin after the uncle," Nick concluded. "If the uncle is convicted, the will would be overturned."

"My thoughts exactly."

Jessica walked into the drugstore and started looking for the items she needed. At the back of the store, next to the pharmacy area, she paused in front of a rack and studied the advertising on the boxes.

Condoms, it seemed, came in many different shapes and…she gasped…sizes. However did a person know that?

Images flashed into her mind. Her with a tape trying to make Brody let her take his measurements. Him laughing as the size changed before her eyes. The two of them meshed as one, their purpose forgotten in the heat of the moment.

She laid a hand against her chest. Her heart was going as fast as it had last night when he'd held her and driven her mad with the magic of his hands and mouth…

She brought her attention back to the matter at hand. Well, she'd get the large size. That seemed, um, about right.

She didn't think color was important, but what about those ribbed things or the ones with the dangles at the end.

No, that looked like a bunch of worms. She suppressed a giggle.

Ah, now here was something interesting.

She read the print on the box with growing amusement. Add fun and excitement to your marriage, the manufacturer advised. Give your significant other a surprise. Impress her with your ardor. She'll know where you are every fun-filled, passionate minute.

Jessica bit her bottom lip to keep from laughing. The condoms were guaranteed to glow in the dark.

She couldn't resist. She dropped the box into her basket, then selected a box of plain ones—in case Brody objected to the glow—and dropped it in with her other items. Then, for good measure—a giggle escaped her—she tossed in the ones with the blue ribbing down the sides.

Brody joined her at the checkout line just as the clerk was dragging her choices over the scanner. The condoms were next.

She felt his quick intake of breath against her arm when he saw the boxes. She met his gaze and, unable to control the mischievous mood, winked.

He gave her a lethal glance, then studied the traffic outside the windows with meticulous attention. His ears were a bit ruddy. One might even say they glowed. Her rugged, supremely masculine, arrogantly confident husband was blushing.

"Very funny," he muttered when they were in the truck and on their way out of town.

She couldn't help it. She burst into laughter. She was still smiling when they reached the ranch.

Chapter Ten

Brody stopped at the stairs. Jessica nearly ran into his back. She looked at him expectantly.

He realized she was planning on coming up with him. She probably planned on moving in with him...and sleeping with him...and using all three dozen of those damn condoms she'd bought at the drugstore...

A cold sweat broke out on his forehead. It soon turned hot as his body sizzled at the idea of making love to his wife, who was gazing at him with the most innocent expression he'd ever seen on a female's face.

Ha. If she could buy glow-in-the-dark condoms, she wasn't half as innocent as she looked. She was a woman with plans. He knew what they were. She'd entrap him with her charms until he didn't know what was what, then she'd walk out when she'd had enough of the bucolic life...and him.

When the case was solved, she'd hightail it back to the

city and her friends there, the charity balls and boozy luncheons—not that Jessica ever drank more than an occasional glass of wine—and all that society junk women loved.

Yeah, he knew how the female mind worked. He'd pleasured her, shown her how good sex could be between a man and a woman. Right now, that was new and exciting. It would pass. Meantime he wouldn't get suckered in.

"Where are you going?" he asked.

She blinked those clear, gray eyes as if she were a sleepy cat, then smiled just as lazily. "With you."

"No way. I like my privacy."

Her expression didn't change. Only her eyes. They opened wider at his announcement, then became a calm, silvery surface that admitted no emotion. He wished he could take the words back so he could see that lazy, sensually content expression again.

She stepped away from the stairs. "Okay."

Going to the guest room tucked under the stairs, she went inside. The door closed behind her.

His frustration level rose to the saturation point. He wanted to break the banister with his bare hands and beat the walls that surrounded him to rubble. Fat lot of good that would do. Maybe he should go on his knees and apologize—

Forget that.

Rubbing the ache that splintered his head, he walked up the stairs, closed the door to his room and went into the office. He placed a call to Denver and checked in with his secretary. He read several pages of faxes, returned calls to a dozen clients or potential clients, then dialed a number in New York.

"Did you get a copy of the grandmother's will?" he asked.

"Yeah, I got it," the attorney responded. "You were right. Everything belongs to Jessica. Judge Parker, who was the executor and prime trustee for Jessica before his death, wrote the grandmother's and the mother's wills."

"You know what I'm thinking, don't you?"

"Yes."

There was a tense ten second silence. "You know what to do if anything happens to either or both of us," Brody directed in a tone of deadly quiet. "You got my instructions?"

"Right."

When Brody hung up, he sat in the executive chair, his hands behind his head, his eyes half-closed as he stared out the window at the snowy peaks of the mountains. He knew for sure who wanted Jessica out of the way. Now he had only to prove it.

And soon.

If his passionate wife was pregnant, no court in the country would let a will stand that excluded her child as an heir. The grandfather was right. Her mother had written a stupid will that meant nothing but trouble for the daughter. He wondered if her attorney had tried to make her see the light...or if he'd been influenced by another family member, and maybe a sweet little packet under the table.

Money. It did strange things to people. In his years of private investigating, he'd seen supposedly close-knit families torn apart by greed or resentment that one sibling had gotten more than another.

He pushed himself out of the chair. Time to see about the cattle and the ranch chores. Then he'd check the perimeter area.

Jessica didn't know it, but he had security devices planted at every location leading into the ranch. He would know if anyone came in by vehicle. If they came by horse, they might slip through his net, so he kept an eye on the trails, too.

He'd also know if his independent-minded wife tried to leave without telling him.

Jessica glanced up when Brody came in. The sky was dark outside and had been for an hour. She didn't ask where he'd been, though.

He passed her with a nod of greeting but without speaking and went upstairs. She heard the water come on in his shower. In ten minutes, he returned, dressed in a fresh jogging suit, his dark hair still wet.

Leaning against the counter, he watched her cook their dinner. She was preparing a quick meal tonight. Pasta with a light garlic-tomato sauce and a salad would be it.

Ignoring his moody presence, she slipped sourdough rolls into the oven to let them brown. "Dinner is almost ready. Shall we call Don and have him over?"

"No. He eats only soup when he's sick."

"What about the students?"

"They're up with the sheep."

"Oh, that's right." She set the table. He opened a bottle of red wine and poured them each a glass.

She couldn't believe they'd gone back to being these cool strangers. Not after last night.

The icy patch returned to her heart and settled in. She couldn't think of anything to say. She removed the rolls from the oven and dumped them into a napkin-lined bowl. The pasta went into a bright red one. She retrieved the salads from the refrigerator and plunked the plates on the table.

"It's ready," she announced.

The silence was oppressive during the meal.

"The weather is supposed to be clear for a week,"

Brody finally said, already half-finished with his pasta and salad. He hardly glanced at her.

"How nice." She swallowed a bite of penne that seemed to swell in her throat as she tried to get it down. If she'd been a crying person, she'd have felt like weeping. She forced herself to eat, bite after choking bite. And keep a pleasant mien.

Her thoughts roamed to the past and the men who had been part of her life. They had all hurt or disappointed her somehow, right up to the present. Poor little rich girl, she chided as she grew more introspective.

They had almost finished before she stopped her internal brooding and spoke. "My father was killed in an auto accident in a winter storm."

Brody gave her a quizzical glance as if he couldn't figure out what had induced that conversational gambit.

"He was supposed to have been at a business conference, but he went to a resort in the Adirondacks with another woman. She was an attorney in his office, a law student studying for the bar exam actually. As a teenager, I never understood how he could do that to my mother…to us."

Brody stopped eating and watched her.

"Mom almost married another man a few months later, but she broke it off. I never did find out why. Kids often don't, but they hear whispers and abruptly stopped conversations, and they worry. For years I've wondered why my mother said I had to marry to take control of my money, considering her past."

"Maybe she thought her experiences had soured you on men and marriage," Brody suggested.

She shook her head. "As a child, I was angry at my father for dying. As a teenager, I hated him for going off with another woman. I'd thought their marriage was perfect. Kids want to believe that. At the very least they accept the flaws in their family as the norm. For them it is. When I was older I decided it was wrong to judge others by my father's actions. I didn't know the dynamics of my parents' marriage."

"Very wise of you." He didn't hide the sardonic overtone.

"What I'm trying to tell you is that I don't expect anything from our marriage." She gave him an unflinching perusal. "So you don't have to worry that I'll start making demands because of what happened last night. I know it didn't mean anything."

To her surprise, guilt flashed over his face, and something that looked like fury. There were other emotions, too, but they were too fast for her to read. But the guilt she recognized.

It rather surprised her, but she'd known Brody was a man of honor when it came to his word, whether in his job or in his personal dealings with another. That was why she'd trusted him in spite of his warnings not to trust anyone. That he also had a conscience regarding the male-female relationship was a bonus.

He took a deep breath and let it out slowly as if reaching for an inner source of control, again surprising her.

"Then it appears we understand each other," he said.

"Yes."

They finished the meal without another word. Brody looked angry. She was merely tired. And sore. And discouraged with life and its cruel uncertainties.

Well, someone was trying to kill her. That was enough to lower the spirits. Her husband regretted making love with her. Another downer. Life was not rosy at the moment.

Brody cleaned up his dishes, refilled his wineglass and

went into the living room and turned on the television to the news. Listening to the reporter, she thought there must be disasters happening all over the world.

"To each his own," she said, lifting her wineglass and toasting her own feelings of doom.

After straightening the kitchen, she went to her room, showered and put on cotton pajamas and a short matching robe.

She lingered there, unsure what to do. Finally she got out a romance novel in which the heroine had been sent to live with the wicked guardian, who turned out to be the hero once she got past his surly ways.

Jessica wondered if she could get Brody to read the book. There was a lesson for him in it. She finished the story at eleven and prepared for bed. She wondered if her grouchy husband had retired yet. Ranchers usually went to bed early because they got up at the crack of dawn.

Just as she was turning back the covers to climb in, there was a knock at the door. Instead of calling out, she crossed the room and opened the door. Brody stood there.

His eyes seemed so very dark and deep and mysterious. Her heart jumped, then beat furiously as he abruptly moved.

Brody stooped and hooked one arm behind her knees and the other behind her back as he hoisted her off the floor. He was relieved when she didn't tell him to drop dead or hit him with something. He turned and headed up the steps.

"We'll move your things up tomorrow," he said.

"This might be an entanglement," she warned.

That one sassy eyebrow hiked up and mocked him and his guilt and all those other feelings he couldn't define.

He nodded grimly and entered his—their—bedroom. "It's already that."

She looped an arm around his neck and snuggled into his embrace. "What made you change your mind?" Her eyes were bright with curiosity.

"I missed you." That was as much as he was going to admit.

She beamed at him and ran her hands over his chest and his abdomen when he set her on her feet beside the rumpled bed. He was already erect and ready for her.

"Do you often go calling on people in the middle of the night in your, ah, birthday suit?"

"Only when it's you."

He unbuttoned the pretty lavender pajamas she wore and pushed the top off her arms. It fell to the floor. The elasticized bottoms were a simple matter, too. When she was naked—the way he liked her best—he gave in to the desire to let his gaze roam over her at will.

"My God, you're beautiful," he murmured. He sat on the bed and looped his arms around her hips. She caressed his shoulders.

When he opened his legs, she stepped inside the V of his thighs and pressed close, showing him in ways better than words that she wanted him, too. He knew as long as she stayed with him he wasn't going to try to shut her out again. She was more than any sane man could resist.

Slipping a hand behind her head, he urged her mouth to his, needing the taste and feel of her the way a dying man needs succor.

She responded fully, with her mouth and tongue and hands and body returning every caress of his. When he left her lips and roamed down her breasts, she rubbed her hands through his hair and down his back. Shifting slightly, she rubbed her thigh against him, nearly blowing his mind as red-hot need flashed through him as if it were wildfire.

He lay back on the bed and, hands at her waist, lifted her to the bed so she was on her knees. She gave a soft exclamation of shock when he pressed his face intimately into the springy mound of hair.

He explored her thoroughly while satisfaction stole over him. He was selfish enough to be glad he was the first to show her the full possibilities of pleasure between male and female and arrogant enough to think he'd made it as good for her first time as it could possibly be. He'd make it better this time.

"Brody," she whispered, her voice strained with the passion he built in her. "Brody, I think…"

"Shh," he told her. "Don't think."

"I'm going to fall…"

He felt the tremor rush over her and knew she was close to completion. He reluctantly backed off. Turning them, he let her fall onto the mattress and rest a few minutes while he fondled her breasts. He saw her eyes go to the lamp he'd left on low. It had been pitch-black in the cabin last night.

"Do you want it off?" he asked.

"I don't know." She gave him a helpless smile. "I don't think I like you seeing me disheveled—"

He chuckled. "Now there's a city slicker word if I ever heard one."

"All right, panting and sweaty and out of my mind from what you do to me."

He shouldn't have been, but he was surprised by her total candor. It was a rare trait in a woman, he was pretty sure. At least, he hadn't encountered it often. But she was different. He'd known that from the first moment, the moment he should have run but hadn't.

"Why not?" he asked. "That's what you do to me."

"You seemed in control last night," she reminded him. "I was the one shaking and carrying on like a banshee."

"Last night I had to be careful."

"But tonight you don't?"

He almost laughed at the avid sexual curiosity in her catlike eyes and the earnestness of her question. "Yes, but not as much as last night. I can go a bit wild myself tonight."

The thought raced through his blood like champagne. He'd let her rest long enough. It was time to take her higher.

He began at her mouth again and worked his way down until she cried out and tugged at his hair. He nudged between her legs, then remembered. "Where are the boxes?"

"What boxes?" Jessica was too far gone to remember anything beyond the last five seconds.

"The condoms."

"I threw them in the trash."

He groaned and moved away from her. "Where?"

"The kitchen."

He kissed her once, hard, then padded out. "Don't go 'way," he advised with a mock scowl.

She took several deep breaths to calm her racing heart while he was gone. It did no good. Her heart took off again when he returned. He dumped the three boxes in a drawer, selected one and prepared himself to come to her.

When she realized she was watching, he faced her so she could see his actions. His dark eyes expressed amusement.

"I'll let you do the next one," he promised.

"Okay." She willed herself not to be shy. Brody was her husband, a very considerate husband. Sex was new to her, but it was natural and wonderful. She'd lied when she said it didn't mean anything. She knew differently.

"Entanglements," she said, aware of the icy patch that lingered in her heart.

Brody returned to her. Lying beside her, he trailed a finger over her tummy and circled her navel. "Yes." He bent and kissed her, then started the process of seduction all over again.

This time she watched while he merged their bodies. She decided she liked seeing what was happening and told him so.

"The possibilities are endless," he assured her, his eyes alight with humor and passion.

She thought maybe they were. And the future? Maybe it was endless, too.

Brody breathed the pure air of the mountains and let the sense of well-being pervade his senses. It was a false one, but for the moment, all was well.

"This is beautiful, Brody," Jessica called out behind him.

He twisted in the saddle and watched her lean forward as her mount climbed the last few feet. He'd put her on a gentle gelding, but he saw he needn't have been so cautious. His wife had a natural seat, and she'd ridden often enough to be comfortable in the saddle.

His body stirred.

She was a spirited and natural lover, too, everything a man could ask for in a partner. She did whatever he did to her and experimented on her own to find out more about what he liked. The problem was he liked everything she did.

He quelled the tumultuous passion. This wasn't a good time for her, she'd told him four days ago.

"I'm not pregnant," she'd said, lifting her orange juice glass. She'd gestured as if making a toast, her smile mocking his worry about a child and the entanglements it would create.

Well, hell, it would.

The funny thing was…this was really weird…but he'd felt sort of…well, like he might have been maybe a little disappointed at the news. It had startled him. He'd never considered having a child before.

Gazing at the three thousand acres of land that were his, he realized he had no one to leave it to. Well, there was Carly and Jonathan and the new baby when it came, but they didn't need any money. He would leave everything to a scholarship fund.

He hadn't even written a will. That was stupid. But people were like that, Sloan Carradine, his Denver attorney, had assured him the last time he'd stopped by the law office. Sloan had a wife and a couple of kids now and was obviously content.

Being married made a man think of the future and the responsibilities it might bring. And the possibilities.

"Brody, look, you can see the clouds forming."

He followed his wife's pointing finger. As the warm mid-May air lifted to flow over a nearby mountain peak, the moisture in it condensed into a cloud before their eyes. He'd seen the phenomenon many times and no longer noticed.

Not so with Jessica. She had pointed out each wildflower and sparkly rock and natural occurrence on the trail.

He pushed the thoughts to the back of his mind and concentrated on the trail ahead. He'd spotted tracks up this way earlier in the week. He wanted to see if there were any fresh ones. So far he hadn't seen any.

He wasn't worried about an ambush. The hired gun was cagey and careful in his moves, using the cover of storms and darkness for his deeds. That was why he hadn't hesitated about bringing Jessica on the trip when she'd requested it that morning.

Besides there was a place he wanted to show her. The Rockies were a young mountain range and still forming. That meant there were plenty of hot spots in them. Water, running through the fissures in the earth, seeped into basins of rock, forming pools. Cowboys' bathtubs, they were called. That's where he was taking Jessica.

"A fern meadow," she sang out when they entered a glen where wild ferns unfurled their long leaf spikes.

He nodded and led them down the incline and up another hill. There, he veered off on a narrow path among a forest of pines. The trail wound down the mountain and became gentler in slope but rockier in terrain.

At last they reached the spot where water burbled out the side of a rocky face and tumbled into a mossy pool. The faint scent of sulfur blended with the balsam scent of pines.

"This is marvelous," Jessica said with awe in her tone. "Utterly charming."

"You ain't seen nothin' yet," he teased. He dismounted and left the rein dangling on the ground, then went to Jessica.

Jessica sighed contentedly when he smiled up at her. He held up his arms for her. She tumbled into them. He held her for a second before sending her on her way to explore with a pat on the fanny.

"I'll see to the horses," he murmured.

Hugging her arms across her chest, she walked to the pool and peered into its clear water. When she trailed her fingers in it, she started in surprise. "It's warm."

Brody squatted beside her. "Yeah. It's a natural hot spring. Even in the dead of winter, it's usually warm enough to bathe in."

"Really?" She sounded like a kid just discovering life.

"Yes, really," he mocked. He sounded like a man who desired his wife and wasn't sure he would be welcome.

Four nights with her in his arms but without making love had put a strain on him. He didn't think he could hold out much longer, especially with her looking at him with something similar to adoration in her eyes. He sucked in a calming breath, but it didn't do any good.

"I brought lunch," he said to distract himself.

She glanced up with a pleased smile. "That was thoughtful."

She said things like that, complimenting and thanking him and Don and the cowboys for little things. Finishing school talk, he called it. He once would have shied from any woman who did that, thinking she was too highfalutin for his tastes. With Jessica, it was different.

Maybe it was because she seemed sincere. It made a man want to do more to win one of her smiles and accolades. Then, too, she always acted surprised when anyone did anything for her. As if she weren't used to servants at her beck and call. Except for the three years she taught in a missionary school in Africa.

His do-gooder wife. He recalled the shine of tears in her gray eyes when he'd brought her a wild rose he'd found growing in the fence row of the horse paddock that morning. He wondered why that would make her cry.

He rubbed his hand down her shiny curls, unable to control the need to touch her. Her hair had grown longer in the six weeks they'd been living at the ranch. It curled over her collar, and the darker color was showing at the roots. Normally she would have had a touch-up by now if she lived in the city. She hadn't once asked to go to town.

"Do you miss city life?" he asked.

She shook her head. "I love it here. I feel free."

When she glanced at him to see if he understood, he nodded. He did. It was the same with him. He dropped his hand and went to get their lunch out of the saddlebags before he did something really stupid. Like make love to her on the spot.

He groaned as his body grew rock-hard in anticipation. The most fleeting thought of her produced the same result no matter where he was. He should be used to it.

When he returned with a blanket and the sandwiches, she had her shoes off and her jeans rolled up to her knees.

"Oh, it's wonderful. Take your boots off," she invited. "You'll love it."

He dropped the blanket behind them, laid the lunch out and yanked off his boots and socks. He wore Western jeans, which were tight in the legs to fit inside his boots.

"Take them off, too," she challenged with a wicked grin when he couldn't get them up past his mid-calf.

Gazing into her eyes, he stood and with deliberately slow motions, unhooked his belt and pants. He peeled them off while her face changed to that hazy glow of passion he'd come to know as well as himself.

He settled beside her, set his feet in the warm water and picked up a sandwich. "Tuna salad with pickle relish," he announced. "Don made them. There're chips and cookies, too."

"And apples." She helped herself.

The silence wafted around them, and the somnolent drone of nature took over, the cadence of bees among wildflowers, the rustle of the wind in the tops of the trees, the murmur of the spring water tumbling over the granite. He ate, but he couldn't take his eyes off her.

"Brody?" she at last questioned.

"Shh," he said. "Just let me watch you."

Pink rose in her cheeks. He didn't understand how she

could be so beautiful and so unaware of it. What was wrong with the men in her life that she hadn't been snapped up long ago?

He realized where that line of thought was taking him. Theirs wasn't a real marriage, he reminded himself savagely. As a husband, he'd been bought and paid for in order to keep her safe from her enemies for as long as she needed him.

He'd do that. With his life, if need be.

"Can we swim in the pool?" Jessica asked, jarring him out of his fiercely protective thoughts.

"Yes."

She was on her feet as soon as she stuffed the last bite of sandwich into her mouth. She had stripped by the time she'd chewed and swallowed.

"Last one in is a rotten egg," she declared and stepped up on a boulder, ready to leap.

He caught her around the waist and hauled her back to terra firma. "Not so fast."

Still holding her, he managed to get his shirt and shorts off while she squirmed and fought and tickled him. Then he slipped his hands under her buttocks and walked into the water with her feet dangling at his ankles.

"My feet are in the water." He peered past her and looked down. "Nope, just as I thought. Yours aren't. Now who's the rotten egg?"

Jessica was enchanted. Brody in a playful mood was so rare and new to her that she thought her heart would expand right out of her chest. His interesting features changed with his smile into stunning good looks. His teeth were brilliantly white against his skin, which had tanned to deeper shades of bronze during their six weeks at the ranch.

He walked deeper into the pool. The water came up to

their knees, their thighs, their waists, then their necks when he found the ledge and sat down with her in his lap.

She saw his eyes survey the area in his usual alert fashion. She ran her hands into his hair and pulled his face toward hers. Then their lips met.

The kiss was searing at the first touch. He let her explore his mouth first, then he took over, thrusting against her tongue in sensuous play. His hands caressed her breasts until the nipples rose in hard little points of desire.

They kissed and tickled and engaged in all the tricks of a lover's trade for a long time.

Finally his hands moved along her body into more intimate stroking. "Are you all right?" he asked, mumbling the words while he nibbled on her earlobe.

She'd never discussed her personal body functions with a man, but she knew what he meant. She'd been blessed with brief, pain-free menses. "Yes."

His chest lifted as he drew a deep breath. "Then shall we see what new venues we can discover?"

The seductive question sent the blood sparkling through her body as if it were pure champagne. It went right to her head.

"Yes." She could barely whisper the word.

He shifted her across his thighs. "It should be safe now, don't you think?" he asked before he adjusted her on his hard staff. At her nod, he guided her down on him.

They spent the next two hours exploring the possibilities of making love in the warm, swirling water. She thought they'd discovered all of them by the end of that time. She expressed this thought to Brody.

"We'll return soon and make sure," he suggested with a wicked gleam in his eyes as he did enchanting things to her with his hands and the glide of his body against hers.

It occurred to her that she'd never been happier in her life. At the same instant, she knew why. She was in love.

Chapter Eleven

"Wait here," Brody said when they climbed out of the pool.

Jessica feasted on the sight of his masculine good looks—the broad shoulders, the muscular back, the slender shanks and long, tapering legs—as he went over to his horse and retrieved a towel from the saddlebag. She shivered with emotion as she realized he'd planned this whole scene.

Her heart soared. He was passionately gentle in his lovemaking. He was protective and caring in a way she'd never experienced from others in her life, except maybe her grandmother and that had been so long ago, she barely remembered.

A woman could do worse in a mate.

Of course he was also stubborn and bossy, but as his aunt Essie might have said, a smart woman could handle that. A smile pushed its way onto her mouth. She wrapped her arms across her chest and let the sun stroke her with its warm rays. She was warm all the way through.

She laughed and threw her arms up toward the impossibly blue sky. Brody shook the towel out and slung it over his shoulder. He returned to her, a smile on his face. "What's so funny?"

"Us. This." She gestured around the glen. "A year ago, could you have imagined yourself standing here, as naked as the day you were born, basking in the sun?"

"A year ago, no, but for the past couple of months it's all I've thought about."

Her breath strangled in her throat as she realized the implications. "Have you ever had another—" She stopped. She had no right to ask questions about his past.

"Another woman up here?" He finished the sentence for her.

She nodded.

"Never."

"I'm glad." She leaned against his bare chest and wrapped her arms around him. "I'm selfish where you're concerned. I want you all to myself."

"I'll be a faithful husband," he assured her laconically. "For as long as we're married, you won't have to worry."

She nodded, her mood switching from expansive to pensive. Maybe the marriage would last a lifetime. Brody seemed to enjoy it now. But all men were probably attentive during the early days of making love.

He dried her back, then shifted so he could dry her front. He lingered on her breasts and finally sucked at her nipples.

"Um, sore," she murmured.

His smile flashed in apology. "Sorry, I couldn't resist." He finished and left her to dress while he dried and pulled his clothing on. A cloud drifted over the sun.

454 HUSBAND: BOUGHT AND PAID FOR

"It's clouding up," she commented when they were mounted and ready to start on the trek to the ranch house.

He glanced at the sky. "Nothing to worry about. It might shower on those peaks, but the rain won't reach the valley."

She kept an eye on the storm on the way down, wondering how Brody knew these things. He appeared to be right. The clouds came no farther than the high peak and were left behind as their horses ambled along. When they reached smoother ground, Brody clucked his tongue and both horses swung into a fast walk.

A little after three o'clock, they came out on the ridge above the ranch headquarters. "Home," she murmured. "How very beautiful it is."

The spring grass was thick and green from the rains they'd had. The cottonwoods had leafed out along the creeks that meandered across the pastures. The place exuded serenity. With Don in the hills with the sheep and the students checking fences and moving cattle in the back acres, not a soul was around.

She spotted the two extra horses in a paddock next to the llamas. Brody kept six horses, she'd discovered. The students were riding the other two.

"That's the only reason they work for me, so they can ride horses and think they're real cowboys," he'd explained the other morning after the two young men had left the house.

Jessica had invited the cowboys over for Sunday breakfast. They had eaten an amount that boggled her imagination...and she was used to cooking for Brody. The biscuits and gravy had disappeared so fast she'd prepared pancakes to make up for the shortage and fried another pound of sausage while they scraped out the bowls.

"The boys will be in early tonight so they can hit town

before the loggers take over the saloon. Can you have supper ready by five, five-thirty?''

"Sure. Let's grill steaks. I can toss potatoes in the microwave to bake and make a salad.''

"Good.'' He led the way down the steeply slanting bluff.

She couldn't keep her eyes off her very intriguing husband. He rode with the ease of long experience, his gaze ever restless as he checked the trail and the woods on the right of them. She heard a strange sound, a sort of angry buzz, then her gelding snorted and lunged so abruptly she hadn't time to prepare.

Her feet slipped from the stirrups. She lost her grip on the reins. She grabbed at the saddle horn, but it didn't help. She and the horse were both going over the ledge. The horse screamed. That was the last thing she heard. Pain exploded in her head. The world went dark.

Brody jerked around, not sure what had caught his attention. He saw Jessica's mount rear up, then they both went crashing over the edge of the incline. He leapt from the horse. For the next two minutes, he alternately cursed and prayed as he pulled his rifle from its scabbard and fired several regularly spaced shots into the woods.

He now knew what had caught his attention. The hiss of a bullet fired from a gun with a silencer. He reloaded the rifle, tucked his handgun into the waistband of his jeans and dropped over the slanted rimrock to see about Jessica.

She lay on her back, one arm outflung as if reaching for something to cling to as she fell. He didn't let himself think of anything but getting to her as he picked his way over the rocks. She turned to her side and curled her legs toward her chest. He breathed freely for the first time since she'd fallen.

He stooped beside her. "Jessica, honey, you all right?" He ran his hands over her arms and legs, then her ribs and collarbone, all the areas of the body he knew were the most vulnerable to breakage. He didn't find the rough ends of splintered bone under her skin, so that seemed okay.

"Honey, can you open your eyes?"

He wanted to haul her into his arms, but he knew better than to move her yet. He checked the rim above them in case their visitor had decided to finish them off then and there. His horse was skittish around strangers. It would snort and dance if anyone came close.

She opened her eyes and gazed up at him. "Hurt," she mumbled. Blood ran out the corner of her mouth.

His heart jackknifed. "Where? Tell me where you're hurt. Don't go to sleep," he warned when her eyelids drooped.

"Head. Shoulder. Arm."

"What about your neck? Can you lift your head?"

She rolled her head back and forth on the wide flat ledge where she lay, then lifted it a half inch. "Yessss." She didn't seem aware that she drawled the word into a hiss. Her eyes closed again.

"Stay alert," he ordered. "We've got to get you out of here and to a doctor. Jessica? Open your eyes, honey. Dammit, don't you pass out on me, you hear?"

But she didn't. She didn't rouse at all when he prodded her arm. He could hear her breathing. It was shallow and swift. Her pulse seemed to skip every other beat. He clamped the useless curses inside and looked toward the gelding.

The horse was trying to get to its feet, but its hind parts wouldn't move. Brody walked over and spoke soothingly as he assessed the damage. The horse gazed at him trustingly. He'd had it since it was born, had trained it himself to the saddle.

But this horse would never be ridden again. Its back was broken. Still talking in low crooning tones, he put it out of its misery. Heaving a grim breath, he returned to Jessica. She hadn't stirred a hair at the shot.

"Come on, baby, we've got to get out of here."

He hoisted her into his arms and as gently as possible descended the steep slope using the slanting layers of limestone as a walkway, moving down to the next layer when he reached a dead end. Jessica was like a doll in his arms, her head and arms bobbing with each step. At the meadow, he hugged her close, let out a piercing whistle that would bring his horse down to the stable and headed for the sports ute.

He folded the seats down to make a bed, then laid Jessica in it. He ran inside for a blanket and pillows. After covering her and cradling a pillow on each side of her head, he headed out. An hour later, he pulled up at the emergency entrance of the hospital. He'd used the truck phone to call ahead. The medics were ready when he stopped. He followed the stretcher inside.

"How is she?" he asked when a doctor who had one of those cherubic faces that made him look about thirteen straightened from his examination.

"She's alive," he said and barked out orders to several nurses for IV setups and other equipment.

Brody clenched his hands to keep from pounding the young medic. "How badly is she hurt?"

The doctor turned to him. Brody saw that his eyes were those of a man who'd seen too much in too short a time. "What happened to her?"

"Her horse fell over a cliff. She was on him at the time."

The doctor nodded. He'd heard and seen worse. "She has a concussion. I'm calling in a specialist."

"Get the best," Brody ordered. "I want the best. I can afford it," he added.

The doctor snorted and walked over to the central station. He put in a call.

Brody took Jessica's hand. It was warm. There were small calluses forming on her palm, the result of the ranch work she insisted on doing. She seemed to actually enjoy helping muck out the stalls and hand-feed the orphaned lambs and calves. She'd cut her nails short and tried milking the cow under Don's supervision. She'd actually squeezed a thin stream of milk into the bucket. The cowboys had whooped and applauded. She'd taken a bow, a big grin on her face.

He shook his head. His city slicker wife was a good sport. He bent over her, disturbed by her stillness and by the tubes snaking into her mouth and nose. Ah, God…

"We're taking her to an ICU," the doctor told him, returning to Jessica. He barked out more orders over the noise of an arriving ambulance.

Jessica's injury wasn't an accident. Someone was trying to kill her. If they'd succeeded, would they have come for him? He would have liked to laid low and found out. If Jessica hadn't been seriously injured, he would have set up a little ambush of his own. But she came first.

The hospital staff tried to make him wait outside, but he stayed with her, leaning against the wall while the specialist was there, then holding her hand after the doc's orders had been carried out. Jessica was packed in ice to control the swelling. If that didn't stop it, they would open her skull next.

He called two of his best detectives and pulled them off other cases. There was one driving thought in his mind—

catch the attacker and get the evidence needed to arrest the two-faced jackal behind the crime. He gave out orders, spoke to his secretary, then sat by Jessica's side.

Midnight came, then the gray of morning. She didn't rouse or move once during the night. Her hand, when he touched her, was as cold as glacier ice. So were her lips. Like the Snow Queen, she was cold all over. He settled in a hard chair and waited.

Jessica became aware of sounds first. Strange voices spoke in the air over her head as if they floated there without being connected to bodies at all. For a long time, she simply lay in the bed and listened, too tired to open her eyes, not interested enough to try. She drew a deep breath—it felt as if it were the first she'd taken in days—and let it out slowly.

Nothing hurt at the moment. Fancy that.

She could remember her head pounding fiercely each time she saw a pinpoint of light move across her eyes. She thought that had something to do with the voices because the light and the pain only appeared when the voices did. Then the light would go away and leave her in peace. This time, when the voices came, the light and pain didn't appear.

The darkness flowed over her, soothing and pleasant. She could feel herself drifting deeper into it. So peaceful. So relaxing. But wait...there was light...at the end of the darkness...

This was confusing. She wasn't sure she wanted to go toward the light. With the light came pain and remembering the terrible thing that had happened...

No, no, this was a different light. A new place... She let herself drift toward it.

I'm sorry, but there's nothing else we can do.

The hell it is. Jessica, wake up. Dammit, wake up.

Mr. Smith, please, you're not helping...

Jessica tried to ignore the voices as she'd done in the past, those hateful voices and their probing light, but that one voice...it called up memories...pleasant memories...laughter...warmth...oh, yes, the warmth.

Jessica, you listening? We have a deal, a full year, remember? A full year, you hear me?

She sighed. Really, all this commotion. The light at the end of the darkness blinked out. Panic swept over her. She would lose the way without that light. She tried to see through the darkness but couldn't. She had to—

Open your eyes. That's an order.

That maddening, imperious voice. She suddenly knew who it belonged to. And she had a thing or two to say about orders.

She opened her eyes.

"About damn time." Brody glared at her, his face hovering over hers, only inches away.

"Don't yell at me," she told him. Her voice was hoarse, raspy. It didn't come out with the force she'd wanted.

The people surrounding the bed laughed as if this was the funniest thing they'd ever heard. It was obvious they were on his side. She tried to remember what they were arguing about. It was too much effort.

"I'm sorry." He grinned at her, not sorry at all. "How do you feel?"

She thought about it. "Thirsty."

That brought more laughter. These were really strange people. But cheerful. She liked that.

Brody held a straw to her mouth. She sucked a few swallows of water, then rested again.

"Thank you." She laid her head on the pillow and

watched him place the glass on the bedside table. "You need a shave."

In fact, he looked terrible. She'd seen him covered with dust from working with the cattle. She'd seen a five-o'clock growth of beard when he came in at the end of the day. She'd seen him with his hair tousled by the wind. But she'd never seen him like this.

His eyes were bloodshot. His face sported a beard that was at least three days old. His shirt looked as if he'd slept in it. There was a spatter of coffee stains down the front.

"I'll take care of it," he promised, rubbing a hand over his jaw. He winked at her.

She tried to smile, but she really was tired now. She yawned, then grimaced as her head started hurting again. There had been no pain in that floating, peaceful darkness, but she instinctively knew she wouldn't find it again.

"I'm going to look at you," a vaguely familiar voice told her. Oh, yes, the doctor. Her memory returned.

"I fell off my horse," she said.

"And over a bluff," Brody confirmed. "You hit your head."

"Is Captain all right?" She couldn't remember the other horses' names, but there were five more.

"He's fine," Brody assured her.

"Good." She let the doctor look into her eyes with his annoying little flashlight. Then she went to sleep.

The next time she awoke, it was Brody's voice again that prodded her to wake up.

"Breakfast," he said when she looked at him.

An aide brought a tray for her and one for Brody. She studied the Cream of Wheat and dish of Jell-O, then peered at Brody's tray. He had a thick round of Canadian bacon, a mound of scrambled eggs, two biscuits and a roll, plus juice and coffee.

"I'll have what he's having," she told the woman, really miffed at the discrepancy in food.

The aide checked the menu chart. "Um, it says you're
on a light diet."

Jessica accepted the inevitable and thanked the woman
as graciously as she could. She stole another glance at
Brody.

He was clean-shaven. His hair was neat, and he wore a
white shirt with the sleeves rolled up and a pair of navy
slacks. Except for the missing coat and tie, he looked very
much as he had when they'd first met.

Including the same all-business manner and an identical
scowl on his face.

On the ranch, she found a different side to her taciturn
husband. That he could laugh. That he was caring toward
his hired hands and his animals. That he was gentle.

She sighed as a depression settled over her. She didn't
know why she was sad, but she was. She remembered the
cold that had encased her in the darkness and shivered.

"Here," Brody said when the aide had bustled out after
raising the bed and moving the tray table within reach. He
brought his food over and forked a bite of egg into her
mouth. "Nobody could eat that pap."

He shared his breakfast with her.

She shook her head after a few bites, refusing more.
"My eyes were bigger than my tummy," she told him.

"You haven't eaten in four days."

"Four? I've been asleep for four days?"

He met her startled gaze solemnly. "You were unconscious for three and a half days. Your sleep was normal
last night, or so the doctor said."

She put her fingers to her temples.

"How's the head?"

"Better. It hardly hurts at all. That's all I recall—that

my head hurt terribly, and it got worse when someone shined a light in my eyes.''

She stole a biscuit and broke it in half before he wolfed it down. He'd almost finished with his meal. He buttered her half, then his, and added jelly to both.

"You didn't react to the light."

"It was too much trouble." She munched on the biscuit and found it very good. "I was so cold."

He picked up his coffee cup. "You were packed in ice for forty-eight hours." He took a drink.

She noticed his hand trembled slightly. "Oh. Everything seemed so strange. Tell me, what have you been doing for the four days I was sleeping my head off? And when do I get to leave? I got a real hankering for home," she said in her best John Wayne drawl.

Emotion, too fleeting to be read, flicked over his face. "I'll ask the doctor about discharging you. As for what I've been doing, I've been sitting here on my can waiting for you to wake up, lazybones. Don and the cowboys said to tell you they've missed you." He scarfed the last bite of biscuit and started on the sweet roll.

She snorted indignantly. "I know what you men miss when a woman isn't around. The cooking."

He polished off all but the last swallow of milk and offered it to her. She drank it. He set the glass on the tray and pushed the table away. He half laid on the bed, his elbows on either side of her.

"There were other things I missed," he told her, his voice dropping to a husky baritone. He smoothed the hair from her temples, then cupped her face. His mouth touched hers, once, twice, a third time.

"Well, I'd say you were feeling better."

Brody moved away when the doctor stopped by her bed. Jessica studied the young man's face. He looked like a friend's younger brother, one just entering puberty. "Were you a child prodigy?" she asked.

He laughed. "Don't let this pretty face fool you. Inside beats the heart of a mad surgeon. This guy wouldn't let me operate on your brain. I wanted to take it out and see if I could figure out what made women tick." He nodded toward Brody. "Some watchdog you got there."

She smiled at her husband. The peace she'd found in the darkness returned. Yet, there were other troubling things. She tried to think, but couldn't bring them to mind.

"When can I go home?"

"In a couple of days. If you promise to stay off horses for the next eight weeks. Also, no choppy boat rides. Um, no high speed chases. No bungee jumping, parachuting…"

She was laughing by the time he reached the end of his list. "What about normal activities?" She glanced at Brody, thinking of their nights together and his exquisite lovemaking.

"You'd better give it another week, then start in slowly." He beamed at her, then Brody, then back to her. "No marathon housecleaning for a month. Easy does it." He slipped her chart under his arm, shook her hand and left them.

Jessica grimaced in disgust. She could feel the heat in her face. When she looked at Brody, he was wearing a big grin.

"Was I that transparent in what I was thinking?" she demanded.

He leaned over her again. "Only to a close observer."

He touched her breast. The nipple jutted against the hospital gown as if it were a little peg. She groaned in embarrassment.

"Now where were we before we were so rudely interrupted? Ah, I know." He kissed her again.

When Brody lifted his head, he gazed into her eyes for a long moment. He could feel the bonds of shared experience wrapping around them, drawing them together. The camaraderie of the foxhole was a well-known phenomenon.

And in this case, it was false.

He and Jessica weren't soldiers. He was her hired gun, and so far he'd done a damn poor job of protecting her. The man had slipped past his network of security devices without triggering any of them.

"I'll do better by you," he promised.

The one eyebrow he had learned to observe for an indication of her temperament rose in question. He couldn't explain what had happened. He didn't think she was ready for the truth yet. But it was only a matter of time before they would know for sure who was behind the attempts on her life.

Her lips curled upward in amusement. "If you do much better, I really will die, right in your arms," she suggested with engaging innuendo. She dropped her lashes to a sexy level while laughter hovered in her eyes.

His heart clenched as if a giant hand had reached inside and squeezed it to the bursting point. He'd protect her, this woman he'd come to know as brave and true, with his life.

"Why the frown?"

"Just thinking," he said.

"Hmm, it's really hard on you, I see."

He feigned a jab to her chin and lingered to caress the smooth flesh. "Show some respect for your betters, woman."

"I will. When I meet them."

"Watch it. Falling on your head turned on your true smart-mouth personality. Maybe I should call the doc back and tell him to go ahead and operate on your brain."

"Huh." The word was a challenge.

Relief swept over him. Her spirit was as plucky as ever. She would be all right, whatever the future held.

"I have some work to do at the office. Can you make it on your own until evening?"

"Of course. I'm going to take a nap." She rolled her eyes. "Can you believe I'm sleepy again?"

He caught the flash of vulnerability in her expression before she smiled prettily and smoothed the sheet, tucking it under each arm as she prepared to nap.

Words caught in the back of his throat. He didn't know what he wanted to say, but they were there, crowding up from some place deep inside. He straightened from the bed and went to the door, reluctant to leave her.

She waved goodbye, then covered a yawn. Her lashes drifted closed. He lingered, something besides words filling his chest, making it tight and achy.

"Hey, chief, I wondered if you were going to leave. I've been here for an hour." Joe Hernandez, one of his best men, was waiting several feet down the corridor.

"Good. Thanks for coming in on your day off."

"No problem."

"Did you or MacPherson find anything more?"

"Yeah. Mac found the casing. It was the same as the one you brought in a couple of weeks ago. The guy makes his own shot, using rock salt as you suspected. That's why there was no mark on the horse."

"I think he was after me this time. I felt the sting on my leg when my mount was hit. Luckily, the gelding didn't panic. Did you find out what happened to the infrared detector?"

"Yeah. He didn't use the trail. He came through the woods. Laid down a track a blind man could follow."

"He's craftier than I thought a city slicker would be."

"Yeah." Joe visually checked out the people getting off the elevator. "He's probably getting a little stressed about messing up. That's not a good image for a professional man. Next time he'll do better."

"My thoughts exactly. You know how to ride a horse?"

"Me? Sure. I was bustin' broncos for pocket money before I was half grown."

"How would you and Mac like a job at the ranch for a while?"

"Great. I hear your wife can cook like a dream." The private investigator was forever trying to cadge an invitation to a meal with the married men's families.

"She does everything like a dream," Brody affirmed.

Joe's eyes opened wide. "Yo, chief, you in love?"

Brody speared the impertinent bachelor with an impatient stare. "Watch your mouth and this room. Anybody gets through to her, you'll be dead."

The younger man sobered. "Nobody has ever got through me."

"See that it stays that way." Brody strode to the bank of elevators and hustled into one of the cars as the door opened. He impatiently punched the Down button. He had things to do and people to see...actually to call. It was time some of Jessica's family came for a visit.

Chapter Twelve

Jessica sighed as Brody guided the sports ute around the last bend leading to the ranch house. She couldn't believe how weak she felt after spending five days lounging around because of a blow to the head. Now that she was home, she expected to feel a lot better in no time.

Brody parked right beside the back porch. "Wait," he ordered. He came around and opened the truck door.

"Thank you, kind sir." She laid a hand to her heart as if overcome by his thoughtfulness.

"Get in the house before I conk you on the head for insubordination," he ordered.

She didn't blink an eye at that threat. Instead she put her arm around his waist and leaned into him, drawing on his strength as she gazed over the acres of pasture that dwindled to a narrow gorge in the mountains. The sky glowed azure. The sun massaged her scalp like warm fingers. The breeze caressed her body and toyed with her hair.

"Home," she murmured. "I didn't realize how precious it could be."

Brody cast her an odd look, at once grim, sort of brooding and yet she thought there was tenderness, too. He'd been quiet and withdrawn again the past couple of days, more like when they first met rather than as the lover he'd been those two weeks before her accident.

That reminded her. Her gaze went to the meadow where five horses munched the spring grass. She could see the two young cowboys working on an electric fence over near the creek. Don would be up in the high country beyond the gorge with the flock.

"Where's Captain?" she asked. "I don't see him."

Brody didn't answer.

"I've been trying to figure out what made him rear up like that. Do you think he got stung by a bee? That happened to me one time when I was riding my bike. I had a wreck. Fortunately, the car I nearly mowed over managed to stop before we crashed."

"Were you hurt?" he asked.

She looked up in time to catch the fierce frown on her husband's face. "Not other than the sting and a scraped knee. The bee flew under my blouse and stung me when it realized it was trapped in a strange place. I found its poor little carcass after I picked myself up off the pavement."

"Huh," he said noncommittally.

"Did you move Captain? You didn't say where he was."

Brody laid his hands on her shoulders and turned her to face him. "His back was broken in the fall. I had to put him down."

Those few minutes of falling through space, the terrified scream of the horse, her own fear as she realized they were going over the bluff, came back to her. Tears welled before she could control them. "I should have known—"

"No. I lied to you at the hospital. I didn't want you to face that the moment you woke. I knew you'd feel guilty." His hands tightened. "It wasn't your fault."

"If I'd been more alert, maybe I'd have seen the bee... Was it a bee?"

Brody shook his head. His expression remained grim.

"Did someone...Brody, I heard something. I remember now. It was close, a sort of pop and hiss. Was it an air rifle or something like that?"

"Yeah, something like that."

"You said the other man used rock salt to stampede the sheep. Was it the same person, do you think?"

He nodded, his eyes never leaving hers. "My men found the salt on the trail where you and the gelding went over."

The brightness went out of her heart. Cold reality set in. "I'm never going to be free. That damned money is going to hang like a curse over the rest of my life...should I live so long."

Her laughter was bitter, the first time he'd ever heard her like that. He let go of her shoulders and slipped his hands down her back. He wrapped his arms around her waist and hugged her close enough to feel her heartbeat.

"You'll live to be a hundred and twenty. I guarantee it."

"How? At the risk of your own life? Let me go, Brody. Let me disappear for a year. Then maybe—"

"Forget that. You'll stay where I can see you."

"Why? I've brought you nothing but trouble. That's all I am—trouble with a capital *T*."

"Yeah, but I like sleeping with you." He tilted her face up to his. He grinned as he lowered his head.

"Well, there is that," she agreed just before his kiss landed on her mouth.

When he let her up for air, he added, "And the cooking. Don't forget the biscuits and homemade chocolate chip cookies and the cobbler you made last week."

"Mmm-hmm."

He kissed her again. "Waffles and potato pancakes."

By the time he lifted his mouth from hers, her eyes had lost the bitterness and were shining like moonstones.

"I'd never give up those dumplings," he added for good measure.

When she laughed, he guided her into the house and insisted she lie on the sofa while he heated the soup that Don had sent over to help her recover. She smiled over the soup, then her eyes teared up again. His wife was emotionally vulnerable today.

His heart clenched tight. Odd how it kept doing that.

Jessica listened to the music on the CD player and drifted into a doze. She'd been home for five days and felt fine, but Brody, brute that he was, wouldn't let her do a thing. He and Don did all the cooking.

She'd discovered there were two other men on the ranch, both from Brody's agency. She'd never seen them, but Brody had explained their presence.

A shiver chased up and down her spine. Brody expected something to happen soon.

Worry gnawed at her. If something should befall him… It was an unbearable thought. Love joined with anxiety and guilt to form an achy ball in her chest. Each night she clung to him, afraid he would be hurt, unable to voice her fears.

"I'm too mean to kill," he'd scoffed when she'd said something to him about being careful.

"You're flesh and blood," she'd reminded him.

"Come on, Jess, don't be a worrywart."

She'd never been called Jess before. She liked it from Brody. She wouldn't have from anyone else.

Her sleepy thoughts were disturbed by the sounds of a vehicle in the driveway. Yawning, she went to see who it was. The housekeeper had already been there that morning.

She blinked, then blinked again when a man climbed out of a rental car. He was dressed in gray flannel slacks, a blue blazer and an open-throat white shirt. She went out on the porch, raising one hand to shade her eyes.

"Uncle Jesse," she called. "Whatever are you doing here?"

He removed a weekender from the trunk. "I came to see how my favorite niece was faring. Your note saying you were married left several questions in my mind."

"I invited him," another voice said.

Brody stepped on the porch from the side of the house. He stretched out a hand in welcome. The two men shook hands and sized each other up. "Come in," Brody invited.

Hooking an arm around her shoulders, he led the way inside. Her uncle was shown to the guest room. She and Brody went into the kitchen. She looked a question at him.

"Later," he murmured, stalling her queries. He slid his arms around her and placed a string of kisses along her temple. "How are you feeling today? Headache gone?"

"Yes. I'm totally well."

A light danced in his eyes, causing heat to rise in her. When he looked at her in a certain way, it made her heart jump around in her chest as if it were a deer leaping on all fours into the air.

Her uncle joined them. Brody let her go and moved away. She poured glasses of iced cinnamon tea and served cookies with it. She wondered if she was feeding her enemy.

Ancient tribes used the sharing of food as a sign of truce and peace. It would take more than food to appease her uncle or whoever wanted to do her in. He wanted her money—all of it.

A chill passed over her heart.

Brody glanced at her when she folded her arms across her waist. She forced a smile. It was very discouraging to distrust one's own relatives. Brody was the only person she believed in completely. She even doubted her grandfather these days. He hadn't responded to her note or her calls in the seven weeks of her marriage.

Seven weeks and two days. Almost two months.

"Earth to Jessica," Brody intoned, leaning down and peering into her eyes.

She impulsively kissed him, then tapped his cheek. "I'm here. I was listening instead of talking all the time, as you men accuse women of doing."

"Are you tired? You're supposed to be taking a nap."

"I'm fine. Really."

"Sure?"

"Now who's being a worrywart?"

Her uncle laughed. "I see I can stop worrying about you two and the quickness of your marriage. I can tell you're in love."

"Yes," Brody said in a husky tone. "Very much so."

Jessica drew a careful breath. When she looked at Brody, he was watching her uncle, his gaze unreadable. But she knew her husband now. He didn't say anything without a purpose. He was throwing her uncle plenty of rope. Now they'd have to wait and see if he used it. And what for.

They chatted the rest of the afternoon. Brody grilled

steaks while she prepared duchess potatoes and salads. The cowboys took their steaks and ate at Don's house, where they also slept in the bunk room.

At ten, Brody declared it was time for her to be in bed. She'd thought he would stay up and talk to Uncle Jesse in private, but instead he came up with her. As soon as they were in the door, he took her into his arms.

"I hope you don't mind about your uncle being here," he said, a question in the words.

"No, but…why did you invite him?"

His expression hardened. "I wanted to see if he'd show up."

She sighed and laid her cheek against him. She could hear the steady thump of his heart and found it reassuring. "Do you think he'll try anything?"

"He wouldn't dare."

The menace behind the bald statement was frightening. "Don't do anything rash, okay? No showdowns or shoot-outs or anything, you hear?"

He laughed, a deep chuckle that rumbled in her ear as if it were distant thunder. "You've been seeing too many movies while you've been lazing around. Time to put you back to work. And I know the first task you need to perform."

"What?" She leaned her head back and looked up at him.

His hands went to her blouse. He began unfastening it. With his usual efficiency, he peeled her out of her clothes, then did the same on his. "Make your husband happy. It's a woman's job," he advised sanctimoniously.

"Ha." But she proceeded to touch and caress him in all the ways she knew he liked. He did the same for her. Lying in his arms, bathed in contentment, she laughed softly.

"What's so funny?" he demanded. His voice was still husky, but with the urgency gone.

"I was thinking of jobs. I shall have to write a glowing recommendation for you. You definitely go above and beyond the expected for your clients."

His arms tightened. "Not for any client. You're the only one I ever married."

"True." She hesitated. "Thank you, Brody. You've been wonderful to me—"

He kissed her into silence. She bit back the words on her tongue. Brody didn't like emotion.

Jessica breathed in the vibrant May air. "Isn't it wonderful, Uncle Jesse? The air is so clear here, the sky bluer than sapphire. I love it."

"It's pleasant," he conceded.

They stood with their arms propped on the top rail of the pasture fence, the one with cows, not the llamas. Her uncle was dressed in blue linen slacks and jacket this morning with a white T-shirt. He, like her grandfather, looked younger than his age, which was fifty. She didn't want the llama to spit on his chic outfit. She had on jeans and a shirt as usual.

He stuck his hands into his pockets. "You seem happy with your detective husband."

"Yes."

"Life can be disappointing. You think you've found everything you could possibly desire and then *poof!* it's gone."

"Have you broken up?" she asked kindly. He and his partner had been together for years.

"Charles thinks he must have a child to pass on his heritage and worldly goods."

"Why don't you adopt? Or have a surrogate mother like in a movie I saw recently?"

"Please," he murmured with a grimace.

"Well, yes, there could be problems, but you should explore the possibilities before giving up."

"I've never considered it necessary. I had your mother and then you. I expect I'll also have a grandniece or nephew soon to leave my riches to." His perusal was sly but pleased.

Jessica started. She hadn't thought more about a child since she'd discovered she wasn't pregnant. "I'd like a child," she admitted. If she and Brody lived long enough…

Her thoughts solemn, she showed her uncle around the home paddocks, then hiked up to the bluff with him. She wondered if she was being a fool, taking him to a place where he could push her off and simply say it was an accident.

She needn't have worried. Brody appeared on the trail the moment they reached the rimrock ledge. He sat on a boulder and spread his legs, indicating she should sit there and lean against him. She did. He wrapped his arms across her waist and rested his chin on her head occasionally while they talked. His Stetson shaded both of them from the rays of the sun.

The morning passed quite pleasantly. After lunch, she did take a nap while Brody took over the duties as host. When she rose, the men joined her on the porch. Brody served a wine cooler he made specially for her. They watched the sunset.

When they went to bed, she turned to him, anxious for his lovemaking. Each moment might be her last with him. She had to grab each one as it came along.

"Don't," he whispered, touching the frown between her eyes. "Trust me to take care of you."

She cupped his face in her hands. "I trust you with my life, my fortune and my..." She paused while she searched for a substitute for heart. "My sacred honor, as our forefathers would have said."

"And did say. Is sex part of your personal declaration of independence?" He nuzzled her ear, then her throat before moving downward to caress her breasts.

"I don't know. Love me, Brody. Just love me."

As if their lovemaking was life itself, he poured his strength and energy into it, laving her with kisses and caresses until she writhed and cried out in soft murmurs of ecstasy, lost to danger and suspicion, aware only of his hands and mouth and body and of her great love for him.

He would protect her with his life. She would do the same for him. She held him desperately, not wanting the moment to be over. The future drew near, ominous and threatening. Worry washed over her, bringing an avalanche of fear.

"Please," she whispered, "be careful."

"Always," he assured her. "I'll always be careful with you. That's a promise."

"I can see the attraction," Uncle Jesse said, scanning the impressive peaks surrounding the ranch.

Jessica stared out the window as the sports ute wound higher into the mountains. Brody was driving, her uncle was in the front and she sat in the back.

They were delivering supplies to the mountain cabin. She and Brody would stay while Don and Uncle Jesse returned to the ranch. Don's nephew was due in that afternoon. Brody thought the shepherd should be there to greet his relative.

Her tough husband was thoughtful that way. She let her gaze caress the back of his head. He was wonderful in more ways than she could count. She fell more deeply in love each day.

Love. She hadn't had any idea how potent and exhilarating it could be.

"You're quiet back there," Brody said.

"I'm admiring the view." She ogled him.

His dark gaze met hers in the rearview mirror. A thrill ran over her. His eyes held the promise of passion to come. They'd be alone at the cabin for two nights. Her blood heated and her pulse sped up at the memories that came to mind. Sleeping two to a cot would always occupy a special place in her heart.

Brody smiled lazily, then turned his attention back to the dirt track. They pulled into the long, narrow valley before lunch. The two collies barked a greeting, but didn't leave their woolly charges when the three of them climbed out.

Don shook hands with her uncle, then gave Brody a report on a wild cat that had moved into the gorge at the end of the valley. "It's a male. He's passing through."

She wondered how he knew that, but didn't question him. She'd learned the old shepherd knew the nature of animals and the seasons better than anyone she'd ever met. He'd taught her some of the signs.

The circle she'd seen around the moon last night could indicate an approaching storm. It was caused by moisture, usually ice particles, high in the atmosphere. In spite of the day's warmth, she shivered slightly as she thought of another storm. Someone had tried to kill them the other time she'd been up here.

She searched the perimeter of the woods, wondering what evil lurked in there—

"Here." Brody broke into her thoughts when he hefted a five-pound sack of flour at her.

Distracted, she went inside and put the groceries away while the men unloaded the ute. She discovered Don had a pot of stew on the hot plate for their lunch. She served crusty Dutch rolls she'd made the previous day and glasses of spring water with the meal. Uncle Jesse had made brownies, his one gustatory skill he assured them, and they had those for dessert. He and Don left soon after that.

Jessica waved them off and watched until the truck disappeared. Brody was already checking out the flock. She went over and sat on a boulder.

"It's just you and me, kid," she told him in her best Bogie imitation.

"Yeah." Brody gave her an oblique glance that had her insides tied into knots in a second.

She stood, restless with energy. "Where's Ram?" She peered over the flock. She was surprised that he hadn't come bounding over to cadge a pat and something to eat.

"He might not remember you now that he's been with his own kind for a while. He's probably found some sweet little thing to occupy his mind."

Laughter bubbled in her. "Ah, yes, the call of nature."

"Mmm-hmm," he agreed, his quick glance once more sizzling her insides to cinders.

Ah, love. The things it did to a person.

Brody abruptly strode off. "I'm going to check the gorge for cat tracks. Do you mind staying here and keeping an eye on the sheep?"

"No." She looked at the ewes and lambs. They were grazing or snoozing or just gazing into the distance. The dogs rested nearby, ready for a command to leap into action. "What do I do?"

He grinned. "Sit there and look pretty."

She stuck her hands on her hips. "No problem."

Chuckling at her frown, he offered instructions. "Let them graze. If anything happens, circle your arm and the dogs will round them up and move them in the direction you point or you start moving. Nothing will happen," he added.

"Do I move them to the dip where we went in the storm?" she asked, ignoring his assurance.

"No. You keep them close to the cabin. If anything does happen to frighten you, drop the two-by-four across the door and stay inside until I come for you. There's a handgun on the shelf over the plates. Use it if you have to. Don't come out for anyone but me or Nick Dorelli. No one, got that?"

She nodded. "Got it."

He loaded his rifle and headed toward the end of the valley. She settled on the boulder.

The brightness had gone out of the day. Brody seemed his usual self, but she could sense the tension in him. He'd never spoken of danger so openly to her before. It reminded her of why she'd hired him in the first place and why they'd married.

Living at the ranch with him, sharing a bed and bathroom, eating all their meals together, all the intimate acts that a husband and wife shared had overshadowed the danger. Now it was brought home to her like a slap in the face.

"I hate it," she said to the collie lying nearest her.

It wagged its tail and turned one ear toward her, but its eyes stayed on the flock it guarded.

"Good girl," she said.

As the afternoon wore on, she became sleepy. She stood and ambled around the clearing, her gaze flicking often to the far end of the valley where the land narrowed into the steep gorge of boulders and loose rock that had been carved by aeons of storms.

The valley had been formed by glacier action. Its bowl-shaped sides and fairly level floor told of a past when great floes of ice had pushed through, scouring the land into its present outline. The mighty peaks spoke of volcanic action deep within the bowels of the earth.

For all the evidence of ongoing violence, she felt as one with this land. Here she'd found peace…and all the desires of her heart. The thought of leaving left her chilled to the bone. She wouldn't go, not willingly—

The ring of a shot froze her in place. She began to run, fear a great ache in her chest. She was halfway up the valley when Brody appeared. She threw herself at him.

"Where the hell do you think you're going?" he demanded, not at all pleased.

"Are you all right? I heard a shot." She drew back and checked him over for blood. None was visible.

"I ran across the cat's tracks and followed them. He was eyeing the sheep. I used the gun to kick up a little grit in his face. He hightailed it back up to high country."

"Don't you ever scare me like that again," she ordered, angry at him now that the fear was unnecessary. "You go off and put yourself in danger without a thought to your own mortality. A mountain lion can be as dangerous as a two-footed opponent."

"Yes, ma'am." His smile was sardonic.

She punched him in the stomach. "Did you see any other tracks?"

"No." He caught her wrist and twisted her arm behind her, bringing her in tight against him. "I think you need to be taught a lesson, too."

"You gonna shoot me?" she challenged, mocking his tone.

"No, ma'am," he assured her in his best cowboy drawl. "There's a shady spot about a hundred yards from here that's nice and private. Would you like to see it?"

"Would you like a black eye?" She wasn't appeased.

He looped his arm around her waist and guided her toward the woods. When they were among the trees, he led the way to a hammock of willows. There he laid the rifle aside and made a bed with his shirt. "My lady," he invited, sitting and opening his arms to her.

She couldn't resist. She went down on one knee and pushed him to the ground, then she fell on him and kissed him for all she was worth.

"Wait, I have something," he murmured.

He rolled her off him and onto his shirt, then dug in his pants pocket. He removed three packets and laid them in a neat row on the mossy turf.

"Take your pick," he invited.

"How very considerate of you," she complimented. She gave the decision serious thought. "The one with the blue ribbing. I think." She lingered over the selection, delighting in the play between lovers that was so new to her and enjoying the buildup of anticipation between them.

Brody watched her with amusement dancing in the flames of desire in his eyes. It thrilled her that he wanted her. It touched her that he willingly followed her lead and that he put her pleasure before his. He was, in so many ways, a remarkable man and a most tender husband.

"An excellent choice," he said when she finally decided. He folded her into his arms and laved her with his hot, exciting kisses. She shivered, then sighed, then caught her breath as his caresses became bolder and bolder.

She heard him chuckle, then he, too, grew solemn as they kissed and the magic worked its spell on them. They stayed in the glen for an aeon or two before they remembered the sheep.

Chapter Thirteen

Jessica yawned contentedly and settled on her favorite boulder. Another rock provided a backrest. She hugged her jacket close and watched the twilight turn the world to pink and magenta. Hints of purple showed in the shadows of the woods.

Brody came out of the cabin. He carried the rifle over and propped it against one of the boulders. In his waistband she saw the butt of a handgun. The evening chill crept inside her.

"Let's walk," she requested.

He narrowed his eyes and surveyed the valley. He watched the dogs for a moment. "All right."

They ambled around the perimeter of the flock. A whistle and a movement of his arm sent one collie off in the opposite direction they walked. The other he motioned to go with them.

She knew the collies would sound a warning long before

the two humans spotted anything in the vicinity. It gave
her a sense of security to have them. She felt the same
with Brody.

"I wonder where Ram is," she mused aloud when they
were about halfway around the meadow. He hadn't come
to the cabin to be fed as she'd expected.

Brody smiled. "I think you'll soon know." He nodded
to the west where a commotion was going on.

One of the collies had routed a bunch of sheep out of a
gully and was driving them back to the main flock. One
lamb, smaller than the rest, butted at the dog, then bleated
and ran to one of the ewes when the collie dropped his
head and snapped at the lamb's heels.

Jessica started laughing. "Oh, yes, still up to his usual
tricks, I see." She observed the rambunctious lamb and
the ewe for a moment. The lamb still had a patch of wool
on his back where Brody had glued some of the ewe's
fleece.

Nostalgia made her grow pensive as she thought of the
days she'd spent hand-feeding the frolicking little bully.
The breeze blew her hair into her eyes. The wind was
much cooler now that the sun was completely below the
horizon.

Ram threw up his head, uttered a plaintive bleat and
raced across the pasture as if pursued by wolves. He leapt
into the air and would have struck Jessica in the chest if
Brody hadn't moved first. He caught the blur of fleece in
midair.

"Hold on, you mangy critter," Brody ordered when the
lamb thrashed to be free. "Ouch, dammit."

The hard head connected with Brody's chin.

Jessica laughed until her sides ached as man and beast
waged war. Brody set the animal on the ground and held
him there while she knelt to pet and caress and make

crooning noises. Ram butted her hands the way he used to do when he wanted food or pats.

"He does remember me." She smiled happily up at Brody.

"You'd be a hard woman to forget."

His gaze was pensive the way hers had been earlier. The cold crept down her neck. She wondered if he was thinking of the future and a time when she was no longer here.

"Would you want to forget me?" she asked.

His face hardened, the angular bone structure becoming more prominent as he flexed his jaw. "I might."

The enigmatic answer did nothing to soothe her heart. It came to her that Brody might wish this whole situation to be resolved so they could arrange for the divorce and each of them return to their real lives.

He stood and moved off, leaving her to scratch Ram's hard head and fluffy ears. She swept the area and the dark woods beyond the valley floor with an intent gaze. Usually she saw nothing but quiet beauty. Tonight she saw the danger.

When Ram grew restless, she sent him back to the flock with a swat on his rump and looked around for Brody. He stood nearby.

"Ready?" he asked.

She nodded. He guided her around the flock and sent both dogs ahead of them as they finished their walk.

When they returned to the cabin, he heated water and let her prepare for bed first. While she slipped into a navy sweat suit, he emptied the basin for her.

"I'm going out for a while," he told her. "I want you to stay inside, even if you hear shots." He smiled to show he was joking. "Bolt the door and open it only for me."

"All right."

She didn't tell him to be careful. He always was. She

knew he'd checked out the area thoroughly before he took her to the glen that afternoon. He had a duty to protect her. He would never let anything interfere with that.

An hour crept by while she read a romantic suspense novel. Maybe she shouldn't have chosen a book with the heroine being chased by the bad guy, a serial killer whose face she could identify. Her hair stood on end whenever the maniac got close.

Nine o'clock came and went.

She needed to go to the outhouse. Standing at the window, she peered through the deepening twilight. There was still plenty of light to see by. She wouldn't need a flashlight.

Brody wasn't in sight. No one was. It should be safe. He'd have surely told her if he'd seen tracks when he scouted the valley that afternoon. If he had, they wouldn't have spent time in the glen making love.

She turned out the overhead light and slipped out the door and around the cabin as if she were a thief.

In less than two minutes, she headed back for the cabin. She'd taken no more than ten steps before she realized she wasn't alone. Someone was coming right at her. Fast.

"I told you to stay in." Brody loomed into view, moving like a racing shadow.

"I didn't see you lurking there in the dark," she accused, rubbing her arms where goose bumps rippled.

"You wouldn't have seen anyone else, either," he said in a snarly tone.

"I had to go to the bathroom." She groaned internally. She sounded like a petulant child.

"I told you not to come outside." He bit off a curse and gestured toward the cabin. "Get in and stay there." The order was spoken in a low growl of barely controlled anger.

She went in, threw the bolt across the door and ran to the window in time to see Brody disappear completely into the deeper shadows of the forest. She listened but heard nothing other than the soft moan of the wind through the valley.

The stark beauty of the landscape emphasized the loneliness of her life. A sense of isolation swept over her. Being in love, not being loved in return, made it so much more poignant. No one wanted her. It was a simple fact.

Poor little rich girl.

She sucked in a deep breath and concentrated on the view from the window where she stood. From it she could see most of the valley. The sheep had bedded down for the night, fuzzy blurs against the dark shadow of the earth. She realized there was no moon. That's why the sky seemed so black.

Clouds were moving in over the high peaks. She could discern where they stopped by the lack of stars. The rising wind whispered of the storm to come before morning.

The goose bumps rankled along her arms again. She was aware of feeling nervy and tense, ready for danger or disaster.

An hour passed. Another.

Brody didn't return. Her anxiety increased as the storm grew closer. Lightning flashed. Four seconds later, she heard the thunder. The storm was a mile away.

The hot clouds moved closer, obscuring the stars as far as she could see. The lightning burned zigzagged trails over the heavens that seemed to linger after the bolt blinked out. Thunder banged directly overhead and rolled away down the valley.

Then, in a split second of crackling light, she saw what she'd been watching for. Brody, moving across the meadow at great speed, heading for the cabin, the rifle in hand.

She rushed to the door and lifted the bar, then released the bolt. She strained to see what was happening through the narrow slit she allowed as she cautiously opened the door.

The heat lightning blasted over the sky almost continuously now. She saw the running figure again, heading for the cabin. She tensed, wondering if she should let him in. Only if it was Brody. He would have to identify himself—

A shot rang out. Then another.

Her heart skipped, then pounded out of control. A pause in the storm reflected the silence in the meadow. She saw someone walking toward the cabin. This time she knew who the person was. She opened the door and stepped back. Brody came inside.

He threw off his jacket and pulled a walkie-talkie from his belt. He spoke to a guy named Joe. "Did you get him?"

"We did." The other man was laughing. "You wouldn't believe how."

"Tell me," Brody ordered, the frown smoothing out.

"The guy got the drop on Mac. I was hidden in the trees wondering if I could shoot him without getting Mac killed when this little guy, one of your woollies who thinks he's a goat, came bounding over and butted the dude in the back of the knees. Mac grabbed the gun and wrenched it away. End of fight."

"Good work. Take him to the ranch. We'll meet you there in an hour." Brody clicked off and turned to Jessica. "It's over."

She wrapped her arms around him and clung for dear life. "Who?" she asked.

"We're going to ask the guy my detectives caught."
Brody shook his head. "I can't believe he was going to
try the same trick he used before. Amateur."

"Right," Jessica agreed, weak with relief that Brody
hadn't been hurt. She'd been so afraid for him.

He must have felt her tremor. His voice dropped from
elation to assurance. "You're safe, Jess. This will put an
end to the danger. You'll be okay now."

She nodded.

"Come on. We're going to the house."

"What about the flock?" She eyed the storm and
thought of hail and icy winds.

He chuckled. "Watch it. You're beginning to sound like
a rancher's wife."

"I am a rancher's wife."

His glance was skeptical as he handed her jacket to her
and grabbed his own. He checked the hot plate. "Ready?"

"My clothes." She went into the bedroom and packed
her knapsack with the clothes she'd worn earlier.
"Ready," she reported, returning to the living room.

They made it to the ranch house in good time. Two
county cruisers were there. Nick Dorelli talked on his radio
to someone in dispatch. The sheriff stood on the porch with
a cup of coffee in his hand. The prisoner lounged with
insolent ease against the porch railing. His hands were
cuffed behind him.

Jessica started in surprise.

"Do you know him?" Brody asked.

She swallowed the lump that insisted on forming in her
throat. "Clive Grainger. He was my bodyguard before I
hired you. He and the woman who went through my
clothes worked as partners."

"Nick, Sheriff, did you get that?" He gestured toward

Grainger. The men nodded. "Get inside, Jess. The rain is heading this way." Brody told her.

"Brody, Homicide is on the way. He'll be picked up within minutes," Nick reported.

"Good."

Jessica shivered as chills spread throughout her body. The cold gathered around her heart. She went inside and stayed. The police left. She prepared a pot of coffee and poured a cup. She took it to the table and sat down to wait for Brody. There were questions to be asked and answered.

After the deputy's vehicle cleared the bend in the drive way, Brody came in. He studied her while pouring a cup of coffee, then joined her at the table. "My men will stay the night, then head back to Denver tomorrow."

"Why would Grainger want to kill me?" she asked.

"Money."

"Uncle Jesse—"

"Sleeping like a baby. He never heard a thing."

"Isn't the sheriff going to arrest him?"

"The perp hasn't named his accomplice." Brody hesitated. "Let's go to bed. I've had enough running around in the dark and cold to last me a lifetime."

Her lips trembled when she tried to smile at his wry grimace. She should be relieved. They'd caught the man who'd been trying to kill her. All she felt was dread. Soon she would find out who wanted her dead. It would be a hard truth. Brody's eyes were filled with pity. He already knew. So did she.

She changed from her sweat suit to her lavender pajamas while Brody took a warm shower. He held her when he got into bed, but didn't try to make love. It was a long time before either of them went to sleep.

The call came before dawn. Brody took it. "This is he

husband. I'll take the message." He listened, then, "Okay, I got it. We'll be there this afternoon if possible."

"What?" she asked when he hung up and looked at her.

"Your grandfather had a massive heart attack during the night. He didn't make it."

Jessica laid her purse on the table in the library and sat at the walnut desk that had belonged to Robert Lacey who had fought beside George Washington in the revolution. Her grandfather had died without a will, and she had been tied up in legal meetings for a month since the funeral.

It was odd—she was the owner of this house and all it contained. She always had been. Her grandmother had stipulated that her husband have the use of it for his lifetime, but it and all her holdings belonged to Jessica.

Her uncle had lingered by her side during the ordeal. Brody hadn't objected. Neither had she.

Since there was no real proof other than a suspicious cut in a tire tread and the fact that he'd been carrying a gun, the man they'd found on the ranch had been charged with trespassing and carrying an unregistered weapon. He'd paid his bail and disappeared. So had the woman who'd been his partner.

Brody entered the room and paced in front of the desk. His dark gaze roamed her face as if looking for cracks or other signs of her falling apart. She returned his stare with stoic calm.

"How are you?" he asked. His tone was kind.

She could take wry or sardonic or harsh from him, but not kind. Kindness was what one showed to strangers in distress.

"Fine. I thought I'd go through the desk and get it cleaned out today. I need to pay the household bills. It's odd. Grandfather wouldn't let the housekeeper or even his accountant do it. He took care of his finances himself.''

Brody nodded. "Mind if I sit here and read?" He gestured at the morning newspaper on a nearby table.

"No. Are you keeping an eye on me?"

He flashed her one of his sardonic glances. "That's what I'm paid to do, isn't it?"

"Yes." She toyed with the pen. "I suppose we need to come to a new arrangement…now that I no longer need protection.''

Brody settled in a leather chair facing the desk. His poise was one of ease, hands in his pockets, his long legs stretched out and crossed at the ankles. He studied her, his eyes dark and rather moody, giving away nothing.

When they'd arrived last month, he'd gone to his previous quarters instead of following her to her room. She realized it had probably been an awkward situation for him. But maybe not.

Brody lived by his own rules and a false sense of etiquette or social niceties wasn't one of them. She didn't know if he would have stayed with her if she'd requested it.

Perhaps he would have as part of this kinder, gentler Brody she was seeing, the one she didn't like. With the old Brody, she would have known where she stood. But of course, her whole life was different now.

"What makes you think you no longer need protection?" he asked with a return of his cynical edge.

"I know the truth."

That got his attention. He sat up straight and leaned forward, his forearms on his thighs. "What truth?"

"My grandfather was the one who wanted me out of the way." She met his gaze without faltering. She'd steeled herself to deal with this fact soon after they received the call about his heart attack, which had confirmed her suspicions. The man Nick Dorelli had said would be picked up had been her grandfather.

Exposure was something he couldn't have borne. If the shock of knowing he'd been found out hadn't killed him, she thought he would have taken his own life rather than face trial.

She looked away from Brody's penetrating study. Outside, it was a perfect June day. The sun was shining. The breeze was warm and gentle. It was summer in the land, but it was winter in her heart.

He didn't reply, only looked at her with that terrible pity in his gaze.

"You knew almost from the first, didn't you?"

He hesitated before speaking. "I had my suspicions." Again his tone was kind.

"That's why you agreed to the marriage—to get me out of this house—and why you insisted we live at the ranch."

"Yes."

A shiver swept over her at his blunt confession. She'd been a blind, trusting fool.

Brody reached for the phone, hit the intercom button and ordered coffee. His eyes never left her. Jessica rubbed her arms and considered the past. Neither of them spoke.

The housekeeper brought the coffee. "I have a fresh apple strudel. Shall I serve that? You didn't eat breakfast," she reminded Jessica.

"Yes," Brody agreed before she could refuse.

The housekeeper bustled out, leaving the coffee on the sideboard. Brody poured them each a cup.

When he placed hers on the desk, she tilted her head back and stared at him, hungry for things only he could give her. His glance caught hers before she could look away. His eyes darkened. For the longest minute, he gazed at her while she waited. Longing became an unbearable pressure in her chest.

He straightened and returned to his chair with his cup.

The housekeeper brought the treat and served them. Jessica thanked her. She ate, hardly tasting the perfect pastry or succulent filling. Brody was silent, too.

"I trusted him," she said. "I loved him. I tried so hard to please him when I was sent here to live after my mother's death. I wanted him to be glad to have me—"

Brody visibly tensed. He set the dessert plate aside and again watched her as if he expected her to fall apart.

"You knew. That's why my uncle wasn't arrested at the ranch. You knew he had nothing to do with it."

He nodded, his gaze never faltering.

"Why didn't you tell me?"

"I had hoped you would never find out."

"Why?"

"What good does it do?"

"I should have known," she insisted.

"If I'd tried to tell you, would you have believed me?"

The icy patch on her heart accumulated like winter snow in the Arctic. The chill reached clear to her soul.

Many fine nuances that she'd never recognized came to mind now that she'd faced the truth. "I think my uncle knew I was in danger. Why didn't he do something?"

Brody shrugged. "Your grandfather was cunning. He had the right friends, thanks to your grandmother."

She looked away from Brody's direct gaze. "Did he marry her for her money?"

"From all accounts, he was a social climber and fortune hunter. No matter how much money he might make on his own, he came from the wrong side of the tracks. He would never have been invited into the inner sanctum of society and high finance without your grandmother's name. She was old money.''

''Money,'' Jessica repeated.

''The *love* of money,'' Brody reminded her.

''I thought he cared for me. He was reserved and rather rigid, but I thought he cared.''

''Parents are supposed to love their children and put them first. Your grandfather wasn't blood kin,'' he reminded her, as if this might make it easier to accept the fact that the person she'd depended on for nurturing since she was twelve had tried to have her killed.

Brody's mother sent him off alone to live with a distant relative he didn't know when he was fourteen. He knew what she was feeling, how deep the sense of betrayal went. He'd been through it when he'd been little more than a boy. At least she had a degree of maturity on her side to soften the blow.

Anger, irrational and destructive, made her want to lash out at the mother who had hurt him. The love of a child was a gift, a most precious thing. To throw it away…

A heart was a terrible thing to waste.

''I've talked to a local judge, an old friend of the family, actually. He says I won't have any trouble in setting aside the will.'' She drew a careful breath so that she could say the next part. ''We can arrange for a divorce at any time.''

Brody didn't move for a long second, then he nodded.

''I'll pay you for the year—''

''Forget that.'' His face darkened.

''You may as well take it gracefully. I'll simply have the money transferred to your account and keep doing it until you give up. You saved my life, Brody. It isn't something I shall ever forget.''

He muttered an expletive, shocking her.

Chapter Fourteen

Brody set the cup aside. The rage he'd rarely felt except in relation to Jessica rose in him. He would have choked her grandfather with his bare hands if the coward hadn't died first.

For Jessica's sake, he was glad things had worked out this way. It had saved her from going through a lengthy, tabloid-hyped trial. There would have been a TV miniseries, no doubt.

He tried to assess her emotional state, but she disclosed nothing. It was something he'd witnessed in her before—this ability to shut herself completely off, to smile and talk and act as if she hadn't a care in the world, even when she knew someone was trying to kill her. She'd never said a word to her society friends, had never asked for help or pity from anyone.

She never would.

A sudden need to touch her had him gritting his teeth

He wouldn't impose himself on her, but he wished she would turn to him... Forget it. She no longer needed him. That much was clear. She hadn't come to him once since that silent flight and their return to this house. He was a hired gun and now his duty was finished.

The anger swept over him again. That was the last thing she needed from him. He headed for the door. "I'm going for a walk."

She nodded in her well-brought-up manner.

Jessica was a lady, he mused, standing on the patio. She'd never cause a scene or engage in a shouting match. Only in his arms did she go wild, shrieking and moaning her ecstasy when they made love.

Now he sensed she was buried inside herself, withdrawing more each moment as she became the lady of the manor again, rather than a rancher's wife.

A hard fist of need slammed into his chest. He'd miss that woman. He hadn't let himself depend on anyone in years. He'd learned that lesson the hard way. But...he'd miss her.

After a long walk he returned to the house, made a couple of calls, showered and packed. "I'm off," he said, stopping at the door of the library where Jessica bent over her books and wrote out the household checks.

She looked up, that one slender eyebrow, the one with the attitude, rising as she silently questioned him.

"I have a reservation on the three-o'clock flight. I'm wasting my time here." He smiled. "I do have a business to run and a ranch to rusticate on, so I'm heading out."

"I see."

No fake protests, no forced explanations. Just that cool acceptance. A class act all the way.

"Keep me posted."

"I will. Brody...?"

"Yeah?"

She licked her lips. "Thank you. For everything."

"Nada. It was nothing."

He watched her, not sure what he was looking for. Men
tally shaking his head at his own vulnerability where sh
was concerned—yeah, he admitted it; she got to him in
way no other person ever had since he'd been grown—h
gave her a half salute and headed out. The family drive
was there with the car. He jumped in and told him to hea
for the airport.

"We're going down for the rodeo. You want to come?"

Brody looked up from the report he was reading. Th
cowboy leaned in the door to the ranch house and looke
at him with all the eagerness of youth in his smile. Th
young pup.

"No, thanks, I have plans. You boys have a good tim
I'll come bail you out on Monday if you're not back :
the ranch."

The grin in the tanned, lightly freckled face broadene
"We'll be back on time. We got our girls with us."

Brody sketched a farewell and watched the students pr
pare to leave. It was a new world. He'd allowed his sun
mer hands to invite their girls up for the Fourth of Jul
celebration. The girls were visiting for the entire wee
And staying in the bunkhouse with the guys. Aunt Ess
wouldn't have approved, although she would have like
the idea of hiring females as wranglers.

The couples' laughter as they piled into the old picku
floated in the open windows, making him realize his year
Thirty-three and he felt old clear to the bone.

Forcing his attention to the wrap-up of an importa
case, he finished the report, tossed it on the coffee tab

nd strode out on the back porch. Don closed the paddock
ate and ambled over to the porch.

"Warm today," he commented. He wiped the sweat
rom his face with his sleeve.

"Yeah."

"You not going to town?"

"Nah."

"Hmm."

Brody grimaced at the disapproval in the older man's
one. He thought Brody should have brought Jessica home
nd had shown his disgust by rarely speaking for the past
week.

"I could hardly kidnap her." Brody voiced his thoughts.

"You could have asked her if she wanted to come. You
ot any tea? I'm out."

Brody poured two glasses and took them outside. They
at on the porch, legs dangling and leaned against the sup-
ort posts.

"Why don't you call and find out what she's doing over
he holiday? She might like to come out for the rodeo."

"Why don't you? You're the one with the hots for her,"
e snarled, his temper exploding as frustration and hunger
eat at him with the fury of an angry mob.

"I would, but I'm not her husband. She picked you,
ord knows why."

Brody snorted. He knew why. She'd needed his protec-
on. She'd paid well for his services. He had the savings
ccount to prove it. He'd done his job. When no longer
eeded, he'd left.

Simple.

He just wished he didn't feel like hell all the time. Or
hat he could sleep one night through. He sighed.

"Call her."

"No."

"Stubborn." Don set the empty glass on the porch non
too gently and returned to the llamas, which he was check
ing for pink eye. Brody noticed a green stain on the bac
of his shirt.

He took the glasses in and put them in the dishwashe
then paced the kitchen restlessly. Oh, hell, it wouldn't hu
to call. She was probably at a lawn party or something lik
that anyway. He wouldn't get to talk to her.

The telephone rang several times before the housekeepe
answered.

"Uh, this is Brody Smith. Is Jessica in?"

"She's at the hospital."

"Hospital," he croaked.

"Visiting," the housekeeper quickly added. "She visi
the sick children. She always takes them gifts on holiday
you know."

No, he didn't know. There were lots of things still to l
discovered about his wife, not that he'd get a chance
discover them, but— "I'm sorry. What was that?"

"I asked when you were coming back. Jessica is ve
lonely. I think she misses you."

"Not me," he started to say. His heart began to be
very hard. "Is she…do you think she's unhappy?"

"Well, sometimes she stays out at night. Henry said s
used to stand for hours at the windows in the Lockha
Building. She has been driving herself of late, so we dor
know where she goes. Her eyes are sad."

"I see. Well, tell her I called. The rodeo is going (
over the holiday weekend. I thought she might like to a
tend."

"I'll tell her."

After they hung up, he stood there, worry eating at hi
It was none of his business. That day in the library she

made it clear she no longer needed him. He'd been expecting to hear something on the divorce any day.

He paced a while longer, then picked up the phone. Nothing like making a total fool of yourself, but he had to check for himself, just to be sure.

Jessica stepped out of the elevator. The building was silent, empty the way she liked it. It was almost two o'clock in the morning. Her favorite hour of the day. Or night.

The loneliest hour.

She pressed a hand to her aching breast. A person got over things. She knew that. Time was the key. She would simply outwait the longing and the loneliness. In a year or so, she was thinking of adopting a child. When she could be sure that her reasons were the right ones.

Leaning against the railing, she rested her forehead on the cool glass and watched the traffic far below. A cab stopped and let a passenger out. Another person grabbed the cab before a couple jumped in. The man shook his fist at the departing vehicle. She smiled wryly. Life in the city...

Her sigh steamed the glass, but the moisture was quickly gone as the cool breeze from the air conditioning wafted over her. The trees in the atrium swayed and rustled.

Inside she was aware of the cold, a tiny frozen spot that would never thaw.

Poor little rich girl.

She tried to laugh, but the sound was hoarse. She pressed her palms against the glass and felt the cold spread over her hands.

The reflection in the glass changed. She stared, puzzled, then she realized the elevator doors had opened. A man stepped out. She turned slowly and watched him approach.

"Are you real?" she asked.

Brody stopped in front of her. "Touch me and see," h
invited in a sexy tone that caused shivers to dart throug
her.

He didn't smile. In fact, he looked so solemn she wo
ried about the news he'd come all this way to tell he
Brody didn't travel a thousand miles to discuss th
weather.

She laid her hands on his chest. He covered them wi
his.

"Cold hands, warm heart," he murmured. The smi
appeared, brushing his lips lightly, and was gone.

"What are you doing here?"

His chest lifted in a deep breath. "I've come to tal
you home. To the ranch. If you want to come."

She blinked, uncertain of his meaning. "Why?"

"There's a rodeo in town. I thought you might like
see it." He frowned as if the answer displeased him.

Her heart butted her rib cage like Ram in one of h
boisterous moods. "Why?" she insisted.

"I've missed you."

"I see." He missed her? Or the sex? Or the cooking'

"You'll come?"

She shook her head. He looked away, but not befo
she'd seen something dark and hurting in his eyes. Sl
pressed her hands against his chest as need, urgent a
hopeful, filled her. "Why, Brody?"

He swallowed. He dropped his hands to his sides, h
fists clenched so tight his knuckles turned white. "I'
missed you," he said again, but with an edge of desper
tion.

She suppressed the wild joy in her heart. She had
know more, to be sure she understood exactly what he w
saying. "In bed? In the kitchen?" She managed a lig

augh, the one she'd learned early so that no one would
now how she felt.

Brody caught her shoulders, his movement so fast she
vas startled out of her society smile.

"In my life," he said in a low, hoarse tone that seemed
ipped from his guts. "In my arms." He clenched his teeth
or a second, then said, "In my heart."

She stared at him, speechless. For all her wishing, she
adn't really let herself think he might love her. But now
he couldn't deny the possibility. This moment was cru-
ial. She had to say the right thing, or else he'd leave and
ever return. She didn't even know how she knew this,
ut she did.

She closed her eyes, afraid to show the need. "Take me
ome, Brody. Please."

She was engulfed in a hug that threatened to crack every
ib she possessed. She didn't feel a thing. There were other
ensations to marvel over—the feel of his mouth on hers,
is caresses all over her back, his hand fisted in her hair,
is chest warm and solid against her breasts—so many
hings.

"Let's go," he said.

"Now?"

"You got something else to do?" he demanded.

She loved the brashness, the masculine arrogance behind
he question, the startling quality of his smile, the light in
is eyes...oh, yes, the light in his eyes most especially.

"Brody, I love you." She gazed up at him anxiously,
fraid she'd scare him away with her confession.

He returned her gaze for a long moment. "If it's a tenth
f what I feel, it'll be enough to last a lifetime."

"Does that mean what I think it means?"

"I love you, Jessica Lacey Lockhart Smith." His eyes

darkened. "Be sure you want this. I'll never let you g
once I take you home."

Her smile was radiant. "I'll never want to leave."

Jessica sat on her favorite rock and watched the activi
below. The llamas were being loaded onto a truck to b
returned to their native country. One of the Andean trib
was taking them as part of a breeding program for the
developing wool market.

Voices rose from the valley and came to her on th
October breeze. The cottonwoods along the creeks and th
aspens girdling the hills were buttery yellow now that the
leaves had turned. She heard Brody cursing as the stubbo
llama male decided he didn't want to relocate.

She laughed. When they got the animals loaded, Brod
washed his hands at the horse trough and scrubbed th
green stain on his shirt with his handkerchief. Then h
hiked up the inclined rimrock to her.

She made room for him to sit behind her to watch th
sunset. He swung a jeans-clad leg over the boulder an
took his place. She leaned against him contentedly. B
not for long. As usual when they touched, the need becam
too much.

"Ready?" he asked.

"Yes."

They ambled down the path to the ranch house. Th
scent of simmering chicken and dumplings and fresh
baked cinnamon rolls welcomed them into the hous
"Supper first?" she asked.

"Yes."

She studied him while she set the places. He had a my
terious gleam in his eyes.

"I'll miss the llamas," she said.

"The stud had to go. He took to spitting on me eve

chance he got. There's room for only two males who are in love with you on this ranch. A third was too much.''

She lifted one eyebrow in question.

He grinned. ''Me and Ram. Well, Don, too, but he's better at hiding it.''

Happiness bubbled in her. She couldn't ever remember being so happy. There was one other thing she wanted. She'd tell her handsome husband later. In bed.

They watched the news and commented on the weather, always an important item for a rancher. The anticipation built. Brody was deliberately dragging out the evening. She could wait.

At ten-thirty, he stood and stretched. After clicking off the TV, he gestured that she should go first. She floated up the stairs.

He read a couple of faxes in his office while she prepared for bed. When she climbed between the sheets, he came over and kissed her, then turned out the lights. He pulled down the room-darkening shades before heading for the bathroom.

A bit puzzled, she watched him until he disappeared inside. The shower came on. A few minutes later, she heard the hum of his electric razor. Then silence.

The bathroom door opened. The room was so dark she couldn't see a thing. ''Brody?'' she questioned, worry creeping in.

A strange light appeared. She raised up on her elbows and watched it float toward her. Then she heard Brody's voice as he hummed a melody she'd never heard. The eerie glow bobbed and swayed in time to the tune as if engaged in a secret ritual.

She realized what was happening.

Clamping a hand over her mouth didn't help. She giggled and chortled helplessly as the show continued. The

tune ended and the glow dipped down, then up. She ap
plauded as her sexy husband took a bow.

She heard him take two steps. There were two corre
sponding bobs of the glow, then the covers lifted an
Brody's masculine length covered her.

"Thank you," she murmured as he planted kisses o
her face. "It was a delightful show."

"It isn't over." He kissed her senseless, until sh
writhed in hunger under him and begged him to come t
her. Finally he pushed up on his arms. "Observe, ma
dam."

She watched the glow disappear as his body merge
with hers. It reminded her of her earlier idea. "When a
we going to start a child?" she asked.

He settled himself deep in her. "When do you wa
to?"

"Soon." She moved against him.

"Tonight is fine with me." His voice was husky, wi
a quiet undertone that spoke of love and his faith in h
not to abuse that love. The gift of a heart...

Tears filled her eyes, and she was glad of the dark s
he wouldn't see. "Yes."

He shifted to her side. The condom shrank to a lin
glow and was tossed aside. Then he came into her agai
flesh against flesh, heart to heart, soul joined to soul. F
made the sweetest, gentlest love to her, then held her whi
their breathing quieted.

She thought of a child growing inside her. Brody mu
have, too. He rubbed her stomach as if it already w
rounded with the new life. There would be many childre
on the ranch next year. Besides their own, they were goir
to open the ranch to other children. The Lockhart-Smi
Foundation would oversee the program for kids to get
new chance on life.

Jessica sighed, unable to believe her happiness.

"Yeah," her husband murmured, his breath warm on her temple. "Life is good."

And so it was.

* * * * *

magazine

♥————————————————————— **quizzes**

Is he the one? What kind of lover are you? Visit the **Quizzes** area to find out!

♥————————————————— **recipes for romance**

Get scrumptious meal ideas with our **Recipes for Romance**.

♥————————————————————— **romantic movies**

Peek at the **Romantic Movies** area to find Top 10 Flicks about First Love, ten Supersexy Movies, and more.

♥————————————————————— **royal romance**

Get the latest scoop on your favorite royals in **Royal Romance**.

♥————————————————————————— **games**

Check out the **Games** pages to find a ton of interactive romantic fun!

♥————————————————————— **romantic travel**

In need of a romantic rendezvous? Visit the **Romantic Travel** section for articles and guides.

♥————————————————————————— **lovescopes**

Are you two compatible? Click your way to the **Lovescopes** area to find out now!

Silhouette® —

where love comes alive—online...

Visit us online at
www.eHarlequin.com

$ **Saving Money Has Never Been This Easy!** $

Just fill out and send in this form from any
October, November and December 2002 books
and we will send you a coupon booklet worth a
total savings of $20.00 off future purchases of
Harlequin and Silhouette books in 2003.

Yes! It's that easy!